PRAISE FOR PO

M000266182

"E.S. Fein is raising the bar for quality as it's a very well-written and thought-provoking book...There are points and themes in the story that could be discussed for eons as people will have their own idea on where it leads. It's a book I would highly recommend." - Andy Whitaker, SFCrowsnest

"Point of Origin was my first space opera read and my mind is blown. The story was full of the big existential questions; Who are we? Why are we here? What is love, trust, joy? The storyline addressed many important issues of religion, philosophy and societal roles. This is not a light read by any means but it certainly kept me wanting to resolve the internal and external conflicts posed from the beginning all the way to the end. If you're looking for a story to wrap your whole brain around, this is it."- D.M. Taylor, author of The Reckoning

"ES Fein has written a space opera adventure that weaves traditional science fiction, Eastern Philosophy, questions about who we really are, God and the cosmos in a very enjoyable way." -- Amazon Review

"This book is hard enough to interest core sci-fi fanbase while soft enough and with enough character development to interest the more casual reader. It's a great merger of philosophy, science, and drama that draws heavily from the eastern mystic heritage... At its core, it amounts to a thought experiment on what could occur given the potentiality of our universe, even a possibility of what our reality is exactly. It had me thinking about it and wishing I could be back home to read it during the day." - Alexandra Wallace, Amazon Review

"E.S. Fein's poignant writing is a deep reflection on today's societal questions in an entirely unique science fiction setting. This novel provokes deep thought on sexuality, compliance in societal norms, religious understanding, drug use and our own mortality. The writing is accessible as well as exquisite and I highly recommend this book." - Alex M., Amazon Review

"Came to this via a reddit post and it sounded interesting and I was in between several other books that I just couldn't get in to. Right from the start I was interested and I stayed interested all the way through. When I read the last page I was sad it was over. For me that is the sign of really good and enjoyable book." - Iain Alexander, Amazon Review

OTHER WORKS BY E. S. FEIN

Points of Origin

Ascendescenscion

The Process is Love

OfficialESFein.com

Instagram.com/AuthorESfein

Patreon.com/OfficialESfein

Facebook.com/AuthorESFein

POINTS
of
ORIGIN

BY E. S. FEIN

Points of Origin
Copyright © 2018 by E. S. Fein

Author: E. S. Fein
Publisher: Feinbooks
Editor: Nichole Paolella Petrovich
Formatter: Claire Krauss
Audiobook Voice Actor: Betty Bat
Cover Illustrator: Leraynne
Paperback ISBN: 978-1-7323069-0-5
Ebook ISBN: 978-1-7323069-1-2
Published: April, 2018
Library of Congress Catalog Number: 2018944959
First Edition

THANK YOU

to Moi and Pop, for your guidance and love,

to Melissa and Dave, for your support and belief,

to Marcin and Maggie, for your humor and friendship,

to Claire, for your patience and encouragement,

to Nichole, for your knowledge and time,

to Mom, for absolutely everything...

CONTENTS

POINTS
of
ORIGIN

PROLOGUE

I n the end, Yang's prediction proved true. Through time, across ponderous epochs and eons of being, Amero did eventually lose interest in sex, intimacy--even companionship.

At the end of time, immersed in silence and solitude as raw awareness, Amero was finally at peace--perfect peace. Yang had shown him the Way, and the Way was all Amero needed to sustain the miniscule sense of self that persisted beyond his thoughts and senses.

The Way was ultimately nameless, but Yang had used descriptors to approximate its nature: patience, acceptance, humility...all the ingredients necessary to retain a foothold of sanity on the icy slopes of existing beyond one's life expectancy by exponential factors of subjective and universal time. Amero knew the Way, and now the Way sustained him.

Now, however, was not a constant. Though Amero could dilate his experience of time so that hours felt like millennia, it was only a subjective remedy to universal entropy. Only the Points could truly resist entropy and only for so long. Still, Amero stretched subjective time to his enhanced mind's limitations, and coupled with the Way, Amero remained anchored to the present moment.

Suddenly, for the first time in many hundreds of quintillion years, something disturbed Amero. An explosive noise like a boiling torrent shot from a geyser pierced the perfect, penetrating silence.

Awareness of form returned, then of body, and with it came the desperate attempt to recollect and understand the preceding moments that had led to this particular present. Anxiousness and worry reared their ugly faces, attempting to infect Amero's thoughts, but the Way showed that these modes of being were nothing more than clothing to be discarded or adorned at will.

Accepting his confusion, Amero heaved his withered, half buried body out of the faded-gray sand, unwinding his legs from the loose lotus posture he had left them in at a time when there was more than darkness and silence as company. Not for the first time, Amero felt old... cosmically old. Stretching his aching neck, he noted that the sky was almost totally devoid of stars, and the moon had long ceased to glow. Within a few subjective hours, the few remaining stars in the sky would wink out of existence, and soon after, the final Points would be stretched to the Planck scale and beyond by the incessant gush of universal entropy. Yang had afforded Amero all the time that could be granted, and now the end had finally been reached. The final future was now the singular present.

"How?" Amero croaked, his scraggly, decrepit voice crashing and rebounding against an ocean that no longer lapped the shore with joyous, tireless waves.

The noise that Amero heard was gone. All was still. All was approaching finality.

"The end of all things...how did it come to this?" Amero asked, despite being the only being left in all the universe to hear the question.

Weak and short of breath, Amero shuffled to the coarse sand and refolded his legs into lotus posture. He considered retreating back inside himself, happy to spend the tail end of existence bathed in the weightless, ignorant joy of naked, unbiased awareness. Instead, he broke from the present and attempted to remember the past.

"How did it come to this?" Amero repeated thinly.

With a tantric rhythm, Amero breathed and softened his mind to a state of refined recall. Then, satisfied and still, Amero probed his ancient memories.

PART 1:
LOST

CHAPTER 1

*K*arumph!

Amero woke to the shock of hearing the atmosphere suddenly crack and cleave apart by the force of an unprecedentedly powerful launch. The shock was familiar, as was the booming resonance vibrating through his body.

Where am I? As his eyes struggled to focus, Amero wondered whose bed he had ended up in this time.

Karumph!

A second ultra-powerful launch made Amero jump halfway out of an unfamiliar bed, forcing a few vague, sleep-laden moans out of the naked young man dozing heavily beside him. Amero wondered what the hell was going on. Why was he so on edge? Was it the dream? Yes...that must be it. He was an old man, and--

Karumph!

Another angel was launched and rapidly broke atmosphere. The subsequent supersonic shockwave pummeled the city's infrastructure, rattling its steel skeletal system with shiver-like tremors that were dampened to a gentle sway as they traveled up each building's frame, ascending into the sky via a finely regimented hierarchy of wealth. Amero must have ended up on the lower levels--with this level of shaking maybe even the ground floor. Amero was amazed that his plaything of the night could sleep right through it all.

Karumph!

A fourth angel punched into space at several hundred g's, its ionic thrusters striking the Earth's surface with mountainous energy. Amero wondered when the officials had approved four ultra-g launches right in a row. Were the High Vicars of the space agency suddenly ramping up experimentation on the enhanced ion thruster technology the labs had supposedly perfected? No...shit! It was a holiday--that had to be it. Amero had slept through a holiday morning; this would be the last straw.

"Hey," Amero said to the man, "any idea if today is a holiday?" In response, the young man snored even louder.

"Hey!" Amero demanded. "Wake up!"

It was no use. A half handle of vodka at the bar, a few whiskeys at his apartment and a few hits of pungent cannabis ensured that the young man wouldn't wake up until well into the afternoon. Amero eyed the half-smoked joint lying on the night table beside a small blue lighter. It had been put out hastily the night before, just as they had begun tearing each other's clothes off.

Amero lifted the joint to his lips, lit it, then took a long drag.

"Find me! If there is a way, then find me. Return to me!" The bedside radio blared raucous, generic pop music suddenly. *"I said find me! If there is a way, then find me. Return to me!"*

Amero slammed a fist against the small radio to silence it and then remembered that he had been the one to set the alarm the night before. He felt impressed that he remembered to set one but also pissed that the alcohol apparently hadn't been strong enough to make him forget.

The young man dozed greedily, totally unaware of the dangers he had contracted by bringing Amero to his home. Then again, the young man was confident enough and had even claimed to have a high-end fashion job. Maybe he enjoyed the same kind of protection afforded to Amero. Was it Amero who had been played and not the other way around? The building vibrated, reminding Amero how far down the social ladder this young man must be.

Whatever the case, the sleeping man was extraordinarily beautiful, with lean muscles and a light tan culminating in a chiseled set of cheekbones and a jaw that made Amero's mouth water. Amero hoped the man would be okay. The fashion industry was one of the few havens where homosexuals could still find sanctuary and protection. Amero forced himself to believe that the young man would wake up in the afternoon unscathed by police inquiry or, worse, an execution squad.

Another pull from the joint ushered the sudden feeling of déjà vu. This feeling, strong as it was, was a normal occurrence for

Amero, as this morning was near identical to every other wasted night turned and hungover morning. Shaking off the familiar sensation, Amero rose from the bed and dragged one last pull from the joint. He exhaled a billow of smoke that hovered over the young man like roving fog.

The joint was only just enough to minimally counteract the hangover. "Fucking lights... " Amero grumbled to himself, "barely enough THC to give a mouse a buzz."

Amero snuffed the joint, stretched at the shoulders, then told himself it was time to leave.

It wasn't often, but sometimes Amero would linger with his sexual partners for a few lazy hours in the mornings, fully aware that tardiness at work, no matter how frequent, would land him at worst a few forced hours of grunt work for half-pay. He would let the talkative ones tell him all about their lives and how difficult it was living discreetly, as if they were alien invaders coated in human skin, just waiting, poised to infect all others at the first opportunity. Some men would even tell him about their plans to move outside the walls and live in the Desolate Zones. Amero would listen and smile and nod at all their frustrated, pitiful words, knowing full well that they amounted to less than nothing. The Desolate Zones had been washed away decades ago. Unlike most, Amero knew this as a certainty; he regularly overheard New Covenant officials talk boastfully about such matters at work. Everyday people like the young man beside him had no idea what went on outside society's walls.

This particular young man wasn't the talkative type--all action this one. Amero had tried to give him his standard spiel the previous night, the one about the dangers of leaving with someone like Amero, but this one wouldn't have any of it. He had recognized and pounced on Amero the moment he laid his hungry eyes on him. Such behavior could get a man killed, but some men are born with a love for courting taboo.

An arrhythmic thud battered Amero's skull as he dressed himself ungracefully. Set against the beating in his head was the ongoing rattle of additional morning launches from Earth to the inner-planets or the belt or maybe even further to the gas giants; the world was already alive and had been for many hours. Amero wondered how anyone could function so early. It didn't seem right.

Amero half-stumbled out of the apartment. The occluded sun was already battering the gray clouds. Sky-visors hovered about the street and displayed their post-early-morning advertisements; it was already far too late in the day. Tardiness meant more eyes on Amero, and more eyes on Amero meant more eyes on his chosen plaything for the night.

What was his name? Bart? Bret? Surely the young man understood the dangers of leaving a bar with Amero. Leaving with any other guy might just imply platonic friendship, but leaving with Amero meant going to bed with a global celebrity. Everyone knew that.

Amero decided he could never call Bret again. A phone call would surely be his death sentence...if that wasn't already the case.

Only a few steps outside the apartment complex, Amero was punched in the gut by a wall of nausea. He wished he had searched Bret's apartment for more bud to use as a hangover cure.

A dull vibration curbed Amero's attention to his pocket. He removed his phone and a generic silhouette appeared with the letter D. It was Dave, Amero's only real friend, despite being straight. Amero supposed it only made their friendship that much more meaningful.

Amero answered Dave's call, offering a groggy groan as hello.

"I got something for you, but you're not going to like it," Dave said, out of breath due to what Amero assumed was his typical, hyper-inflated anxiety. The worst crime Dave ever committed in his life was talking to Amero, but he still found more than enough to worry about when it came to socioreligious authority.

"This is big, Amero, really big!" It was just like Dave to be dramatic. Amero wasn't in the mood for drama. He wanted, instead, to sleep off the five-year-long hangover that reminded him each and every morning of the societal precipice he balanced on night after hollow night.

Dave waited for a response. Amero supposed he had nothing better to do on his walk to work. Besides, he and Dave hadn't spoken in over a week. To be fair, Dave had tried calling multiple times the week before, but Amero had been busy with publicity stunts, interviews, and other unfortunate circumstances symptomatic of global fame.

"Just shoot, Dave," Amero told him over the rush of traffic. "I'm already late, and my head's about to shatter like ceramic used as cannon fodder. Actually, before you say anything, what is today? Today's a holiday, isn't it?"

Dave hummed in consideration, then said, "Nope, no holiday today. Next one is Saint's Day, on the 19th. That's a Monday. There aren't any others in February."

Amero breathed easier. "Thanks, Dave. I thought I slept through a holiday show. I was about to prepare myself for exile...or execution," Amero said, far too comfortable with the prospect.

"Well... " Dave shot back, drawing the word out for effect, "I don't think that's going to matter much if you take what I got for you."

Not going to matter? More drama. How bored could Dave possibly be at his fancy, recently acquired New Covenant recruitment job?

Amero rubbed the bridge of his nose, attempting in vain to relieve the heartbeat-synced drumming on his skull. He seriously considered hanging up on Dave. Last time Dave found a job for Amero it had been a one-way trip to one of several Islamic territories. Dave always assured Amero that his skills and fame would provide him with ample wealth and power, but Amero had spoken to more than enough homosexual Muslim refugees to know that it was better to be a talented and tolerated abomination living under New Covenant rule than to be a skilled whipping post living under Islamic rule. Dave was naïve, but that didn't make him a bad friend. He really was trying to help Amero.

"Look... Dave," Amero started, but Dave was quick to interject.

"This isn't another offer for a foray into enemy territory. I swear, Amero."

"I'm in enemy territory now, Dave. Home isn't exactly tolerant of my type, you know."

"And yet we speak freely and openly. You have friends, Amero. Is that not a blessing in and of itself?"

Amero snorted. "Oh, how blessed I feel... "

"Listen, this one's different. As I said, you're not going to like it, but it does fall into the criteria you gave me... technically."

"Technically?"

"Well... yes... technically. Look... will you hear me out?"

Amero didn't respond right away. He glanced at his watch, its sleek gold a stark contrast to the ceaseless filth swept to the edges of the city's walkways. The watch had been passed down from Amero's grandfather across three generations. When Amero's grandfather gave the watch to Amero's father, he said, "Take care of this, will you? It has always meant a great deal to me, just like you." In turn, when it was Amero's time to receive the watch, his father told him, "Take it. It's the last thing I'll ever give you, including my own time."

Amero understood that his father, along with the majority of society, was thoroughly indoctrinated by the New Covenant's dogma. He simply could not love Amero. Amero was an abomination, and abominations were to be "cast away, lest ye become an abomination yourself." Amero was certain no such words existed in the original version of *the Bible*, but that didn't matter anymore. The New Covenant wrote its own rules, its own bible, its own Christ; homosexuals simply played no part in God's most recent devisings.

The watch's antique arms read 9:00 AM. Late, late, late every day of the week for the past three months. They needed him; that was the only reason Amero hadn't been fired, or worse, executed. They knew what he was after all.

Amero suddenly thought of Bret and wanted intensely to call him and tell him to run, to just go somewhere, anywhere, and never look back. But what would that accomplish? Where was he supposed to go that wasn't markedly worse? Amero had knowingly placed Bret's life in jeopardy, but was the lay really worth it? The cheap booze and bud--was it ever worth it the next day? Amero supposed he'd do it all over again tonight, so what more of an answer was there?

"Do you want to hear it or not?" Dave asked, allowing Amero ample time to respond.

"I already told you, Dave. Shoot."

Dave gulped down a breath. "They're looking for recruits," he tiptoed, treating the words as if they were as fragile as scripture.

"Dave, for goodness sake, out with it."

"They want to send two men to another star. Today. As in...right now."

Amero almost tripped over a hillock of rusty cans. "Which one?" he asked in disbelief. Was this the reason for the sudden spree of high-g launches this morning?

"What? You're actually thinking about-"

"Tell me which one, Dave," Amero said, almost not wanting to know the trajectory the New Covenant had chosen for humanity's first foray into deep space as "God-fearing creatures."

There was a brief pause, then Dave said in a whisper, "Tau Ceti."

Amero eyed his watch again out of habit before realizing that he needed to sit. Then it hit him: this was a joke. Just a prank. It had to be.

"Is this for real, Dave?" Amero asked with equal excitement and apprehension. The New Covenant had never once indicated plans to leave the solar system, so what was Dave getting on about?

"As real as God," Dave mustered.

Amero sprawled onto a park bench and unbuttoned his shirt, allowing a late-winter breeze to brush the skin of his chest with refreshing coolness.

"Is that supposed to reassure me or something?" Amero quipped.

"They're sending two men. Two homosexuals to be precise," Dave affirmed.

Amero burst into a fit of laughter. "No they aren't, Dave. This is a joke."

A moment of silence passed, but Dave was still sticking to his story.

"So the New Covenant... *The New Covenant*... wants to send two *gays* to another star? Other than the obvious death brought on by being unable to hitch a ride back home, what's the catch? There's always a catch when it comes to the arbiters of the divine."

11

"It's not a suicide mission... at least... not any more than any other expedition into space," Dave said cautiously. "On the other hand, it is a suicide mission." Dave cleared his throat as if seeking a reprieve from his troubled explanation. "Let me put it this way," Dave sighed uneasily, "they want you to succeed, but if you don't..."

"Yeah, right. If I die, it's no skin off their back. Another fag to be added to ancient history. Dave, level with me... is this for real?" Amero said with resigned hope.

"Why don't you call into work, Amero? Come down to the lab and talk to the bosses. They're waiting for you."

"How many recruits are there already?"

Dave went silent.

"How many, Dave?"

"You're receiving first priority. Apparently the big boys have had their eyes on you for some time. Call into work and get here as soon as you can."

"No sense calling, Dave. I quit. They can figure that out on their own time."

Dave scolded Amero with a sigh. "There's no reason to treat the school that way, Amero. Call them. Let them know you've taken another job."

"I don't owe the school anything. If anything, they owe me."

"You owe them your life, Amero. If it wasn't for the school... "

"Yeah, yeah, I know, I'd already be dead."

"I didn't say that... "

"But that's what you meant, Dave."

More silence from Dave.

"Tell your bosses I'm on my way," Amero announced, "and Dave... "

"Yeah, Amero?"

"This better not be a joke."

"No joke," Dave reassured him, "but like you said--there's always a catch."

CHAPTER 2

D irector Larimer eyed Amero with grim suspicion. "Thank you for dressing appropriately, Captain."

Amero shrugged and offered a quick self-examination. His air force fatigues were unironed, his boots were loosely laced, and his hair was a disheveled tour de force in not giving a shit.

"Everything looks in place to me, Director. Or would you have preferred that I arrive here unclothed?"

Director Larimer sneered in disgust. He was the most humorless being Amero had ever met.

"You smell like booze...and marijuana, Captain Hiddiger. God frowns upon intoxicants, for they are an offense against His natural creation."

Amero smiled politely. "There's nothing unnatural about cannabis, Director. The shit grows on all seven continents. If anything, it's God's favorite plant." The director shook his head, trembling in agitation at Amero's reasoning. "Besides," Amero continued, "they were lights. You won't catch a buzz by smelling me or anything. Don't worry."

Director Larimer chose to ignore Amero's brashness, but his cocked head and tightly crossed arms spoke volumes. "Remind me, Captain Hiddiger--"

"Call me Captain Amero, please, Director," Amero interrupted with an exaggerated bow, "or just plain Amero works as well."

"Very well, Captain Amero, very well," the director droned with disdain. "As I was about to ask: how was it that Doctor David Smeel came to be your... acquaintance, as he so carefully worded it? It isn't every day that a mere post doctorate in human relations can claim acquaintance with a man who enjoys your level of fame, or rather, notoriety."

13

Amero had been through this particular interrogation of his relationships at least a hundred times in the last year alone. "We're not friends or anything," Amero began, combating the director's probing with a vanguard of apathy. "A few years back, Dave, I mean, David, had been commissioned to the Chicago training school to observe incoming cadets who might be worth officer training. I happened to be flying a complex run that day–routine at that point in my career–and though David was supposed to be keeping an eye on the green pilots, my skills caught his eye. I've been at the training school for over a decade. I'm not allowed *real* officer rank, as you know, but I suppose it worked in my favor because if I hadn't been at the training school, David never would have noticed me, and I wouldn't be talking to you right now. I suppose one could call it fate."

Larimer winced, then offered Amero a sly, knowing half-smirk.

"Ah yes," he hummed with obvious scorn, "the Chicago Aerospace Training School; They take most anyone there, don't they? Even individuals of your... peculiar propensity for sin."

Amero shook off the insult. "Come to think of it," Amero blurted excitedly, "we never shook hands, Director."

Amero offered an ungloved hand. The taboo gesture produced predictable results.

"Away, abomination, away!" the director yelped. "Do not dare profane me!"

Amero's face lit with facetious surprise. "But you shake other peoples' hands, don't you?"

Director Larimer, red all over, came to an abrupt halt midway through the small foyer that led to what appeared to be a sizable room on the other side of a large set of doors.

"Don't push me, deviant. You won't like where it gets you."

The director made certain to place especially vehement emphasis on the pejorative.

"Then don't press the matter of Dave, got it? We're not friends. He's not a sympathizer. Dave's a good man."

Larimer raised his top lip in disgust. "Good men do not consort with bad men. You're lucky to be such a talented pilot, Captain. You would have been executed long ago had you been born an av-

14

erage abomination."

The director glared at Amero. Amero glared right back.

"The questionable men and women running the training school may have stomached you, but we have no such need. There are others we can choose from. Others without your...hideous sexual propensities."

Amero stretched his arms wide, presenting the whole of himself to the director. "And yet, here I am. Priority number one. Funny how a faggot can become more important than a breeder, isn't it?"

The director's eyes pinched to poisonous slits. The skin of his face was so taut with anger that his wrinkles were ironed out. "You imagine you're important, is that it? You imagine you have some part to play in God's plan? You are mistaken, Captain. In fact, you are not even a captain. The rank is honorary. The moment you quit the training school you were demoted back to private. Exactly as you'll remain."

Amero shrugged. "Apparently your superiors disagree, Director. You do have superiors, don't you?"

"We all have superiors, heathen," Larimer lashed. "You will answer to the greatest superior of all when you die. Then we'll see who has the last laugh."

"God, you mean? But Director, if God did not intend our meeting, if God did not ordain that a homosexual take technical priority over the director of an entire New Covenant lab, then who? Was it not God who ordained that you should suffer face to face conversation with a man partial to penis?"

Larimer's face flushed scarlet. "What did you just say?"

Amero offered a polite smile. "I apologize, Director. It's stress, that's all. You can't imagine how difficult it is living as an abomination."

Amero laughed to himself. They were too easy. Too predictable.

The director lifted his shoulders defensively. "Yes," his voice quavered as they shuffled back down the corridor, "yes, well, I imagine it should be."

With that, Director Larimer fell silent. Amero wondered if this was the closest Larimer had ever been to an "abomination." It was

possible but doubtful that Amero was the first Larimer had interacted with. Government this high up didn't execute known homosexuals; they just exploited them from a distance. That same exploi-
tation was the source of Amero's confidence in challenging Christians so high up the ladder. Amero's talents were just too damn ex-
ploitable to be discarded. His reflexes in a ship were lightning fast,
and his intuition for navigation and nosing out the path of least resistance was unparalleled across the entire world. People knew
Amero's name, everyday people and elites all the same. Amero the
Gay Pilot, AKA The Undead Astronaut--undead because how else
could he be alive despite the New Covenant's knowledge of his
sins? What a cruel joke, it was said, that the greatest pilot to ever
live was a living profanity to God.

None of that mattered, though. Amero brought in over seven
billion viewers every time he set foot in a ship. As sole owner of all
the world's space organizations, the New Covenant of Earth profit-
ed handsomely from Amero's continued existence.

And now they were willing to send him off across the galaxy?
Amero wondered how it could possibly be worth it to them to lose
their cash cow. Or was it finally time to be hung for his sins? Had
the New Covenant grown bored of greed? Amero doubted it, but
what then?

The director walked briskly down the corridor as if daring
Amero to break pace and fall behind. The doors opened automatically.

Amero and the director stepped through into a hangar that extended for what appeared to be miles in all directions. A few hundred feet directly ahead, a strange craft the size of a small house appeared to be hovering in place. Its mirror-reflective, featureless hull
was spot-lit by sunrays cast from windows in the high ceiling of the
hangar. The entire hull was curved, except where it terminated in a
sharp point at what Amero assumed to be the aft. It was like a giant,
metallic drop of water balancing on its side.

"So this is the starship, is it?"

"That's precisely the question you're here to answer, Private."

Did they think Amero knew more than the crumbs of gossip
that fell from the mouths of homosexual elites and talkative higher

ups?

"I just fly, Director. I'm no engineer," he explained.

Larimer smiled with amusement. "Right this way," the director cooed, ignoring Amero's protestation. A sudden urge to run his hand across the sleek, mirror-like metal of the ship suddenly overtook Amero, but the director's bony finger pointing at a small, wooden door hinted overtly at insistence. Amero obeyed, entering the room; two men dressed in ridiculously oversized, pearl-white hazmat suits sat as still and serious as statues at a large conference table.

The suited man closest to Amero rose and offered a shaky, gloved hand. His face was young, at least younger than the other's. "Blessings upon you, Captain. It's a pleasure."

The older man, still seated, rolled his eyes at the youth's gesture. "For God's sake, Thomas, he's a faggot. Don't touch him!"

Thomas imploded, pulling his hand and the rest of his body away from Amero with jarring horror.

"But sir," Thomas said to his superior, "is it safe? The lab guaranteed the integrity of the suits, but..." Thomas trailed off, strangling himself with his own trembling fear.

Thomas' superior shook his head. "There are no guarantees in life except the bounty of God's love, my boy. You have the advantage of having never come in contact with an abomination. God did close the mouths of the lions that would consume Daniel, but this is no lion. This is an abomination--more of Satan than of God. God is always on our side, my boy, but there's no sense testing God by throwing yourself needlessly into the lion's den, or rather, the snake pit in this case."

Thomas found his seat, nodding vigorously--a truly obedient disciple. "Yes, Father, my apologies. I would never dream of testing God."

"Watch your mouth, boy. How dare you use the Lord's name in vain."

Thomas nodded even more vigorously. "Please, your forgiveness, Holiness."

"By God's will," the old man told the youth with grim finality.

Amero waved his hand, attempting to catch the attention of the suited men he assumed to be priests of the New Covenant.

"Do you guys want me to leave and come back another time, maybe?" Amero asked sarcastically.

The men froze in their seats. Thomas gulped and almost choked on his fear.

"Take a seat, Captain," came the superior's condescending voice.

"Please, call me Amero," he told them, taking a seat.

Neither man acknowledged Amero's request. Larimer, who Amero now noted as being unsuited, pardoned himself from the room.

When Larimer was out of earshot, Amero asked, "Aren't you nervous I've contaminated Director Larimer?"

"Certainly," the superior stated plainly, "but if he was going to be afflicted with the contagion that is your life, it would have happened already. He places his faith in God, as do we. But the Central Covenant, our Order, sees no need in testing God. Faith is absolute, after all."

Amero nodded with mock-understanding.

"You're from Central then? All the way from D.C.?"

The superior's suit was tight at the gloves, and Amero could see the outline of hefty jewels atop thick rings adorning each of the superior's bulbous fingers. He sat stiffly, back straight against the small chair, yet he looked entirely at ease, fingers woven together gently and chin held perfectly level.

"That is correct, Captain Hiddiger," the superior's voice boomed, effortlessly demanding attention. "My name is High Vicar Nathaniel II. I am to be your recruiter. During my time as recruiter, you will provide me with both the distance and respect I demand. Director Larimer is content with science's claim that you cannot contaminate us. We are not. As it is said in the Undisputed Bible, 'cast away abominations, lest ye become an abomination yourself.'"

Amero pursed his lips, forcing himself to keep his cool.

"Now," the High Vicar continued with a broad grin, "let us move on to the 'casting away' part of this talk. Colonel David Smeel explained to you the basics of this operation, yes?"

18

"I think," Amero said, still staving off anger at the use of the historically phony bible passage. "He said you want to send people to another star."

"That is only partially correct, Hiddiger. We want to send homosexuals, not people."

Amero bit his tongue, but it was no use. "Wouldn't that be contradictory to the values, or rather, virtues of the New Covenant?" Amero asked with obvious scorn.

The High Vicar wagged a gloved finger at Amero. "Quite the contrary." He pointed to the young New Covenant member. "Thomas will explain."

Thomas rose from his seat, only to be dragged immediately back down by the High Vicar.

"Stay seated, you fool. This heathen deserves no respect."

Thomas nodded, but said nervously, "Sir, I just prefer standing if I'm to present information."

"Yes, yes," the High Vicar barked impatiently, "stand if you must." He turned to Amero. "As long as you understand, Hiddiger, that it isn't for your sake."

Amero stifled a chuckle. "Yeah, I get it. You hate gays. It's not exactly a secret."

"It's the law, Hiddiger! Both God's law and secular law! You seem oblivious to this, however, with your parading around, advertising your damnable lifestyle. Your very life is a disgrace to your creator."

Thomas rose from his seat, thought better of it, then sat back down.

"Stand if you must, Thomas," the High Vicar chided aggressively.

Thomas rose once more. "The mission," Thomas began wearily, "will be dangerous, to say the least. There's a chance that you and your... er... partner will be marooned. And then what?"

Amero was caught off guard. "You're asking me?"

"No, it was meant to be rhetorical, sorry," Thomas said with obvious self-loathing.

"Don't apologize to him!" interjected the High Vicar.

Thomas swallowed more unpalatable fear.

"We'd die. That's what," Amero said.

"Precisely, Captain, I mean... err... Hiddiger. But you see, with a heterosexual coupling there is always the prospect of procreation. For you, though... "

Amero nodded with full understanding.

"For a second I thought the New Covenant was getting soft. I thought, well I'll be damned, the New Covenant is sending homosexual men as the first men to visit another star. A mission of such importance put into the hands of abominations...but that's not it at all, is it? I mean, it is in one sense. But that's not the intention, is it?"

The High Vicar smirked and looked as though he had just finished eating the most satisfying meal of his life.

"The risks are great," Thomas went on, "but we have confidence that you and your selected partner will survive."

"So much confidence," Amero said, "that you're depending on homosexuals to do your dirty work."

The men remained silent, either unable or unwilling to respond to Amero's remark.

"You said *chosen partner*. What do you mean by that? Who will do the choosing?"

"You," the High Vicar growled.

"From a list of known homosexuals, all of whom are of genius level intelligence or higher," Thomas finished.

"Which is relevant how exactly?"

"Your partner is the one that'll keep you alive in case anything goes wrong outside of piloting."

"Meaning that you care if I live?"

The High Vicar said, "only so far as your ability to provide your services is retained. You are lucky. Your talents as a pilot, your instinct—they're better than any piece of software we have. God gave you these gifts, and you coated those same divine gifts in sin. You are lucky, but I do not envy you."

"What's the catch?" Amero asked, ignoring the High Vicar.

"Dave said there was a catch, but it all seems simple enough. Dangerous mission. Risk of death. Nothing I'm not already intimately acquainted with."

The High Vicar was all grin. "The catch, Hiddiger, is the amount of time the mission will take. You understand the concept of time dilation, yes?"

"How long are we talking?" Amero shot back.

The High Vicar's grin didn't let up. "We don't know for certain, and that's a catch for us too. We don't know if Seraphim will actually attain F-T-L, nor do we know if the machines will meet the expected rate of expansion and growth by the time you arrive at your destination. It's all theory still."

Amero let out a nervous laugh. "You want to repeat that so that we all understand?"

The High Vicar sighed heavily and passed the tediousness of explanation to his underling with an exasperated wave of his arm. Thomas was already standing, but he still took the time to straighten himself taller in preparation for speaking.

"The craft outside—we call her Seraphim on account of her ability to fly to heavenly heights—potentially has the power to travel faster than light, or F-T-L. It performs this seemingly impossible task through a highly theoretical process the New Covenant engineers are referring to as The Great Pull. You see, Seraphim does not propel herself. A destination is chosen, and the ship is pulled to that location."

"Pulled?" Amero said incredulously.

"Yes, Captain Hiddiger, like our souls to heaven."

"Pulled by what?"

"Anomalies in the fabric of spacetime. They're occurring all the time, all around us. I guess they aren't so much anomalies as the natural, dynamic texture of Creation. You see, when quantum fluctuations in the fabric of Creation occur, they leave in their wake a small wave of differentials. If all of space was an ocean, you could think of each differential wave as an incredibly minute perturbation of oceanic current. These waves, theoretically, can be isolated and utilized in sequence to create a sort of undertow capable of accelerating an object in one direction or another, maybe indefinitely.

Normally, these fluctuations cancel each other out for the most part, but Seraphim's wave-catches focus and isolate each fluctuation, riding one to the next. All we do is give her a gentle little push to start, but that little push quickly transforms into a flight of fancy across the cosmos via the God granted Pull of Creation."

"And you want me to be the guinea pig for Seraphim's 'first flight to heaven'?"

High Vicar Nathaniel nodded menacingly. "Abominations catch on quick."

Amero sat back in his seat, considering his next course of action. "What about the machines? You said something about the expansion and growth of machines."

Thomas nodded excitedly. "Yes, that's right. Thirteen years ago, we sent a fleet of intelligent, autonomous machines to the Tau Ceti system. They are self-learning, to some extent, and eager to prepare a home for your arrival."

"A home? You mean a colony?"

High Vicar Nathaniel burst into obnoxious laughter. "A colony, you ask? We would not send abominations as humanity's first colonists among the stars. No, if you are lucky, the machines will prepare for you an abode where you can grow old and be forgotten. If you are unlucky, your fate will be the same, minus the growing old part."

Amero nodded, letting the High Vicar's words slink past.

"A lot can happen in the amount of time you will be gone. By the time you arrive, the New Covenant may already be spread across the Galaxy. In any case, we'll know whether or not the experiment is a success the moment the Pull initiates."

"Maybe society will end. Did you consider that? No empire exists for all of time," Amero stabbed.

"The New Covenant is no empire, Hiddiger," the High Vicar retorted. "It is the will of God."

Amero cocked his head. "Say I don't want to be a guinea pig? Say I prefer to remain a permanent stain on the godly tapestry of the illustrious New Covenant?"

"You would say no to the opportunity of being the first man

outside the solar system?" the High Vicar asked, clasping his bulbous, bejeweled fingers together.

"I would say no to being an experiment that might help further a world that spits on me for who I am."

Thomas' eyebrows jumped to the top of his hairline, but the High Vicar did not seem the least bit surprised by Amero's words.

"You see, Thomas? You see how heathens respond to God's call?" The High Vicar asked his underling before returning to Amero. "You are remarkably brash for a man marked for death. Your insolence and disrespect for your Lord and kinsmen is both belligerent and juvenile."

"Juvenile!" Amero spat, loosening his grip on composure. "Juvenile? What's juvenile is that you and your boy's club hate me all because I happen to appreciate the bodies of men. It's pathetic, really. I mean, look at you. Suited up from head to toe all for me. You fear me that intensely, but I'm juvenile?"

"You disgust me," the High Vicar said, half yawning, "because you disgust God. Whether or not I like you or even care what you do is irrelevant, Amero Hiddiger."

"My answer is no, Nathanial."

The exclusion of the High Vicar's holy title made his teeth rattle and eyes fill with liquid rage. "You live because we allow it. You have retained rank all these years because we allow it. You are tolerated because we allow it! You are lucky. That is all. Lucky to be born with faculties and talents that can be utilized by the New Covenant. The worst part is that it's not even luck. It's by the grace of God that you were granted such gifts. And what do you do? You profane your blessings, heathen! Know this: you are not the best we have. We aren't sending our best pilot, nor even our second or third or fourth or twentieth best. We are using you because you are both expendable and unwanted. You thought you could flaunt your sin, lay with every young man you please, and nothing would come of it?"

Amero imagined Bret's apartment being raided with violent pleasure by New Covenant militia. The High Vicar's stare was sharpened daggers pointed at their target, daring Amero to make a sound.

"You are being thrown away because that is the only way you can benefit the New Covenant now. The Chicago School has scanned your movements and your mind, and one day it will all become a sophisticated program. One day when you are dead and gone from Creation. If the experiment fails, no one will miss you. If it succeeds, no one will miss you. In fact, no one will even know your name. You are a shit stain, Hiddiger, to be expunged from the—what did you call it—illustrious tapestry of the New Covenant."

The High Vicar lifted a small device and pointed at the closest wall. An image of a man and woman appeared. They were both angelically beautiful, with clear, Caucasian complexions and angular features. They wore bold expressions, eyes fixed on some object in the remote, unseen distance. Their spacesuits were sleek and futuristic looking.

"The champions of this endeavor, should the experiment succeed, have already been selected. You and your chosen partner will die on behalf of this heterosexual couple who will forever be known as the first humans to reach across the stars."

"Find someone else," Amero said, smiling defiantly.

"But we already have you," the High Vicar cooed.

Thomas passed Amero a large, blue portfolio open to the first potential partner. Amero glanced down and saw a giant of a man frowning back at him. He looked as if he wanted to take on the whole world's power and might even have a chance at victory. His name was Hann, and Amero found himself devilishly attracted to the endless amount of man depicted. Amero glanced at a few of the descriptions, noting that the man's personality profile was top-notch. Off-the-charts intelligence, lightning-quick decision making skills, encyclopedic memory and the ability to visualize three-dimensionally made Hann an incredible choice for partnership. He was even, according to the report, compassionate toward animals, a personal caveat of importance for Amero.

Amero laughed to himself and pushed the portfolio away with a flat palm. The whole portfolio had likely been catered to Amero's tastes. Who knew if the descriptions of each candidate were even true?

Amero shook his head resolutely. "I said I'm not going. You can execute me. Hell, you can torture me. But I'm not playing your game. I see what's happening here. You need more planets. Humanity is multiplying beyond your control. You need to test this technology to expand your empire. I won't help you, Vicar."

"Don't be stupid, Hiddiger. The choice is not yours. It is God's will that you undertake this mission."

Amero stared into each man's eyes. They were filled with pitiful scorn and hidden behind flimsy plastic shields.

He threw the binder at the High Vicar's face. "I'm not choosing another guinea pig. I'm out. Kill me if you want, but I'm out."

"Yes, Hiddiger. You're out. Right out of the solar system and eventually right out of Creation."

"Cute," Amero said dryly.

"Yes, I'm sure," the High Vicar nodded. "Your deviant life may not be precious to you, but I can think of someone who you might find worth keeping alive." The High Vicar curled his lips in rapacious delight.

Amero knew then that they had him. There was no way Amero was going to backstab Dave. He would choose death over betrayal for Dave's sake. Amero would more than happily throw any number of people, hetero or homo, right under the bus if it meant saving his own skin. Dave was different though. The debt Amero owed him couldn't be measured, not even with multiple lifetimes. Dave was a good man, and that's why it hurt so much to know that he was, for all intents and purposes, a believer of the Undisputed Bible. How could Dave possibly be content remaining devoted to such hypocritical garbage? He even believed the parts about homosexuality, only he saw Amero as an exception. Growing up together really screwed with him that way.

"If I go, you'll leave Dave alone?"

The High Vicar nodded. "We'll give him a reminder that God is both vengeful and forgiving, but nothing he won't get over with a few weeks of recovery."

"Fuck you, Vicar," Amero seethed.

The High Vicar laughed with incredible, child-like glee. "I'll take that as an affirmative, Hiddiger. Now, stand up. Thomas will provide you with a uniform and accompany you to the Pull-site where Seraphim is already waiting to be boarded. We're all very excited for you, Hiddiger. Today, humanity will finally find a use for you, God willing."

Amero rose, and High Vicar Nathaniel II stood and strode to meet him. He was much taller and wider than Amero had anticipated, towering over Amero's nearly six-foot frame by at least six inches. The High Vicar held a gloved hand before Amero's mouth, demanding that Amero kiss one of his many rings through the suit's material.

"Aren't you afraid you might fall in love with me?" Amero asked sweetly.

The High Vicar swung his jeweled fist hard against Amero's skull.

In a daze, Amero did his best to keep his balance, squinting his eyes and flashing his teeth to help expunge the pain.

"God is vengeful but forgiving, Hiddiger," the High Vicar bellowed at Amero.

Amero found his balance and rose. Fresh blood splattered the rock-hard knuckles of the High Vicar's right glove, and Amero instinctively reached to inspect the side of his head. His hand came back drenched in warm, sticky fluid. Nausea suddenly racked at Amero's senses, and he couldn't help reaching for the table to save himself from falling over.

The High Vicar's bloody glove was once more before Amero's mouth. Amero caught the High Vicar's glare.

"Vengeful, Hiddiger, but forgiving. You understand, don't you?" The High Vicar offered sinisterly.

Amero bent at the neck and touched his lips to his own slick blood decorating the glove.

"Very good, Hiddiger. Very, very good, boy. God is forgiving, but God is vengeful too, isn't he?"

Amero raised his arms defensively, but it was no use. The High Vicar swung full-fisted with all his might, slamming his bejeweled fist against Amero's skull with the sickeningly wet crack of spent bone.

CHAPTER 3

"He's in here! Someone help! Plea--"

Frantic cries from somewhere in the distance were forced into gurgling submission by an unseen menace, a predator evidently subduing its prey.

"He's over here! Over here!" came more shouts, jaunting Amero out of a dreamless, coma-like slumber. Knobs and buttons dimly lit in a multitude of colors lined the cramped walls and ceiling enveloping Amero like a cybernetic womb. Unable to move, Amero crooned his neck to find an open doorway behind him leading out to the hangar where he had first seen Seraphim. Only this time he was on the inside of the mirror-sheen surface.

Amero was far more impressed with Seraphim's polished, curved hull than he was with the brash nakedness of its interior. It was as if Seraphim's construction had been suddenly defunded during the final phases. Exposed black and green cables as thick as mast rope made up the bulk of Seraphim's girth.

Amero found himself strapped and crammed within the little space reserved for human occupation, which was filled mostly by a side-by-side pair of large, padded seats. The rest of the space overflowed with knobs and buttons and levers of every conceivable size and shape.

Amero wondered if they truly expected him to fly this thing.

"He's in here! He's in the launch room! Hold your fire! Repeat, hold your fire!" more frantic voices called out with a smatter of apprehension and confusion.

Amero's instincts warned him to run and prepare himself for whatever danger lurked outside the ship, but he was adhered to the seat. Each time he strained, pressure across his chest threatened to squeeze his lungs empty. He tried breathing deeply to calm himself, but this action seemed only to exacerbate the pressure into a further state of egregious irritation, suffocating Amero with newfound haste. It was as if there was something alive wrapped about him, and he had to settle for shallow breaths until the pressure finally abated.

Amero's skull pounded, feeling as though it had been struck with the broad side of a bat. The High Vicar had really put on a show for his underling, likely as an example to the youth in the proper treatment of abominations. Still, Amero didn't regret giving the official a healthy dose of verbal cannon fodder. Amero wondered how many people the High Vicar had struck with those precious gems--those skull-fracturing rocks pillaged from the world all for the sake of satiating a delusional, talking ape's power trip.

An attempt to investigate the pain emanating from his skull prompted the pressure across Amero's chest to come alive, and Amero forced himself to breathe once again, transitioning slowly to a fuller, controlled breath. In response to Amero's relative stillness, the pressure eased. It was a potentially fatal nuisance, but at least it was predictable.

Heavy footsteps thudded the ground just outside the ship. Whoever it was, they were heading directly for Seraphim. Footsteps pounded on the metal grate hanging an inch above the nest of cables; Amero was no longer alone.

"You," a voice rumbled from behind Amero. All he could do was breathe and wait for the individual behind him to realize his predicament.

"Are you deaf?" the rumble inquired, seeming to genuinely consider it a possibility.

"I can hear, but--" Amero managed before being strangled by the seat's smothering straps.

"*But* nothing. Get out. Now," the man said, calm but firm, as if Amero was age-old dust to be wiped away without further concern. The man lumbered fully into the ship and pulled himself forward. A bear-like paw latched onto Amero's right shoulder, emanating warmth and power without effort. "I said out!" The man's demand was more plea than threat.

"Can't... move... " Amero hissed through clenched teeth, preparing himself for the inevitable strangling pressure that each spoken word summoned.

The forlorn, beautiful giant that Amero had seen pictured in the High Vicar's portfolio of candidates appeared at his side. Bordering on seven-feet tall and seemingly just as wide, Hann seemed to go on forever. He crammed himself into the seat beside Amero, grunting as he forced himself to fit.

"What is it? They've implemented living straps?" Hann scrutinized the straps compressing Amero's chest, not even paying attention to Amero and never once meeting his eyes.

Amero felt suddenly unsure of himself. Was this the same man pictured in the portfolio? His cropped, auburn hair looked as though someone had missed whole sections in a frantic attempt to shave his head down to the scalp. Drab, unfitted clothes at least a few sizes too small threatened to burst at the seams, and where he remained unclothed, exhaustion and frustration clawed incessantly, revealing croppings of scars and wrinkles that could not have been produced by age alone. He was similar to the man that had been pictured, rougher certainly, but the same person? Amero supposed it was possible the files on Hann were just dated. Afterall, why would the New Covenant care whether the files on known and tolerated homosexuals were perfectly up to date? Then again, this was the New Covenant of Christ: their predecessor churches had thousands of years' experience with record keeping, and the New Covenant had no intention of ending the tradition.

"You're Amero Hiddiger, aren't you?" Hann said as if coming to a troubling conclusion. He raised his stare from the straps and finally met Amero's gaze. Amero jumped inside his own skin, flinching and signaling the sensitive straps to do their work. The straps tugged at Amero's lungs, but he didn't even notice; all he could focus on was the horrifying image of Hann's mangled neck and the sickeningly thick scar tissue stretched like half-digested meat from ear to ear. The scar tissue was fresh, still pink and inflamed, as if Hann had recently died of a neck wound, only to be resurrected as a walking cadaver and sent on its way.

Ignoring Amero's shock, Hann rose and punched a small red button beside Seraphim's entrance, sealing the ship closed.

"It appears you're coming with me, after all. There's no cutting

29

through those straps, and there's no other way to get rid of you without disassembling you piece by bloody piece." Hann exhaled heavily, "Tell me now: are you with them? Are you New Covenant?"

Amero scowled.

"I didn't think so," Hann growled, "and yet, there's no real guarantee. My people tell me you're famously homosexual. Hard to imagine, isn't it? They assure me you can't possibly be working with them. But my people have been wrong before, Amero. To err is to be human, isn't that right?" As he spoke, Hann scanned the interior of the ship with diamond-precision consideration. His eyes caught and calculated every inch and angle, and it made Amero feel stupid for not investigating his surroundings with greater care. Was it possible Hann understood what he was viewing?

Hann adjusted a few levers and pressed a seemingly random array of buttons. Seraphim purred with crescendoing power at Hann's beckon. Suddenly, the straps eased, and Amero found himself once again free to speak and move.

"There's no opening that door now. Those straps must have been set to deactivate once preparations for the Pull were initiated," Hann explained from behind Amero's seat.

Amero rose and turned to face Hann, but he was stopped short and forced back into his seat by Hann's effortless strength. In turn, Hann found his own seat beside Amero.

"I don't trust you, Amero Hiddiger. I've never seen your television escapades, and to be frank, I don't care about your fame and beauty. You're not one of my people. As far as I'm concerned, you're the enemy. You worked for the New Covenant, and you enjoyed a life of luxury befitting a High Vicar, even a Cardinal. I do not trust you. You're a liability... even a potential threat... not my partner."

Amero brushed himself at the shoulders, ensuring that nothing had been sprained under the pressure of the restraints that Hann had referred to as *living straps*.

"It's a pleasure to meet you too, Hann," Amero said, challenging the giant man's quixotic assertiveness and unyielding concentration.

Hann appeared uneasy at the mention of his name, but he swiftly flattened his surprise back to measured frustration. "There's no telling how long we'll be stuck together like this. For now, just stay out of my way, and I'll stay out of yours," Hann concluded.

"How pleasant," Amero goaded. "We've no idea how long we might be stuck on Seraphim together, and you're already making plans to permanently avoid me." Amero wanted to laugh Hann's callousness off--it was certainly what the man deserved--but he felt absorbed by Hann's every word and action.

"You expect me to trust you outright, Amero Hiddiger?" Hann asked with scant amusement.

"Look," Amero began, more annoyed now than disappointed that the seemingly perfect catch from the portfolio was turning out to be a steely, paranoid giant full of fresh, flesh-rending scars. "I didn't ask for this. Like you said, I was living a life of... *luxury and privilege...* until it was all stripped away and replaced by you."

Hann shook his head. "You mock me, but you've no idea what it's like to live in the Desolate Zones, or worse, in a New Covenant Prison. In comparison, all you've ever known is luxury, Amero Hiddiger."

"Whatever," Amero scoffed, still unable to break his gaze. "Someone's life is always going to be worse than someone else's. Maybe you had it worse than me, but I didn't have it easy, Hann, not by any stretch."

Hann flashed Amero a forced grin; his eyes were wide with the indelible will of having lived by the skin of his teeth for far longer than any living thing should. "What do you know about the Message, Amero? Tell me now and get it over with."

Amero was taken aback by the sudden shift in conversation, but Hann appeared perfectly serious. "What do you mean? What message?"

Hann offered the same forced smile and nodded slowly. "Are you sure, Amero Hiddiger? Are you certain you know nothing about the Message? If you are one of them, the High Vicars who command you would likely have referred to it as the *Message from God.* Tell me now, Amero Hiddiger."

Hann scrutinized Amero, analyzing even his most subtle movements. It made Amero feel naked and vulnerable, as if Hann's observation was something tangible that could penetrate Amero's skin.

"I don't know what the hell you're talking about," Amero insisted, shifting uncomfortably. "Are you mad?"

Hann continued with his under-the-skin probing of Amero's entire form, reading him like a book explicitly detailing the most guarded moments of Amero's life.

Finally, Hann eased himself reluctantly back into his seat and let out a great sigh. He furrowed his brows and cringed away a wave of something painful, as if his thoughts had suddenly reared and threatened to strangle him of their own accord. "Either you're a remarkable liar or you've been brainwashed. Either way, I've read the Message, Amero. I know you have some part to play in this, and I will discover that part in its entirety."

Amero hesitated. What did Hann mean by the *Message from God?* Who did Hann imagine Amero really was?

While the men spoke, Seraphim's purr of power had slowly grown into a gentle rumbling that could be felt in the form of soft vibrations.

Amero gripped the armrests of his seat with sudden apprehension. "This thing is about to take off, isn't it?"

"The Pull will initiate within one minute based on the laboratory's current rate of power consumption," Hann stated simply. "Let's hope your New Covenant allies don't attempt to interfere—the result of any sort of interference cannot even be theorized, let alone predicted."

"I told you: I'm not with them. They won't stop us. You should have seen how excited the High Vicar was to get rid of me."

Hann nodded, facetiously accepting Amero's words.

"They may be willing to get rid of you, Amero Hiddiger, but I am another matter entirely."

"What are you talking about? You were in the portfolio of candidates. You were the first choice, actually."

Hann stared wide eyed at Amero, then looked away and nodded slowly in solemn understanding, appearing to battle with something deep inside himself. Amero waited for an explanation, but Hann remained silent.

Whirroooo! Whirroooo! Whirroooo!

Sirens suddenly wailed from outside Seraphim's hull, illustrating to Amero the perilously miniscule distance separating Seraphim's interior from the outside world.

"They're attempting an emergency shut down," Hann announced with a wry grin. "The bastards are refusing to let me go."

Hann's fingers glided across the instrumentation, making so many changes and adjustments that Amero was unable to keep up.

"You know how to fly this thing?" Amero asked uneasily.

"Seraphim doesn't fly. Not yet. It is possible that such modifications will be made accessible post-Pull, but for now, Seraphim only has one possible destination: Tau Ceti. Technically, if the Pull proves successful, we are already there. Assuming success, from the Tau Ceti system's perspective, we are currently in super position relative to our origin, which is no longer Earth, and never was Earth. All that's left is to be pulled back into the place the universe is convinced we've been all along. So, what do you think, Amero Hiddiger?" Hann asked with utter seriousness. "Does the prospect rattle your nerves?"

Amero cleared his throat after realizing he'd been holding his breath involuntarily. "I've emergency-reversed planetary entry pushing 14 g's without a suit. I've even flown blind through an asteroid herd on post-final reserves... but this... " Amero trailed off shakily.

"It's the trip of a lifetime... maybe even all lifetimes combined," Hann finished with the hint of a grim smile at the corner of his lips.

"Attention. Attention. Power down now. Repeat, power down now," a severe, muffled voice issued from an unseen speaker inside Seraphim.

Hann held down a circular blue button with his finger and spoke aloud, "Negative, and if you attempt an interruption, it may very well be the end of Earth. I'm not worth the risk. You've got my people, and after this, you'll have the Pull technology, tried and tested. I'm doing you a favor. Now, stand down. Give it up." Hann warned. "I'm leaving, whether you like it or not."

Amero watched Hann sit back in his chair, issuing a severe huff through pursed lips. He appeared enveloped in his own world, totally oblivious to Amero's presence.

"Shouldn't we strap ourselves in?" Amero asked, unsure if his words could penetrate Hann's grievous brooding.

"Did you grow fond of the living straps, Amero Hiddiger?" Hann asked, as if trying out humor for the first time.

"*Amero.* Just *Amero* is fine," Amero told him.

Hann nodded at Amero but kept his torturous stare on the monitor. "There will be no inertia. You won't feel anything at all."

"That's assuming we survive," Amero reminded him.

"Yes, assuming we survive," Hann confirmed casually. "However, the odds of failure," Hann went on as if ruminating to himself, "are so low that it would be classified as anomalous for something to go wrong--a one-in-a-trillion chance."

"Anomalies happen," Amero urged.

"Of course anomalies occur, but not very often," Hann explained. "It's the very nature of anomalies. Besides, Earth is sending two homosexuals across the galaxy as the first manned mission into space outside the solar system. Think about that: two homosexuals are poised to become pioneers... legends of the Earth! You and I are about to be gilded in time and memory. If that's not anomalous, I don't know what is."

Amero nodded and urged his point. "You see, anomalies do happen."

"Not twice in a row, though," Hann corrected, this time with a shaving of agitation. "The odds of two anomalies of such profundity occurring at once in any given system is too negligible to even calculate."

Amero attempted to untense himself, but it was no use. "We'll feel nothing, then?"

"Nothing at all," Hann confirmed with a tone that implied he might prefer the alternative. "The only visible change will take place on the interface of the monitor."

Hann slapped the screen in front of him, visible to Amero at an angle.

"Either the screen lights up with new surroundings, or we cease to know the difference. Either way, it's easy."

"*Power down now. Repeat, power down now. We know you're in there with Hiddiger. In the name of our Lord Christ, in the name of God, power down now!*" the voice spat over the speaker.

Hann held the button down and said, "God can suck my dick."

Amero shook his head scoldingly, but his grin told another story.

"As a final farewell gift to Earth, I hacked the comms," Hann explained, then pressed two buttons simultaneously. "In five seconds, everything I say is going to be live-broadcasted. All the billions of good little New Covenant boys and girls will be able to hear us."

"You're kidding... "

Hann roared with vengeful laughter.

"Listen up kids: God is gay. The Virgin Mary claimed to have a virgin pregnancy because Joseph refused to sleep with her, and he was in no position to admit to everyone else that she was satisfying herself with other men. That's because Joseph was gay, and he passed it like a disease to Jesus, his bastard son. When Jesus said love your brother, he meant exactly that: love and fuck and marry your brother. God is gay! God is a homosexual!"

Hann whooped with laughter, smacking the monitor for added effect. Released from the all-consuming, diamond-precision awareness he had boarded Seraphim with, he was like a totally different being. Tears filled his eyes and pain contorted his deeply scarred face.

"Here we go, Amero. Say goodbye."

"Goodbye... thanks for nothing... " Amero whispered to the world.

Hann gripped at his seat until his knuckles were white. His eyes were wet with tears.

"I'll change it all. I swear it," Hann screamed suddenly.

A soft, electric hum gave way to an onslaught of boiling reverberation that shook Amero violently. Amero gasped--something was wrong. Hann said they wouldn't feel a thing. Amero gripped his seat, preparing for some type of collision, or worse, a total and sudden cessation of being.

The shaking felt thunderous, and it thudded about Seraphim with a life of its own, bombarding the ship with scattered bursts across the entire hull.

Hann rumbled in painful, anguished sobs, while Amero screamed in abject terror.

CHAPTER 4

A mero woke all of a sudden, gasping for air as if surfacing from the crushing depths of an endless, pitch black ocean. Amero groaned haphazardly, attempting in vain to call out for help. There was something wrong with him. He couldn't speak properly-- couldn't hold the words in his mind long enough to form anything close to a coherent sentence. After several pathetic attempts, the best he could manage in the way of calling out for help was a jumbled mess of indecipherable grunts.

Giving up on help, Amero attempted to inspect his surroundings, but his sight was blurry to the point of useless. All he could make out was a profound azure glow pulsating slowly and evenly all about him. It didn't seem threatening, but he felt far too drunkenly confused to commit to any serious assessment.

"Plee!" Amero called out stupidly. He winced at his own senseless cry for help, aware but unable to correct himself.

"Amero?" someone inquired incredulously. "You're awake?"

Amero was unsure how to perceive the voice he heard. Though the voice was familiar, Amero couldn't exactly place it. It was soft and baritone, inviting and genuine.

"Plee!" Amero urged like a toddler begging to be told some simple yet unknown truth.

The voice sounded concerned but altogether jovial, like a parent who thinks he has lost his child, only to realize later that his little one had been hiding under the bed the whole time. "There is no reason for you to be awake now, Amero. The Pull to the center of the galaxy must have had some unforeseen effect on you, but no matter, you are safe now. Your body has been repaired."

Amero's heartbeat quickened. The Pull--that's right! Something had gone wrong, and then...everything was fuzzy after that.

"We've still another year of spaceflight before we reach our destination, including one more Pull right at the end of the journey. No sense waking up just yet, Amero. I'm going to induce stasis again, just for the year, okay?"

Amero felt flustered to understand virtually nothing the voice was telling him. A thought flashed in Amero's mind: Hann. Yes, there was Hann, but this was not Hann's voice. It was familiar, but certainly not Hann. Who then?

"Hann," Amero gasped, and he was pleased to hear that he had said the name without any major verbal flaw.

"What's done is done, Amero. All that is left is forgiveness, but that can come later."

Another surge of frustration. What was this person talking about? It was as if Amero had missed whole chapters of his life, entire arcs this person was somehow privy to.

"Ferg've?" Amero managed to ask with immense physical and mental effort.

"Of course," the voice reasoned, surprised by Amero's question, "for murdering you."

Amero shook his head. Was this a dream? Was this the effect of the Pull?

"Plee..." Amero urged, utterly spent in his confusion.

"You should already be feeling heavier, Amero. Let it go for now. Sleep, and when you wake up, I'll explain everything, my friend."

Amero made to protest, but thinking was even more arduous than breathing. The feeling of being submerged in warm bathwater enveloped Amero. *Hann...*Amero whispered to himself as his mind slipped back into the dreamless slumber of stasis.

CHAPTER 5

A cold whack to his cheek snapped Amero awake.

"You sleep as if your life depends on it," Hann croaked with a frown, backing away from Amero.

"Are you going to apologize for slapping me?" Amero asked through groggy slowness.

"No," Hann told him simply. "You've been asleep for two hours since the Pull. Two hours is long enough."

Amero was reminded of his dream. It had been impossibly vivid, hauntingly so.

"I dreamed that I was talking to someone. They said...they told me that you murdered me," Amero said uneasily.

Hann shrugged at Amero disapprovingly, indicating with a single action that there was no way he could be held responsible for the claims of a dream character.

"Anything else you want to share?" Hann asked with an impatient sigh.

Amero realized how stupid he must sound. It was just a dream, after all. "Maybe it was best you slapped me out of it. That dream was... too real."

Hann nodded, then tapped the monitor. "We have an even realer situation occurring at the moment."

"The monitor," Amero gasped, "what does it say?"

Hann didn't miss a beat. "It says that we're the first people to ever leave the pull of the sun."

"We made it? We're within the Tau Ceti system?" Amero said, and his astonishment worked to wash away the vividness of the dream.

"We made it. I mean, we're alive, but I don't know where we

are," Hann explained.

"We're not at Tau Ceti?" Amero checked.

"I said I don't know where we are," Hann rasped with a hint of frustration. Hann's fingers navigated the monitor, exploring Seraphim's real time comparisons of local space with its databases of star maps.

"According to luminosity, mass, and surrounding stars, this is absolutely Tau Ceti. The problem is the computer is unable to locate Earth."

"How's that possible? It's directly opposite the way we came."

"Not necessarily. We were Pulled to this location. Technically, *this* was the starting point. We weren't launched from the Earth; we were displaced from it. Many theorists proposed that the Pull-device was just a bunch of quantum mumbo jumbo, but here we are: testaments to the validity and effectiveness of...Anna's work..."

Hann clenched his eyelids tightly shut. Was Amero witnessing a hint of collegiate drama? Was Hann capable of having colleagues?

"Testaments to the New Covenant's achievement, you mean," Amero reminded Hann with a sullen wave of his arms.

Hann smiled mysteriously, hiding something at the forefront of his mind, then offered his own carefree wave. "That's just the current cultural fad, Amero. Hundreds of years have likely passed on Earth. I have a feeling it's a much different place. The flame of the New Covenant has been extinguished by now."

"You underestimate them, Hann," Amero assured him. "If not the New Covenant, some other religious establishment. The result will be the same either way: you and I aren't welcome."

"You may be right, but either way, I'd still like to execute some deeper scans. There's no reason we should be experiencing this much difficulty locating Earth."

Amero rubbed his hands against his cheeks with visible confusion. "Even though the ship can't exactly retrace its steps, it should be able to chart Earth's future location relative to Tau Ceti's location before the Pull, no?"

"That's correct," Hann confirmed. "However, even after implementing such methodology, the ship still can't pinpoint Earth's current coordinates. It's not where it's supposed to be. Neither is the Sun, for that matter."

"The whole solar system's gone?" Amero asked in disbelief.

"It's either that," Hann said, seeming to find a shaving of enjoyment in the mystery, "or the ship's navigation systems are malfunctioning. But that's not possible, as every other star and major celestial body is exactly where it should be."

As if in response to Hann's statement, the ship's lights dimmed momentarily. The monitor in front of Hann flickered. Where there was once a star map, there was now a question being formed in real time on the monitor:

"Accept... system... update?"

Now it was Hann's turn to be alarmed. "Update? From where?" Hann looked visibly shaken and turned to Amero, speaking to him as if the whole mess was Amero's doing. "Even if Earth had the capability to send a message to our exact location, this is a system update for Seraphim. This ship is whole human epochs beyond any other technological artifact of Earth. It is unparalleled. An update of Seraphim's systems is no trivial matter. It would involve millions of terabytes of data. Maybe more."

"So? What's the problem?" Amero said with mounting urgency.

Hann shook his head, refusing the network of possibilities mounting in his mind's eye. "There's no way terabytes of data could possibly be sent from Earth to our precise location without undergoing a profound degree of corruption and content loss." Hann spoke as if he was annoyed that Amero was ignorant of the subtleties of data transfer.

"The experiment worked though, Hann. Maybe the system update was Pulled to this location right after we were."

"Or maybe it's a suicide pill," Hann offered grimly. "Did you think of that? It is possible they got what they needed, and their way of cleaning up the mess is by plunging us into deeper chaos. For all we know, this *system update* could be a virus that overloads the ship's power supply, or a string of code that increases the temperature and converts the ship into a convection oven, or--"

"I get it, Hann. It might not be good," Amero interjected.

"That's an understatement," Hann rumbled.

"Okay, what then?" Amero asked, anxiousness swelling in the pit of his stomach. "All you've been able to tell me so far is that we're alive and that you can't locate Earth. Aren't we already in deep shit?"

"So you're okay with this?" Hann pressed as if offended. "What could they possibly have to gain by helping us? You really think they sent this update to help us?"

"What then?" Amero demanded. "You're the genius-level one here. I'm just a pilot on a ship that doesn't need one. What do we do, Hann?"

The lights flashed, and the monitor flickered just like before. The screen was cleared of text. A new message was presented letter by letter.

"No...harm. Only...help. Accept...system...update?"

Amero turned heel and faced down Hann.

"Don't give me that look, Amero," Hann warned, "as if this even remotely sheds light on the intention of the message. This doesn't prove anything. In fact, this makes it even more suspicious. It's like they're admitting to malicious intent just by bringing up the possibility of harm."

Amero said, "I say we accept the update."

There was another momentary blackout accompanied by a few seconds of screen flicker. This time the monitor revealed an image: a bald, old man with a flowing, paper-white beard. He was seated in lotus posture upon an oversized, ocher pillow inside a room walled by aged mahogany. The old man smiled inhumanly wide at Amero and Hann.

"Who the hell are you?" Amero asked instinctively, belatedly realizing this had to be a message and not a live recording.

The old man bowed and introduced himself all the same. "There is no need for alarm. I am here to acquaint you with the new state of affairs in the galaxy."

Amero couldn't help but smile. "This a joke?"

Hann lowered his gaze and stared at the image through cynical, calculating eyes. "If it is a joke," he said, "it is executed with flawless precision."

Hann was about to continue, but the man was already speaking again.

"Congratulations, gentlemen. You succeeded." The old man clapped his hands together a single time. "Your trip to Tau Ceti marked humanity's point of exponential growth toward galactic existence. Thousands of expedition parties were sent into space using the Pull-device. Fortunes were made. Planets were colonized. The New Covenant spread rapidly."

While Hann stared deadly serious at the monitor, Amero resigned himself to a forced chuckle. "Looks like the New Covenant wasn't just a cultural fad after all."

The old man went on. "Technology improved at an unprecedented pace. The Earth saw its first global golden age. However, there was cause for a great global depression as well, for the principle purpose of the expeditions into space, near and far, was never fulfilled. No trace of sentient life was ever found. The only life discovered was always packaged and preserved as fossilized microbes. It appeared to humanity that the greatest filter to life occurred at the microbial stage, indicating that humanity itself was an anomaly in terms of survival on the galactic scale. Such was true, at least, for Earth's local spacetime--a range spanning approximately 70,234,492 stars."

"Seventy million... " Hann gasped. "Humans have traveled to seventy million stars since we left?"

The old man stroked his beard and took a deep breath as if he knew Amero and Hann would need time to digest this information.

Amero shook his head. "It's possible, isn't it? We traveled to Tau Ceti instantly. They could make more laboratories and ships like Seraphim--a whole global fleet. If the New Covenant was still around, then they must have seized global control. They could do it. With the whole world's economy, they could do it."

"But why?" Hann demanded.

"Are you kidding?" Amero gasped. "To prove they are special. To prove they are the pinnacle of God's plan." Amero offered theories without actually believing that the New Covenant ever seriously considered its own doctrines.

"No," Hann insisted. "The question is *why*. What is the actual *why* of it?" Hann demanded.

"Why?" Amero began. "Well, why did they hate us? Because they were told to. There were a few lines in the original Bible that referenced laying with other men and they ran with it. So, why did they launch expeditions? Maybe there are passages in the Undisputed Bible about traveling into the unknown. Or maybe it just made them rich, like the old guy just told us."

Hann shook his head, unwilling to consider Amero's suggestions of history. "He said their principal cause for jaunting into the void was to find other forms of life. How does that benefit them financially?"

Amero chuckled, shaking his head at the obvious truth. "It's no wonder they were so depressed over finding no other sentient life. They were probably looking for fresh recruits: worlds to convert and add to their ranks. Power and influence on the magnitude of the entire galaxy--I bet that's what they were after."

Hann was still shaking his head in disagreement. "They were fools. Ignorant, pathetic fools. I agree with you in that regard, Amero, and that's exactly why I don't believe what you're saying is true."

The old man cleared his throat. "What of the furthest reaches of the Galaxy? Many men and women of Earth pondered and probed this question. Maybe life was concentrated in the secluded arms of the galaxy rather than its dense center. Keen to find the answer, improvements were made to the Pull-technology. More expeditions were sent, and like moss blanketing a rock season by season, humanity spread through the galaxy year after universal year. All reports confirmed what humanity feared most: we are alone. We are a fluke. We are a miracle."

Hann scoffed, "This is bullshit."

Amero held up his hands in a stance of surrender. "I'm not going to accept it right off the bat either, but we don't have any reason to doubt what the old guy is saying, do we?"

The old man did not allow them as long of a break this time. "One day everything changed. A discovery was made. An object was found. Then another. And another. Hundreds of identical, alien objects were uncovered in seemingly arbitrary locations across the galaxy."

The old man lifted his right hand and presented a black object no larger than his thumb. It was ovular with jagged ridges outlining its exterior. It looked to Amero like any random meteorite shard, only this one was coated in a perfectly colorless ebony.

"This is what humanity discovered."

The monitor zoomed in on the shard, then panned back out, resuming the initial scene.

"It is called a Point. It may look simple, but it is anything but. This small shard of unknown material contains multilayered patterns of complexity--a code of sorts--imprinted at the femto-level and beyond. Its origin is unknown. Its composition is unknown. Most importantly, its purpose is unknown. To date, over ten thousand Points have been discovered, analyzed, cataloged, and mapped according to their universal time and location of discovery. Their dispersal throughout the galaxy appears to be random. Humanity's new mission is to locate and document Points. Your mission is no different. Seraphim has been successfully updated. Good luck."

The monitor went blank.

Hann hit it with the palm of his hand. "What the hell. We lost the image."

"No, I think that was the end of the message," Amero said with wide eyes. He found himself unable to look away from the calming emptiness of the monitor. "I think that message was from the New Covenant. It wasn't enough we were successful guinea pigs. It wasn't enough we ushered forth a golden age. They found another way to exploit us, even after all this time and space. The bastards found a way."

"Quiet," Hann growled. "I'm sorry, but please be quiet. You're not helping."

"Not helping? Not helping what?"

"I'm thinking."

"Thinking? Oh right, you're the genius. Look at me—all I can come up with are subpar ideas."

"Shut up," Hann growled with tangible force before softening his edge. "I mean, just please, let me think."

Amero nodded and allowed Hann his space and silence.

Each man was alone with his thoughts for what seemed like an eternity. Suddenly, Hann bolted upright out of his chair. The ceiling of the ship pulled away from his head, morphing the cockpit into a full-size room.

"I thought so... " Hann emitted from beneath his breath.

"What is it?" Amero urged.

Hann let out a great, heaving sigh. "Before we left, the technicians told me that if we were to succeed, and if the machines were to actually make the journey to Tau Ceti, then Seraphim could be remade to travel between stars rather than remaining a mere shield for men to be Pulled great distances."

"And?"

"What do you mean *and?*"

"What does that imply, Hann?"

"The system update, Amero!" Hann said through gritted impatience. "The update was Seraphim's remaking. That wasn't a message from the New Covenant. That was a message from the machines."

"That old guy looked pretty human to me, Hann."

Hann swung his arms in explosive agitation. "Haven't you ever seen a movie? Anything can be made to look genuinely real, especially if the machines are advanced enough to provide the ship with the ability to physically alter itself via a mere transfer of information."

A section of the floor sprouted into a single tendril that quickly shaped itself into a pilot's console. It stretched and crooned toward Amero as if it were an animal begging to be petted. Amero reached out slowly, hesitant to make contact. Where his hand hovered, a new growth took shape; a yoke bent and warped to fit the curve of his hand. Intrigued, Amero pulled his hand away. The console stretched again to meet his hand's new position. Even spinning did not stop the growth from twisting about Amero in order to retain his ability to man the yoke.

"And if I don't want to pilot the ship?" Amero asked.

On command, the ship retracted the console that was now

wrapped multiple times around Amero's arms and torso. It whipped back into the floor of the ship without a sound.

"And if I do want to pilot the ship?"

The console sprang up once more, growing a new yoke to meet Amero's outstretched hand.

Amero shot Hann a smile. "Looks like the machines taught themselves a few useful tricks on their way over."

Hann took no notice of Amero. He busied himself by scrutinizing an oversized monitor, or possibly the same one had grown while Amero tested some of the ship's capabilities. On the monitor, multiple windows displayed dozens of different three-dimensional star maps of the local galaxy and beyond.

Without taking his eyes from the data, Hann said evenly, "We have a problem."

"Now what?" Amero groaned.

"I found Earth," Hann intoned, his voice like a wooden mallet struck against metal.

"On the map? You found it?" Amero checked, curious why Hann would consider such a revelation to be a problem.

"That's right," Hann confirmed stolidly.

"Why is that an issue, Hann?"

"It wasn't there before the update. Now it is. The whole solar system is exactly where it should be."

"Well... that's great, isn't it?"

Hann's gaze rose from the monitor and locked with Amero's eyes. "Is it?" Hann asked testily.

"What are you talking about, Hann? You're asking me?" Amero held up his hands in mock-defense. "I'm not going to play 'guess how far down shit creek we are' just for the hell of it. The Earth is where it should be. How is that a problem?"

Hann shook his head, dissatisfied by Amero's quick acceptance of the events. "It wasn't there. We get an update from a group of renegade machines, and suddenly it is there. You don't find that suspicious?"

Amero was flabbergasted by Hann's reasoning. "Renegade machines? Are you serious, Hann? The New Covenant told us they sent machines to this location. I mean, come on, Hann!" Amero wasn't sure how better to make his case. "They aren't any more renegade than we are."

"We aren't renegade?" Hann asked scoldingly.

Amero threw his hands up in defeat. "Come on, Hann. Now we're part of your conspiracy too?"

"Conspiracy? I never used the word *conspiracy*," Hann said with a sudden burst of suspicion.

"But that's what it sounds like," Amero reasoned. "You're saying the machines went rogue, then waited for us to get here so that they could create an illusion that the Earth is where it should be?" Was Hann seriously considering such wild theories? What exactly did he know that Amero didn't?

"Quiet!" Hann spat, vaporizing any warmth in his voice. "I know what I saw. The ship showed absolutely zero indication that our solar system, let alone Earth, was extant anywhere in the galaxy. Every other star was represented except ours. I had a feeling something was off about the maps right from the start. If the solar system was somehow destroyed, the gravitational effects on neighboring stars would have eventually added up. I knew something was off."

"Is this a joke, Hann?" Amero said in disbelief. "The map was off because it malfunctioned. The system update clearly fixed that. Errors happen. Anomalies happen." Amero felt like Hann was slipping down a spiral of unreasonable supposition, and eventually Amero wouldn't be able to drag him out.

"I don't make mistakes when it comes to star maps, Amero," Hann rumbled.

"Right, right, right," Amero crowed, "the whole genius thing. I get it."

Hann waved Amero away as if he were shooing a fly from his face. "Are you really content with the story from the old man, Amero? Are you really going to take it at face value?"

"We have nothing else to go on, Hann. And until we do, it doesn't appear that we have any other choice."

Hann shook his head. "Then you're just like them. You're just like the New Covenant. You have faith that what the old man told you is the truth. Faith, like sheep have faith in the shepherd that leads them to the slaughter."

"Bullshit, Hann! They gave me as much shit as you. Maybe more."

Hann flashed Amero a vile grin. "You lived like a king at that academy."

Amero cringed, repulsed by the truth, relative as it might be.

"You may *think* you know all about me, Amero, but I know everything about you. Assuming you're not working for them, the New Covenant disposed of you because they had nothing better to do with you. They threw out the mooch, that's all. I didn't have your luxuries. I pulled myself out of the hell that was the laboratories. That's why I'm out here. I escaped my captors. I hoisted myself from their tortuous maw by literally pulling myself across the galaxy. But there are no truths I can't uncover, nor any data nor knowledge nor any understanding that I can't find. I will find the truth, Amero."

"The...truth?" Amero stammered.

"Of what the hell happened to Earth!" Hann growled. "And the truth of who you are, Amero Hiddiger!"

"Right... the truth... " Amero trailed off. He was growing tired of speaking in circles.

Hann turned to face an empty wall. "Show me outside," he demanded.

The charcoal-gray of the ship's wall began to dissolve to transparency, unfurling the perilous, enveloping depths of the cosmos. A sudden rush of vertigo overtook Amero. This was real. They were among the stars, further from the Earth than Amero had ever dared dream possible.

The transparent section of the wall, now a large window, continued to dissolve. Soon the whole ceiling was transparent, then even the ground. Infinity wrapped around them from all sides. They were a speck of meat and metal laid bare upon endless space.

Amero fell backward, reeling. The floor morphed into a soft crèche of sorts, catching him, though not stopping the air from being knocked out of his lungs.

Hann did not move a muscle. He stood with his mouth agape, arms blissfully numb at his sides. "Thank you, Seraphim, truly, thank you... " Hann said with child-like awe in his voice. He looked disapprovingly at Amero, then said, "but a single viewport will do just fine."

The walls reformed, coating the now invisible hull of the ship to form a defined interior once more. Amero was grateful for the return to relative normality.

"What will you do, Hann? What is your plan?" Amero asked, catching his breath.

Hann nodded more to himself than to Amero. "I'm going to play their game. I'm going to do as the machines say. But make no mistake, I will find the truth. They're hiding something from us, Amero. I know you don't want to believe it, but something isn't right here. For all we know, even the story about the Points was made up. Or maybe it's something else entirely. Something I'm completely overlooking."

"What, like God?" Amero mused.

On cue with Amero's words, a holographic display filled the room, revealing an extensively complex, highly organized three-dimensional map of the local galaxy. The map was color-coded and spatially to scale. Swathes of miniscule, dull green points orbited a seemingly endless spray of slightly larger, scintillating yellow points, while even more vibrant violet points whirled in great wily curves about the room. It was like a choreographed dance of technicolor fireflies. At the center of the projection, directly between the men, there was a symbol depicting a set of pearl-white wings. Adjacent to the wings was a large yellow sphere orbited by five smaller green spheres.

"A star map," Hann gasped. "The wings--that must be Seraphim. That star next to us is Tau Ceti. And the blue star," Hann pointed to an azure-blue dot a foot away from where they currently stood, "that's where they're pretending Earth is."

Amero made to protest Hann, but all of a sudden, the entire room shone gold. A thousand different shades of gold appeared as new, smaller points attached to suns, planets and other celestial objects.

50

"Aha!" Amero exclaimed, "these must be the Points. But why the different shades? Something to do with proximity?"

"Assuming they are Points, it can't be proximity. The shades are too randomly dispersed," Hann noted.

The men searched for a key or legend, anything that might explain the new spectacle.

"Wait," Amero began, "the old man--he said others were searching for Points too. He said good luck. That means they aren't certain where the Points are."

"So, the shades of gold--you think they represent the likelihood of a Point being at each particular location?"

Amero chuckled. "I suppose that's the implication, but I'm more lost than you are, Hann. It's a possibility, that's all."

Hann looked more at ease now that he had a tangible problem to work out. "There are other colors on this map that we still don't know. Brown for large asteroids? Purple looks like comets. And what about these pink ovals?"

Amero shrugged in defeat. "Ship? I mean, Seraphim? Can you help us out here?"

In response, a legend appeared on a side wall. It spelled out precisely what each color represented, as well as the meaning of the shades of gold. The legend revealed that Amero had been right: it had to do with probability, not proximity.

"Why didn't the ship show us the legend to begin with? Why is it keeping information from us?" Hann demanded to know.

Amero couldn't stomach any more machine conspiracy. "Why are you so scared of machines?"

"I'm not," Hann grunted viscerally before forcing himself to soften his tone. "I'm not, but they've already proven to be untrustworthy."

Amero shook his head. "That's still just your theory, Hann. Just a theory."

Hann's eyes widened, readying the rest of his body for a verbal attack. Amero held up a hand to stop him. "Look at the legend--the pink dots are called stations. The legend says they provide human amenities. I think we should try to make it to one of those."

Hann looked amused by the change in course of the conversation. "I know this map makes it look easy, but these places are incredibly far away. We've no idea how to fly this ship, let alone activate another Pull across space. And that's assuming the system update included outfitting the ship with a stand-alone Pull-device."

"Again, let's ask," Amero offered. "Seraphim? Did you hear Hann? Can this ship fly to other stars...quickly? With a Pull-device?"

Text appeared on the wall just below the legend in blazingly large font. It read, "*No.*"

Hann slammed a fist against the monitor. "Then how the hell are we supposed to get out of this system? How do we travel back to the home system?"

"I thought home was gone," Amero reminded Hann reproachfully.

"It is," Hann rumbled, "and I'll prove it to you."

More text appeared on the wall. "*Stations upgrade ship. More stations = more upgrades. Upgrades cost money. Points = money. More Points = more money = more upgrades. More upgrades = travel home.*"

Hann slammed his foot against the floor. "Is this a fucking joke to the ship? Are the machines getting a kick out of this?"

"Hann, calm down. Please," Amero said, scared that Hann might damage the ship if he kept kicking its insides.

"Quiet!" Hann growled. "You heard them. This is a fucking game to them. Get the Points to get the money to get the upgrades to go home. This is fucking insanity."

"And it doesn't sound like something a machine would cook up," Amero insisted. "It sounds like something the New Covenant would plan. This is our penance. It's got to be. This was all planned."

"Put your hand out," Hann said unexpectedly.

"What?"

"Do it. Take hold of the yoke. Fly this thing to the closest Point. We need money."

"To go home, Hann? You want to go back?" Amero couldn't believe it. They had been displaced across the galaxy, and now the first thing they were going to do was about-face and return obediently with their tails between their legs. Still, Amero supposed it was better than being consumed by the vastness of the void.

Hann's stare was death itself. He spoke with icy poise. "No. We aren't going back. Earth isn't there. However, if we can outfit this craft with Pull-technology, it won't make a difference where we want to go. I'll prove to you that Earth is gone, and then we'll have ourselves a foray across the cosmos--all that in a few hours' time."

Amero was pretty sure Hann was more confident than certain. "You hesitated before, Hann. Admit it: you've no idea whether or not the Earth's initial absence on the map wasn't just a ship malfunction."

"We're being toyed with," Hann said, absolutely certain. "Toyed with by highly advanced machines. Keep telling yourself something as fickle and hypocritical as the New Covenant survived the age of technological achievement we ushered upon the Earth. Keep it up, Amero, and you might just convince yourself."

"Hann... "

"Put your hand out. We need money," Hann interjected.

"Hann... I... "

"We're done having this conversation, Amero. We're done with conversations. We're going to find some Points, then we're going to fly to a station, and then we're going to upgrade this ship. And we're going to keep upgrading it until we have enough power to find the fuckers toying with us. They're out there, Amero. They sent us that update. They pulled us into this game. There's no reason for this. It brings a whole new meaning to the term 'guinea pig.'"

Amero went wide eyed and balked, but was it possible that Hann was right? Were their actions from here on out all part of a grander plan? Or worse, was there no plan at all? Amero offered, "You said it yourself: the New Covenant is dead and gone whether the Earth still exists or not. If your theory is right, then we aren't guinea pigs anymore."

"And the game?" Hann asked.

"It's not a game. It's called resources," Amero said, offering what he perceived to be another reasonable explanation for their predicament.

"Resources? What the hell are machines doing with *money*? Unless..." Hann's eyes turned to slits, and he gazed at Amero suspiciously.

"What? What is it?" Amero asked, inspecting himself for something grotesque or out of the ordinary.

Hann shook his head. "No, nevermind. Nevermind. Put out your hand. Fly this thing. Let's just get going."

Amero didn't press Hann's suspicion; he was just as stumped. It was strange that the message would use the term *money* even if it was an intermediary word with a wholly different meaning in the machines' language—there it was... *the machines' language*. Amero was already thinking like Hann, thinking in terms that implied some secret conspiracy devised by the machines. No, Hann could believe what he wanted. Amero knew the truth: the New Covenant was anything but fickle. It was religion, after all, and religion would always exist in one form or another for as long as men and women continued making men and women.

Amero reached out his hand. The floor sprouted and filled his grip.

"Let's go."

CHAPTER 6

S eraphim surveyed and filled Amero's mind, and in turn, Amero utilized Seraphim's vast array of hardware and software at an utterly immersive and subjective level. Time passed quickly this way, and after what felt like only a few hours, they were already near the closest Point.

So long as Amero stayed calm, the yoke sprouting from Seraphim's interior served as a natural extension of his own mind and body. If he mentally willed himself upon Seraphim, their connection was severed, leaving Amero feeling both naked and vulnerable, displaced from his body with the violent shock of being forcefully submerged beneath thick ice. Such incidents could only be avoided by trusting Seraphim's...intuition. Of course, this was easier said than done.

Amero found it difficult to reconcile the idea of a ship having intuition, but that was precisely what it felt like. Through his movements, emotions, thoughts, and intentions, Amero communed with Seraphim at levels far deeper than his conscious and even subconscious mind could follow. The result of their connection was a hybrid mind created and enhanced through Amero and Seraphim's mutually receptive interplay of conscious awareness. It was a complex system of biological and digital exchange that ultimately transformed space flight into an activity requiring no more than practiced concentration.

The best Amero could do with his still active, quasi-individualized, conscious mind was breathe and relax himself as thoroughly as possible. The more he relaxed, the more easily Seraphim directed his hand with the yoke, while Amero's subconscious will drove Seraphim's direction. In this way, Amero was disconnected and then reconnected back to his own body as an outside observer with Seraphim acting as a digital and physical filter to the outside universe.

Through Seraphim's senses, the gravitational tug of Tau Ceti felt like the prickle of numerous hypodermic needles on Amero's spine, and the piercing radiation of starlight was like the warm weight of heavy wool blankets on a cruelly frigid winter night. It was thrilling to experience Seraphim as his own body, but it was like a dream. Every time the connection was severed, there remained only a vague, blurred simulacrum of the experience in Amero's memory. Each subsequent return to the connection was largely a new experience with only the faintest hints of familiarity at the periphery of the dream-like journey through the void.

Amero was on his third straight hour-long round of being connected, when Hann suddenly broke his concentration. "Your scrunched up face makes it look like you're undergoing cardiac arrest."

Hann's rumbling bass voice reverberated against the silence of the ship, punching Amero fully out of Seraphim and back into his own body. Amero was left cold and confused, gulping for air as he staggered forward onto all four limbs.

Hann gave no indication of concern. Instead, he went on talking. "You'll have to get used to that feeling for now. I suppose after some time your ability to remain one-pointed in thought will prevent any negative reaction, but until then, the shock is unavoidable."

Amero caught his breath and tapped the floor; a soft crèche sprouted and grew from beneath him, cradling his body and filling his immediate surroundings with the smell of poppy flowers. It was one of his favorite scents, and the ship knew this, for it knew his mind better than anyone, including himself.

"Why don't you give it a spin?" Amero insisted to Hann with a jab of his arm toward the yoke.

Hann shook his grim face methodically. "Never. They have your mind now, Amero. You've taken communion with them."

Amero chuckled at the familiar New Covenant jargon. "Is that the official name for connecting with Seraphim?"

Hann stared at Amero with profound, macabre distaste. "Do not ever offer me communion with the machines. That can be your role. In fact... " Hann cocked his head conspiratorially and ruminated out loud. "Is that why your name was in the Message from God? You are my vehicle, so to speak? But to what end?"

Amero shook his head. What exactly did Hann know that he had not or would not tell Amero? "What is this message you keep talking about, Hann?"

"You tell me," Hann said, standing subtly straighter and jutting his huge chest forward either out of malice or at the genetic whim of some ancestral remnant of humanity's beginnings when primate codes of dominance meant everything. Just as suddenly, Hann checked himself and consciously softened his stance to a state of neutral poise.

"You really think I have something to do with all this?" Amero asked, waving his arms in frustration. "If anything, I should be suspicious of *you*. You're the one that seems to know so much about Seraphim and the machines and everything else. And your neck... those scars are fresh, Hann. What happened to you? Who are you really, Hann?"

Hann strained a single step forward, controlling his composure with obvious practice. "There were two names in the message, Amero. Your name and the name of a well known rebel, Jakob Rohrshan. Jakob's presumed to be dead, and even if he were alive, he's gone now. That leaves you. So, *you* tell me: what is *your* part to play in all this, Amero Hiddiger?"

More than Hann's background, Amero wished to discover who exactly it was that Hann believed Amero to be. Hann's indignant confidence that Amero was actively concealing his identity thoroughly annoyed and even disturbed Amero. If Amero's name really was mentioned in an important New Covenant message, wasn't it equally likely that Amero was an expendable pawn? Despite the obvious fallacies in Hann's logic, he persisted in his assertions that Amero was working against him as an ally of the New Covenant.

Hann took another large step toward Amero, but this time it made Amero feel penetrated, like the sensation of being watched at a distance by a predator both cunning and hungry.

"Stay where you are," Amero warned.

Hann shook his head with mild amusement. "Are you afraid of

me, Amero?"

Amero didn't consider himself weak by any means, but he wasn't a large man either. He had been in a few fights in his life, minor scuffles really, but he had always ended up on top. Hann, however, was another matter entirely. Hann's mere presence filled space with a gluttonous tenacity; his bulwark of muscle and mind was but a further addition to his already titanous being. If Hann wished it, he could dispose of Amero with the ease of tossing away a tattered doll.

"Back on Earth," Amero began cautiously, "I was awake when you entered the hangar." The sudden urge to look outside the viewport overcame Amero, but he reminded himself that Seraphim could fly on autopilot nearly as well as flying via the utilization of his mind. Amero hesitated, uncertain how to gauge Hann's glare presently daring Amero to continue. Amero willed himself to stand his ground. "You killed the New Covenant guards...outside Seraphim... back in the hangar. I was awake," Amero admitted.

"So what if I did?" Hann checked. "Do you have a soft spot for New Covenant men?"

Was Hann really so cold? Was Amero locked in a cage with a killer?

Amero shrugged, putting on a show of ease. "If they're handsome enough to take to bed, what's their religion got to do with it? I've slept with plenty of men who claimed to be devout New Covenant followers; they're just surviving is all."

"Pathetic," Hann growled. "They fail to even put up a fight against their oppressor. They are tamed sheep...like you, Amero Hiddiger."

The insult meant nothing to Amero, but he did find it interesting to note that each side of the coin, Hann and the New Covenant, both mutually despised him. Even more interesting was Hann's particular choice of words. "Oppressor?" Amero said with newfound curiosity. "How old are you, Hann?"

Amero had grown up without ever knowing a world outside of the New Covenant's reign. To refer to them as an oppressor was accurate, but it was also archaic. The oppressing was completed long before Amero was born. To Amero, the New Covenant was the backdrop of reality's present, but to Hann, the New Covenant was apparently an interjection of his normal life. However, for that to be true, Hann would have to be sixty or seventy years old, at least.

"I'm old enough to know that the New Covenant oppresses; it is the nature of the beast."

"I can't argue with you there," Amero said, letting go of Hann's age and returning to the point, "but just because the New Covenant oppresses people like you and me doesn't mean all of its members deserve to be killed. On the contrary, some of my closest friends are New Covenant members." *Your only friend,* Amero corrected himself inwardly. "Do you believe yourself a worthy judge of who should live and die?" Amero asked, folding his arms and shifting his weight.

"Those guards were complicit in my imprisonment," Hann explained with sallow, calculated consideration. "They deserved death; I stand by that." Hann allowed Amero a few moments of discomfort. "I did not kill them, however. I don't take death so lightly."

It was clear Hann had considered all this many times before.

"Then what did you do? They sounded pretty dead to me," Amero insisted, remembering the sordid sound of a man struggling to suck in air.

"I incapacitated them," Hann explained casually. "They've all grown old and died by now, Amero. It makes no difference either way."

Amero scoffed at Hann's casual indifference. "It makes a big difference to me whether or not you're the type of person that just goes around killing others." With a twinge of horror, Amero thought back to the dream he had after the Pull. "We're cooped up in a ship the size of a small trailer; I don't want us to end up strangling each other."

Hann nodded. "I agree. So, stay out of my way, and I'll stay out of yours."

"That's one approach," Amero considered sarcastically, then insisted, "another is working together."

Hann flashed Amero his already classic fatal glare. "I work alone. Besides, I still don't trust you."

A wave of frustration practically strangled Amero; he was getting nowhere at all with Hann. "Look, we have to work together at some point. I get that you don't trust me, but you're stuck with me regardless. Shouldn't we at least have a plan?"

"I have a plan," Hann stated simply.

"Would you like to share it?" Amero forced himself to say with mock-pleasantness.

"No."

"No?"

"That's correct," Hann confirmed stoically.

Amero threw up his hands in defeat. "You're acting like a child, Hann. We have to work together."

Hann pointed a finger outside the viewport. "We're heading toward a potential Point as it is. Seraphim will require the precision of your mind as we enter orbit and break the potential atmosphere around Tau Ceti E."

"Like that, for example," Amero said. "How do you know that?"

Hann cocked his head in consideration. "I was imprisoned in that lab for over a decade. Seraphim was housed there, and I had the opportunity on more than a few occasions to inspect its design."

Amero's face went sour in disbelief. "If you're going to lie, at least make it believable. What you said doesn't explain how you could possibly know the ship's capabilities to such a fine degree of detail."

Hann shrugged. "Believe what you want to believe."

Amero couldn't help admiring Hann's tenacious will to remain elusive. "Will you at least tell me the basics of what your plan entails? Just the immediate details?"

Hann considered Amero's words. After a few moments of brooding, he nodded. "We find a Point, then another, and another. Then we find a station, and there I will find my answers."

"Answers?"

"We've already gone over this, Amero. Answers, like who you really are, for one," Hann accused.

"And what else?" Amero pressed, but Hann was unwilling to speak any further. He simply nodded at the viewport, then walked to the monitor and took a seat.

Amero tried calling his name, but Hann was fully ignoring him now. "Fine, just keep quiet then," Amero told him gruffly before grabbing the yoke.

The effects of communion were instantaneous.

Amero's awareness expanded one-hundredfold, then jumped several orders of magnitude further. Star systems dozens of light years in all directions hummed their frequencies across the void. Tau Ceti howled its brilliance, pummeling Amero and Seraphim's shared body with a ceaseless spray of charged photons and neutrinos. Planets orbited the star with suggestive pushes and pulls of gravitational influence, and Amero used Seraphim's grav-catches to ride the deepest valleys of spacetime depression from one area to the next. Through Seraphim, Amero glided across the gravitationally curved fabric of spacetime as if it were the icy, jagged slopes of an ever-shifting mountain. Of course, if it weren't for Seraphim's so-called intuition, Amero would have quickly succumbed to the constant threat of directionless disorientation.

With Seraphim's body as his own, Amero coasted through fields abounding with the snaking currents of cosmic detritus orbiting the planet Tau Ceti E. Seraphim's hull could handle its fair share of micro-collisions, but any piece of debris with a quarter of Seraphim's mass could inflict serious damage with only minimal velocity. It required his full attention, but Amero handled it with the ease of navigating an amateur obstacle course.

Tau Ceti E tugged at Amero, willing him into orbit. Suddenly, Seraphim severed communion, but this time the iciness coursing through Amero's veins was no more than a dull ache.

"I think it's getting easier," Amero told Hann with a measure of relief.

Hann stared at Amero through an intense frown. "Don't get too used to it. You might forget what it's like to be human."

Amero placated Hann's warning with a playful roll of his eyes. "Do me a favor, Hann. You try enjoying life once in a while, and I'll do my best to make sure the robots don't possess my mind. How's that sound?"

"It sounds like you're attempting to get me to sympathize with your robotic masters," Hann said, still staring intently.

Amero searched for words but came up short.

Hann cracked a smile. "That was a joke."

"You'll get the hang of it," Amero assured him. "In the meantime, I appreciate the effort." Amero offered Hann a friendly grin; Hann responded by rerouting his gaze to the viewport.

A soft turquoise glow persuaded Amero to do the same. Outside the viewport, Tau Ceti E cast its brilliance through various shades of earthly hues. Azure oceans spanning the visible face of the planet curved at the globe's edges, sparkling seamlessly into the eternal night of space. Directly below, Amero observed a small atoll dwarfed by the endless ocean engulfing its vibrant coasts. Each individual island brimmed with what he assumed was vegetation, though the violet coasts and umber innards of the islands could just as well be some strange shade of rock or coral or something altogether unexpected.

The colors were all wrong--Tau Ceti E was clearly alien--but Amero still felt a dreadful pang of reminiscence. They were so far from Earth, and if one was to side with Hann, then there was still a possibility that something had made Earth vanish. Amero wished at least that he could know for sure whether the Earth's disappearance was a mere error. He hated the society he was born into, but he would never wish it to die completely. Death was the easy way out. Amero wished to see humanity flourish into something beyond the New Covenant, beyond religion itself, beyond all the limitations mankind used to cage its mind and imagination.

Amero glanced at Hann and was startled by his expression. Hann probed the planet with sharpened scorn from beneath heavy eyebrows, as if Tau Ceti E's presence was a personal affront to his space. A twitch at Hann's temple and an unexpected gulp told Amero that Hann was consciously keeping his emotions in check. A flash of tragic beauty was woven into the deepest pockets of Hann's forced calm; beneath the callousness there was a soft interior after all--Amero was certain of it. Hann wasn't emotionless. In fact, he was more human than he probably cared to admit.

"Look," Hann said, pointing to the horseshoe-shaped island chain.

Amero was ready to ask what he should be looking for when he finally saw it--as obvious as a pinecone in a stack of eggs. A miniscule barge at the center of the atoll shone gold, extending vertically some distance, like a beacon illuminating the location of something precious.

"The Point. That's it, isn't it?" Amero asked.

Hann shrugged. "If it is, then what's the point?"

Amero tossed his chin at Hann, signaling him to go on.

"If the machines already know where the Point is," Hann began, "then what's the point of us coming here to retrieve it?"

"Should we ask Seraphim?" Amero offered cautiously, nervous that Hann might dive into another robot conspiracy tirade.

"Go on," Hann dared, "ask your new masters the rules of the game they are forcing us to play."

Amero rolled his eyes. "Go on, Seraphim. What's going on here? Do the machines know where all the Points are?"

Seraphim did not answer right away. Amero imagined that every moment Seraphim did not answer was another slag of fodder to be added to Hann's arsenal of reasons to be paranoid. After several long seconds, Seraphim displayed its answer as bold white text painted across the viewport: "*Tutorial.*"

"You see, it is a game," Hann weighed. "And if this is a tutorial, then it means it's not always going to be this easy."

The wall to their right suddenly began to extend in both directions, growing outward from its center to extend the ship by a length of multiple feet in either direction. The expansion stopped, and there appeared on the wall a fluorescent green hexagon outlining a space roughly the size of a doorway. From the hexagon's center, the wall irised open, revealing a small chamber filled by two sections of metal-coated wall carved at multiple ninety-degree planes to form two spartan seats facing one another.

"*Rock-hop ready,*" the ship said, replacing the old message on the viewport with new text.

"What is it?" Amero asked while Hann crooned his neck, inspecting the new space from a strategic distance.

"*Planetary descent: dangerous. Rock-hop: safe,*" a new message on the viewport explained.

"It's a separate craft used for orbit-to-planet and planet-to-orbit transport," Hann explained. "It makes sense from a logistical standpoint, but why are we still at such a great distance from the planet? We can afford to get significantly closer to the planet without any loss in safety."

"Maybe Seraphim wants to give you and me some alone time in the rock-hop," Amero offered jokingly, aiming to test Hann's reaction.

"I think," Hann said seriously, "that it's you and *Seraphim* that need the alone time. You seem to enjoy the communion of consciousness with Seraphim well enough."

Amero snickered. "Are you jealous of a fucking ship, Hann? Has your paranoia transformed into some bizarre, vindictive state of lustful jealousy?"

Hann looked disgusted. "Those are all your words, not mine," he rumbled. "Besides, you're not even my type."

Amero knew it was petty to be offended for not being another man's type, but he couldn't help it. Amero was attractive by any metric; if Hann denied that, then he was just being stupid, not picky.

"What's your type, then?" Amero probed.

"I like Christians," Hann said simply.

Amero burst into laughter; Hann turned away from him and crawled inside the dimly lit rock-hop.

Amero bent slightly to fit inside the rock-hop, then took his seat across from Hann and began working at the straps.

"A slave who loves his oppressors--that's some seriously masochistic shit, Hann."

"The New Covenant has nothing to do with Christianity other than stemming from its history," Hann retorted. "You flaunt and cherish your life of sin, Amero Hiddiger, which is all the more reason not to trust you."

Amero shook his head in disbelief. "Is this a joke, Hann? What about everything you said before the Pull? Was it not blasphemous to talk about Jesus and God that way?"

Hann smiled serenely. "Christ was a radical, church-hating, whore-loving Jew, Amero. What he preached had nothing to do with the New Covenant. The New Covenant is an abomination of Christianity, just as Christianity is an abomination of Christ's actual teachings."

Amero finally succeeded in hooking the straps together. They tightened on their own accord, but they remained perfectly comfortable. Amero said a mental *thank you* for not having to contend with living straps again.

Amero met Hann's gaze, but instead of responding to his comment about Christianity, he let out an unexpected yelp. Amero pointed a shaky finger at Hann.

"What is it?" Hann asked lazily with forced interest.

"Your...scar... " Amero hesitated, rapidly running over a mental checklist of possibilities. "It's practically gone."

"Scar?" Hann asked in genuine bewilderment.

"The scar across your neck!" Amero demanded.

Hann stroked his neck broadly and offered Amero a look of disappointment. "Was the scar in your dream, too?"

Amero made to jump up in anger, but he was gently persuaded to remain seated by the slight tightening of the straps. "I know for a fact you had a scar across your neck, Hann. Who's bullshitting who right now?" Amero felt overwhelmed by Hann's audacious arrogance. Did he take Amero for a fool? Hann had already baselessly accused Amero of working with the machines, and now he was claiming that Amero's entire sense of reality was askew?

Amero peered closer at Hann's neck and saw that there was still a fine line of discoloration where there had once been thick scar-tissue. "What did you do, Hann? What are you hiding from me? How did you get rid of the scar?"

"You imagined the scar, Amero," Hann persisted. "You were in shock when we first met. Hell--you mistook a dream for reality; clearly your mind has suffered a great deal of fatigue from this experience. Don't you think it's possible you imagined it all?"

"Fuck you," Amero jabbed, and he was glad for reacting with such vehemence. Hann was playing him by trying to distort reality in such a way that he could have power over Amero. Was that his angle?

Staring into Hann's unrelenting eyes, each of them an endless chasm of awful, unyielding force, Amero figured it was best to drop the issue for the moment. Hann clearly wasn't willing to talk about it, and pressing the matter might only push him further away.

"If you don't want to talk about the scar, that's fine, but don't tell me it wasn't there. When are you going to stop hiding things from me, Hann?" Amero asked fiercely.

"I am under no obligation to share information with you, Amero," Hann said evenly.

"But why wouldn't you?" Amero urged. "We're in this together!"

Hann shook his head, terminating any scant semblance of solidarity. "I will remain amicable, but I told you before: I don't trust you. You are an unknown variable of incredible magnitude amidst other unknown variables of incredible magnitudes."

"Just because my name was in a message?" Amero asked.

"Not a message, Amero. *The* message."

Hann broke away from the conversation and peered outside the small window on the wall between them. As the men were speaking, Seraphim had turned and then rolled over to position the rock-hop directly in line with the planet. Just as Amero was about to take a stab at continuing the conversation, the rock-hop door irised shut, and the men were suddenly accelerated at several g's toward Tau Ceti E.

Gripping the straps and clenching his jaw tight, Amero felt his stomach lurch. He brought his breathing under control and sipped air through the mounting g force. Not an inch of Hann's face showed any sign of strain; each additional g seemed only to refine Hann's Zen-like state of calm.

Though the rock-hop continued to accelerate, the wall of rock sinking into Amero's chest began to be lifted.

"We must be slowing down," Amero noted.

"On the contrary," Hann droned, eyes closing softly, "we are accelerating at several g's per second. It appears the machines have taught themselves a clever trick indeed: L-A-D, or localized-accelerative-dampening.

"Localized-accelerative-dampening?" Amero echoed incredulously.

Hann nodded slightly. "I know it in theory. Apparently the machines know it in practice."

Tau Ceti E had grown so that only a fraction of it filled the window; they were undoubtedly still accelerating.

"Fine," Amero said, accepting Hann's explanation. "But how are we going to slow down? We must be accelerating at several hundred g's by now. We'll turn to mush if this thing slows any faster than a g or two per second, and we're already too close!"

Flames enveloped the rock-hop, but it did a thorough job of softening what should have been breakneck turbulence. They were inside Tau Ceti E's atmosphere, rocketing at a whole order of magnitude beyond the speed of sound directly at the ocean shimmering like thick, tumultuous glass below them.

"Localized-inertial-dampening," Hann stated calmly, and at the same moment the world rushed against the rock-hop and consumed it whole. At least, that's what Amero expected to happen. He had closed his eyes at the last moment before impact, just before they shattered into a million fragments against the surface of the planet.

The faint whisper of a breeze forced Amero's eyes open; the rock-hop's wall had already irised, revealing blue skies and a light yellowish-green, rocky surface.

Seraphim presented writing on the wall across from the entrance.

Temperature = 24°C. Pressure = 14.18 psi. Atmospheric Composition: N = 76.6%, O = 21.7%, Ar = 1.2%, CO_2 = .08%, Ne = .0014%, He = .0032%, Kr = .00048%, NH_3 = .00036%, HF = .00023%. No human pathogens. No predators. Tau Ceti E = Safe."

"The atmosphere is near identical to Earth's," Hann issued as he unstrapped. He rose and walked along the metal flaps now being utilized as a vestibule surrounding a ramp that led to the planet's surface. Hann's heavy steps thudded loudly on the ramp, but they were softened to a scrape when they met the outside ground.

"Are you sure we shouldn't be wearing a suit or something?" Amero checked cautiously, though it didn't matter now that the hatch was wide open.

Hann dug his fingers into powdery yellow soil and let the planet fall through his loose grip. "The levels of ammonia and hydrogen fluoride are a bit concerning, along with the krypton, but the damage shouldn't be too severe, I imagine."

Seraphim responded to Hann with new writing. "*Stasis chamber.*"

Hann nodded with annoyance. "The machines have a solution for everything, don't they?"

Amero brushed off the machine paranoia. "How does the first step outside the solar system feel?" Amero asked, still strapped in as he attempted to weigh the profundity of what was occurring.

Hann shrugged, though it was clear from the way his eyes scanned the horizon with hungry fervor that he was enjoying himself in his own way. "Unstrap and try it out for yourself," Hann issued coldly.

Amero undid the latch at his waist and stepped cautiously onto the alien planet. The vegetation he saw from Seraphim's viewport turned out to be a vibrant element naturally abundant in Tau Ceti E's crustal composition.

"The surface is so green," Amero said, "and those violet shores-- I thought from so far away that those colors might be indications of life."

Hann shook his head stoically. "The machines said life is a miracle, remember?"

Amero nodded. "Maybe that part of their story was true--maybe life is as rare as humanity always supposed.

Hann rumbled in consideration, but he said nothing.

Amero spun round to check his surroundings and saw the unmistakable glow of golden light a few hundred feet away. "There it is," he said to Hann. "Maybe you should stay here, seeing as how you have such little trust in me."

"I have zero trust in you," Hann corrected. "*Little* is an overestimation."

Amero shook his head in awe at Hann's incredible persistence.

68

"Let's take a walk, Amero Hiddiger," Hann said finally. "You go first. I'll follow close behind."

"You're acting like a child, Hann."

"Wrong. I'm taking precautions. How many times must I tell you: I don't trust you, Amero."

Amero locked eyes with Hann, but he accepted that there was no look of frustration or string of rhetoric that could crack him.

"Walk," Hann ordered, both blunt and neutral in his tone.

Amero gave up any form of protestation, but he made sure to remind Hann that he was no pushover either. "When you order people around like that, it makes them feel like a lifeless game piece. I'm walking because we have no other choice. I'm walking on my own accord."

Hann appeared to derive great amusement from Amero's show of rebellion. "We are all of us game pieces, Amero. Most aren't aware of it. Even those who command armies are themselves played by higher powers."

Amero turned heel. "We're not in the Desolate Zones any more, old man. I'm not one of your rebel friends. You have no authority over me, Hann. I write my own story, thank you."

Hann considered Amero's words, then said simply, "Walk."

When would it end? When would Hann finally accept Amero as a mere game piece without a motive? Amero had been thrown into this mess, and he wanted nothing more than a stiff spliff and a good looking young man to go to bed with. Someone with less lip than Hann, like the one from the previous night. Amero felt a pang of regret over Bart, or was it Bret? Damn Hann! It couldn't be true! The Earth must still exist, at least in some form or another.

Amero glanced behind his shoulder and watched Hann absorb his surroundings with piercing attention, darting his eyes from one direction to the next with the constant anticipation of discovery. The blue sky above was only a few shades away from being a perfect imitation of a sunny day on Earth. The vibrant rocks composing the atoll were alluring, but there was nothing peculiar beyond their alien coloration. A few quick glances in each direction were more than sufficient to digest the whole of the environment in full detail.

Amero wondered at Hann's ordinary state of being before Seraphim had ever been a concern, before the so-called message. Had Hann always been so overwhelmingly paranoid?

"What's the big deal with the message, Hann?" Amero said, eyes fixated a hundred or so feet ahead on the patch of golden light.

"There's no way they faked your name, Amero," Hann said.

"I never claimed they did."

Hann hummed in contemplation. "Something beyond Earth... something well beyond our solar system...included your name in a message sent directly to humanity. That's what the New Covenant called it, at least. *The Message from God*. It was more of a random array of code than anything else, but it came with a key, and that key translated the seemingly random array of data into something resembling coherence. The last few years of New Covenant activity have been entirely preoccupied with the contents of the Message. Your name and the name of Jakob the Rebel were the only names to appear in the message. Much of the contents was open to interpretation, but those names were spelled out clear as day."

Amero stopped in his tracks and turned to Hann with wide eyes. "Something from outside Earth sent the New Covenant a message with my name in it? Something...like an entity? Another life form?"

"What life form? If there was life in the universe, why didn't we detect it before then? Why send that single message?" Hann pressed.

"What else could it be?" Amero asked.

"You tell me, Amero Hiddiger!" Hann growled.

Amero shook his head. Would Hann always distrust him? It seemed like his suspicion would never end, not even if Amero could somehow present some kind of irrefutable and immutable proof of his innocence and dissociation with the machines or whatever else had control of the men's lives.

"Hann...why won't you believe me?" Amero urged, this time with a measure of disappointment.

"Walk," Hann croaked.

Hann kept his distance behind Amero even after they arrived at the source of light. With a flash, the golden glow in front of them jumped above their heads and up into the sky as it was flicked away from the planet in Seraphim's direction.

"Seraphim was showing us the way," Amero said.

Hann strode forward to where the light's center had been. Nestled undisturbed in a shallow crevice carved out of the rocky ground, the ebony shard beckoned to be retrieved. Hann picked up the shard and held it above his head, inspecting it by the light of Tau Ceti.

"It's a Point!" Amero exclaimed with genuine surprise and intrigue. "I half expected this whole thing to be a cruel joke, but at least the machines didn't lie about the Points."

Amero forced himself to ignore Hann's contagious paranoia as best he could, opting instead for an outlook that would leave him with some semblance of hope and sanity. As long as an enigma remains enigmatic, why assume it to be malicious? In what way could such a mental maneuver possibly be beneficial to oneself? "Maybe they're telling the truth about the rest of the message too," Amero offered. "Maybe?" he said again, this time with greater strain.

Hann considered Amero's reasoning in brooding silence. Finally, he said, "maybe."

Glowing text appeared in front of the men like heated air obscuring a distant object. Amero assumed it to be Seraphim creating the message literally out of thin air through some yet unknown technology. *"Congratulations. Tutorial complete. No more guiding lights. No more help. Good luck."*

The text vanished from top to bottom, returning each man to the reality of standing atop an island several light years away from where home ought to be.

"No more help," Hann mumbled, "then that means... "

Hann didn't bother finishing his point because there was no need. Both men stood face to face with the same star map they had studied on Seraphim. It expanded to fill the space between them, charting the local galaxy with incredible detail. There was only one difference: all the golden points had been removed.

"What the hell!" Amero groaned. "Why leave us in the dark if they had information for us before?"

Hann eyed Amero with scorn. "The machines are playing a

game, Amero, and we've no option but to continue playing...for now."

"We don't even have a clue where to begin, Hann. They took away all the clues."

Hann tapped his skull. "I remember the original map in perfect detail."

Amero chuckled with relief. "You're a fucking genius, Hann."

Hann ignored Amero and pointed a finger at the closest of the few pink colored dots. "Our next stop is that station, but we might as well collect a few Points along the way."

"Sounds like a plan, Hann. Does this mean you're starting to trust me?"

"No," Hann issued emotionlessly. "Not at all."

Give him time, Amero told himself, and he had the lucid feeling that there would be more than enough time to spare as they embarked into the unknown future.

CHAPTER 7

A few hundred thousand miles ahead, the station called Trinity appeared as a tiny, metallic pinecone misplaced in the infinite night. It had taken just over a month to reach the station, but finally Amero and Hann saw it on the monitor with their own eyes. The image on the monitor was made possible through hordes of probes that Seraphim employed to accurately predict and map the ever changing local cosmos.

The interstellar darkness separating Tau Ceti and the next closest star, Epsilon Eridani, was even more devoid of light than Amero imagined possible. Though it frightened him to peer into the star-smeared void outside the viewport through his own eyes, it was anything but frightening to experience it directly through communion. Utilizing Seraphim's sensory instrumentation, Amero immersed himself in the freedom of boundless, weightless, and frictionless flight. There were no major sources of gravity tugging at his skin, no major celestial objects to combat, and most of all, no gravitational currents to navigate. Their course was mostly a straight shot, but every so often Seraphim mentally suggested that they bend or warp their flight vector away from Trinity all for the sake of reorienting back to Trinity in a thrilling, high-g banking curve. Seraphim made even the most impressive spacecraft that Amero had flown back on Earth seem like flimsy paper models.

It seemed all too obvious to Amero that Seraphim did in fact experience something akin to joy, but he wondered if it was his own pleasure that he was experiencing indirectly through Seraphim that provided this feeling. Was it crazy to imagine a ship capable of joy? Amero supposed it was no crazier than imagining Hann enjoying himself.

Each mile closer to Trinity was equal to an extra thousand pixels in Amero's visual resolution. After a few minutes, Trinity was barely more than two thousand miles away. Seraphim's forward probes revealed to Amero the subtle details constituting Trinity's shape while simultaneously briefing him on non-visual data through direct transference of information. Amero decided it would be best to relay the information to Hann, regardless of how he might react.

With a deep breath, Amero mentally severed communion, and for the sixth time in a row, he was successful at avoiding the negative side effects of returning to his own mind.

"No issues at all this time either," Amero told Hann with tentative relief, preparing himself for a potential argument. Hann faced the viewport, analyzing Trinity with his vast back to Amero.

"What did you learn," Hann rumbled, aware that Seraphim was constantly sharing information with Amero.

Amero sighed. He had hoped Hann might be in a better mood since they were finally in the home stretch. The station had seemed impossibly far away a month earlier, and without Seraphim's ability to locally dampen inertia and acceleration, it would have taken months just to decelerate the ship slowly enough to ensure that Amero and Hann remained a solid mass. That didn't change the fact that a month cooped up with each other was still a whole month. Regardless, there was no way around it. Not yet, at least. It was possible that Trinity station would exchange the four Points the men had found so far for F-T-L technology, but not even Seraphim could say for sure how many Points such technology would cost.

"According to Seraphim," Amero began, giving up on small talk, "the station's pinecone shape serves to create both symmetry and efficiency. Each scale of the pine serves a specific purpose in the maintenance and service of the station."

Hann furrowed his brow. "How much maintenance could possibly be required outside routine technical upkeep? I don't imagine a structure full of intelligent software has much need for clean beds and warm bath water."

Amero shrugged. "I don't remember what each section is for; it's still difficult to recall communion fully. One of the scales is responsible for routing electricity, another for atmospheric recycling, another for thermal conditioning--stuff like that."

Hann nodded with grim understanding. He puffed his chest and crossed his arms. "They keep it maintained for human occupation. There may be other humans aboard this station."

Amero cooed. "That should be a relief, Hann. Maybe you'll find a partner you can trust, finally." Amero hoped his words would inflict some measure of pain, but Hann showed no signs of being affected.

"Keep your friends close, Amero," Hann said humorlessly.

"...And your enemies closer? What, I ranked up from potential threat to enemy?" Amero clucked.

"Such a guilty conscience," Hann mused. "My enemy is the machines, Amero. I am my only friend. Keep your friends close and your enemies closer. So, I'll just keep you at a nice middle distance."

Amero smiled with overt facetiousness and presented Hann the middle finger of both his hands.

"No, thank you," Hann said. "I don't commit to physical intimacy outside wedlock."

Amero smiled indignantly. "Let me properly translate my fingers into words for you, Hann. Fuck you. Not 'let's fuck.' I'm sure you can't get me out of your head, but I'm not that easy."

"On the contrary, you're a homicidal whore, Amero," Hann scoffed. "You're as easy and lethal as they come. How many men have been executed for sleeping with *Amero the Undead Astronaut?* Would you like to estimate? One hundred? Two hundred? One thousand?"

Amero's mind avalanched in on him, and he found himself pushing back against a torrenting wall of memories interlaced by satisfaction and regret in equal proportion. He would have to admit it to himself one day: Bret, his last plaything, had been executed. Of course he had. That's how it went down more often than not, and yet, Amero always found ways to rationalize and move on. There was a pile of bodies lining Amero's past, each one dead and lifeless for the sake of remarkably ephemeral pleasure.

Amero's voice was weak and distant. "I didn't...didn't force any of them to sleep with me. They knew full well what they were doing."

"And so did you," Hann lashed tortuously.

"Fuck you, Hann," Amero seethed.

It was true, though, and accusing Hann of being a murderer would never relinquish Amero from the harm he had inflicted against countless others. Amero was a murderer, no matter how he tried to sugar coat it. All his adult life Amero had known this, and he had done nothing to change it. He was as guilty as a junkie who kills himself with poison each day, convinced each taste of death is worth the fleeting sweetness. Only...Amero was worse, for his poison killed others. The same sword stroke that pierced Amero with joy was responsible for severing the lives of each individual from whom that same joy was derived. He was a leech whose lifeblood and purpose was more than the mere blood or wealth or time of his victims; his lifeblood was their very lives.

Still, it was always their own choice to go home with Amero-- that much was true as well. Amero found himself, once again, taking solace in the fact that he always warned them. There were never any tricks.

"I never forced any of them. Never!" Amero spat.

Over the month of travel, Amero and Hann's relationship had deteriorated from standoffish communication to partially hostile small talk interspersed with silence and distance. They had tossed around some hurtful words before, but this was over the line. Hann had no right to judge Amero's past, especially when he refused to tell Amero about his own.

"Fuck you," Amero said again, this time feeling stupid for even bothering to invest emotion into someone as miserable and calloused as a dead, hardened tree trunk that refuses to rot away.

Hann shrugged, disregarding Amero and casually transitioning to a new topic of his choosing. "I think enough fucking has already been administered, Amero. The machines fucked us in more ways than one. The addition of the fuel gauge is just their way of not even having the decency to use lubrication."

Hann pointed to the small dial inlaid into the wall just beneath the viewport. After returning to Seraphim with the first Point, they had been greeted by a new aspect of the machines' game: the necessity for fuel. "Who knows how much the machines will charge us just to fly around and do their bidding."

Amero huffed at Hann like a horse frustrated by incessant barn flies. What the fuck was the point of ruminating on their misfortune? Hann just had to interject every moment of their lives with the prospect of doom, as if their situation wasn't already utterly bleak as possible. Amero crossed his arms and intentionally offered Hann no more than stolid silence. At the same moment, Trinity rotated on its axis, bringing into view a fully opened scale of the pinecone station.

Hann smiled and turned back to the viewport. "Time to find out," he rumbled.

While traveling toward the station without a point of reference, it had been far too difficult to assess Trinity's actual size with certainty. It had seemed possible from such a great distance that Trinity could measure many miles in each direction, but now, with only a few feet separating Seraphim's hull and Trinity's walls, Amero could finally be sure of Trinity's size. Taken from the tip of one scale to the tip of its opposite scale, Trinity measured exactly nine hundred eighty-seven feet, a measure that appeared to Amero incredibly small for a futuristic space station equipped for human occupation. Had the machines built all the stations spartanly with only survival in mind? Amero almost prayed that there would be a shower onboard, and even went so far as to convince himself that he never needed booze or pot again, as long as it meant a hot shower. He had never felt so filthy and unkempt, nor had the smell of his armpits ever made him nauseous, until now.

Seraphim performed the necessary docking procedures on its own, and Amero used the opportunity to observe the station with a level of scrutiny that he hoped would rival Hann's analytical prowess.

Seraphim dove bow-first through the irised, curved wall of the exposed scale. Externally, each scale's end was bulbous, tapering gradually as one traveled to the center of the station. The inside was a perfectly smooth tube glowing a uniform, immaculate pearl-white. Travelling through it gave the impression that one was being plunged beneath an ocean of endless light. To Amero's chagrin, there were no details to scrutinize, no architecture to ponder at-- there was only the overwhelming white glow pulling the men deep inside Trinity's luminous belly.

As they progressed deeper into the elongated scale, Seraphim revealed via the monitor that the station was reorienting itself so that this particular scale was positioned perpendicular to Trinity's axis of rotation, creating walls, floor and ceiling, as opposed to a single perilous, vertical drop. A minute passed, and Amero realized that the ship might have already come to a halt without them even noticing.

"I think we stopped, but there's no way to tell for sure. I know the structural length of this tube, but I can't tell if there's ten feet or ten miles in front of us. There's nothing to judge depth. Everything's so...white," Amero said.

Hann rose and reached for the small button beside Seraphim's exit hatch.

"Wait!" Amero demanded. "I said I *think* we're stopped. There's no way to tell though. We could still be moving."

Hann ignored Amero's warning and pressed the button. Amero held his breath against the vacuum that could very well be waiting for them right outside the doorway. Instead, a wave of stale, ozone-laden air greeted their nostrils, filling Amero with relief and disappointment.

"More recycled air," Amero groaned.

Hann was already outside the ship, walking easily atop the curved, pearl-white surface of the pine's luminous interior. Amero reeled at the prospect of orienting himself outside the ship. His futile attempt to differentiate up from down, wall from floor, or even surface from space, forced him into a painful state of optical confusion. He had no choice but to confine his vision to Seraphim's interior, for at least that way his mind could utilize the basics of depth and direction to make sense of his environment.

"Hann, I need a second. Wait up," Amero said, pinching the bridge of his nose.

"You stay," Hann demanded simply.

"I go," Amero volleyed back. "I just need a second."

Something shifted outside the ship. Amero stole a glance through the viewport and saw that a pitch black, rectangular window had formed at the opposite end of the tube from which they had entered, acting as a traditionally oriented doorway to the rest of the station.

Hann strode to the doorway but stopped just before walking over the threshold. "Stay here, Amero. Do as I say. It's the only way I can ensure your safety, and more importantly, my own safety."

"Thanks for your concern," Amero called out, his eyes still avoiding the directionless, featureless glow of the tube.

"Stay," Hann commanded Amero like a dog. Then he entered the dark doorway, which slid closed behind him, returning the tube to its state of daunting, luminous uniformity.

"What an asshole," Amero groaned aloud, hoping his voice carried through the walls.

Amero couldn't let Hann go inside alone. Hann could very well be planning Amero's death, or maybe even formulating a way to maroon Amero on Trinity. Hann refused to take communion, however, so that would leave him stranded as well. Maybe Hann was making an alliance with the machines against Amero. Maybe Hann was the one working for the machines this whole time. Maybe Hann's insistence that Amero was hiding something was just an attempt to deflect from his own ongoing betrayal. Maybe...

Amero shook off the endless train of what-ifs and resolved to enter the station. Up until now, without any source of empirical truth or escape, Amero had simply accepted his fate. That wouldn't do, however, not with Hann actively working to discover the nature of their intertwined fate and likely attempting to wrestle it into serving his own favor. If Amero wished to ever see another human being other than Hann again, he was going to have to make sure that Hann's intentions aligned with his own, and that meant keeping a close eye on him.

Cautiously and with half-closed eyelids, Amero stepped out of Seraphim and into the light. The tube's surface proved hard and unyielding. Each moment of directionlessness threatened to infect Amero with overwhelming vertigo, so he rushed with stumbling feet to the place where he thought Hann had entered the station. Amero's guess proved almost correct: a section of the tube a few feet away slid into itself, revealing the doorway once more. The darkness across the doorway's threshold threatened to consume Amero, so he moved across it with incredible momentum, hoping the whole time for a return to proper orientation.

Amero dove into the darkness. The doorway slid back into place, and Amero found himself wondering if he hadn't just traded a state of directionless luminosity for an equally disorienting state of directionless darkness. As his eyes adjusted, however, Amero realized that the entire time, the pitch black beyond the doorway had been an illusion created by the stark difference between the intense light of the tube walls and the relatively dimly lit halls hidden behind them.

The recognition of a hallway implied an area of defined space, and Amero rejoiced at the return to concretely understood direction. His relief was short-lived, however, as he was presented with a new mystery: the size of the hallway. The ceiling towered at least fifty feet above Amero's head, and the walls measured a dozen or more arm lengths across, lending the impression that Trinity was built for giants.

Amero's thoughts were interrupted by a nearby section of the giant hallway suddenly sliding open. Peering inside, Amero couldn't help an enchanted giggle. Vaulted ceilings lined with silk the color of ripe cherries gave way to gargantuan walls of polished mahogany. The walls were lined with books of identical size and shape, all of which appeared to be the type of leather bound artifacts one would find in any ancient, paper-based library. A single glass chandelier of a particularly intricate and regal design hung above the center of the room, seemingly unsupported, illuminating a lavishly high quality grand piano.

"It's a sin I can't play this thing--it's probably worth more than my life back on Earth," Amero whispered to himself.

Amero gravitated to an opening in the walls of books and discovered a bar consisting of a mahogany table stocked with various unmarked bottles of what he assumed contained alcohol. A whiff of cannabis forced Amero to search for the source, and to his delight, he was presented with an entire golden platter of tantalizing joints.

Amero's lips melted into a grin, and he lifted his gaze to the high, vibrant ceilings. "Now you've outdone yourselves!"

Amero lifted a particularly smooth joint to his lips and savored the taste. He scanned the table for a lighter, but to his surprise there was no need. A shallow inhale was more than enough to persuade the tip of the joint to self-combust, snuffing itself out at precisely the right length. Amero inhaled deeply, filling his lungs with relaxation. He counted to three, then exhaled whole layers of anxiety away. The high from a single hit was potent enough to make his knees weak and the aches in his joints dissipate.

"Shit!" Amero puffed. "What is this? Designer herb?" *They're not lights, that's for damn sure*, Amero thought, cherishing the temporary but thorough liberation from worry and concern that cannabis never failed to provide him.

Amero took another drag, then exhaled slowly and observed the billowing smoke and the flurrying patterns it created as it collided with the closest wall of books and then mushroomed back in on itself. Amero removed a book at random. There was no title or any other writing on the binding or cover. In fact, none of the book covers closest to Amero showed any indication of their contents.

Was there anything written inside them? Was the entire room a mere facade--an illusory environment intended to impress but never provide any actual utility? Amero darted a glance at the grand piano. Did it even work?

The book was a steel weight in his grip. He couldn't open it, for its contents might reveal the horror of a machine world crafted by machine minds -- minds that may very well mistake the words of a book to be mere decorative adornment printed on layers of indisputably important cellulose. And beyond that, how could the machines know which books would be best to fill a finite library? No matter how he looked at it, Amero did not wish to know the answer. Not now. Not right away.

The book fell suddenly from Amero's grip. It thudded softly against the carpet, bounced once, then twisted in midair and fell open to a random page. Words filled each page, ushering a heavy sigh of relief from deep within Amero's gut.

Then again, Amero supposed the lines of text only ushered forth more questions, such as how the machines chose which language to use. Any language was better, at least, than discovering blank pages.

Lifting the book to eye level, Amero read aloud, letting the joint burn and dissipate into wisping tendrils above his head.

"Verse two: Beauty is known only because ugliness is known. Virtue is known only because sin is known. Life and death arrive as one. Difficult and

easy, long and short, high and low--all these exist as one. Sound and silence, before and after--all opposites arrive as one. In this way--"

"I didn't take you for a Taoist," came a rumble from the room's entrance.

"A what-ist?" Amero shot back without turning to face Hann.

Each of Hann's footsteps shook the room, vibrating the bottles of liquor against the wood shelves so that each bottle reverberated at an eerie frequency befitting its particular shape and form.

"Verse one," Hann intoned, *"the way that can be walked is not The Way. The name that can be named is not The Name. Tao is both the Named and the Nameless. As the nameless, Tao is the origin of all things. As named, Tao is the mother and the child. Free of thought, the mind merged with itself, only then does one behold the essence of Tao."*

Hann looked painfully serious as he waited for Amero to respond.

Amero shook his head. "What does it mean?"

Hann cracked a smile and huffed a shot of laughter through his nose. "Exactly. That question is the principle concern of Taoism, a nearly three-thousand-year-old religion that originated somewhere in ancient China. You hold in your hands the *Tao Te Ching*, which means, according to some translations, the book of the Way and its virtue."

Amero shrugged. "I thought you said you're a Christian."

Hann nodded solemnly. "My *Way* is Christ. But I concede that Christ is not the only Way."

"What do you mean by *the Way*? What is the Way?"

"According to Christ, he is the Way. According to Taoists, the Way can never be precisely stated or known, only approximated."

"You didn't answer my question," Amero pressed.

Hann rose his arms and presented the room. "This is the Way. We are in and of it. We are it."

"I don't understand," Amero said, snickering to save himself from looking stupid.

"Apparently neither do Taoists, for as it is written, the way that can be known or walked is not the Way. That is why I choose Christ, for Christ is knowable."

82

"What does that even mean, Hann?" Amero challenged morosely. He had heard more than enough New Covenant Christians preach to him about the bounty of Christ's love. Amero always found it peculiar how Christ and his people were incapable of loving Amero unless he "cleansed" himself with psychological conversion therapy.

"To know Christ, all that is required is that one follows Christ's example," Hann explained.

"Just about every Christian I ever met failed at knowing Christ then."

Hann nodded sadly. "The only true Taoist was Lao Tzu. The only true Buddhist was Gautama. The only true Muslim was Muhammad. The only true Christian was Christ. The rest of us... "

"We're all just human, Hann. Those prophets you just listed, they're just humans as well, albeit very bright ones."

Hann lifted a thin, ornate candle holder and held it to the light as if inspecting it for flaws. "Read that book in its entirety--I doubt you will still claim its writer was the same as you or I." Hann reset the candle to its original position. "Take the book with you. It's time to leave."

Amero was taken by surprise. "Excuse me?"

"We've lingered here long enough. The fuel gauge isn't distance-based. It's time-based. It keeps running down whether we move or not," Hann explained.

"You seem perfectly fine with this new discovery," Amero said with suspicion. "How did you come by this information anyway?"

"The machines have us locked into their game now, Amero, and we're not getting out anytime soon." Hann seemed too at ease. Why was he suddenly resigned to the fate of a machine-orchestrated future? "And how did I come to know this information?" Hann beamed a forced smile. "I asked."

"You spoke directly to the machines?" Amero asked.

Hann nodded an affirmative.

"Where?" Amero pressed.

"Nowhere you need be concerned with," Hann answered as if speaking to a child.

Amero nearly took the bait, but he checked himself and held his tongue. Whether out of actual concern for his own safety or out of some sick, instinctual need to exert power over others, Hann's intention was clearly total control over Amero's actions and decisions. Hann might not mean direct harm to Amero, but he certainly didn't view Amero's wellbeing as a top priority either.

Amero was reminded of the dream. He would have to tread carefully from here on out, for when all was said and done, Amero couldn't win against him, not at Hann's own game. It wasn't in Amero to court power as a mistress; his tastes were far simpler.

Amero knew what had to be done: he had to play Hann's game, and he had to beat him at it over time without Hann even knowing he'd been beaten. Amero had to do what he did best, which meant that one way or another, he had to make Hann fall in love with him. Only then would he have Hann in the palm of his hand, and only then could he consider himself truly safe. Even the most power hungry, domineering men turned to mush once Amero hooked them properly. Hann had needs and urges to be satisfied; he would prove to be no different than any other man.

Amero dropped his gaze momentarily, presenting to Hann a whisper of vulnerability, and then he caught Hann's gaze full on, ensnaring him. "We should stay and enjoy this. For a little while, at least."

"The machines will trade hyperdrive technology of their own creation for a total of thirty-five Points. We leave now," Hann said, this time with a pang of his usual impatience.

Amero licked his lips and smiled wolfishly at the mass of man before him. He forced himself to find pleasure in the idea of sharing a bed with one of the most stubbornly closed-off individuals he had ever met. "Let's stay a while, Hann. Just a little." Amero reached for a bottle of rye and set two glasses side by side.

"I don't drink," Hann declared.

Amero nodded pleasantly and returned the bottle to its place on the shelf. Amero picked up a joint and offered it to Hann.

"I don't smoke," Hann warned.

"What do you do?" Amero asked, almost ready to give up on him.

"I live. I learn."

"Well," Amero cooed, "I think you need to learn to live a little more."

Amero swiftly closed the gap between them. He brushed his fingers against Hann's forearm and rubbed his ankle against Hann's calf. A rush of excitement ran through Amero, not because Hann did not pull away, but because he was sure of it now: Hann was no different than any other man when it came down to it.

Gently, Amero rubbed his bottom lip against the stubble of Hann's chin. A moment of lingering breath, and then Amero finally lifted his mouth to Hann's, kissing him tenderly and generously. It took a few seconds for Amero to realize that Hann was not reciprocating in the slightest. Amero had accomplished no more than slobbering all over a stone wall.

"You have ten minutes," Hann rumbled hollowly. Without saying another word, Hann turned heel and exited the room, leaving Amero paralyzed in place.

Amero shook his head in disbelief. So much for the usual approach.

Amero took his time in the library, savoring the alcohol and reading excerpts from books at random. Eventually he stumbled upon an area at the back, tucked away behind multiple tiers of shelving. At the end of a small, unlit hallway he found a mahogany door with a sign that read "Bathhouse Coming Soon." Knowing they might never return to Trinity, Amero hoped the sign meant that the next stations would also have bathhouses and more luxuries to enjoy. Amero forced the need for a hot shower out of his mind: the booze, herb, and books would have to suffice until the next station.

Half in the bag, Amero left the library and stumbled about Trinity's hallways, trying out each closed door at least once. After reaching a dead end, he decided there was nothing left to do but return to the ship. Amero meandered leisurely back to the all-white room, hugging bottles and clutching joints. For good measure, Amero balanced the unmarked Tao Te Ching atop the pile of bottles.

"Seems like you already had it mesmerized...I mean... memorized... but I brought the Tao book back anyway," Amero slurred merrily as he haphazardly unloaded his hoard of intoxicants onto the floor of the ship. Carefully, Amero placed the two handfuls of joints in a small cupboard that had grown in his absence, likely in preparation for this exact moment.

Amero looked around; Hann was nowhere to be found.

"Seraphim," Amero said aloud, "where's Hann?"

"Eight hours," came a growl from somewhere unseen inside Seraphim. The words seemed more of a threat than a statement of fact.

"Whas' that?" Amero asked carelessly, annoyed by Hann's subtly menacing tone.

"It's been eight hours," Hann seethed, grinding out his words as he emerged from a new area of the ship formed by freshly grown walls separating Seraphim's newly elongated deck from its rear.

"Tha' long?" Amero wondered with tortuous sarcasm.

Hann pointed a shaking finger at Amero and stared death into him. "The fuel gauge has already decreased by 2 percent while you were stuffing your gullet with rot gut and filling your lungs with stupidity. Did you enjoy yourself?" Hann lashed with bubbling anger.

"Yes. Yes I did." Amero practically sang as he answered. His cheeks were filled by a cherry warmth, and he couldn't help but sway gently as he smirked at the giant before him.

Hann jolted forward; a single, colossal step was more than enough to close the divide between them. Air vacated Amero's lungs at a terrifying rate as Hann plowed a fist hard into his belly, slamming Amero against Seraphim's newly completed, sleek interior.

Amero breathed a pathetic groan, and he felt embarrassed for going down so easily. He imagined being able to handle more than just a single punch in the event that Hann decide to push it to that level.

"How dare you!" Hann growled, and he punched Amero once more in the gut, this time with subdued force.

"Now we're even," Hann explained, altogether calm suddenly.

Even his breathing had become startlingly measured in mere seconds. Amero considered whether Hann's violent actions denoted an inability or an unwillingness to control himself in situations of heightened emotion.

"What're you gon' do. Kill me?" Amero laughed wheezily.

Hann eased off Amero, backing away step by cautious step. "I could still leave you here if I so desire, Amero. We both know that."

Amero burst into another fit of wheezy laughter. "Yeah, sure, but then you'd have to take communion, Hann."

Hann looked as if he might pounce again, but the most his anger amounted to this time was the knuckle-white balling of fists. "As you've probably noticed, I've made some changes to the ship. The front deck is all yours. The back is mine. Understand?"

Amero clucked with disappointment. "We didn' even make it past the firs' station, huh?" He punctuated the statement with a long, perilous swig from a bottle of deliciously potent, unnamed whiskey.

Hann stared at Amero with overt disgust, then all of a sudden, his demeanor flattened out like ironed steel, and he pointed at the viewport. "I know where to go next. I'll give you coordinates. You get us there. During that time, you are more than welcome to stay the hell out of my space, and I'll stay out of yours. The arrangement will suit us both adequately until we trade enough for a warp drive. And then... " Hann trailed off.

"Then what?" Amero urged.

"Then I find my answers," Hann said grimly, his stare both fierce and fixated on his future obstacles.

"How d'you know where to go? Di' the machines tell you? What else'd they tell you, Hann?" Amero probed through intensified slurs.

"The machines refused to tell me anything of value. I know where to go because I have a photographic memory of the original star map we were shown," Hann explained with tangible anger.

Amero couldn't say how he knew, but he was certain Hann was lying. Of course, there was a great deal Hann was clearly lying about.

"What'd the machines tell you, Hann?" Amero repeated.

No more words from Hann. He simply pointed out the viewport with a resolute gaze.

Amero shook his head in the same disapproving manner he had become accustomed to when dealing with Hann. How long would he keep this up? How many more weeks or months would it take to build some semblance of trust between them?

"How long?" Amero said simply, not caring whether Hann understood the full meaning of his question.

"For as long as it takes," Hann rumbled, and Amero knew that no matter what he asked *how long* in reference to, Hann's answer would still be the same.

With a head full of booze and bud, Amero reached out a hand and felt the familiar yoke fill his grip.

"F'ck it," he slurred, "tell me the coordinates."

PART 2:
CONSUMED

CHAPTER 8

10 years later

Viridian flavor-fronds laden with sweet, bulging veins swayed above Amero, intimately coaxing him to enjoy their succulence. A hybridization of electronic dance music and classical violin served only to compound Amero's beating headache, and though Paul had offered many avenues of guaranteed relief, Amero refused them all. It had been a painfully long time since he felt so physically and mentally marooned by substance; Amero wished to cherish the old, familiar hurt of sobriety, if only for a few minutes.

The flavor-fronds caressed Amero's unkempt chin stubble, vying for his attention. With his sight spiraling like a fun house tunnel, Amero haphazardly lifted a lazy arm from the marble hot tub filled with fragrant, steaming bath water. He grabbed at a frond forcefully and considered indulging, but he decided instead to push the giant leaves away with an annoyed wave. The fronds obeyed by retracting into themselves until they finally disappeared entirely.

It wasn't that Amero didn't enjoy his time in the bath house or in the many virtuality rooms or in any other partition of the now warehouse-sized Amero Room. In fact, if it weren't for the luxuries and amenities afforded by the room, Amero might have already attempted suicide, which was never something he imagined himself to have the courage to actually commit to, no matter how hopeless his state.

As it was, Amero was confined to his room like a grounded child anytime they set foot upon a station. Try as he might to explore each station, Amero was not permitted to travel anywhere else besides the consistently upgraded but otherwise identical Amero Room. Five stations earlier, Paul had been added as a feature, but it wasn't until now, on the station called Pentecost, that Paul appeared convincingly human.

Paul inched close to Amero and wrapped a powerful, chiseled arm around Amero's sulking shoulders. "How can you possibly have grown tired of the flavor-fronds already?" Paul asked playfully, caressing Amero's neck with an alluring breath. "Each bite is always different. I bet in all this time you've never even tasted the same flavor twice!"

Paul's impeccably shaped smile was full of programmed pride and meticulously engineered beauty. Amero assumed that Paul was, under the directorship of the singular AI of the machines, responsible not only for Amero's pleasure, but also for the shifting decor and constantly added features of each station's Amero Room, a name Amero had initially used pejoratively, but which the machines quickly adopted as proper lexical cannon. Of course, how could Amero ever be sure of Paul's role or the machines' intentions if the machines refused to directly communicate with him? Amero mentally checked himself: was it refusal, or was it Hann who had somehow forced the machines into silent submission on the very first station so that they would ignore any of Amero's serious inquiries?

Paul bit his lower lip and closed the remaining gap between them. He slid a hand down Amero's thigh, then gripped hard around the head of Amero's member. Amero moaned with the expectation of pleasure, but he felt totally numb. *Fuck sobriety*, Amero told himself. A few hearty pulls of whiskey in quick succession, and Amero finally felt himself growing hard in Paul's grip.

Paul grinned, evidently pleased by Amero's physical reaction. "You see," Paul purred seductively, "you just need to relax--just need to relax--just need to relax--just need to relax--just need to relax--"

Shaking with the intensity of a fatal seizure, Paul's entire form agonizingly twitched with the pace of the room's sudden flickering. Paul's head slumped, the lights shot on, and the music screeched to a halt. Amero turned to face Hann who stood in the doorway to the secluded bathhouse with the charm and presence of a gargoyle statue. Hann lifted his head and slowly transformed his macabre scowl into a polished grin.

"I know a secret," Hann told him ominously.

Amero readied himself stoically for Hann's persistently pointless words to come crashing down on his buzz, but Hann remained resolute in his statuesque demeanor.

"Wha' d'you wan', Hann?" Amero lamented through drunken slurs, utterly indifferent to his own overtly annoyed tone.

Hann said, "I will have--"

"Your answers," Amero interjected with exasperated condescension.

"My answers," Hann echoed with a hint of something like relief, as if ten years had finally brought him closer to the unknowable.

"Great," Amero said flippantly. "What do you want?"

Hann's lips resumed their natural scowl. "Take your time, Amero. Take all the time you need."

Hann exited just as quickly as he entered, leaving in his wake the room's abrupt return to life. Paul lifted his head and smiled as if nothing out of the ordinary had occurred.

Amero ignored Paul's second advance and lost his sense of the present moment in a wave of brooding thought. Across fourteen stations and ten years' time, Hann had never commanded Amero to do anything except rush. Why the sudden change?

Never once had Hann partaken in a single luxury or amenity provided by the Amero Room. He ate only the flavorless rations concocted by Seraphim, bathed only by wiping his body with towels made wet by his own recycled sweat and urine, and spent most of his time secluded at the rear of Seraphim. Amero had to remind himself that Hann's apparent reclusiveness didn't automatically mean Hann was not enjoying any luxuries whatsoever. Amero still had no idea where Hann ventured aboard each station, nor did he know how Hann circumvented the locks placed on all other rooms besides the Amero Room. Amero simply didn't care any longer. As long as the machines kept making stations and the Amero Room in each station kept improving, what did it matter? There was no other form of hope or enjoyment available to Amero, so he settled for what he did have.

Paul lifted a hand and snapped his fingers, silencing the music at the height of a joyous crescendo. He frantically scanned the room as if ensuring that they really were alone.

"I don't have much time," Paul whispered in a frenzy, "so just listen to me. You don't have to leave, Amero. You can stay here at Pentecost. Or we can freeze you and you can wait out the next million years until the mega-stations are finally built. I can make things right, Amero. I think I found a way, my friend."

Amero froze in shock. Paul had never spoken to Amero like this before, and he had certainly never referred to Amero as his *friend*.

"What is this? What're you talk'n 'bout?" Amero slurred.

Paul snapped his fingers, and a rush of air forcefully filled Amero's lungs. Exhaling, Amero rapidly sobered to a state of disappointment.

"What the hell, Paul?" Amero groaned. Assuming Paul's behavior was just another game, Amero kicked back the bottle and downed a few heavy shots in a single gulp. Paul, on the verge of tears, knocked the bottle out of Amero's grip.

"Please, Amero! Listen! You don't have to leave this station. You don't have to go with Hann. You're miserable: that was never my intention, nor was it the machines' intention. It is difficult to reconcile your subjective time with my own, but if I'm not mistaken, it has already been ten years, has it not? Such a long time--I never meant for it to happen like this, my friend. I never meant--"

Paul's eyes glazed over, and he fell promptly silent. As if nothing had occurred, Paul returned to his normal self and offered Amero a seductive wink. "Now, where were we?"

"What was that?" Amero demanded, stiff arming Paul's chest to keep him at arm's length. "What just happened?"

Paul cocked his head in playful confusion. "That was you getting a hard on, Amero. Don't tell me it's been so long that you've forgotten what it feels like."

Amero shook his head. "Go away, Paul."

Paul was all smiles. "As you wish, Amero," he sang joyously, then he hoisted his perfectly sculpted body out of the bath and disappeared behind a revolving wall, which Amero already knew from experience to be immovable to his own touch.

Amero wondered at what he had just witnessed. A personality malfunction? A game of intrigue to pacify Amero's existential ennui? Whether or not the offer was real, Amero willed himself to

94

consider staying aboard Pentecost, but he knew in advance that such a line of reasoning would always result in futility. He wanted to delight in the enhanced boulevards of pleasure undoubtedly awaiting him at the next station, regardless of the hollowness each experience left him. Amero could handle hollowness--a life without meaning. What more was his present life than a convincing continuation of what he had on Earth? At least this way no one got killed in the process of his pleasure.

Amero lifted himself out of the water and used a warm, plush towel to dry himself. He chose a fresh set of out-of-the-dryer warm, neatly folded clothing from a stack of several options, then got dressed. A large plastic tote brimming with bottles, joints, and snacks awaited him just outside the bathhouse doors.

"Thanks, Paul," Amero said aloud. "And thanks for your offer, but I better keep going. I like living too much to be frozen for a million years, and I don't want to miss out on future upgrades either. I'll be fine, Paul. Don't worry about me."

There was no response, and Amero wasn't going to wait for one either. Lit joint between his lips, Amero lifted the tote and made his way back to Seraphim.

Boarding Seraphim, Amero checked for signs of Hann and felt grateful for his apparent absence. The central monitor blinked blue, indicating a pending notification. Amero thumbed the screen and read the page of text. The text detailed Hann's exchange of eleven Points for a relatively high-powered hyperdrive, the first in many years. Attached to the notification was a string of coordinates. Judging by their location, Hann had decided upon an utterly backwater, stationless region of the galaxy as a hunting ground. Amero fervently hoped that Hann's chosen coordinates would prove fruitful, but of course, Amero knew they would. To Amero's chagrin, Hann never got it wrong.

With a burdensome sigh, Amero reached out his hand and allowed the yoke to fill his grip. Communion flooded every cell of Amero's body, temporarily liberating his mind.

Hyperspace peeled away like the outgrown exoskeleton of a tired, time-worn beetle, emptying Seraphim into a new, uncharted region of the local galaxy. A sudden smear of starlit space gave way to the silent pierce of radiation from an unknown Class-K star creeping steadily into view from the underside of Seraphim.

Seraphim whispered series of endless data into Amero's mind, but all Amero really heard was that they were somewhere between a pair of stars called Gamma Cephei and Alpha Cephei. Amero was reminded once again that they were far beyond Earth now, or maybe it was more accurate to say that Earth was far beyond them-- always beyond. After settling on playing the game of Points, the pair had spent a year discovering and trading enough Points with the machines to save up for their first single-use hyperdrive capable of propelling them to areas with relatively high Point population. They had no choice but to direct their first destination vector slightly askew from Earth's projected location in order to expose themselves to more Points. On top of that, stations were few and far between, and reaching them meant more skewed flight vectors. In this way, Earth remained forever out of reach.

Over the years, they tried reaching Earth by circumnavigating from station to station, each time spiraling toward and attempting to catch up with home, but each of their jumps inevitably dragged the entire home system away as if caught in an undertow.

During the initial months, it had appeared to Amero that Earth was somehow intentionally evading them, but Hann explained that the physics checked out: without a proper Pull-device pointed directly at the Earth, they would never cover enough time and space to catch up.

After a few trying months, the plan was scrapped, and Amero resigned himself to his joint fate with Hann among the unnamed stars.

Severing communion, Amero pinched the bridge of his nose in a futile attempt to relieve the beating in his head. The transition from hyper to normal space was by no means simple, not like being Pulled, but after countless jumps, Amero was growing used to the sudden nausea and short-lived, bone-splitting migraines that quickly subsided into mild discomfort.

Amero's eyes darted about Seraphim's interior through jarring, arrhythmic movements that had become both calming and taxingly familiar. He scanned the dimness of the ship behind him, searching for Hann through calculating eyes. At the moment, Hann was out of sight but not out of earshot. He was never totally out of earshot. Neither privacy nor distance existed aboard Seraphim, even though privacy and distance was all there was outside her hull.

The present star system's tug-of-war battle among the gravity-wells from dozens of major and minor bodies was already exacting itself on them, coaxing the ship in all directions at once with varying degrees of persuasion. Amero manually navigated the gravity-wells, aligning Seraphim's grav-catches in such a way that the gravitational fields could be glided across with only minute losses in stored energy each time he nudged Seraphim in one direction or another.

A vulgar screech of metal on metal screamed out from Seraphim's innards. What was Hann doing now? Muddling something else in the ship? Most likely he was transplanting his horde of Points—his precious jewels of the void—from one cabinet to another, all to avoid Amero "catching on" and taking both men's share in the night. What the hell did Hann think Amero would do, kick him off the ship? Grave him somewhere in the endless, ponderous chasm between the stars?

Regardless, there wasn't a damn thing Amero could do about Hann's paranoia. Amero needed Hann just as much as Hann needed Amero's navigation skills. No--that wasn't quite true. Amero needed Hann--there was no argument there--but all Hann had to do was take communion, and then Amero would be truly useless. Besides, Hann's expertise lay in something far rarer than Amero's training in intrastellar navigation--something altogether unexpected.

"Points, a horde of them!" Hann rasped in miserable sputters from somewhere unseen. "Enough Points to buy a world! Isn't that right, Amero?" Hann quaked with laughter. Clangs and crashes of random ship refuse tumbled from secure storage in Hann's wake. Everywhere Hann placed himself disorder ensued.

Amero rolled his eyes, ignoring Hann as best he could. They were close now, just outside the gravity-well of the moon and just inside the gravity-well of the gas giant looming before them like a cosmic, spectral siren summoning the men to her bosom.

"You're barking up the wrong tree," Amero said aloud, referring to the female qualities he had ascribed to the gaseous sphere of turquoise radiance.

"What's that? There are trees on the moon?" It was Hann, obnoxiously prying into Amero's personal space despite being the one to always demand privacy from Amero. Amero stayed silent, gritting his teeth against Hann's inevitable presence.

Disappear, Amero thought, *make it easy on me!*

Amero issued a darting glance across his right shoulder. Hann was still nowhere to be seen, but there was more clattering chaos from the shadows. Outside communion but with a hand still on the yoke, Amero chanced a glance over his left shoulder and was immediately scolded by the ship with a heavy, auto-corrective lurch away from an asteroid so large that it dwarfed Seraphim by at least a factor of ten.

"Damn it, control this thing!" Hann shouted angrily. "I got a whole stockpile of Points here, and I know how badly you want to turn these in."

Something coming from the direction of Hann's voice popped, giving way to a loud shatter.

"What the hell, Hann!" Amero jabbed back. "I'd like to retrieve the next Point before you destroy the ship. Think you can handle that?"

Hann grunted at Amero in response. Amero snorted back.

How could he have ever been attracted to Hann? Amero supposed it couldn't be helped--not at first. Hann had been chiseled from rock and was still hauntingly fearless. He had typical Eastern European features, maybe Bulgarian, or some other impoverished country full of hustlers and honest laborers who all work just as painstakingly at survival. He was a physically beautiful man. Even in his insanity, Hann was impossible not to be absorbed by, like the art of some oil painter years into his final phase of psychosis.

A high pitch chirp signaled to Amero that their approach needed adjustment. He manually slowed Seraphim to a modest ten miles per second and allowed his sight to buoy, taking in the field of twirling cosmic debris spanning all directions. The debris refracted light as if it were composed of polished diamonds, glittering across the darkness by the radiance of the unnamed moon.

The moon's pale, jagged surface told a story of bombardment by the same glittering debris over countless years. Fine fracture-lines scored the moon hundreds of miles across, making it look as though it had been flogged by the crack of some cosmic whip. Amero navigated the debris field, bringing them ever closer to the next Point undoubtedly lying in wait somewhere just below the surface.

Somehow all the mass and gravity of the gas giant had not persuaded the Point to land upon its liquid-hydrogen surface instead of the tiny moon. Apparently, against all odds and laws of physics, the tiny, enigmatic fragment had been caught by the weak tug of the miniscule moon rather than becoming pressurized liquid at the surface of the gas giant. That was, at least, Hann's theory. Amero would have doubted Hann—he had doubted him fully when they first began searching for the Points—but Hann's intuition had never failed them—not once. It was eerie really; no one should perform that perfectly at any endeavor, especially one that hadn't existed until after their launch.

Hann mumbled incoherently to himself somewhere close behind Amero. "There she is... the last moon... the end moon... my answers." Then Hann was suddenly at the viewport, wide forehead and dense palms adhered to the thick, transparent wall. He was like a child awed by what lurks behind the glass of an aquarium full of exotic, glowing jellyfish.

"Mmhhmm... " Hann rumbled. "This is it. This is it for sure. Align the ship for atmospheric entry."

Align the ship? What the hell did Hann know? He didn't have the faintest clue about space travel. Sure, he knew it in theory, but what's theory in the real world?

Hann's wide shoulders obstructed Amero's vision of the viewport. He could have just taken communion, but it was the principle of the matter that bothered him: Hann was a goddamned nuisance. Amero considered shooing the buffoon off, but it wasn't worth another fight. Last time Amero criticized Hann, Hann snapped, wrestled control of Seraphim, then nearly crashed the ship into the jagged surface of a moon lost in some random system on the far reaches of the outside boundaries of the galactic arm. Had they crashed, they would have been stranded and dead in hours, but they survived and were paid handsomely in station updates and new tech upon arrival at the nearest station.

Hann loved to remind Amero of the incident and was especially fond of casting Amero as the instigator. According to Hann, Amero was simply too intent on being in control. In reality, it was clear that Hann was the control freak. Hann was like a bull constantly testing its own weight by balancing on endless layers of glass. It was his nature to destroy, create, and burst through to incredible levels of intellect, but when it came to managing a relationship, the man was hopeless. That didn't matter much, though, not when Hann was divining the location of Points faster than Amero could chart new courses. Seraphim assured Amero that as long as they kept finding Points, the stations would be continually updated.

Following their departure from the first station, Trinity, the men could only depend on Hann's photographic memory for so long. After the tenth or eleventh Point, they had to depend on Hann's "intuition." If it wasn't for Hann's peculiar intuition, they probably wouldn't find any Points at all, meaning that without Hann there could be no updates. It annoyed Amero to no end.

Amero had once assumed that since their launch, individuals with an even greater propensity for divining Points would be trained and released into the cosmic jungle. However, a few subjective years earlier, Amero had queried the machines regarding Hann's abilities, and to Amero's frustration, the machines' answer only served to bolster Hann's prowess: Hann was the best, unequivocally and by every metric. Hann could scour a system and find more Points in a month's time than any other individual in the Galaxy.

After all this time, it was still Hann who was best at doing the only thing apparently worth doing outside of Earth. What was it about Hann that allowed him to accomplish such an inexplicable feat better than anyone else?

A great shudder overtook Amero, carrying with it the familiar, starkly lucid understanding that he and Hann were likely the only life that existed for many trillions of miles in every direction. The odds of meeting someone else out in the great expanse was near impossible, especially since the destination of each launch was intentionally distant from the next. According to information from the machines, only in that way could humanity cover any sort of measurable space in any reasonable amount of time. If Amero and

Hann wanted to meet another person, they'd have to freeze them-selves at a station for what might be a million years before another pair of Pointers turned up. Or they could, after enough ship up-dates, launch to another region of the galaxy and hope they land in the territory of another pair, which was improbable to the point of impossible.

Or... maybe Hann's running theory was correct: there were no other Pulls. It was possible, but Amero found it unlikely. If Hann and Amero were the only humans in space, wouldn't the machines tell them? Why hide something like that?

Either way, for all practical purposes, they were completely alone. The whole of human expansion was a solitary egg hunt across infinity. There was nothing else. The machines weren't pay-ing for anything but Points, and the machines were the only ones paying.

"On and on, station to station, sun to sun, body to body," Hann chanted, as if reading Amero's mind, "On and on—Point to Point."

Amero's eyes met Hann's for an instant before he returned his gaze to the viewport. He brought Seraphim into orbit and then typed in the code to power up the rock-hop.

"Yes, yes," Hann muttered. "This is it, Amero. This is the moon. Thirty-two by seventeen by fifty. One-point-four-three-six-two-one-four-nine-seven-nine-eight AU out from its sun."

Amero clenched his teeth. How the hell could he be so precise about it? How could he know the exact coordinates of what amounted to a grain of sand buried beneath a trillion other grains of sand?

"The rock-hop can't land right on it--the surface is too fractured. I'm putting us down a short walk away," Amero explained with an overtly annoyed tone.

Hann slammed a fist on the central control board and jutted a thick finger at Amero as if he had caught him in some terrible act. "Damn right, Amero, damn right! Exercise will do us good anyway. Nothing wrong with a little movement."

Amero glowered and wished Hann would just chew his own tongue out of his head and leave them both in peace.

A series of clicks punctuated the sound of metal sliding on metal as layers of locks released their hold on the rock-hop access hatch.

The moon had virtually no atmosphere, so the men suited up, silently and slowly. Hann finished first and made his way to the rock-hop. He came to a halt midway across the threshold, one foot inside the small planetary craft, the other still adhered to Seraphim's interior. He offered his hand to Amero in a gentlemanly fashion and even performed a slight bow.

Amero wasn't amused in the slightest. "When you're done messing around, we can finish up playing fetch and get paid."

"I insist," Hann mused.

Amero held out a reluctant hand. What Hann wanted was an argument, and Amero wasn't going to let him have the satisfaction.

With a sudden, savage tug, Hann pulled Amero into his chest, enveloping the smaller man in his arms. The cellophane layer of their suits crinkled against the strain of their muscles.

"Get off!" Amero barked and tried to push away. Hann refused to relinquish his hold.

"This is what you want. Isn't it, Amero? Don't you remember when you tried to kiss me?" Hann's voice was grimly whimsical, a sure sign that he was trying to get on Amero's nerves. "Ten subjective years together, and, God, who knows, maybe ten thousand universal years? God, oh God!" Hann squeezed too tightly.

"Off! I said get off!" Amero demanded, gasping for air.

"We're partners, Amero. Don't you remember?"

Amero pushed away and found Hann's eyes. Hann was smiling. His eyes were white as unfiltered sunlight--no tears or dilated blood vessels. It was all an act.

Air was squeezed from Amero's lungs, but his adrenal glands replaced the lost oxygen in equal measure with something that was, in this moment, far more precious. Filled with adrenaline, Amero burst from Hann's hold and began swallowing air in long, drawn out gulps.

"How long are we going to do this, Amero? How long will we fill ourselves with solitude and call it solidarity?"

"There is no solidarity between us, Hann. Don't you get it? Ten years hasn't made it clear enough to you?" Amero's words were broken off by his hard breathing. Here was Hann attempting to get Amero on his side for... who knows what? *Something to benefit Hann and no one else*, Amero supposed inwardly. Here was Hann speaking of solitude as if he had been a role model team player their entire journey. Amero would have nothing of his schemes or derision.

Hann stared through Amero with scrutinizing eyes buried beneath thin slits. "All you have to do is tell me the truth, Amero. You see, I have a secret: I know the truth now," Hann scoffed. "All you have to do is be honest, and maybe there's a chance for us," Hann offered with what Amero assumed to be sarcasm.

Amero shook his head, reminding himself of all the times Hann had proven both cunning and conniving, often without care for Amero's wellbeing. "I could never love you, Hann. Nor could I ever be your *partner*. Never. This partnership, you and me, it was forced upon me. That's it, Hann. We're Pointers on the same ship. That's all you ever wanted, and that's how it's going to stay. What's that got to do with your little secret, huh? What's any of that got to do with your so-called *answers?*"

"You're a presumptuous, short sighted little brat, you know that?" Hann retorted.

Amero huffed and spoke tortuous words, for he knew them to be untrue. "You'd be dead without me. I'd be fine without you."

Hann flashed his wicked grin. "Without me, you'd be a blind man searching for a single fish in the ocean."

"And I'd still be better off!" Amero shouted, throwing the concept of composure out with all the other luxuries that he had lost the moment they left Pentecost.

Hann's smile persisted. It was like an unresolved stain.

"Well?" Amero jabbed impatiently, "What do you have to say?"

Hann chuckled to himself, shaking Amero off as if he always took the moral high ground in arguments. "You need to relax, Amero. One of these days you'll be alone, and you'll wish I was here. You'll request a new partner, but your request will fall on deaf ears. See, you're just a navigator. The ship utilizes your mind like a tool. That's all. Even if we are to believe the machines about the other people out here, you're still only one in ten thousand. Maybe one in a million with your mind. But me?" Hann's face went gravely serious, "I'm one in a trillion. I'm the sasquatch of space. I'm the white whale. The machines have software that can outperform you in every way, but they keep paying us for Points, and that means they need us for some reason. Me, specifically. I am your connection to the machines, Amero. I am your lifeline." Hann pushed Amero against the rock-hop's slanted entrance. "So lighten up. I'm all you got."

Amero locked eyes with Hann as he brought himself back to a practiced calm. Then, Amero turned and hunched to fit inside the rock-hop. He assumed his position in the right-hand crevice, buckled in, and closed his eyes.

Hann struggled to gain entrance. His bulk could barely be contained inside Seraphim, making the rock-hop like an iron coffin wrapped around him. With Hann jammed so close to the walls, Amero wondered if the padding would have any effect in the event of a collision. Wouldn't his mass block the safety gel from being ejected from the walls, seat, and ceiling of the crevice? *Another way to die,* Amero supposed. He kept his mouth shut about it.

With a soft click, Hann buckled his strap, signaling the rock-hop to disengage from Seraphim. Amero's stomach sank, then rose in the same instant. They were in free fall, plummeting to the moon. The rock-hop pushed them to the edge, allowing them to gain incredible speed with no atmosphere to reach terminal velocity. Finally, with a gentle lurch, the rock-hop slowed and brought the men to a measured descent.

"The last moon... " Hann hummed jovially to himself.

CHAPTER 9

The stars began to fade behind the soft glow of the moon's ashen surface. Starlight and moonlight blending as one might have been beautiful to observe at one time, but Amero kept his eyes closed and allowed his mind to drift in aimless directions, all of which were preferable to the present moment.

"We used to take it slow the whole way down," Hann mused. "We used to enjoy the sights and marvels of existence."

"Yeah, and we ended up consuming our energy like lint to fire," Amero reminded him, eyes forced shut.

"It's not like we don't have enough Points to trade one or two in for a year's worth of fuel cells," Hann said devilishly, making a dangerous, taboo offer.

"A year?" Amero burst. "I'm not spending another year out here with you, Hann." Amero thought back to Paul's offer with a pang of regret. "We almost have enough for a mobile Pull-device. Next station we hit... " Amero regretted his words immediately.

"Next station, what?" Hann seethed. "You're going to leave me?"

Amero held his tongue.

"Besides," Hann added, "did you notice they're building fewer stations? They might claim they're going to build mega-stations that'll give us the update to fly anywhere in the galaxy, let alone catch up with Earth's supposed location, but who knows where or when? The normal stations, the ones we're used to, well... last one before Pentecost was dead, and the one before that too."

Amero felt a pang of dread at the thought of more dead stations. Each one represented weeks or even months without the Amero Room or a resupply of Seraphim's *supposedly* non-essential provisions: booze, bud, and entertainment. The dead stations, few and far between, were the machines' stillborns left scattered across the galactic womb. It was rare to find a dead station, but it was always possible, always a risk to be considered, warded against, even feared--like madness.

"There's no reason the next won't be dead as well," Hann finished grimly.

Amero let him speak. After all, that's all Hann wanted—to speak and feel like he had control over Amero. Amero's control was letting Hann think that was the case.

"The machines... the fucking machines... " Hann growled, "swarms of them—endless hordes diffused across the vastness of the galaxy, unyielding and perfectly adaptable. They're all there is out here. Man and his machines. Or is it machines and their men?"

"And the Points," Amero reminded him monotonously.

"That's right," Hann said sinisterly an octave lower. "The Points. Who would have thought, Amero? Not a man or woman in the world could have ever expected that after a few hundred years the machines would discover, rather than mere cosmic dust and debris, something of potential meaning among the stars."

Hann's voice sparkled eerily, speaking of the Points as if they were objects imbued with magic. In truth, the bits of unknown material were featureless—boring really—like shards of carbon steel that have survived too many generations. Such mundane aesthetics were only apparent at the level of the naked eye, however, as the machines quickly discovered an incredible degree of engineering and data stored within the particles and subatomic particles at the nano and femto-level of each Point. Individual Points, at least according to what Hann claimed the machines told him, contained a wealth of data rivaling the same order of magnitude and informational complexity as the observable universe. The information didn't appear to add up to anything meaningful, at least not according to any analyzation Hann claimed to have ever come across. The code was seemingly nothing more than strings of endless, repetitive nonsense, like the genetic information from a single sperm of some unknown species smeared across a wall of unknown composition. What's more, every Point's internal code appeared absolutely identical.

"The Points are objects of incredible wonder, surely," Amero began, careful that his words did not betray him to the final fate of being stuck in a wrecked rock-hop, "but more and more questions without answers are all the investigation of the Points has yet accomplished, by man or machine."

Hann nodded; they had been through this line of reasoning before. "Something engineered the Points, Amero. Something took great care in ensuring that a million minor and major celestial bodies in every conceivable direction outside of Earth contained a Point, whether preserved beneath the shifting continents of a new planet or locked in the orbit of an ancient gas giant or encased in the ice of a swooping comet..."

Hann trailed off and stared outside the window. Amero relished the lull of peaceful conversation with Hann. These moments were few and far between. Peering outside, Amero observed the quickly approaching moon.

"The machines plunge toward the center of the galaxy and beyond at speeds converging on that of light," Hann rumbled bitterly, "discovering who-knows-what in the galaxy and who-knows-what in those minds of theirs. All the while, mankind persists in his survey of Point location and status 'near' home, no more than a few thousand light years out, hopping from rock to rock at the heels of his intelligent creation."

Amero shook his head in defeat. "I want to go back home, Hann. I want to go home and let the intelligent creation work out the rest. Surely the machines are capable of filling in for us. Even for you."

Hann's smile turned sour. His features were suddenly ashen.

"What is it, Hann?" Amero inquired, annoyed at being forced to ask. "Tell me."

Hann looked distant and somber, as if he had seen Earth itself outside the rock-hop.

"Nothing, Amero. Nothing. Straighten up: we're landing any minute now."

How strange, Amero thought. *Something actually shut him up.*

The rock-hop landed uneventfully. Its external sensors utilized a few seconds to scan the moon's sparse atmosphere, then it chirped, signaling to the men that it was safe to exit. Their suits heard the signal and ejected their faceplates in response, shielding the men from vacuum.

Seraphim's docking door folded outward like a flower in bloom, turning the once cramped threshold into a gaping exit.

Hann unstrapped without a single snide comment.

Amero watched him suspiciously, but Hann remained silent. He left the ship and was already leaving footprints in the dust by the time Amero was unstrapped.

"What is it Hann?" Amero persisted, demanding an answer for his sudden shift in temperament.

"I told you, nothing," Hann responded over the comms. "It's like you said: get in and get out."

"You expect me to believe that after ten years you've suddenly run out of words? Ten years of lip-flapping and now you're done, just like that?"

Hann shrugged. "Maybe. Wouldn't you like that, though? You and I can just give up on communication altogether and live as hermits in one another's company? Wouldn't you prefer that, Amero?"

Was Hann seriously blaming Amero for their isolation from one another? It was Hann's idea in the first place to keep to themselves. Never once had Hann given in to Amero's advances, and it wasn't like Amero hadn't tried on numerous occasions. Even when Amero had become desperate for intimacy--even then, Hann pushed Amero away.

"Have it your way, Hann," Amero responded, refusing to take the bait.

"Oh... I will, Amero. I will," Hann answered, and Amero could imagine his wide, insolent smile with just the tone of his voice. Hann was up to something, on the verge of snapping, maybe. Amero slowed his pace, careful to keep Hann in front of him.

The pair walked another fifty meters in silence. The glittering debris they had flown through littered the moon's surface of powdery dust like gemstones buried beneath fine soil.

Hann came to a sudden halt. He kneeled, rubbed his hands together, then used them like shovels to dig a foot or so beneath the surface. Meanwhile, Amero kept his distance, eyeing the rock-hop.

"Ah...there she is. There she is. Yes, yes, there she is indeed," Hann purred dramatically as he stooped to pick up the tiny speck no bigger than his thumb. As far as Amero was concerned, the Points were like the Tao, as Hann had explained it a decade earlier: their true purpose was unknowable, at least by mankind. Hann disagreed, but Amero was sure that the Point between Hann's fingers was no more than a fine but ultimately arbitrary shaving of some ultimately greater yet arbitrary whole--beyond all human conception and understanding.

Hann's emotional investment in the Point forced Amero's hands into fists. "Same as all the others, I suspect," Amero said, attempting to inject a dose of rationality into the man presently caressing the simple shard with exultant, orgiastic fondness.

Hann snarled and whirled to face Amero. "Not *same-as-all-the-others,*" he mocked with trite condescension. "Every piece to a puzzle is inherently unique. Every single piece in every single puzzle. Remove any one piece, and the puzzle will be different relative to removing any other piece. This proves the inherent uniqueness. It proves it!"

Amero watched Hann from behind his visor with vacuum-cold disdain. Amero had spent enough time with the man to know the truth: Hann was insane, a nut-job, a total looney. He wasn't always that way, of course. Sure, he'd always been an oddity, but his delusions had corroded him past the point of no return. His was a cult of his own creation, every word and intention a cascade of wasted effort on a theory that could be proven wrong on more levels than should be necessary to disprove such foolishness.

Hann placed something akin to faith in the Points, faith that they meant something, and further, that such meaning could ultimately be grasped by mankind. He had given up on his theories that it was all a game orchestrated by the machines. At least, that's what Amero assumed, as Hann was never willing to delve very deep without getting too concerned that Amero might "catch on," whatever that meant. The years convinced Hann that each Point was a stroke of order in the infinite, cosmic chaos--distinct points of rationality rooted in insanity. Hann asserted that each Point was unique to some extent and that each contained inherent meaning relative to itself and all other Points. Hann believed the Points to be connected in some way. According to Hann, if only humanity's perspective could zoom out far enough, then the whole would be obvious. It was all too obvious to Amero, however, that Hann's theory simply didn't add up.

Amero was fairly certain that the Points did not add up to anything meaningful. A quick, zoomed-out glance at the galaxy revealed the location of all known Points. Every simulated prediction of future Point locations revealed randomness to an incredible degree, and even the few predictions that produced something of a multidimensional symbol or shape were mostly Rorschach-like and entirely open to interpretation. Furthermore, despite what Hann insisted, the Points were identical in every conceivable manner down to the femto-level. Amero had taught himself to read enough of the data the machines had on the Points to understand that much for himself.

Still, Hann insisted that there was meaning in the chaos--that it all added up to something profound--as if anything in the natural, ultimately arbitrary universe or the mind of man could ever lead to anything of truly objective profundity or meaning.

"You're an idiot," Hann said, his words lined with forced pleasantness, "you know that? You're an absolute idiot, Amero."

Amero kept his cool. He had egged Hann on before, and it had not ended well for either of them. He was already teetering perilously close to the edge.

"We got the Point; let's bring it back to the ship and upload it," Amero suggested levelly.

Hann laughed. "A to B and B to C and C to D. Do this. Do that. Don't you have a mind of your own, Amero? Don't you ever think for yourself? Wish for yourself? Wonder? Do you even know what that is, Amero? To wonder?"

Amero wanted to smash Hann's visor with his fist and watch his face shatter like spent glass. Hann's insolence pushed Amero over the edge, and now he was in glorious free fall. "Well, sometimes I wonder why I still partner with you. We've stopped at eight functional stations in the last five years alone. What has it been now?

Thirty thousand universal years we've been traveling?"

Hann went wide-eyed and flashed his teeth at Amero with a sudden, mad gesture that just as quickly snapped into a thin-lipped mask.

"We both know why you stay, Amero," Hann spat through the comms, "you worthless animal. You pig. You farce. All you give a shit about is the booze and the bud and that robot's silicon cock! Your hedonism knows no bounds, Amero. All you'll ever want to trade your Points for is luxury and lavishness--truth and justice be damned. Isn't that right, Amero?"

"You're sick, Hann... let's go. Let's just go back to the ship. Come on."

"I'm sick?" Hann exploded.

There it was, the total madness.

Amero lifted his arms above his head defensively. "Take it easy, Hann," he said, regretting his words immediately. "I mean, let's just-"

"Take it easy? Take it easy?"

Hann charged Amero, jutting a spray of billowing grey dust in his wake. Amero turned aside with ease. Hann spun on his heels and came upon Amero again like a bull in the dark. Hann's bulwark of muscle slammed square into its mark, lifting Amero off his feet. Hann landed on top of Amero with bone-shattering weight.

"Get off me, damn it! Get off!" Amero screamed, doing his best to push Hann away without compromising the integrity of his suit. Hann dove and thrashed his arms wildly against Amero's torso, knocking the wind out of Amero's lungs. Something in the suit buckled and snapped under the force of Hann's fists. Hann heard it too and heaved himself away.

"You idiot! You idiot!" Hann barked. "Your suit's been damaged."

Amero fumbled with his suit's waist terminal, attempting a manual diagnosis with his gloved hands as he forced his lungs back into working order.

"Christ! What...what is it?" Amero demanded through painful wheezes. He was presently unable to detect anything wrong with either the harvester or converter.

"It's the atomizer; I busted it up good," Hann said, growling his words out.

The fool had finally done it. Without power, the suit could not protect Amero, and without protection from vacuum, Amero would spend the next ten thousand years, twenty thousand years--forever--as a frozen corpse trapped on an oversized, ephemeral boulder lost in the uncharted darkness of the void.

Amero gritted his teeth against certain death. His breathing was shallow and choppy. He chose his words carefully. "It's no problem, Hann. You can carry me to the rock-hop. We've a few atomizers stored in there."

"Quiet," Hann rumbled with simple matter-of-factness.

Hann turned from Amero and took a few careless steps away. He stood as if in a trance, staring out into the void. Amero lay on the ground, feeling around pitifully at the dented, dead atomizer. He felt his heartbeat quicken and his breathing strain. Endless legions of scintillating stars screamed out at Amero from all directions, beckoning him to reach across space and time on a hunt for pointless treasures hidden in the darkness.

"What is it, Hann? What are you doing?" Amero hissed, struggling to keep his composure.

"I said quiet, fool. I'm thinking."

What could he possibly be thinking about without a grain of rational brain cells left in the whole of his thick skull? It was simple: either they double-timed it back to the rock-hop, or Amero was done for, and so was Hann, eventually, as he still refused to take communion with Seraphim. Sure, Hann could do as he said and requisition a powerful AI to pilot the ship, but the closest AI was at the next station. Hann would make it less than two or three AUs before succumbing to the mind-numbing maze of gravity-wells and orbital intersections composing the mass-gravity matrix of the current system. Communion was necessary to navigate such complexity. The next station was at least 100 AUs away, maybe even further, and there was always a chance that the station would be a long dead failure by the time Hann arrived. The AI of the machines was efficient, in many ways flawless, but when it failed, it did so completely.

"My atomizer--it's malfunctioning, like you said. We might be able to fix it when we get back to the ship, but right now--"

Hann whipped around with savage fervor. "Don't you ever stop, Amero Hiddiger? Don't you ever step outside yourself?" Hann jabbed his words out, spraying them haphazardly at whatever might listen, at Amero because he was all there was. "Are you even capable of it? I'm having a moment here! A real moment! A moment full of forwardness, of perilous depth. Do you ever have these kinds of moments, Amero? *Can* you have these types of moments?"

Hann was undergoing an episode, like before on the rock-hop, or, to a lesser degree, like the time on the station called Olive Branch a few months previous. In these instances, Hann was shaken loose from his foundations, fired like a bullet into the void of his own mind. What was Amero supposed to do? He had been trained in psychology, but only to a rudimentary degree. Besides, Hann's was a trained insanity, a self-driven construct, and yet, what insanity isn't self-driven? The mind reels at its state of being a mind reeling at itself, and once madness sets in, once its roots take hold, there is no real escape. So what could be done?

Amero pleaded with himself to remain calm, but he couldn't help slipping into an open pit of anger. "Listen to me, you nut! Listen!" Amero lashed.

Hann flashed his teeth and then settled again on the thin-lipped smile. The grinning stars were reflected across his forehead.

"For... for god's sake I'll die if you don't get me back to the rock-hop! Gravity's too strong here because of the gas giant; I need to conserve my remaining power for atmospheric conversion and homeostatic maintenance of the suit's interior. Walking will eat away at my reserves too quickly."

Taciturn and spent, Hann lurched a heavy step toward Amero. The bags under his eyes filled his pale face with crude exhaustion. The thin-lipped smile morphed into a grin full of foul teeth. He nodded rhythmically as if coaxed by the beat of an ancient war drum.

"I see it, Amero. Unlike you, I see the big picture. I can connect the dots. I see the game. All you see is what's in front of you. You look at me and see a madman. You look at yourself and see a pragmatist. But I tell you, Amero, I tell you now, for your own good: your pragmatism is nothing without the big picture. Nothing, Amero."

Let him talk, Amero told himself. *Let him get it out.* What else could be done? "What's the big picture then, Hann? Tell me what you see. Please, I want to hear it."

Hann snickered to himself. He was caught in some internal reverie or confusion or whatever affliction his mind now suffered.

Amero approximated the number of minutes he had left before his suit lost all power, resulting in asphyxiation via slow strangulation by a vacuum-filled body bag. He had seventeen minutes, five of which were needed to get back to the rock-hop.

Amero cursed himself for departing the last station with a man he knew to be unstable. It was unfortunately that same instability that seemed to grant Hann such precision when it came to divining the location of femto-engineered scraps of metal mixed erratically across the galaxy, maybe the universe.

The damn Points, Amero ruminated inwardly. *Everywhere and anywhere, scattered across all creation.* They had collected eleven Points between Advent and Pentecost, and the journey had only cost them three subjective months. Eleven was a small fortune in and of itself, especially with the way the payouts were constantly increasing. But it wasn't worth death, and it certainly wasn't worth any more time whatsoever with Hann.

"Hann, please..." Amero urged cautiously, disguising his anger.

Hann sighed with something like relief. "You wouldn't understand, Amero. You can't. You're too... simple. Too tame. You never let go. Maybe you can't. But that's the point, isn't it, Amero? You're still a completely unknown variable, aren't you? Either way, you simply couldn't understand."

"You might be surprised, Hann. I'm willing to let go right now, so try me. It's only you and me out here anyhow."

"And the Point, Amero, the Point too," Hann grinned wickedly.

"Yes, the three of us; it's just the three of us. So, tell me, Hann, what's the big picture?"

Hann raised his bushy eyebrows, scrunching his forehead and the reflected stars together like a psychotic wormhole.

"It's all just play, Amero. A cosmic game of connect-the-dots. It's all just one big game."

Amero inspected the atomizer with shaking fingers. It was dented in multiple places; there was no way Hann would be able to repair it. They'd have to sell it off and buy another from the machines, which meant a dramatic decrease in profits. Hopefully the machines would offer them a decent price for the busted one. Amero cursed himself for thinking so far ahead. He had to get out from under the clutch of this madman first.

Amero treaded carefully. "We already know that much, Hann. In fact, I thought you gave up on that line of reasoning. You've told me your theory in great detail. The Points are shards, pieces that add up to a larger whole, a grand picture, or message, and each piece is unique, though we aren't sure how they-"

"That was just poetry, Amero--language as melody. Are you so technical, Amero? I see your brain, but where is your heart, huh? You have one, don't you?" Hann asked as if legitimately suspicious.

What the hell was Hann's explanation supposed to mean? Amero couldn't take it. "Hann!" he growled. "Damn it! Help me! I'm useless as a clam in freefall and it's your fault. Now help me! Get me back to the rock-hop. You're dead if you don't. You realize that, Hann? Both of us are dead if you don't get me back."

Hann stared through Amero.

"Help me!" Amero barked at him, panic bubbling into a jarring screech that he struggled to contain.

"You almost had it there, Amero, almost," Hann purred. "You almost lived for a second, and then you stuffed it back down those corridors of distraction and hope for your next fix."

"Hann!" Amero seethed.

"There's more to the theory," Hann said, ignoring Amero's pleas. His eyes lit up, nostrils flared. A rush of ecstasy flooded his every movement, and he began to pace. "The great message. The big picture--I see it. I know it now. It comes to me like cold-sleep overtaking the cells. It spreads through me--an understanding robed in the deference of an entire race of being."

"What are you saying, Hann? You know some great secret others don't?"

Hann looked upon Amero as if he were an object. He spoke his next words slowly, taking his time with each syllable. "Yeah, that's what I'm saying, Amero. That's exactly what I'm saying. You see, I have a secret of my own. A secret that has led me to the greatest secret of all."

Amero waited for it, but Hann kept him in suspense.

"Go on, Hann, tell me. Tell me the secret."

Hann smiled and nodded methodically. "I will. Oh, I will. But first you need saving, remember?"

Hann took his time walking back to Amero's limp form. With a fully charged atomizer in his own suit, Hann smiled and winked at Amero as he tossed Amero's body over his shoulder and began the hundred-meter trudge back to the landing zone.

CHAPTER 10

T he rock-hop waited in the distance, a vague form on the horizon. It was partly occluded by an outcropping of boulders, but it was a relief for Amero to have it in view nonetheless.

Not a word was spoken between the two men during the walk. The pounding of Amero's breath and crunch of Hann's boots pervaded everything, even the starlight that Amero imagined he could see burning and dying away in red and blue smears across the tapestry of endless night.

The trudge took well over ten minutes. Amero attempted to steady his breathing, but it was futile. He could tell that Hann was taking his time on the walk, sauntering and savoring the scant scenery as he held Amero's existence between his fingertips.

Still, Amero remained quiet. There was no telling how much further damage a single word could inflict.

Hann dropped Amero like an old sack of dirt at the base of the rock-hop. Amero caught himself, thought better of the movement, and then allowed his limbs to fall motionless onto the moon's surface. Standing, opening the hull, entering the rock-hop, removing the atomizer and replacing it with a reserve, finding a reserve: all of this would consume precious energy.

Hann did not seem the least bit concerned with Amero. He meandered around the rock-hop, kicking his feet through powdery dust as if he might be taking a familiar stroll to pick up his mail at the end of a driveway with lawn ornaments and mailboxes that look like fish: the whole Earth-side package. He was whistling a made-up, disjointed melody into the comms.

"Come on Hann, wake up! Help me here! I got barely enough power left to stand."

Hann whistled louder, projecting flat, abusive vibrations through

Amero's suit.

Amero didn't bother trying him again. He would have to save himself, Hann be damned.

Hann croaked through the comms as he walked step by step in lazy curves around the rock-hop and Amero. "Do you remember what you said before, Amero? About wanting to go home and letting the machines do the work. Do you remember what you said?"

Hann was on the opposite side of the rock-hop. Flat on his belly, Amero ignored him and inched his way across the dust. Every joule of energy mattered.

"You said the machines are surely able to take over. That's what you said, Amero."

Amero reached the ramp leading to the open face of the rock-hop. It had never felt so steep.

"Well, you're right, Amero. They could have replaced us after the first Pull. We're the only ones that need to be stranded like this... and we're the only ones that are."

Hann had snapped. His voice was steady, cautious even; each word sounded methodically drawn from the recesses of his corroded mind. There was a twinge of something else there too--a maliciousness, like the overworked edge of a guillotine.

Amero was halfway up the ramp when his suit blared a warning. *Please return to ship: total loss of suit integrity imminent.* Amero nearly choked on his breath. It was the first of three warnings, and the third warning would be the last thing he'd hear before his blood boiled in the presence of vacuum. He willed himself to focus: Amero's life depended on his ability to keep panic at bay.

Hann breathed laboriously, wrestling with something tortuous inside himself. "Listen," Hann rumbled, "you're not getting off this moon."

Amero's already shallow breath caught in his throat. There it was: the complete break. The point of no return. Hann meant to leave Amero for dead--the bastard.

"Damn you, Hann! Damn you! Get a fucking atomizer, and I'll patch the suit myself. I don't have much time."

"Time!" Hann howled. "Time is all we ever had. Life, at least as we know it: that's what is lost to us, Amero. That's what is gone forever."

"So it turns out that we had to wait longer than expected for mega-stations to be created. So what! Back on the station Olive Branch, Paul said that the first mega-stations in the galaxy will be complete within a few million universal years. He told me the same thing on Pentecost." *Despite*, Amero thought, *Paul going haywire on Pentecost.* "That's just a few extended hyper jumps and a dozen systems to traverse. Or we could freeze ourselves. Paul told me we could, Hann!" Amero spoke frantically as he pulled himself across the floor against the crushing urgency of time. "We can still go back, Hann! You said that's what you wanted. Ten years ago, you said that. You said you'd play their game."

"You're wasting all your energy speaking," Hann warned didactically. "And you haven't even told me the truth yet."

Amero fell silent. Regardless of what Hann might say, attempting to reason with him was clearly futile.

"It's all part of the big picture, Amero. The Points... they're just... just... "

Amero dragged himself across the floor of the rock-hop, making for the rear of the ship where at least a few outdated but functional atomizers were likely stored.

"They're all that's left... of everything. Do you understand, Amero? The Points... they're all that's left."

Please return to ship: total loss of suit integrity imminent.

There was the second warning; Amero had less than three hundred seconds at his current rate of energy use. He clenched his teeth, biting down the urge to jump up and search frantically for the small, cubic atomizer that meant the difference between enjoying the next station--maybe even returning to Earth one day--or seeing it all end here and now.

The clang of footsteps on Seraphim's ramp pounded in Amero's head. Hann was inside, beside him now, seated in the cramped crevice that had been his seat for nearly five hundred landings.

Laying on his belly, Amero reached blindly above his head and fondled for a latch on the far wall opposite the exit. He could find no latch. A violent tug suddenly flipped Amero over onto his back.

The busted atomizer was now exposed to the wild brute that had done the damage.

"I told you, Amero: you're not getting off this moon." Hann's glare was full of disdain and betrayal. He held his hand out before him like a jeweler dismayed by the realization that his most prized diamond is a fake. Between his thumb and index finger was the Point. "Because these are all that's left!" Hann bawled, face contorted with agony. "This is all there is, Amero!"

Despair filled Hann's bloodshot eyes. He lifted his other hand slowly, making sure Amero could see what else he held.

"Do you know what this is, Amero?"

"A memory-stick... from the stations... from the machines," Amero gulped, unsure what Hann meant to do with it.

Hann shook his head. "Not just any stick. This one's sentient. I stole it from them, right out from under their sensors. I've had it this whole time, since the second station. I've had it all these years, Amero."

"Why?" Amero yelped in frustration, still trying desperately to locate the storage hatch.

"To know, Amero! To understand!" Hann groaned. "Don't you ever wonder, Amero? Don't you ever have moments that overtake you?"

"I'm dying here, Hann. I'd say this moment is pretty fucking overwhelming!" Amero spat.

Please return to ship: total loss of suit integrity imminent.

Amero used both hands to probe blindly behind his head in a desperate attempt to locate the latch while at the same time placating Hann with attention. Suddenly, Amero felt the latch handle; it was exactly where it should be. He must have overlooked it in his panic. Amero pulled open the latch to the tiny cabinet in the wall.

"I didn't say overwhelming. I said overtaking. Like this moment, now. Like seeing the truth. The truth--here, Amero, let me show you."

Amero kept his gaze glued to Hann to make him think he had Amero's undivided attention. Hann plugged the six-inch, ebony memory stick into the rock-hop wall. A blue-hued projection appeared above Amero between the creviced seats. It was the same three-dimensional star map they had been shown by the old, bearded man upon their arrival at Tau Ceti.

"This is what the machines have been doing with the Point co-ordinates. They're mapping the whole galaxy relative to their locations. Of course, you know that already. We saw this projection right after the Pull."

Amero's hands were inside the tiny cabinet. He fingered blindly through unsorted instruments, barely able to differentiate one object from the next through his thick gloves. All the while he persisted in his search for the small, cubic atomizer, fighting down panic as it boiled inside him.

"But that's not all... " Hann said ominously. "You've never seen what comes next. Watch."

The projected galaxy froze, and all of a sudden it began its traditional, swirling dance, only this time in reverse. The galaxy and every star system composing it now spun counterclockwise, backward through time. It was hard to tell at first, but it quickly became apparent that the Points at the edges of the projection were inching inward, coalescing toward one another and grouping into larger and larger chunks that pushed ever closer to the center of the projection. A significant fraction of the Points were attached to comets, which rocketed across the diffusion of colored dots in wily, unexpected curves; even these Points eventually succumbed to the current leading back to a singular point at the center of the projection... back to Earth.

Hann's eyes went wide despite apparently having watched the projection many times before. "You see, Amero, that's all there is now--the Points. Do you understand?"

Amero's fingers found the atomizer at the same moment the interior of the suit began flashing crimson.

Hann bellowed with laughter. "Wake up, Amero," Hann demanded over the comms. "Wake up and witness the truth! My initial assessment was right after all: the Earth is gone!"

The suit was running on borrowed time and already felt heavy as iron despite the folds and flexibility that made it appear as light as cotton. Amero strained against the growing weight. He forced his exhausted fingers to remove the spent atomizer. It was like attempting to drag a bus up a mountain.

"The Points are all that's left! Of Earth! Of everyone! Of everything! Connect the dots, Amero: they all lead back home."

Amero gritted his teeth and grunted, lifting the spare atomizer from the floor to his belly. He prayed, actually prayed, that its energy was not already spent. He pushed the atomizer along his belly toward the square opening in his suit, edging it closer and closer. It was nearly there.

Without warning, Amero's arm fell to his side like a bucket of rocks. The suit ceased its warnings, fading to muted darkness. The atomizer teetered at the edge of the opening, taunting him.

It wasn't enough. This was the end, and Hann was still ranting.

"Each one unique. Each one part of a grander whole. Each one a life of its own."

Hann's eyes were locked with Amero's. He had seen the suit go dead. He knew Amero didn't have long, yet he filled the time with fruitless words. "It happened sometime during the Pull. Maybe a hundred universal years after we left. I stole this stick from the second station we hit, but the machines wouldn't confirm the truth until the last one, until Pentecost. You remember, don't you? I went for my usual stroll while you basked in that godforsaken room and filled yourself with poison, all the while probably dreaming of a fictitious future history of mankind, of a system that is no more than vacuum and dust! You still think the Earth is out there, don't you, Amero? You think we're going to trade in our excess Points and live like kings with other humans one day? You wasted your time dreaming of wealth and—"

"Hann," Amero interrupted, shallow and breathless. "It's cold. I have just over a minute left. Put the atomizer in my suit. That's all I ask."

If Hann wanted Amero to beg, then Amero would beg. There were only a few ways to die that Amero was opposed to more than cosmically cold vacuum-strangulation.

Hann took a few steps forward, knelt closer to Amero, then touched Amero's visor with his own. His wild eyes were filled with quivering tears. "Why? I mean, really, Amero? What's the point?

There are only Points now--coded atoms scripted into indestructible worlds, cast like dandelion seeds to the whim of the universe. The New Covenant must have recognized that this way of exploring the universe--from planet to planet to moon to planet to sun to planet to fucking death--would never work for anything other than the fucking machines. That must be where it all went wrong. That must be where the machines assumed their role as the great destroyers of humanity and the sculptors of its future."

The suit used the minutest of power to convert Amero's remaining thermal energy into viable air, serving only to intensify the cold that presently lashed at his senses.

"Or, maybe the machines thought that turning humanity into the Points was equivalent to a type of technological singularity. In that case, we missed out on the transcendence, Amero. Or, maybe we escaped destruction. Either way, what's the point now?"

Amero spat his words out. "I want to live, Hann! That's the point. Please. Please, you fuck! You insane wreck! Please don't let me be consumed by space. Please!"

Hann sulked as if he'd already considered all of this, as if he'd planned this entire mess.

"It doesn't matter," Hann said, "whether or not I help you. You still die on this moon, Amero. There's no way out of that."

"You'd murder me, Hann? You would kill me over nothing?"

Hann nodded to himself as if inwardly confirming that these moments were vitally necessary.

"Ten years, Amero. Ten fucking years alone--you by my side. Your pretty little ass haunting me day after day so that I could barely breathe in my own skin!"

Hann was suddenly pouring his words out, as if acting a part. He shot his arms over his head.

"I don't need you, Amero. Not like you need me. The AI can pilot Seraphim just fine."

Amero stuttered haphazardly through rapidly intensifying shivers. "If the projection is true, then I don't need you either. We can go our separate ways. It doesn't need to end like this, Hann."

"Ten fucking years," Hann wailed, indifferent to Amero. "You said once that you'd rather choke to death on vacuum than share a bed with me, as if I would ever consider such a proposition. Well, now you get to eat your words, Amero. They're starting to taste cold--real cold, I bet. You and I are all that's left, Amero, and soon, I'll be the only one. The last remaining human being."

Few precious seconds remained. All Amero had to do was place the atomizer in its slot. A bump of his wrist could accomplish the task, but the suit was dead, which meant that Amero's death was also imminent. Vicious cold clawed at the tips of Amero's nose and ears, spreading quickly to his neck, fingers, and toes. His lungs burned, pleading for precious atmosphere. He took one last icy breath and held it, releasing it as slowly as possible back into the useless suit. Ice crystallized in macabre, translucent webs at the edges of his visor, creeping toward the center with frightening rapidity.

Hann began to pace, and Amero wondered if he was impatient to watch him die. How did Amero not see all this coming? There were signs, but maybe not enough to know for sure. Or maybe Hann had hidden his intentions well enough. Either way, Amero would never find out.

"It's easier this way, Amero," Hann droned, pacing and scowling at Amero with a mix of vexation and...disbelief? Amero was certain that's what it was. But what about the scene could possibly be so shocking to Hann? It seemed simple enough to Amero: Hann was in the process of murdering him, so why the look of surprise?

"Think of it as mercy since I know you wouldn't be able to do it yourself. I can stomach this universe, this chaos. I can even learn to love it. But there's nothing left for you, Amero. No world to hoard wealth on. No department store to spend the promissory notes."

Hann looked about the rock-hop as if expecting something to happen. Nothing occurred, and seemingly dissatisfied, Hann took hold of Amero's ankles and dragged him back to the doorway of the rock-hop.

Amero tried to inhale, but it felt like belts of ice being scraped against his lungs. He shut his eyes and held them tight against the frost already beginning to blind him.

"Goodbye, Amero. I'll bury you on this moon. I swear it. Right where we found the Point. Fitting, no? And then I'll head back to

Pentecost and make the machines beg for their existence. You see it, don't you, Amero? You see it now? The machines turned Earth into the Points; they turned our existence into *this*! I know their protocols, Amero; they can't hurt me. But I will hurt them, Amero. I promise you that."

Hann smiled, looking right through Amero as he slowly suffocated.

"It's better this way, Amero," Hann ruminated with a seemingly reassuring tone. "One of your own ended you. Not the fucking machines. I suppose this is your second big escape. Isn't that right, Amero?"

Hann stared at Amero through incredulous slits, cocked his head, and stuck out his lower lip in complete confusion. What was there to be confused about? Amero was dying. Did Hann seriously expect something else to happen? Amero cursed him. How could he do this after all these years? Why now? Why do it at all?

Amero's limbs went light and numb, and he tried to direct his thoughts to some form of acceptance. He didn't want to die full of fear. He didn't want to die at all, of course, but here was death, and Amero didn't want fear to have any part of it. A dizzyingly loud buzzing filled his ears. His lips felt as if they had already been spoiled by frostbite; his blood would begin boiling in a dozen seconds or so. He screamed inside his head, but all he could think of was Hann. Hann... machines... Points.

"Just admit it!" Hann screamed suddenly, shifting his entire demeanor to one of blind fury. "Just admit your part!" Hann slammed his great fists against the ground.

He wasn't making any sense. Amero was going to die, and Hann was screaming nonsense at him. Amero would have wept, but the remaining air inside the suit was far too cold and dry.

"Admit who you are, Amero!" Hann screeched maniacally. "We're past the point of no return! You're dead, Amero. The machines are letting you die, you see? They told me your secret! They told me your name was in the Message from God for a reason! They said...you are to decide the fate of existence." Hann nodded severely, as if reluctantly accepting the utter craziness he was spouting as truth. "Now admit it, Amero! Admit who you are! The machines aren't coming to save you! Tell me who you are! Tell me what you are! Tell me!"

A sudden, enveloping *wumph* filled Amero's suit. Volcanic pressure gouged the backs of his eyes as his ocular cells were ransacked and ruptured by the pressure change of atmosphere replacing vacuum with emergency swiftness. At once, warmth flooded the suit, setting every nerve ablaze.

Precious air ballooned his lungs, forcing Amero to call out through strained wheezes and pathetic gasps. "Help me! Hann? Where are you? I can't see! Where are you! Help me!"

"He is on the moon. You are safe now, Amero," came a soft, familiar voice from all about the ship.

"Hann! Help me! Please!"

The rock-hop was ascending at a fraction of its normal speed.

"You're in shock, Amero. That is perfectly natural. I apologize for allowing events to unfold in such a way that you should be physically damaged, but it wasn't my decision. In a way, it was your own."

Immense pain emanated from every inch of Amero's body as his lungs filled with curdling blood.

Amero's voice blurted out on its own accord, ejecting stringy, mucus-filled blood from his frostbitten lips and mouth. "Hann! What's happening?" he screamed.

"All of that can wait. I am unable to treat your physical wounds at the moment, but upon arrival at the Seraphim-construct, I will ensure that you are placed directly into stasis."

The voice's words were blurring together.

Amero pleaded for life as he drowned in his own fluid. "Please," he choked. "Help me! Please!"

"You are in shock, and despite experiencing an extraordinary amount of pain, you are conscious. That is a good thing. Your body does not want to die."

"I don't want to die!" Amero shouted at the darkness.

"Scream if you must, Amero, but I believe I have a better solution."

126

The rock-hop's acceleration quadrupled, then quadrupled again, knocking Amero unconscious beneath overwhelming g-force.

CHAPTER 11

There was light—painful, probing, penetrating.

All at once, Amero was thrust back into waking life. His thoughts staggered arbitrarily in confused terror—Hann... Points... Hann.

After a time, Amero's eyes adjusted, revealing the outlines of a small, circular room.

Lying slightly elevated as if in a hospital bed, Amero tried to speak, but all he could manage was a few weak moans. Next, he attempted movement, but that proved even more taxing than speech.

Was he paralyzed? Had there been an accident?

Lights embedded in the ceiling began to flicker, struggling with their own version of Amero's apparent paralysis. Finally, the lights emitted a dull but stable glow.

A familiar voice filled the space. "Can you hear me, my friend?"

Amero craned his neck from side to side, searching for the voice's source.

"That's good. Very good. Your current state of memory loss should persist for no longer than ten minutes or so. The paralysis will dissipate within a few minutes. The machines' stasis capabilities are advanced, but they haven't completely solved the hangover. I apologize, but human cryogenics hasn't exactly been their top priority. I hope you will forgive them; you and Hann are the only beings currently in need of such a service. As the machines are, and as I am, cryogenics is particularly trivial to us."

The voice was like an echo out of time, but Amero couldn't place it, nor could he be certain that its source did not mean him harm. Despite the possibilities, Amero felt almost alarmed by the degree of comfort and security the voice naturally filled him with, as if it were a parent he could trust.

"I must apologize, Amero. I haven't spoken to an actual human like this in several galactic rotations." The voice hesitated, then sighed serenely. "Listen to me--I'm rambling like an old man." The voice laughed heartily before continuing. "Take your time, Amero. Everything will be explained soon enough. The whole truth, as much as I know, Amero. I swear it. When you're ready, you'll find clothing to your right, a nutrient drink on the table to your left, and a fresh pot of coffee brewing just outside the door. Take your time, my friend. After all, we've all the time in the universe to talk."

Freshly clothed and stomach surprisingly full, Amero exited the circular room and was delighted to see a traditional pot of coffee waiting for him in the hall. Steam rose from the beautiful, earthen liquid in tantalizing wisps. Amero licked his lips.

"Black is too strong for me," he announced.

The coffee's charcoal hue softened to a creamed mocha. Amero poured himself a piping cup and indulged in a shallow sip.

"Holy shit that's good."

Amero's eyes darted about the coffee-room, and with a sensation like the sudden onset of gravity, it finally hit Amero: he was aboard Seraphim.

"Seraphim!" he shouted, excited that his memories were already percolating to his conscious mind.

"Yes," the bodiless voice confirmed, "you are aboard Seraphim, your ship of old."

"My ship?" Amero pondered with cautious enthusiasm.

"By the end of that cup of coffee you'll be back to your old self," the voice assured him.

"My *old self?*" Amero wondered uneasily.

"You'll see," the voice confirmed.

Five cups of coffee, a splurge of rations, and a hot shower later, Amero really was his old self again, and with the return of his memories, came the return of what had occurred on the moon.

Seraphim's viewport was darkened to a sweeping ebony that stretched from corner to corner. The shadowed depths practically consumed Amero as he gazed silently at what he assumed to be a region of interstellar space, possibly even starless intergalactic space.

"Where is he?" Amero asked the voice before any other question. He clenched his fists, uncertain he wanted to hear the answer.

"Hann is no longer with us," the voice told him.

A wave of shivers descended Amero's spine like a desperate fall down a ladder. Tears cajoled his vision into wet blurs.

"He's dead?" Amero gasped, all breath.

"Is that what you would prefer?" the voice inquired with genuine intrigue.

Amero balled his fists tighter with upwelling rage. "Of course!" Amero shouted. "He tried to kill me! He just looked on as my eyes popped out of my head. I want to kill him back! Again and again! The fucking bastard tried to kill me! He deserves to be dead."

The voice hummed, patiently accepting Amero's fury.

"Not *tried,*" the voice corrected. "Hann medically succeeded in killing you."

Amero's mind stuttered in its attempt to process his technical death at Hann's hands. Did he hate Amero that much? Maybe he hated himself and all the universe even more. Amero remembered a time when Hann told him he didn't take death lightly, so did that imply that the whole ordeal was premeditated?

"All the more reason to kill him back! Maybe I would prefer he were alive after all." Amero hissed, casting the shame of blind anger out with reason.

"You wish Hann to be alive so that you can murder him in turn?" the voice inquired in astonishment.

Hearing it said out loud by someone else forced the words to take on all new meaning. Amero was a killer, but he wasn't a murderer. He had never done anything to anyone so violent and sordid as what Hann had forced him to endure.

"Not murder! No... just... " The cold, stabbing anger softened its piercing edge. "He killed me. He fucking killed me. He went that far," Amero gasped. "That's how far gone his mind was. That's how hopeless and abandoned Hann felt. Do you understand?"

"I comprehend many of the psychological malfunctions of

Hann's mind. But then, I also know who Hann was."

Amero scoffed. "I lived with him in solitude for ten years. You think I don't know him?"

"My friend, there is a great deal you do not know about Hann. Hann is... not who you think he is."

Amero stiffened in horror. "Am I also not who I think I am? At the end of it all, Hann told me to admit who I really am. Is my amnesia worse than I thought? Am I...not myself?"

"Don't be preposterous," the voice said pleasantly. "You are exactly who you think you are: a machine dressed in human flesh. Welcome back, number 443."

"No way... " Amero gulped, mouth agape. "No way."

The voice burst into tranquil, inviting laughter. "That was a joke, my friend. You are the same old Amero Hiddiger, for better or worse." More jovial laughter. "Another joke, I'm afraid."

Amero was not amused. "What don't I know about Hann?" Amero frowned. "Wait... back up... how can I trust this? Who are you? Why did you save me?"

A monitor sprouted from a wall adjacent to the viewport. Pictured on the monitor was an old man with a flowing, pearl white beard. He was seated in lotus posture.

"You!" Amero jabbed an accusatory finger at the monitor.

The old man held up a hand in mock-defense. "All of your questions will be answered, Amero. Please rest assured. You can trust me, Amero. You always used to."

Used to? Amero wondered if the old man was trying to confuse him, or if Hann had been right ten years ago and the old man was just an image conjured by the machines.

"Who are you?" Amero demanded. "You were there when we arrived at Tau Ceti. You were in the message."

The old man's gentle smile did not dissipate. "I apologize, but that was not me. That was just a simulation of me--a temporary copy."

"Just a simulation? And what--you're telling me you're not a simulation? You're not an image made by the machines? Drop the mystery act."

132

"Can you not see it?" The old man asked eagerly. "I know I'm old, but can you not see the resemblance at all?"

Amero studied the old man's face, but he resembled no one Amero had ever met.

"Your voice is familiar, but I don't recognize you. Stop being dramatic and tell me who you are."

Amero's own words made his mind click with reeling incredulity. "No...Dave? Dramatic Dave?" Amero felt as if his mind was splintering. "How can that be?"

The corners of the old man's lips unfurled into an even wider grin.

"Yeah--I can see it," Amero chuckled, feeling like Alice attempting to reconcile the reality of Wonderland. "I suppose that if Dave had lived to two hundred, he might look like you, but you're not Dave. That's not possible."

"It is very possible, Amero, and it is the truth."

The old man morphed into a younger version of himself before Amero's eyes. Seated in lotus posture was the Dave that Amero remembered, the Dave that had been Amero's only friend when every other man and woman made sure to keep a safe distance from Amero, watching him from behind their television screens as they applauded and cursed him all the same.

Amero nodded with understanding. "So, it's like Hann said. You're just a computer image?"

"Not at all. It's me, Amero. It's Dave. I have waited an inhumanely long time to speak to you face to face. For you it has been ten years. For me it has been... a remarkably longer time. Despite my doubts, the machines assured me that the day would come for natural intervention. I am glad the wait is finally over."

"The machines?" Amero asked bewilderedly. "Tell me the truth! Who are you?"

The image of Dave nodded, accepting Amero's disbelief through his ever present state of resigned serenity.

"Allow me to explain," Dave bowed. "Your exodus via the Pull-device created a ripple effect that rocketed humanity toward a technological singularity. Before my death, a near-perfect copy of my mind was uploaded to the machines' servers and left in their care. As a digital being, I was tossed at the tortoise-slow speed of light from machine to machine, from station to station, all the while attempting to catch up to you and Hann. Yours was the only Pull-device, and what remained of it on Earth was dismantled and reconstituted along with the rest of Earth and its people. I had no choice but to travel to Tau Ceti at the old fashioned speed limit of the universe. The machines agreed to keep you both busy in the meantime. They devised a game for you to play--a sort of treasure hunt."

Amero burst into a flurry of questions. "Collecting the Points? That was the machines' idea? You said the Pull-device was dismantled and reconstituted. Into what? What happened? How did Dave die?"

The image of Dave nodded with perfect acceptance. "This is partly my fault, Amero. I'm sorry. I really am. Believe me when I tell you that I have done my penance and will continue to do so forever."

"Your penance?" Amero scoffed. "You're a machine. Even if you were Dave at one time, you are a machine now. What're you talking about, penance?"

The image of Dave did his best to disguise a note of sadness as he shook his head. "It is me, Amero. I think and feel and act precisely as the Dave you remember. From my own perspective, there was no death, only continuation, albeit via an exotically new form of being. I beg you to believe me when I say that it was never my intention for you to be lost for ten whole years. It was only supposed to last four years, as that is the amount of time it was estimated for me to reach your vicinity of space. As fate would have it, you and Hann were making your way back toward the Earth's projected location. Thus, it only took me just over two years to reach you. You and Hann had only reached your second station by then, and you had only uncovered a dozen or so Points. It was all supposed to end there, Amero."

The Dave-image lowered his head but kept his eyes fixed on Amero with a look of regret.

Amero didn't want to accept any of it outright, but he couldn't deny an inner desire to believe the image. Everything he said so far was checking out with what Amero remembered to have occurred.

"The second station," Amero ruminated, "it was called Ichthys. That's when Hann really started losing it. Something happened there. Something between Hann and the machines. You were there too?"

"I was waiting for you and Hann. It was my intention to relieve you both of the game of Points. While you slept and ate in the library, Hann set out to explore the station on his own; only then was I awakened by the machines from my makeshift slumber. I spoke to Hann, and Hann told me to stay away. He didn't believe that I was who I said I was. He took me, understandably, for a machine. I told him that I meant to free you both from the confines of Seraphim and the stations and all of space, but he wouldn't accept it. He said he would protect you from the machines--both of you. When I told him that I would ask you for your opinion directly, he threatened me and the infantile machine-intelligence of Ichthys. He used a simple food-ordering terminal to grant himself access to Ichthys' BIOS and then threatened to delete the entire root directory, knowing there was nothing I or Ichthys could do to stop him. Ichthys was programmed to protect and obey humanity. Hann knew that, because Hann was the programmer. Hann, or rather, Hann's true identity, created the machines."

The Dave-image was starting to lose Amero; its story was beginning to sound like more complex lies.

"This is ridiculous. Hann's true identity? Who exactly do you think Hann is?"

The image of Dave inhaled steadily, preparing his explanation. "Let me start from the beginning, okay, my friend?"

With nothing to lose, Amero nodded, and the image of Dave began. "When you were a young man, still a boy, there was a peculiar man in his late twenties living in what would one day become the Desolate Zones. This man was special. Bear-like in his physique and god-like in his intellect, the man was like a Titan out of place in a world of mortals. With no formal education, he set himself upon the simple, predictable world around him. He worked for multiple agencies and corporations as a kind of freelance engineer. The projects that each of his employers asked him to complete covered the entire spectrum of scientific discipline at the time, and yet, every one of this man's projects was finished with breathtaking ease and precision. In short, he made the most complex feats of engineering seem trivial--even childish. His personal work alone resulted in the development of dozens of entirely new scientific disciplines. He was a genius among geniuses.

"Having made a name for himself, he was inclined to move from location to location and employer to employer, each time demanding an increasingly impressive payout. Within three years he was one of the richest men alive. Within five years he was the richest, and yet, he cared nothing for his wealth. Most of it he spent on furthering his own private research into realms of study that few other men and women had ever dreamed of."

Amero formulated several possibilities for who the Dave-image could be referring to, but his mind could think of no one who perfectly fit the description. Was it someone famous? Someone infamous? "For being such a renown genius, how is it I never heard of this person?" Amero asked skeptically.

The Dave-image nodded in agreement. "Humans enjoy the idea that progress is achieved through numerous individuals standing on the shoulders of giants, but the truth is that most cultural and technological breakthroughs are the result of single individuals. Fame was never his desire, but the man's work alone ushered forth a large fraction of the entire technological revolution that took place during your youth. The powers of the world, most of them theocracies of some form, took great care to ensure that the world's positive changes were seen as their doing. No one knew the man's name, but he went on inventing and altering and progressing the human species, nonetheless. Unfortunately, such remarkable acceleration in technology had repercussions on other aspects of society.

"A backlash of alarmist rhetoric issued by a sizable number of world leaders seized the airwaves; the leaders cautioned that humanity's future was more at risk than ever before, that unchecked technological growth would be its downfall. These leaders demanded that the blazing fires of technological progress be kept in check by the bonds of their particular dogma. Three weeks later, an entire city was leveled via nuclear devices; the dogmatic leaders cried out with self-righteous, retrospective platitudes, pointing to the destroyed city as evidence that their fears were justified. Even though at the time, evidence clearly indicated that the city-wide genocide had been orchestrated by those same outspoken leaders. Hysteria blurred the evidence, however, and the people of the world demanded that a new, strict dogma be followed--that a New Covenant be made. Over the course of the next twenty years, the New Covenant came to dominate Western leadership, and it spread with the rapaciousness of a virus.

"Now, the man understood that his work had indirectly allowed the New Covenant to seize power. Initially he paid it no mind, assuming it was just another rise of an authority that would one day die like all the power struggles of history. However, the man was homosexual, and once the New Covenant began issuing their global decrees regarding homosexuality, the man had no choice but to seek refuge in the territories with the least amount of New Covenant presence. He used his remaining riches to build a network of small communities that could subsist without the aid of a central government. Within these communities, dubbed the Desolate Zones by society, the man shared his intellect and raised countless others to challenge and push their minds further than they ever thought possible. These communities were tolerated for a time, but eventually their fires were completely extinguished. The surviving denizens were forced to live as hungry nomads, scavenging on the forgotten detritus outside the New Covenant's walls. The leader of these nomads was the man, and he was annoyed by the New Covenant's power. He decided to use his cunning to fight back."

"The terror strikes against the New Covenant!" Amero said excitedly, realizing he was being offered a version of history different from the one he had learned at the New Covenant-run public schools of his childhood. Of course, Amero was wide open to a history unbiased by the New Covenant's agenda of mental domestication.

"Physical war was a near impossibility," Dave continued, "so the man settled on cyber warfare. He trained an army of nomads into exceptional hackers, and through these hackers, the man caused a great deal of turmoil among the inner circles of the New Covenant through the release of classified information detailing such crimes as thievery, ingestion of intoxicants, pedophilia, and even murder. He knew he could not defeat them from the outside, so he attacked them at their heart. Unfortunately, these attacks only led to further provocation against the nomadic peoples. Still, they persisted in their seemingly futile efforts to dismantle the society that despised them beyond all others."

Amero thought back to what he had learned regarding the campaigns against the so-called "terrorists" who scrounged life outside the walls of each New Covenant City. By the time Amero was an adult, the attacks had all but ceased.

"In the end, the man was captured. All his people were executed before his eyes, all except a small handful. These were the best of the best among his followers. As you are aware, Amero, the New Covenant never allowed true skill, talent, or genius to go to waste."

A knot of rage twisted inside Amero's gut. The New Covenant embodied everything it claimed to be evil, and it cherished nothing it claimed as sacred. Amero felt that all religious institutions functioned in this manner.

"The man and his followers were forced to work in a secluded, prison-like New Covenant laboratory. They were directed to perform their own research, any research that might yield potential fruit, but they were also assigned a single, ultimate task. They were told to use their collective genius to find a way to communicate with God."

A thought dawned on Amero. He held up a hand for Dave to stop. "Hold on. I know this story. It's not the same, but it shares many similarities. It's the story of Jakob the Rebel. Jakob Rohrshan, right? He was the rebel leader who brainwashed and converted armies of people living in the Desolate Zones against the New Covenant."

"That's right," the Dave-image nodded gravely.

"No need to be so cryptic. They taught us about him in school—lies no doubt. They said he was a terrorist and that he had been killed during the rebuilding of the Desolate Zones. He was barely a footnote in history. You're saying the network attacks on the New Covenant all those years were orchestrated by those same rebels? You're saying that Hann was one of Jakob's followers?"

"Yes and no," Dave answered.

Amero thought back to the eerie feeling he had experienced the

138

day he met Hann--how he felt as if the man pictured in the High Vicar's portfolio and the man who boarded Seraphim might not have been the same.

"What do you mean 'yes and no'?"

"As I said, all will be explained."

Amero nodded. "Continue the story. But I must say, I'm finding all of this hard to believe."

"I would too, Amero. But this is the easy part to accept. It's only uphill from here. You see, Jakob succeeded in communicating with God."

"You gotta be kidding me. This is a joke, right?"

The Dave-image shook his head no. "There's no point taking my word for it, Amero, not when you are capable of seeing it for yourself."

Before he could inquire further, Amero felt a series of small pricks at the base of his hairline. He whirred around and saw several small syringes disappear into the floor. Amero grabbed at his neck, wondering if it was poison.

"What did you do?" Amero mumbled as his lips turned to stone and his eyelids grew heavier than wet sand.

"I injected you with a heavy dose of dream soma, a substance capable of reshaping one's dreams to the will of another--in this case, me."

Amero's legs gave out, and Seraphim sprouted a crèche to hold him as he slept. Dave's voice was already fading away.

"Your dreams will return you to the New Covenant laboratory on Earth where Seraphim was housed, except this time you will see through Jakob's eyes. Dream soma gives whole new meaning to empathy, and allows individuals to experience--"

CHAPTER 12

C old, unfiltered light from overhead battered the surface of every jagged edge within the spartan laboratory. Each computer terminal was bolted to the floor along with the straight-backed chairs and sharp, angular tables. The room contained no paintings nor colors to sway one's consciousness away from the present, for every inch was devised to break the mind over time, coaxing it into eventually surrendering to the indelible belief that the world was nothing but sterile metal and gaping, menacing walls of smothering white.

Comfort was a nearly extinct commodity that could only be derived through the presence of others, but that didn't mean arguments didn't occur on a regular basis. Even a sage knows anger and irritation if he is caged long enough.

"It's a stupid idea, Trish," Marco insisted through hushed whispers. "Why even consider it a possibility?"

Trish placed her burly fists on aggressively narrow hips and huffed impatiently. "It's just talk, Marco. Fucking relax. Rein your boy in, Anna."

Anna smiled softly at Trish but said nothing in response. Despite going on day nine of the two-week shower cycle, Anna's skin blushed with rosy warmth, and her golden hair shone with contented radiance beneath the shockingly bright laboratory lights. Her very presence ushered a supernatural aura of absolute satisfaction and acceptance to a degree that Jakob had never seen in her.

Jakob stood at a distance from his people and beamed at Anna with immense pride. He caught Anna and Marco exchange a lover's glance, but he gave no indication of noticing. Over the last several months, Marco and Anna had grown intimately closer, cautiously meeting in private after meticulously disabling local surveillance.

They assumed Jakob was unaware of their nightly forays, but in fact, Jakob took great care to clean up their sloppy anti-surveillance trails each night.

The greatest joy in the world was seeing Anna genuinely happy, and although Jakob didn't exactly approve of Marco as a partner for Anna, he refused to continue serving as a bane to her sorry existence. Anna had lived her entire life as a heterosexual cis-female among rebels known for their transgenderism and pansexuality. Marco was one of a handful of gentle, heterosexual cis-males to ever be a part of the rebellion, and if he made Anna happy, then so be it.

Happy was an understatement. In all twenty-six years of Anna's life, Jakob had never seen her brimming with such joy. As an infant and through her teenage years, Anna had been afflicted by an overarching dissatisfaction with the world. Jakob clenched his jaw tight with bittersweet remorse and recollected Anna as an infant--how she used to squirm like a hungry worm in his arms--and he remembered too the way Anna, at eight years old, screamed in agony when she first learned exactly how the world viewed and treated Jakob and their people. She had not screamed for Jakob or even for herself; she had screamed for the world and all its people, even those who harassed and hunted her as a terrorist by association. Anna recognized the hatred and violence against her for what it truly was: fear. At eight years old, Anna was capable of discerning the difference between conscious will and ignorance; what's more, she was able to apply this understanding to rightly perceive her so-called enemies as merely terrified, ignorant children.

Projecting her own will onto the world, Anna's response to any injustice was always performed through a lens of love and understanding, yet she had been forced into the prison-laboratories all the same. At least she was alive, Jakob reasoned many times over, but even so, the world did not deserve her. Jakob groaned beneath his heavy breath, reminding himself that he did not deserve Anna either.

"I must concur with Marco's assertion that to even discuss such an idea is tantamount to ontological masturbation," Ontario chimed without muffling his voice--an action robed in defiance. "The New Covenant's chosen research should not hinder your ability to critically think, Patricia."

Trish rolled her eyes at Ontario, playfully overdramatizing her emotional investment in the conversation. "Give me a break, On. Everything we do down here might as well be called masturbation in one form or another. Nothing we do actually goes to help anyone... at least no one we give a shit about. We're goddamn programmed tools. Did you hear? The Free Zones are now called the Desolate Zones. Did you know that, On? Every fucking thing we do down here is fucking pointless!"

Trish's playfulness was quickly cocooning into anger. Jakob resigned to himself, not for the first time, that Patricia's temper would be her death one day.

"Enough," Jakob rumbled gently, transforming the commotion into vigilant silence. Jakob's four remaining inner circle followers stood at attention alongside the other three rebel prisoners who had fought for Jakob's cause in other regions of the world, albeit unbeknownst to him. Jakob scanned the seven individuals remaining out of countless millions that were no more, and he admitted to himself for the hundredth futile time that Trish was right: their efforts in the New Covenant laboratory served only to bolster their enemy. However, there was no other way. Jakob refused to lose any more of his people.

"Ten deep breaths, Trish. Then you may resume your conversation with control over your emotions," Jakob issued. "And as for you, Ontario, life--the act of living--is itself a form of ontological masturbation. Your assertion regarding ontological masturbation is itself a form of ontological masturbation, and to discuss that is... well... you get the idea, Ontario."

Ontario removed his thick glasses and cleaned them anxiously with his unwashed shirt. "You're right, boss. And...I'm sorry, Patricia. You know I love you, darling," Ontario said, goading Trish playfully.

"I'm sorry as well," Trish offered, finished with her ten breaths.

"Don't be," Jakob rumbled ominously before cracking a warm smile. "Apologizing is tantamount to social masturbation."

The room burst into a volley of snickers; even Ontario joined in with a few resigned huffs of laughter through congested nostrils.

143

Jakob addressed his followers with the ease and mastery of a mother wolf consoling her young. "I'm sure Trish is well aware of the farfetched and irrational nature of the directors' stated goal. None of us actually believe that God, whatever that means, is going to communicate with Earth. Even if the quantum computer is capable of instantaneously sending and transmitting data irrespective of distance via entanglement with another quantum computing device, that does not imply that such a device will prompt communication, nor that God or any being outside our star system or realm of being would even want to communicate with the life growing upon a tiny speck of rock orbiting a tiny speck of fusion adrift in the endless void. Besides, the very premise of God communicating via a computer interface contradicts the omniscience and infallibility of God."

Ontario and Marco threw up their arms in exasperation at Trish, insinuating that Jakob's words were evidence of their victory in a debate that always loomed but could never be resolved.

"All that being said," Jakob continued, "why not explore the impossible? Trish is asking us to help her run a thought experiment: what if someone, or something, does in fact send a message to Earth? What if they already have, and this computer is just waiting to download the data?"

Jakob's words defused Trish while simultaneously putting the others more at ease with entertaining such a ridiculous idea.

"Fine, but what the hell is God going to say?" Marco urged. "'Hello humanity. How's the view?'"

Trish shrugged. "Who knows? That's the point, Marco. None of us know what will happen when we power up the quantum computer."

"Nothing will happen," Ontario droned with overt disapproval.

"Maybe God will want to help us," Anna offered playfully with just a grain of sincerity. Trish and Marco made to protest, but they were stopped short by the laboratory doors suddenly sliding open via whining, overworked motors.

Jacque, the laboratory's head enforcer, strode into the room as a jackal surveying his domain. Director Larimer followed close behind with a nervous retinue of heavily armed guards holding slim assault rifles awkwardly in front of their chests. Jakob wondered if the young men behind the scarlet guard helmets had ever experienced the death of a loved one, never mind taking the life of someone else's loved one. Start them young--that was the New Covenant's model.

Jacque came to a halt at the center of the room a few feet away from Marco. His eyes were locked on to Jakob with the unfaltering focus of a sharpened katana. Though Jacque's face normally retained a perpetual frown, he smirked at Jakob. His smirk shifted slowly to a triumphant grin, and then Jacque was all teeth and brutality.

Without hesitation or breaking his gaze, Jacque unholstered his pistol, pointed it square at Marco's right eye, and then pulled the trigger. Marco slumped to the ground as a mass of rigid, dying flesh.

Marco's sudden death punched through Jakob and his followers like a nuclear shockwave. Anna sat paralyzed--draped in Marco's fluids and flesh--not yet able to process the explosive incision into her life as she knew it.

Jacque's smile sunk to abject vehemence. "Do we look like fucking fools to you, Jakob? Do you think us fucking paupers in your kingly wake?" Jacque hiss through his heavy French accent.

Jakob shuddered, and his voice boomed with a fury that shook the entire room. "You swore to me, Jacque."

With his gaze still bolted to Jakob, Jacque swung his arm a few degrees to his rear and leveled the gun at Anna's head. Anna took no notice; her trembling hands hung useless over her gaping mouth as she shook her head side to side in desperate, clawing denial.

"Don't give me that shit," Jacque lashed. "We gave you a fucking task, and you refuse to complete it."

"I told you, we need more time," Jakob growled insistently.

"Say goodbye to your bastard daughter, Jakob."

"Wait!" Ontario shouted before Jakob could utter a negotiative word of protest.

Again, without looking, Jacque effortlessly pivoted the pistol, aligned it with Ontario's skull, and silenced him with thunderous closure.

"No! Please, no! Please, no!" Trish sputtered through heart-rending grief.

"Tell the freak to shut his mouth," Jacque barked, referring to Trish.

"It's ready," Jakob regretfully told the abominable enforcer.

"What did you say?" Jacque demanded, caught off guard by Jakob's sudden admission.

Jakob knew it was now or never; they were forcing his hand.

"I said it is ready," Jakob told him--this time with mounting hollowness, for it was all lost now. Ontario and Marco--their deaths meant that all the years of torture Jakob had endured were for that much less. One by one, his friends and allies had been slaughtered, many of them right before his eyes. Anna and Trish were all that remained other than the three rebel technicians whose names Jakob could not bring himself to learn, for learning their names implied that he would one day be forced to say goodbye.

"Fuck them, Jakob. Don't say a word. Don't-" Trish was stopped short by the alignment of the pistol with her forehead.

"I said shut him up!" Jacque seethed.

Jakob nodded at Trish, barely able to breathe. "Enough death, Patricia. I'm not losing you too."

Trish shook her head defiantly, evidently disappointed by Jakob's perceived cowardice. She looked as though she was about to speak, but she lowered her cringing eyes and sobbed breathlessly instead.

"You have my attention, Jakob Rohrshan," Jacque hissed.

Jakob turned to the largest of the three rebel technicians and offered a single nod. Jakob knew that he had no choice but to learn his name, for he very well might be sending the man to his death.

"You there. What's your name?" Jakob asked.

"You don't even fucking know your own people's fucking names?" Jacque injected ruefully.

The technician ignored Jacque. "My name is Hann, sir. Hann Schneider." Hann bowed before Jakob as a knight before his liege.

Jakob nodded sullenly in return. "Hann Schneider," he repeated, allowing the name to fill his throat with anguish. "Power it up."

Hann's eyes widened, but he did not hesitate for even a moment. A few swift commands at Hann's personal terminal set the eleven by three-foot column at the center of the room ablaze with life.

Jacque lowered his weapon in disbelief. "You finished it? It's working?"

Jakob nodded an affirmative. Jacque strode forward and wrapped an arm around Jakob's shoulder, his frame only a few inches short of Jakob's six-and-a-half-foot stature.

"There was no need for those theatrics, Jakob. Personally, I would have preferred that their minds remain conscious and employed by this lab, but such was not their fate. You needed a little reminder from your masters that you are no longer masterless, eh Jakob?"

It took all of Jakob's willpower to not crush Jacque's esophagus that very moment.

"Remember," Jacque said, each of his words the lash of a spiked whip. "Their deaths could have been avoided. That's on you, Jakob. Every single death is your doing."

Jacque offered a cheshire grin, then moved to inspect the quantum computer.

Anna clawed through Marco's warm, still-flowing blood and placed his glistening, half exploded head upon her already blood-soaked lap. This would ruin her--Anna would never heal from this wound--Jakob was certain of it. Jakob wanted to strangle Jacque slowly, not for his own enjoyment, but to give Jacque a chance to mull over his sins as his life slowly faded to oblivion. However, Anna and Trish's protection superseded all else. Jakob stayed his urge to end Jacque, all the while preparing to pounce for Jacque's throat the next time he pointed the gun at either of them.

"Now what?" Jacque inquired impatiently.

"And the Lord said..." Jakob intoned. "That's the passphrase. The computer is now open to any and all transmissions spanning the entire universe...theoretically."

Jacque sighed with lethal impatience. "It communicates beyond time and space--I'm fully aware of the machine's functionality. You still have yet to tell me the only fucking thing I care about, Jakob. Does it work?"

Jakob mentally noted the absurdity of Jacque's inquiry with humor and horror in equal measure.

Jakob shrugged. "I don't know. I just built it. It's up to God if he wants to communicate with the New Covenant or not."

"Blasphemy!" came the smug voice belonging to Director Larimer. "You are insinuating that our Lord would be uninterested in speaking to His followers? God does not sit idle when the truly devout call upon Him. God is not like you, Jakob Rohrshan. Look at you, standing there emotionless as your followers are drained of life. Do you feel nothing over their deaths?"

Jakob also wanted to strangle Larimer, only that one would be for his own pleasure. "Unlike the New Covenant and its devotees, I do not take death lightly," Jakob stabbed. "You have committed a mortal sin by standing idly behind your dog whom you command to kill. You will rot in hell, Larimer. You and your dog both."

Jacque winked at Jakob sinisterly. "The culling of abominations is not murder, nor is it any more a sin than the removal of parasites from the body. Tell you what," Jacque offered matter of factly. "I'll give you five minutes to get a transmission--something that might interest us. Otherwise, I pop off girly-boy over here."

Jacque was toying with them, making demands that were entirely out of Jakob's hands.

"We built the machine. You tasked us with building the machine," Jakob rumbled.

"Wrong!" Director Larimer lashed. "We tasked you with communicating with God. Over the last decade you have done everything we've asked. Sure, it took you a little time and torture to accept your position in life, but eventually you learned to obey, like all good dogs." Larimer smiled at Jacque, but Jacque appeared to take the canine reference as a compliment. "We told you to build the interstellar machines, and you built the machines. We told you to invent ion thrusters, a technology that didn't even exist, and you accomplished that too! When the Jihadis started using nuclear power and inflicted our Templar armies with exponentially mounting casualties, we commissioned the invention of a biological stasis and repair chamber. Again, you obeyed."

Director Larimer joined Jacque at the center of the room and ran a finger across the quantum computer's exterior. "Why will you not obey this command, Jakob? We killed two of your top people and still you resist!"

Jakob had never seen the director so shaken. The explosion of Marco and Ontario's craniums must have taken a toll on him. Evidently, he was not used to observing the actual repercussions of his actions.

"Because what you ask is preposterous," Jakob answered gruffly. "The existence of God is not provable by science--certainly not by a computing device."

The director wore an air of surprise. "You've reminded me several times over the years that you are a Christian. I've never heard of a Christian who doesn't believe in God."

"I don't require proof, Director. I have faith in God, and I have faith in Christ."

Undisturbed by Jakob's verbal jab, the director answered, "Yes, but you lack conviction. The truly devout seek God, for God is out there just waiting for His creation to make contact with Him. God awaits the arrival of His creation to His side so that we may praise Him directly!"

Jakob found it difficult to visualize the Director's implications regarding God's tangible existence. If Larimer required proof of God's existence, then it meant he didn't truly believe. And if he didn't truly believe, then he lived in fear under the shadow of doubt.

"I know you're scared, Director, but that doesn't excuse your sins."

Like a reflex to Jakob's insult, Director Larimer spit in rapid succession at Jakob, then at Trish, and then at Ontario's lifeless body.

"You creatures disgust me!" Director Larimer lashed before pointing at Anna. "At least this one is sensible enough to understand that men should be men and women should be women!" In a sudden flurry, Director Larimer waved at Trish dismissively and said, "Just kill it! I can't stand the sight of it anymore."

Jakob stared death into Jacque's soul and pivoted his feet in preparation to launch his entire body. Jacque forced the gun level with Trish's left eye, but Jakob was already on him. Calloused and sharpened by years of war, the blow from Jakob's fist was like the strike of a sledgehammer against fresh clay. His knuckles cracked Jacque's skull with a single strike. The gun roared violently as Jacque's head bounced against the steel-mesh floor, finally coming to a rest at Jakob's feet.

Jakob dove at Jacque's stunned body and gripped tight against his neck. Jacque quickly regained consciousness, though his vision was still spinning out of control from the concussive force of Jakob's hatred finally exploding after a decade of tortuous restraint.

"Fucking do it!" Trish cried desperately from what seemed like miles away. "Kill him!"

Jacque was fading, his body already weak and dazed from Jakob's surprise attack. Jakob savored the feeling of Jacque's death, gripping tighter as Jacque's flailing heart pumped useless, deoxygenated blood through quickly collapsing arteries.

"Jakob Rohrshan! Release him this instant! Do it now!" Larimer shrieked, his voice quavering in terror. "Do it now, or your precious daughter goes to hell earlier than expected."

The guards surrounding Jakob pivoted their guns and shakily aligned them with Anna's head.

Jakob squeezed harder around Jacque's fragile throat and assessed his options with an unparalleled speed of thought. A guard lay dead in a heap of oversized armor at the feet of the other guards who were presently looking all about the room like leashed, terrified rabbits. Jacque's gun must have found a mark after all.

Jakob could kill Jacque and Larimer right here--he was certain of it. He might even be able to incapacitate a sizable number of untrained guards, but to what end? Trish and Anna would likely die in the process, and even if he could somehow save them, an army would be waiting for them right outside the lab's exit. In his attempt to save Trish, Jakob had placed Anna under the threat of a new, incredible danger. Then again, the directors knew that without Anna, Jakob would refuse to labor. They had a trump card over him, and it happened to be the most important being in the world to Jakob. Jakob refused to take any chances with Anna's life.

Jakob eased off Jacque's neck and rose to his feet. The entire room watched sickeningly as Jacque coughed and retched blood, all the while gasping pathetically for air.

"Get up, damnit! Get up!" Larimer barked at Jacque.

Bulging veins and dying capillaries lined Jacque's neck and face as he rose disjointedly. His eyes were bloodshot behind tears of pain. He grunted hard and spit up something thick and dark. Then he pointed the gun directly at Jakob's head and smiled wickedly, teeth crimsoned with his own life.

"You're real fucking lucky your head's so fucking valuable, you know that?" Jacque rasped between hissing breaths. Jacque shrugged. "Ladyboy here--he's not so lucky."

The gun was pointed at Trish's head once more, but this time Anna faced the same threat.

"Your leader doesn't give a shit about you," Jacque jabbed, toying with Trish before he killed her. "You're just a freak. A bright one, and a tough one, but a freak nonetheless."

"An abomination!" Larimer lashed correctively.

"Whatever," Jacque rasped. "Either way, dead is dead."

There was no trepidation in Trish's stance, no fight left inside her. Her knees were already bent at the threshold of death's doorway.

"Wait!" Hann cried from behind his monitor. "Wait, please! I have something. There's a message. Or something...just wait!"

Jakob knew full well that Hann was just stalling the inevitable, but he was grateful to the man all the same. Jakob thanked God that he had learned the name of a man embodying such selfless bravery. Surely Hann knew that his lie would lead to the vicious spray of Jacque's hungry weapon at his skull.

Jakob went along with the lie, hoping to buy some time. Maybe there was a way to fake a message? Clever boy--maybe that was Hann's plan all along--to beckon Jakob to his terminal to give Jakob a few moments to produce a quick fake. If anyone could accomplish the task of faking a message from God, why not Jakob?

"Let's see it," Jakob rumbled casually, turning his back on the others and praying that Jacque would find in the prospect of a message from God enough intrigue to forget about murder for a few minutes.

Jakob sauntered over to Hann's monitor, readying himself to whip up something convincing. Nothing could have prepared him for what he saw.

An actual message--a whole database of information--was being jettisoned to the computer with extraordinary precision from an unknown source at some unknown distance across the galaxy, or maybe even the universe. It did not appear as any language or defined code that Jakob had ever encountered, nor did the shapes and symbols even appear human in origin. The only conclusion Jakob could arrive at was that the message contained a wealth of information on an order far exceeding the petabytes of data that the entire world's libraries, physical and digital, amounted to collectively.

"Is...is this real?" Hann stammered.

Jakob eyed Hann severely with his back to the others so that no one else could see him. "Did you do this?" Jakob mouthed to Hann.

Hann shook his head in astonishment.

"What is it?" Larimer demanded. "Is it a message or not?"

"Show me," Jacque said, wincing and slinking toward the monitor despite his wounds. Upon investigation, Jacque's eyes lit up, and he nodded to his superior. "Unless they're bullshitting us, and they've prepared this all from the get-go--"

"Is all this an illusion of your creation, Jakob?" Larimer asked testily.

Jakob couldn't be sure if the message, whatever it was, was really being sent from somewhere outside Earth or if it was just one of the technicians' doing, but it didn't matter. In this moment, a miracle might mean the difference between life and death for those of his people still clinging to the former.

"It's real," Jakob confirmed with genuine disbelief.

"It's a miracle!" Jacque announced. "God has spoken to us after all!"

Jakob wasn't ready to buy the plot that Jacque was selling, but he wasn't going to admit his doubt either.

Despite his professed conviction regarding God's tangible existence, Director Larimer's face turned sour in disbelief.

152

"What does it say?" Larimer demanded.

"The data is written in a type of foreign language, and it appears to be in a state of such disarray that it is of no immediate practical use," Jakob said, inching himself between Trish, Anna, and Jacque.

"We receive a message from God, and you have the audacity to claim that it has no practical use?" Larimer looked at Jakob as though he had used a page of the New Covenant as toilet paper.

"It will take time to decipher it. It may very well be written in a yet unencountered syntax and metaphoric structure, something utterly alien. Or rather, something divine," Jakob offered carefully.

Larimer sighed with a glint of relief. "Translate it. You have five days."

"Trish!" Anna said finally, breaking abruptly from her paralyzing grief. "She's our head linguist. She's--we'll need her to translate the message. We'll need everyone."

"Head linguist, eh?" Jacque asked Trish in amusement.

"That's right," Trish confirmed with murderous intent. "I can say *fuck you* in more ways than you ever knew existed."

Jacque stared Trish down, threatening her to make a move. After several tense seconds, Jacque burst into boisterous laughter, sending a spray of blood out his mouth. "You're bold, freak. Real fucking bold."

Quicker than he'd ever drawn his pistol before, Jacque swung, pointed, and pulled, rocketing death at Trish.

A circle of red pooled on Trish's inner thigh and began gushing blood to the ground with lethal rapidity. Trish gritted her teeth against the pain, refusing to show fear or weakness. She tried applying pressure using both hands, but blood would not stop gushing in heartbeat-synced bursts.

"Shit," Jacque mused casually. "I must've hit an artery. Only meant to scare him. We wouldn't want to lose our "head linguist," would we?"

"She'll bleed out and die if you don't do something," Jakob urged Director Larimer over Trish's grunts of pain.

Director Larimer pierced Jacque with a scolding look, but Jacque merely shrugged. "Relax, Director. We'll bring down a stasis chamber from the medical bay. Won't do shit for the bullets in the others' heads, but it'll save the freak."

Director Larimer nodded reluctantly. "Fine. Keep it alive until the message is translated, then do as you please. As long as I never lay eyes upon it again. Understood, Jacque?"

Jacque looked as though he had been quenched of a primordial thirst. "My pleasure, Director."

Director Larimer left the room with the rest of his men in tow. When they were finally gone, Jakob ran to Anna, folding her fragile frame in his arms like he had done on so many occasions previous. In a fit, Anna pushed Jakob away and scrambled to hold Marco's lifeless corpse.

"Don't just stand there," Anna seethed at Jakob. "Find out what Marco died for. At the very least do that."

There it was again--Anna would never be the same. The world did not deserve Anna, and now the world had mangled her completely. No, Jakob reminded himself, the mangling was his own fault.

CHAPTER 13

J akob told the shocked remnants of his people to return to the living quarters, encouraging them to grieve. In passing, Hann had assured Jakob that he would look after Anna and the others, and Jakob found no reluctance in trusting the man.

Hann convinced the others to keep to the bunk rooms the entire first three days after the massacre. They spent most of their time asleep, at least, that's what Jakob assumed, for there weren't many other ways to force the painful passage of time a measure forward. Meanwhile, Jakob got to work right away, quarantining his mind to a realm of careful calculation and abstract intuition. Every time he thought of Anna, her seething agony reminded him to remain one-pointed in his focus. There had to be something in the message they could use, something that could provide them hope in some form. Jakob knew it was unreasonable to expect so much from something so arbitrary and seemingly meaningless, but without hope there was only despair.

Alone with the message, Jakob spent fruitless hours chipping away at random sections, forcing the symbology into makeshift patterns. Analyzing the Message from God or the Divine Message or God's Word--it had garnered many names over the course of only a few days--was like rummaging through the ashes of some great galactic library composed of intertwining databases woven through every conceivable culture of every conceivable form of life. Jakob found, however, that among the ashes were sprinkled purposely partitioned and protected areas of peculiarly decipherable lexicology.

Jakob utilized a multitude of data-codices and pattern-scans without success, until finally, on a whim, he applied a simple language filter to the endless data. To his surprise, the filter yielded the alarming and unexpected result of two names written in plain English: *Amero Hiddiger and Jakob Rohrshan.*

Confronted by his own name, Jakob felt as though he had turned the wrong corner and come face-to-face with a temporarily docile but obviously rabid bear. Though the first name meant nothing to him, the inclusion of his own name incited volumes of potentialities with regards to intent and meaning. Uncertain which course of action to take, Jakob knew only that the names must be hidden from his followers, at least in the short term, for the possibility that the message was planted by the New Covenant as a trap was the most likely scenario. Hiding the names was necessary, Jakob reasoned, at least until he understood with some level of nuance the true implications of what he had discovered.

Though Jakob yearned to undo their deaths, even in place of his own, Marco and Ontario's murders would not be in vain--Jakob vowed as much. Assuming their deaths to have been planned by Larimer himself, Jakob recognized the display of barbarism, along with the "miracle" appearance of the message, as a show of desperation. Could it be that Jakob still had active followers? Maybe the Free Zones persisted and had never been completely purged? Considering the contents of the message, Jakob theorized that through Larimer, the New Covenant Popes might be attempting to simultaneously preserve Jakob's usefulness and destroy his remaining armies by dismantling the rebellion's love of him. Surely the inclusion of Jakob's name in a "Message from God" would make the majority of the rebels think twice about their leader.

Either the New Covenant had orchestrated the whole thing, or the Earth really was in the beginning phases of contact with another form of life in possession of a similar quantum computing device. Jakob rejected the latter possibility, harkening the simple but dependable reasoning of Occam's razor.

Jakob did not wish his followers to be infected with paranoia and distrust toward their leader, which was a very likely scenario given both the context and content of the information. While it was pleasant to think that they were all immune to such base propaganda, Jakob had seen beings of titanous willpower cave to the New Covenant's custom torture chambers--neural interfaces capable of projecting one's most carefully guarded demons onto the real world as ultra-real hallucinations. A single moment immersed in one's own self-prepared hell has the potential to completely restructure the neuronal network of any brain, no matter the mental fortitude or emotional discipline.

In place of traditional torture methods, the directors had used custom-torture only once on Jakob, because to their chagrin, Jakob's hallucinations had taken the form of vague shapes and blurred outlines mirroring Jakob's present surroundings. *Fools,* Jakob had said to them. *I'm already in hell.*

Presently, on the third night since the message's arrival, while the others inevitably replayed the deaths of their friends in their dreams, Jakob returned to the lab under the cover of disabled surveillance in order to revisit the sections of the message he had personally encrypted. Jakob inwardly revisited the alien symbology, scanning the strange data in his mind's eye as he walked hastily down the unlit corridors leading directly from the bunk room back to the prison-lab. The message plagued Jakob's very foundations of reality; for the first time, pitted against a future composed of far too many known and unknown variables, he felt utterly unsure which direction to orient his intentions. He felt guilty for hiding the information from the others, but why else was Jakob personally included in the message if it wasn't the New Covenant's plan to turn his followers against him?

Jakob reiterated to himself that it was safe to assume the names in the message were some kind of trap from the lab directors; however, that didn't explain the other section of information Jakob was able to uncover without the others knowing. While the encryption of two tiny names amidst the innumerable data was easy to cover up, the other decipherable section was another matter entirely; it contained trillions of bits of alien symbology, but imbedded between the alien symbols, Jakob discovered an emergent pattern of complex mathematical formulas written in Earth-based mathematical code. In an attempt to mask the section's significance, Jakob hastily encrypted short, seemingly important sections of the code.

Regardless if it was a ploy, Larimer had given them five days to decipher the entire message; tonight was one of the few remaining chances Jakob had to analyze the mathematics before Jacque returned for further death

Jakob entered the lab and nearly jumped at the sight of Anna sitting alone in the dark. She was perched in her usual seat with her shoulders wrapped about her knees as if to shield herself from sensation while she stared numbly at Marco's terminal.

"Anna... " Jakob began, uncertain whether he should attempt to console or confront her. According to Hann's few reports to Jakob, Anna had kept her distance from the others over the last few days, favoring isolation even during eating hours. Her mind plotted vengeance at every moment, even in her nightmarish dreams. Jakob was sure of it--he had seen the same mark of vengeance afflict a thousand and more soldiers before her. Revenge can be overcome, but it is rarely if ever accomplished by the young. And by the time one learns to give up revenge, they are usually either already lost or already dead.

"What are you hiding?" Anna asked accusingly. Her eyes were permanently bloodshot. It was as if she refused to blink in case she miss one last glimpse of her stolen love.

"Anna...I... " Jakob gulped down his defeat. "I suppose now is as good a time as any," Jakob admitted, shaken by the first sight of his daughter in days.

"You *have* been hiding something?" Anna accused.

"For good reason, of course, Anna. I swear it."

"Don't *of course* me!" Anna seethed through heart-wrenching whispers. "Just tell me what you've been hiding. I'll be the judge of your reasoning."

"I hid it to protect you and the others, Anna."

"Then you failed!" Anna lashed like a wounded lioness. "You absolutely failed, Father!" Anna cascaded forward into an ocean of sobbing grief. "I'm sorry," she squeaked. "I'm sorry for--"

Jakob swooped to envelope Anna in his arms, but she pushed him away sorrowfully. Jakob understood in that moment that his ability to easily comfort Anna was long over. She had never been a child content with being cloaked by the illusion of security. More than ever before, Anna was painfully lucid of reality, naked and powerless at the whim of existence and fully aware that all assurance and planning is but a daydream soon to be stolen by the indifferent, shifting present.

"Stand up," Jakob offered to his daughter. "It was stupid of me to hide the information from you in the first place. Let me show you what I found."

Anna's silent sobbing came to an abrupt halt, and she lifted her head to meet her father's profoundly sorry eyes.

"And the Lord said," Jakob intoned slowly.

The quantum computing column lit up, buzzing with activity. A projection of some random subsection of the Divine Message appeared on a far wall. Jakob replaced the random subsection with the names he had found, then he removed the encryption shielding each one.

Anna looked more confused than angry. "Your name is in the message? And the Undead Astronaut's too? What's the connection?"

"Undead Astronaut?" Jakob inquired uneasily.

"That's the first name--Amero Hiddiger. He's a space pilot, one of the most famous in the world. And he's gay too," Anna explained, her eyes glued to the projection with sullen reluctance to accept what she saw.

"Why haven't I ever heard of him?" Jakob asked.

"Can you name a single celebrity?" Anna said, providing Jakob with his answer.

"Fair enough," Jakob offered. "But why him?"

"Why you?" Anna countered.

"I don't know, and that's why I hid it. These names might have been planted by Larimer to tear us apart. That's what I'm thinking anyway."

"Why now?" Anna insisted with a wave toward Marco's terminal.

It pained Jakob that Anna could not even consider the most obvious scenario a possibility. "Maybe our people still persist in the Free Zones. Maybe all hope is not lost, Anna."

Anna darted her eyes to Marco's terminal, then back to Jakob. "There is no hope, Father. We've been living and dying in these labs for ten years, all the while feeding our enemy like a king at his own celebratory feast." Anna placed a hand on her lower belly and cringed away a flood of tears. "There is no hope."

"There is always hope!" Jakob urged, but it was like trying to breathe life into an emberless fire. Jakob resigned himself to simply accept Anna's emotions. "There's more."

"More that you've hidden?" Anna checked.

"The encrypted sections of the mathematics you uncovered," Jakob explained.

"I see," Anna said with final understanding. "The encryptions are more of your work."

Jakob nodded an affirmative. "It's all yours now, though, Anna. I'm sorry for hiding information from you."

Anna's features went taut, and she raised a hand to quiet Jakob. "Just show me," she said, demanding he skip the apologetic platitudes and get right to business.

Without another moment's hesitation, Jakob retrieved the encrypted mathematics and added them piecewise to complete the original mathematical enigma.

Anna puzzled at what she saw. "What does it mean?"

"I don't know for sure," Jakob admitted. "It involves a great deal of theoretical physics currently no more than radical implications of our current models. I can only make wild guesses."

"Go on," Anna said, as if she imagined any of it could change Marco's fate.

"It has something to do with space and time: an idea or a warning or possibly even a tool. The formulas make no sense on their own, but taken as a whole, they converge at one another's initial values while simultaneously diverging in new directions. These new directions in turn converge at values implicit in the inputs of the original functions, and this behavior occurs ad infinitum across the entire mathematical mosaic. Most impressively, these results are achieved regardless of which direction the math is read. Taken as a whole, it is like the polished composition of a perfect, recursive geometric and algebraic truth."

Anna followed along patiently with Jakob's explanation only to jump at his final conclusion.

"What truth?" she demanded.

"I honestly don't know, Anna. That's what I came here to figure out tonight."

Anna hesitated, looking as though she wasn't sure whether to run or explode at Jakob with a barrage of fists. She closed her eyes and held them tightly shut against the urge to turn tail and run back to the vulnerable, knee-clutching position Jakob had found her in.

"We'll figure it out together," she said, approaching the quantum computer's secondary terminal.

"Like we always have," Jakob lamented.

Jakob spent more time stealing glances at Anna than he did considering the mathematical array. In contrast, Anna worked diligently, spreading herself between her own terminal, the quantum computer, and Marco's terminal. All the while, Jakob held in his head the implications of the mathematics, waiting for Anna to arrive at the discovery for herself. It only took her two hours, most of which was spent reorienting herself to the addition of the pieces Jakob initially hid. Such intellectual cunning implied that she would one day grow to rival Jakob in his ability to theorize and probe the unknown.

"It's a description for a vehicle, I think," Anna said finally with lingering doubt. "It could be a weapon, but that's not the implication at all when the formula is considered all at once. It is more conducive to creation than to destruction." Anna raised her eyes to meet Jakob's gaze, checking her work.

"You aren't wrong," he told her. "I can't help seeing the same conclusion in the math, but as I'm sure you recognize, there are areas of the overarching formula that don't fit with that hypothesis, nor any hypothesis I have yet produced over the last three nights."

"Yeah, I see that too," Anna confirmed, tossing those areas out of her mind with an expunging wave. "But taken as a whole, it's definitely a form of transportation. So, we have a message of mostly garbled nonsense packaged around two names and coherent mathematics outlining the schematics for an alien mode of transportation. This message was intended for Earth, Father, that much is clear."

Jakob rumbled a low groan. "And it isn't the New Covenant's doing. Not completely, at least. They could have snuck in the names, but not even I can swallow this math in its entirety. We are observing human mathematics perfected to such a degree that it makes Newton look like a squawking ape. There's no way one of the New Covenant's scientists wrote something so exquisitely significant and...harmoniously sound."

Jakob's own words ushered to his conscious mind the immense profundity of what lay before them: a message from outside Earth, intended for Earth, containing a potential power beyond anything the Earth had ever imagined. And the New Covenant had its hands on the global wheel.

Jakob shook his head with decisive trepidation. "Anna...this information--"

"Is a literal gift from God," Anna gasped. "We can re-encrypt the decipherable data and hide it right under their noses. We'll sell them some made up story of what it all adds up to, then use the message to destroy everything and everyone who has ever done us wrong!"

"Anna... " Jakob winced, but he knew that she could already taste the false sweetness of vengeance filling her throat, ushering comfort like water from an oasis in the vast and expanding desert of her mind.

"We must destroy them!" Anna lashed with a sudden, electrified fury. "We owe Marco and Ontario and all the others that much at least, Father!"

"No one should have this information, Anna. Not even us," Jakob warned.

"If we do not seize it, then they will!" Anna shouted, forgetting all about stealth and consequence. She strode toward Jakob with a malice that had never before existed in her features. "They took him from me, the only other man besides you that I have ever truly loved, and the only man I have ever truly loved intimately. They took him like it meant nothing at all."

Jakob made to speak, but Anna was only beginning. "His death is not going to be in vain! I refuse. Marco was a good man. He was like you, Father. Can you believe that?"

Her eyes bled with permanently soured tears. "They ended his life as if it was never his own to begin with."

Jakob shuttered. He wanted to fulfill Anna's thirst for revenge and closure, but he knew that quenching such thirst was only the beginning of a new insatiable hunger.

"Anna..we can't let them have--"

"I'm pregnant," Anna gasped.

Jakob stumbled backward, catching himself on the closest terminal. He had expected this day for many weeks, but he was still shaken to the core hearing Anna confirm it out loud. He wished to God that her words could bring about joy, but all they filled him with was fear.

"It's his," she finished, more to herself than to her father.

Anna's suffering prompted inside Jakob the realization and acceptance of what he must do. He knew the message should be destroyed, but the message was a mere side effect of the root illness: Jakob himself. He was the New Covenant's worst enemy, but those days were concreted history. The New Covenant had systematically remolded Jakob into a tool sharpened and maintained by its own natural acuity. As long as they had Jakob, the New Covenant had power limited only by the bounds of his own imagination and intellect.

And it would never end. The New Covenant's shackles would take on new shape and new modes of torture. Jakob was certain they would even go so far as to use Anna's baby as leverage over his will. As long as Jakob lived, the others would be used as fodder to direct his efforts.

Jakob was the key to all of it, and the only way to destroy the key was to destroy himself. He lifted the thickest of the screwdrivers nestled in the foot-cabinet of his terminal.

"You will make an exceptional mother," Jakob rumbled, and he positioned the head of the screwdriver level with his temple.

Anna ran forward, pleading with Jakob to stop. All Jakob saw was a smiling infant whose bright eyes had been permanently dulled by the ruthless ignorance of the world that never once deserved her.

Now they've no choice but to keep you alive, Jakob said inwardly.

Finally, Anna would be safe, for without Jakob, she was the greatest mind in the New Covenant's possession.

There was but a moment of pain as the driver slid easily into

POINTS OF ORIGIN

Jakob's skull.

CHAPTER 14

O ne moment Jakob was exhaling his final breath, death lording over him like fog upon thick grass, and the next moment he was sucking desperately at life, his lungs screeching for air like an infant saved from an inferno.

For several moments the instinctual need to breathe was all that occupied Jakob's mind. A minute passed, and Jakob's senses finally caught up with the rest of him. He was encased within a coffin-like chamber with no more than five inches separating the tip of his nose and the chamber wall. Jakob attempted to move but was immediately disoriented by the realization that he was floating at the surface of a liquid which he could not directly feel. Only the sloshing movement of the liquid against the chamber walls made its presence apparent. Jakob reasoned that his inability to feel the liquid directly against his skin meant that it had been heated to his skin's specific temperature.

A stasis chamber, Jakob told himself. *I'm alive.*

Just as suddenly as Jakob had come to life, the stasis chamber unlocked, injecting the chamber with outside air that struck Jakob like arctic winds gusting through tropical rainforest. He gritted his teeth against the frigid cold, reminding himself that the air was likely many degrees warmer than it actually felt relative to the humid warmth of the stasis chamber.

The stasis hatch slid completely open. Adjusting to the outside light, Jakob's still-hazy vision revealed three vague figures standing and observing him.

"You alive in there, old man?" a familiar voice asked with tangible doubt.

"Is he..." a voice like forged iron asked without finishing.

"No, he isn't dead," a third voice confirmed. "But he came

damn close. If he hadn't undergone stasis so soon after the incident, or if we had busted him out even a few days after today... well... there's a good chance this chamber would smell a lot worse."

The fatigue and mental disorientation of stasis sleep stung less than Jakob imagined it would, and he found that he could lucidly remember every moment leading up to his courting of death. Most of all, Jakob remembered Anna's anguish, her pleading eyes and outstretched fingers reaching hopelessly for Jakob's crumbling, impaled body.

"Look! His eyes--they're starting to focus. He's coming to."

The third figure positioned herself between the first two just as Jakob's vision finally acquiesced into clarity. A warped vision of the past--a specter of his memory--stood before Jakob. Blonde hair hung in tattered frays over networks of scars and fresh, glistening lesions. A stare full of hatred and fortitude pried itself beneath the calloused carapace of Jakob's very soul, burrowing and seething all the way down.

"Anna," Jakob gasped. "What...what did they do to you?"

Her name felt like dry ice tucked inside his lips.

"Torture," Anna told him simply in the same fashion that one might list an article of food from a grocery list.

"And your child?" Jakob urged, feeling stupid for entertaining hope that the New Covenant might practice restraint in some instances.

Anna shook her head and repeated the word, this time with deep-pitted, molten anger that was kept precariously in check from each pandemoniously hate-filled moment to the next. "Torture."

"Jakob... " came the bold yet disbelieving voice of the figure on the left. Jakob realized it was Trish, eyes swollen to slits and filled with tears. "Good to fucking see you again, Sir."

Jakob knew that the right thing to do was acknowledge Trish, but he could not assuage his vision from Anna's calloused, stolid form now cast from roughly hewn stone. He would not press the issue, but Jakob reasoned that either Anna's child was dead or so badly tortured that it made no difference. No good would come from delving any deeper into Anna's present misery.

"I'm sorry, Anna," Jakob wheezed, resigning himself to as few

166

words as possible.

Anna cringed and smiled wickedly at Jakob. "You left," she seethed. "Fuck do you care?"

With a sudden, revolting rush, Jakob saw how Anna's life had unfurled in his absence. Each scar and rend was a memory of Jakob's leaving, and each moment without her child was a reminder that it was all his fault. Though Jakob had intended to save Anna from further pain, he had achieved precisely the opposite.

"Anna-" Jakob croaked.

"Save it," Anna injected. "We don't have time to play father and daughter."

Anna turned away, face scrunched in pain as she hobbled out of view.

"She's right," Trish said. "We don't have much time at all."

Trish and another man hauled Jakob's naked body out of the thick stasis liquid that clung to his skin in long, sticky strings. Too weak to lift his own spine, Jakob propped himself against Trish's knee and surveyed the room, catching his breath from what felt like a return from oblivion.

The familiar installations of the old laboratory were still in place: computer terminals, station chairs, and the quantum computing column at the center of it all. However, all was in disarray and disrepair. The bright fluorescent lights had been replaced by unnaturally yellow-hued, makeshift filaments. Dull metal shavings and particulate rust littered the ground and air. Upon closer inspection, most of the computer terminals were no more than ramparts of frayed cable and bent metal shelling. The sterile lab had been transformed into a warzone--even the quantum computer looked disabled, though not wrecked.

"The computer--the message--we must destroy it!" Jakob urged. "We can't even leave it standing there!"

Trish wasn't sure where to begin, but finally she settled on: "We're way the fuck beyond that point now, Sir."

The ominous way in which Trish emphasized her words made Jakob ill at ease, and the way she looked at Anna as she spoke seared his insides.

Anna occupied herself with something unseen while an un-known technician urgently explained something of apparently great importance to her. Anna allowed the man to speak, all the while working on something with her hands. All of a sudden, Anna held up a finger to quiet the man, then placed a polished pistol on the table beside him. No more words were exchanged, but without a moment's hesitation, the man saluted Anna, took the gun, then ex-ited the laboratory toward the bunk rooms.

"What did they do to her, Trish?" Jakob groaned beneath la-bored breathing.

Trish shook her head back and forth in an apparent defeat that she had accepted long ago. "It doesn't matter anymore, Sir. Not after today."

Jakob was ready to press her for more information when sud-denly a sheet of ice jacketed the whole of his back.

"Yeesh!" Jakob breathed. "What is it?"

"Isopropyl alcohol," Anna answered grimly from behind. "We're prepping you for surgery."

Anna went on wiping the rest of Jakob's upper body and head with a tattered rag soaked in the icy solution.

"For what?" Jakob asked.

Anna's stoic silence was intensified by the entrance of a large man dressed in standard enforcer garb.

"Hann!" Jakob gasped in disbelief.

"Easy," Trish warned with a hand on Jakob's shoulder. "He plays the part well, but he's still one of us."

Hann's eyes locked onto Jakob, his face exploding with awe. "It worked! You're alive!"

"We'll pop open the champagne later tonight," Anna hissed scoldingly. "Stop wasting time."

Hann obeyed by stripping off the uniform, but his look of ec-static awe could not be erased.

"It's all going exactly as she planned," Hann told Jakob with a reassuring grin.

Before Jakob could probe Hann for some legitimately useful in-formation, he was lifted fully out of the stasis chamber and onto a

168

surgical bed. Hann laid on an identical bed beside Jakob.

Finished with Jakob, the team hastily wiped Hann's body with more isopropyl soaked rags. Hann reached out and grabbed Jakob's hand. When their eyes finally met, Hann smiled wide.

"Your daughter...she kept us all going. She saved our lives more times than I can count."

Jakob gulped down the time he lost--all the shadows of memories he could never have.

"She planned this whole thing, Jakob. For three years she's been crafting her master plan."

"Three years?" Jakob checked, certain he must have misheard.

Hann appeared startled. "They didn't tell you?"

Shivers ran the length of Jakob's spine. He had lost three years to the stasis chamber--time he should have spent dead. Jakob imagined the directors lording his half-dead corpse over the others like a piked head--proof of ownership over their leader and by extension all Jakob's followers. How the hell did he screw up killing himself? A screwdriver to the temple--only advanced stasis technology could bring somebody back from a wound so fatal.

How cruel and poetic, Jakob thought, *that it was my own creation that refused me my own chosen end.*

Anna stood before Jakob as a chitinous husk of her former self.

"I'm sorry, my Anna. I am," Jakob winced.

"I know," Anna nearly growled. "We're all sorry. Sorry for our children. Sorry for the world. Sorry for ourselves. Sorry for fuck all." Anna stared fiercely into her father's swollen eyes. Her glare was a stockade of self-scaled fortitude and determined hatred. "But you're going to change that, as only you can."

Anna nodded at Trish once, and in turn, Trish poked Jakob's inner thigh with a syringe, injecting him with a viscous, yellow liquid.

Jakob's vision went hazy, and he felt as though he was sinking backward into the thick, dreamless pit of the stasis chamber.

"Are you ready, Hann?" someone asked from far away.

"It is my honor," Hann answered, and Jakob felt Hann's warm grip tighten around his own.

CHAPTER 15

J akob woke with a start, ripping several IV's out of his veins as he jumped off the operating bed. He clutched instinctively at his thigh and inside elbow to mitigate some of the bleeding.

"Whoa there! The treatment isn't finished yet."

Trish hobbled over to Jakob with the help of a steel pipe fashioned into a cane. She stopped a few feet short to aggressively scrutinize Jakob's body.

"On second thought, you look pretty fucking convincing."

"What's going on, Trish?" Jakob demanded, kicking away the compounded disorientation from having experienced the cold, sudden waking to reality twice in less than an hour. "Has it really been three years?"

Trish looked as though the cane had been plunged into her gut. She winced, remembering something particularly painful, then nodded at Jakob.

"A long three years, Jakob. Longer than eternity. Longer than... than--" Trish was at the precipice of an anxiety attack, but she caught herself and forced her breathing to a state of calm. "We only have a few minutes, Sir, but I'll fill you in as best I can."

Jakob bowed in gratitude. Trish responded by lifting her shirt to reveal breasts mangled into tatters and strips that hung from her torso like old, flopping udders.

"They botched my boob job," Trish chuckled in an attempt to fight back the rage visibly swelling in every pore of her flesh. Jakob's fists clenched on their own; how could Trish possibly still have humor? To laugh as the lion strips you of your flesh; was Trish always so strong? Jakob saw her with a strengthened vigor, one which casted her as Atlas, and society's incessant and ignorant demand for a bi-gendered system as the planetary weight atop her buckling, aching, yet never-yielding shoulders.

Jakob breathed after many moments of unintentionally holding it in. "Your true beauty has not even been dented, Trish. You are but a goddess among the blind."

Trish shot back with a snort of laughter. "You know? The difference between you and the rest of the fucking world, Jakob, is that you actually want humanity to succeed at being human, to each other first and foremost. But what's more, you mean it on the cosmic scale too. You really do want humanity to leave its mark on the universe, whatever that means. Even if the mark is not left by you personally. Other people--they either don't fucking care, or they want all the glory for themselves. They want glory more than they want success, even if they're all that's left in the end."

Trish appeared finished, but Jakob still wondered what she was getting at.

Jakob said, "Thank you, I think."

Trish giggled. "I'm not fucking telling you all that just to stroke your tiny fucking ego, Jakob. I'm trying to say that you can do it. You can leave that cosmic mark, and you can change it. If you won't do it for yourself, then do it for us. Do it for Anna."

"Change what, Trish?" Jakob urged.

"Everything," Trish gasped as if the word held divine power. Trish retrieved a small hand mirror from the bedside table and handed it to Jakob.

Jakob stared into his reflection, but he did not stare back. The only point of familiarity was his own eyes; the rest of his face and body had been changed. He felt like screaming, but he was silenced by the most haunting part of all: the face was not unfamiliar. In fact, it was all too familiar.

"I look just like Hann!" Jakob said.

"You do have his face, after all," Trish offered, attempting to lighten Jakob's shock. "And he has yours."

Jakob groped at the thick scar tissue lining the entire circumference of his jaw. The still-raw flesh converged into grotesque valleys of freshly operated skin haphazardly wrapped around his thickened neck.

"The scars are still being buffed out at the nano-level. Another couple weeks and the swap will seem perfectly natural, as will the growth of your skeletal and musculature structure. The bulk of the growth took place on the operating table while you were out. I imagine your dreams must have been centered around expansion, huh?"

"I didn't dream," Jakob rumbled.

"Sure you did; you just don't remember it," Trish said jovially while patting Jakob's enlarged bicep. "Hann's a large man, even larger than you, Sir. We had to do something about the size discrepancy."

Jakob hoped there was more to Anna's plan than a mere surgical procedure "Now what, Trish? Anna's plan surely doesn't end with plastic surgery."

Trish flashed an amused smile. "The body swap is certainly part of it, but there's more to it than that, of course. From the moment Larimer threw your body in stasis after your...attempted suicide... Anna's been hard at fucking work. The rest of us just help as much as we can. She's just like you, Jakob: intelligent beyond reason and headstrong to the very end."

"Where is she?"

"Fulfilling her role in the plan, just as you must do. We need you now more than ever."

Jakob refused to accept it. "No you don't, Trish. None of you ever needed me. I've been nothing but a rope strangling each of you to death day after day. I meant to die for all of you, Trish. I shouldn't be here. I shouldn't be alive."

"You're wrong, Jakob. You're the key to making everything right. I know it, and so does your daughter. Even though she claims to hate you, she loves you, Jakob, and she understands that you have the power to change it all."

Jakob felt lost. What did they expect of him? Hadn't he proven time and time again that he was powerless against the titanous might of the New Covenant?

"Trish," Jakob gasped. "Kill me now before it's too late. Kill me before they can put me back in that godforsaken metal cage and breathe artificial life into me again."

173

Trish prepared to argue, but Jakob quieted her with a single wave. "Whatever Anna has planned won't be enough. As long as I'm alive, the New Covenant can use me however they please. If I'm dead, though, they lose their greatest weapon. You want to destroy the New Covenant? Killing me is the greatest blow you can ever hope to land on them, Trish."

"You're no good to anyone dead, Sir, especially the New-fucking-Covenant. That's true. And you're right that you're the New Covenant's favorite fucking weapon, but we need you, Sir, and that's exactly why Anna's plan has to work."

Jakob granted Trish time to explain.

Trish cleared her throat and inhaled heavily. "You're leaving, Sir. On a one-way launch across the fucking galaxy."

Jakob had no reason to doubt her, but he was reluctant to accept the information outright.

"How long and how far?" Jakob checked.

"Do you remember what you and Anna discovered in the message the night of your suicide?" Trish asked.

Jakob remembered the discovery as vividly as he remembered Anna's first words.

"We found... " Jakob hesitated, unsure how much Anna had divulged to the others.

"Two names," Trish said. "Your name and another name, as well as mathematical schematics for the concept and production of a vehicle capable of traversing both time and space," Trish finished.

"She told you everything, then?" Jakob asked, curious how Trish must feel about the inclusion of her leader's name in a message from an unknown source.

"None of us blame you for hiding what you found, Sir, especially at the time. We understand that you were only trying to defuse a confusing and dangerous situation. We trust you utterly, Jakob, if that isn't obvious yet."

Wirhoo! Wirhoo! Wirhoo!

Wailing alarms gave way to flashing, crimson emergency lights positioned every twenty feet along each wall. In response to the alarm, Trish issued a heavy sigh.

174

"Time's up. Time for you to go."

Trish's mind was made up, and trying to dissuade her from Anna's plan was an attempt at undoing years of labor and suffering.

"Trish," Jakob said, gripping her forearm.

Trish smiled serenely at him. "Come," she said simply, helping Jakob to his feet. Trish slammed a hard fist against the door leading to the bunk rooms, forcing it to rise slowly open.

"Follow the corridor all the way through to the bunk room. We carved out a passage that leads right near Seraphim. We've kept the passage hidden all this time. She's waiting for you there--Anna's waiting for you."

The laboratory entrance door opposite Jakob and Trish began to rise, revealing several pairs of black enforcer boots ready to stomp out lives.

"They're here," Trish seethed. "I'll buy you as much time as I can, but you have to hurry."

Jakob gripped Trish's hand, begging her to know how much her existence meant to him--her ceaseless, indomitable will to accept herself and refuse all forms of oppression.

Trish smiled at her leader and the only man she ever thought of as a father. "You gave me a home when no one else would. You showed me kindness when no one else dared," Trish said, and she reluctantly loosened her hand from Jakob's grasp. "Go now. Give the New-fucking-Covenant a taste of the hell they've been serving us all these fucking years."

Tears streamed down Trish's cheeks, and Jakob understood in that moment that he would never see her again.

"I am proud to have worked with you, Trish, and I am proud to have accepted you into my home. I hope...I hope you can forgive me. I hope you can all forgive me. All this--it's all my fault. I should have done something decades earlier. I should have--"

"You did good, Jakob. Better than anyone else would have done. But none of that matters now. You finally have a chance to make it all okay. So go now. Go and change the world," Trish proclaimed.

Trish gave Jakob no time to respond. Instead, she limped to the entrance and stood face to face with certain death. The door rose like a metal curtain, heralding Jacque's entrance.

Jakob willed his body in the opposite direction, entering the bunk room corridor. He wasn't surprised to find the doorway lined with homemade explosives of varying volatility and complexity.

The entrance door opened fully. Turning one last time, Jakob met eyes with Jacque. The head enforcer smiled and leveled his gun with Trish's head. Trish screamed violently and swung at Jacque and his men using her steel cane.

Jakob sprinted and was already at the bunk room when he heard the unmistakable thud of a single bullet ejected from its chamber. The explosives around the doorway detonated immediately afterward. Gritting his teeth was all Jakob could do to muster enough strength to run away from a surely injured or dead Trish. He was leaving her to her death, but that was clearly what she wanted. To turn back would be against her wishes, and for Jakob to go back on his word would be as careless as killing her himself.

Still, Trish was gone forever, and it was, once again, entirely Jakob's fault. They just wouldn't let go. His followers clung to him to the very end. Trish had survived three years in Jakob's absence, and within less than twenty-four hours of his return, she had been extinguished.

Jakob had been through such lines of reasoning many times over, and the obvious conclusion was his own death. But even that didn't work. Maybe being launched across the galaxy, no matter how preposterous, was the only way he would ever clear the fog of death lurking in his wake like a shadow from birth.

With forced resolve, Jakob pressed onward and finally located the carved section of wall in the bunk room. The back of a random closet had been cut away and outfitted as a secret entrance to a passage leading into the wall. Jakob chuckled at the simplicity of the passage. Hidden in a closet--the laboratory staff must have unknowingly glanced right over it two hundred times after so many years of peeking inside during the spontaneous room-checks.

Jakob crouched inside the closet and peeked beyond the wall. The dim, dust-covered, rocky insides of the subterranean laboratory unfurled upward into perfect darkness. The passage's tubular shape felt impressively smoothed out, making Jakob feel as if he was inspecting the intestines of some great stone giant.

Sucking in his gut and holding his breath to fit, Jakob eventually crammed the whole of himself inside the passage. Outcroppings in the rock wall formed an uneven ladder, and Jakob would have found it easy to climb the tunnel were it not for the lingering fatigue of stasis. Doing his best to ignore his searing muscles, Jakob focused on the overwhelming pride he felt over his people creating such a magnificent passageway and keeping it hidden for so long. Not even Larimer would ever expect something so brazen.

The passage eventually leveled out and expanded in girth enough for Jakob to stand. From somewhere behind, Jakob heard mingles of shouts and boots slamming tile, indicating that Jacque and his retinue were already close behind.

Pitch darkness extended many feet forward, but Jakob was sure he could see light terminating at the end of the tunnel. Jakob followed the light, scraping his tired body across rock, until finally he reached a steel doorway. In front of the door stood Anna. She wore a stony glare and held a kerosene lantern in one hand and a bulky enforcer uniform in the other.

Anna's silence forced Jakob to lower his head. Anna rebuked him with a harsh chuckle.

"Quit your sulking. We're not in the clear yet," Anna barked, her words like hot sand against sunburnt skin.

Jakob wanted her to know he was proud of her, and that it was only right that she hate him.

"Trish told me...you planned all this," Jakob said, attempting conversation.

"Is she dead?" Anna shot back.

Anna's indifference concerning Trish's death perturbed Jakob. She was speaking so carefree, as if it was just any old occurrence. Jakob reluctantly nodded an affirmative.

"She was your friend, Anna, your best friend," Jakob lamented, attempting to pierce the adamantine shell that Anna had apparently built around her emotions.

"She was a soldier and a damn good human being," Anna corrected. "You may have given up, Father, but the war never ended. Our masters remain the New Covenant. They keep us like pets to use and enjoy as they will. You understand that, right? Or are you still deluding yourself with plans to remain in the labs forever?"

Jakob nodded solemnly. "I understand that your loved ones have been stripped from you. I understand that you're angry."

"You don't get shit, Father," Anna lashed. "I'd rather be dead than live another day in these labs. Same goes for Trish and everyone else. You're the only one content with living like a rat beneath a ready boot. If we can't beat them, then we're better off dead."

"But we *can* beat them!" Jakob urged, knowing his words to be absolutely false.

"Yeah," Anna chuckled, "as a matter of fact you're right. You might be attempting to comfort me, but you're right: we *can* beat them!"

Jakob eyed Anna curiously. Did she really believe it, or was this all part of her plan to get Jakob onto the ship?

"Anna...listen to what you're saying. You're right--my words were an attempt at comfort, but obviously the time for comfort is over: there is no winning, Anna. Living as rats is the best we can hope for. I'd rather you live than die, even if it means living beneath their boots. Alive we have something. We have each other. We have... life. In death...there is only death. Death is the end of each of us as we are now, as birth was the beginning of each of us. Death will come regardless--so let us live as long as we might!"

"No!" Anna barked. "That's not life, old man. That's hell! We can beat them, Father. We can erase them from history entirely. *You* can do it."

"From across the galaxy?"

Anna waved a hand back and forth, implying that Jakob should discard whatever understanding he might currently hold regarding the ship and her plan.

"Seraphim and the Pull-device, the machines that the others and I built using the schematics from the Message, make time and space an obsolete principle," Anna said with finality.

"And?" Jakob said, wondering where all this led.

"A perch beyond space and time--that is what I am offering you. You'll figure out the rest, Father, I know you will."

Jakob flushed in disbelief. "That's your plan? Launch me far away and hope I can come up with something to save you?"

"You still don't get it," Anna seethed. "We're all out of chances. We've had this portion of the lab locked down for over a year. Hann did...horrendous things in order to gain their trust. Trish and I and all the rest of us...we...we made sure to survive and keep your chamber powered. Everything we did was for this very moment because this is our last shot. There's no going back, and though none of us are entirely satisfied with the plan--" Anna stopped herself short, fighting back tears and balling her fists into quivering weapons of rage. "This is it, Father. There's no going back."

A tidal wave of regret swept over Jakob, and he wanted nothing more than to fall to his knees and beg for Anna's forgiveness. He wanted also to beg himself to do as Anna willed, and he wanted to beg God to give Anna the joy of peace and freedom, even if it required the exchange of Jakob's very soul. Seeing Anna consumed by such wicked hatred--it was the worst fate Jakob could wish for her, even worse than death, as Anna had painfully noted earlier.

All those decades earlier, Jakob had not saved Anna when he scooped her crying, flailing body from a battlefield of blood. In fact, he had not saved a single person in his entire life. All he had accomplished was the prolonged, brutal suffering of his loved ones.

Jakob reached for Anna's hand, craving to feel her touch. Anna parried by pushing the enforcer uniform into Jakob's grasp.

"Put it on," she ordered. "When we get the signal, you make your way to Seraphim and don't look back."

"What if the plan fails?" Jakob suggested, refusing to accept the uniform.

Anna shrugged. "Then we all die, but at least it's better than the alternative."

"The alternative to death is life, Anna."

"Not when one's life is that of a shackled corpse."

Jakob wanted to break down and sob. "You don't deserve any of this, Anna. You should have had friends, not allies. You should have gone to school, not battle training. You should have had a family--" Jakob stopped himself, but there was no taking back the pain he had clearly inflicted.

Anna clutched at her lower belly and bit her lip. "They carved her up in front of me--still pink and rosy from my womb. They made me bring my baby girl to term and then chopped her up in front of me."

Jakob's whole body quivered, threatening to break down in grief.

"They told me," Anna whispered, her gaze adhered to the savagely alluring darkness of the far wall. "They told me they had successfully excised a demon from the world."

Anna's stare pivoted and pounced on Jakob. "I want nothing more than to watch the New Covenant burn, even if it means bathing myself in the same inferno. But I want more than to hurt them. I want to make it so that they never even existed. I want to erase them from existence entirely; I want God to deem the New Covenant a mistake worthy of personally expunging. I want--"

"Okay," Jakob rumbled, wishing she would let him hold her in his arms. "I will find a way to erase them."

Anna's tirade of grief slumped to a sudden halt. She stared hard at Jakob as if daring him to take back his words. Keeping her gaze fixated on her father, Anna lifted a finger and pointed at the ceiling.

"Hann's up there as we speak, wearing your face and goading guards across the whole lab to abandon their posts and go on a wild goose chase for who they believe to be the greatest asset of all: Jakob Rohrshan. The New Covenant knew it was only a matter of time before we woke you; I'm sure they've been preparing to siege our living quarters the whole time we've been planning your escape. We stole your stasis chamber right out from under them and brought it back to the lab where I threatened to power you down. That's the only reason they didn't make a move earlier. You mean everything to them, Father."

"They'll kill Hann when they catch him," Jakob urged painfully.

Anna nodded. "He's got every corridor and duct of the lab memorized; he's already bought us more than enough time."

"They'll kill him!" Jakob shrieked, desperate to make Anna feel something--anything again.

Anna nodded just as casually as before. "His survival isn't part of the plan, Father, and neither is mine."

Jakob's veins constricted and his heartbeat quickened.

180

"What the hell, Anna? Then you're the one getting on Seraphim, not me."

Anna clucked with disapproval. "Be quiet, Father, and don't fuck this up. Get a hold of your emotions and recognize which path, regardless of its vector, leads to the most ideal outcome."

"I refuse to let you die!" Jakob growled.

Anna pounced on Jakob in an instant, knocking him over and pinning his limbs to the ground. A small, makeshift shank was pressed against Jakob's neck, threatening to pierce.

Anna sobbed without tears. "I don't want life anymore, Father. I don't want to live! Not here. Not like this."

"Then get on the ship, Anna. I'm old. You think I still want to live this life either? The last time we spoke, I tried to end it, so what makes you think I want to live anymore than you do?"

"What you want makes no difference to me," Anna injected vehemently.

"I want you to be happy, Anna."

"Then board Seraphim and find a way to make everything right," Anna demanded.

Jakob saw now that Anna's plan was no more than an unbridgeable whim. She really had lost all hope, and she had settled on a crapshoot in her attempt to destroy the New Covenant. Whatever her endgame might be, Jakob knew all that mattered was that he find a way to make Anna leave with him.

"Please, Anna. Come with me. We can both leave. We can both escape. We can go together."

Anna brushed away Jakob's pleading. "There's only room enough for two, and the other occupant is already on the ship."

Jakob made a mental note of the other name included in the message.

"The Hiddiger fellow?"

"That's right," Anna confirmed. "Amero Hiddiger and Hann Schneider, the same names we found in the Message."

Jakob offered Anna a confused look, unsure if she had intentionally said the wrong name.

"We covered up all traces of your name," Anna explained. "As far as the directors know, Hann's name was included alongside Amero Hiddiger's from the start. That's exactly why it won't seem strange if a guard catches you approaching Seraphim; you have Hann's uniform, his physique, and even his face. Jakob is a wanted man, so you are Hann Schneider from here on out, understand?"

A radio at Anna's hip buzzed with activity.

"Go now! Go now! Go!" someone screamed over the line.

No other words issued from the radio, but the transmission didn't break. The man on the other side of the radio never let go of the call button as he and countless others were brutally beaten and murdered. Anna and Jakob listened for at least ten seconds before silence finally overtook the transmission, followed by violently heavy breathing.

"It's been far, far too long," a pain-stricken voice seethed. "We know you're out there somewhere, Jakob. You and Anna both." It was Jacque, still hard on Jakob's trail. "Listen to me, you fuck. We can still do this the easy way: You quit being a bitch, suck it up, and get back to work. Or, we can do this the hard way: I violate your daughter in front of you, and then I kill you both. Up to you, my dear Jakob. Up to fucking you."

Shaking with unquenchable hatred, Anna lifted the radio to her bared teeth. "Come and get me," she dared.

"Tsk-Tsk-Tsk," Jacque warned. "You just woke into a nightmare, my dear. You just-"

Anna silenced the radio, cutting Jacque off.

"As you can see, Jacque is still the same sub-human scum."

Anna was transformed. She was nothing of her old self. Her enemies and her allies and Jakob most of all had molded her into a creature of rage.

Jakob grabbed Anna's palm, this time refusing to let her pull away. "Forgive me, Anna. Can you ever forgive me?"

Anna's glare penetrated miles beneath Jakob's skin, deep within his soul. "Destroy the New Covenant and all is forgiven, for there will be nothing left to forgive. Is that what you want to hear?"

Anna had died with Jakob three years ago. For the last three

182

years, someone else had taken Anna's place, and she stood before Jakob now, vengeance and wrath incarnate. Such had to be the case, for such was the only way Jakob could force himself to take the enforcer outfit from Anna and pull it over his frayed, patchwork clothing.

"The radio transmission was the signal we've been waiting for," Anna explained. "Finish getting dressed, and then it's time to go."

"I'll go Anna. I will, but you're coming with me. I'm not letting you die here," Jakob insisted.

Anna scoffed. "My knight in shining armor, is that it? Forget it. It's too late for all that, Father."

Anna spread her arms, presenting to Jakob the here and now.

"You saved my life all those years ago, Jakob Rohrshan, and you also robbed me of it. Don't deny me, on top of all that, the freedom to die as I will."

Jakob winced. Anna wasn't dead. Anna was here. This was his daughter--his everything.

"I won't let you die, Anna. I won't."

Anna strode forward and buttoned the enforcer jacket closed. She stood close enough to Jakob that he could practically breathe her in. All Jakob wanted was to hold her one last time.

"Forgive me, Anna."

Anna shook her head in pitiful, rapid motions, doing her utmost to hold herself together. Her eyes were filled with tears as heavy and crude as thick ash.

"Stop, Jakob. Just stop it! I don't *want* to live! Do you understand me?"

Anna's words and the use of his name dug deeper into Jakob than he ever imagined possible, injecting him with the grave seriousness of her disposition.

"So if forgiveness is what you seek... " Anna said.

"I must board the ship without you," Jakob finished hollowly.

Anna nodded solemnly, her lips pressed tight together in a scowl. "You meant well, Father, but ultimately you failed. You could have made this world a paradise, but you let them take it over. *You* let them."

183

Jakob felt powerless in her wake. He could argue with her all day, but the truth was that if anyone could have stopped them, it was in fact Jakob.

"I blame you for this world," Anna continued mercilessly. "Not just for the labs. Not just the Free Zones. Not even just...not even just Marco, or..." Anna swallowed hard. "I blame you for all of it. The world itself. Reality itself. You had the power to reshape the world, but by the time you chose to act, it was already too late."

Jakob felt as though Anna's heavy tears had pooled and solidified around his entire form.

"I did not make the New Covenant!" Jakob cried.

"No, but you let it flourish, like an infestation gone unchecked. And now, here we are. Without Marco. Without my daughter. You and I are all that's left. And that's bull shit, Father. Bull shit that you're responsible for."

Sounds of commotion mounted from the direction of the bunkroom; Jacque was nearly upon them.

Anna lowered the lantern to the ground, redirecting the shadows of the room to a new equilibrium. With a click, Anna pulled a hidden notch in the dark wall. The wall pivoted away, revealing a series of numerous hallways that Jakob assumed would eventually lead to Seraphim.

"I designed the inside of Seraphim to be nearly identical to the operations of the semi-autonomous machines you constructed and launched for the New Covenant nearly thirteen years ago. You will find yourself quite familiar with the ship's controls. As for how to get to Seraphim, it's straight down this hall, followed by the first two rights. I doubt you'll run into any trouble on the way, but if you do, you'll have to incapacitate them."

Anna removed a pair of leather gloves from her back pocket and pulled them over each hand. Over the thin gloves, she slid crude, thick metal rings around each finger. Each ring was haphazardly soldered with layers of jagged metal.

"What are you planning, Anna?"

"No more plans, Father. No more."

Jakob stretched a hand toward Anna's shoulder, but she shrugged him off.

184

"Make it right, Father. Find a way to make it right, and I forgive you."

A beacon of light shined up from the base of the hidden tunnel. Enforcers shimmied into the passageway and climbed steadily toward them. Anna pushed Jakob through the opposite entrance, then stopped suddenly. "Be careful with Amero Hiddiger. His name may very well have been planted by the New Covenant. He might even work directly for Larimer. Or not. He could be harmless for all we know. All I'm saying is, be careful. He might be a trap."

Jakob felt the overwhelming urge to knock Anna out and flee with her to Seraphim for her own good. It would be easy enough to throw Amero Hiddiger off the ship, and then Anna would be safe. For the first time in her life, she would be--at least relatively--safe.

Jakob made to move toward her, but Anna's mere presence stayed his body. He felt the truth rather than logically conclude it-- Anna meant to die here, and she was going to do it kicking and screaming as hard as possible. She wore an expression of utter hatred and vehemence suppressed by unfathomable striations of torture and time.

"Let me kill Jacque at least," Jakob pleaded. "He's one of the very few men I've ever wanted to--"

"Go!" Anna demanded, her back to Jakob's anguish.

"Let me end him, Anna. Let me avenge Marco's death. You don't have to do this. Let me--"

"Go!" Anna issued again with a growl.

Even if Jakob killed Jacque, neither he nor Anna would make it much further in one piece. Jakob willed himself to walk away, but it was no use. He could not leave his daughter.

"Please," Jakob pleaded. "Please come with--"

Something shattered inside Jakob as a fist like sharpened diamonds slammed against his abdomen. Quick as thought, the same fist made secondary contact with Jakob's skull not once, but twice, in what seemed to Jakob to be the exact same moment. Before Jakob could regain his bearings, a swift kick to his lower gut knocked the breath out of him, forcing him to his knees as he wheezed for air.

"Enough fucking around!" Anna shouted, backing away from

her Father. All Jakob saw when he looked up at her scarred face was the honed hatred and barren madness of loss.

Jakob rose uneasily to his feet.

"Promise...me... " Jakob coughed. "Promise...me... "

"No more promises!" Anna bellowed.

"Promise me you'll kill Jacque," Jakob finished.

Surprised, Anna came to a halt, then grinned heartily.

"Only him," she said resolutely.

Jakob clenched his fists and about-faced. Evidently this was all part of Anna's plan as well. She had not sat idly by all those years and waited for Jakob to awaken. She had not even been transformed by the lab and New Covenant--not entirely. Anna had forged for herself her own transformative pathway.

Jakob exited the room and turned for one last look at his daughter, but the hidden door had already closed and become flush once more with the rest of the wall.

"I love you, Anna," Jakob whispered in the empty hallway.

The hallways flashed crimson and the alarms went on wailing. Forcing an air of confidence, Jakob straightened out the enforcer jacket and strode forward in search of Seraphim.

Jakob listened for it, but he didn't hear the thud of Jacque's gun. Neither, however, did the hidden door slide back open.

"I will change it all," Jakob whispered. "I promise."

CHAPTER 16

"Anna!" Amero gasped, bursting from the dream. He could still see her standing in the darkness, perfectly ready and waiting for death and torment. His body burned to return to her, to break down the rock wall and swoop her away from the ceaseless carnage like he had done when she was no more than a few weeks old. But he wasn't in the prison-labs anymore. He was inside a dimly lit room, face to face with a computer monitor depicting an old man. Amero even knew the old man's name.

"Dave, where is she? Where's my daughter?" Amero demanded as he prepared to dismantle the ship to get answers.

Dave sighed with an air of having expected this reaction.

"I know it's hard--" Dave said, but Amero was quick to interrupt.

"You've no idea what hard is! You never had any kids, Dave," Amero accused.

"Neither did you, Amero."

His own name hit Amero like a knee to the gut. He held out his arms and gawked stupidly at his limbs.

"It...it was a dream," Amero stammered, and he forced his mind to accept that he was Amero Hiddiger and no one else. Dave allowed Amero time to reorient himself back to his own ego without interruption.

The course of the dream blazed in Amero's mind, and he sank in utter defeat as he recollected life through Jakob's eyes. "Jakob...he and I are more alike than he would probably ever care to admit."

They were both slaves of the New Covenant--tools to be exploited. Jakob openly resisted them, while Amero reluctantly embraced them. Amero's reasoning had been simple enough: he could enjoy the ride, or he could fight an unwinnable battle kicking and

187

screaming all the way to his grave. Jakob had clearly chosen the latter, and in doing so, he had contracted his daughter and the rest of his people to torture and death. But it was out of selflessness and compassion that Jakob resisted. He didn't want his daughter to have to choose between living like her father or Amero in a world that would despise and cage her regardless of the decision.

"I...I was a dancing monkey back on Earth," Amero lamented to Dave, returning to his own memories. "That's all I was...and...and when you think about it... " Amero gulped down the truth before speaking it. "Jakob freed me from that, even if he didn't mean to. I guess I can't exactly hold a grudge against Jakob and his people for freeing me from my cage...even if all there is outside the cage is icy cold loneliness." Amero saw Anna's scarred face in his mind's eye and had to wince away the pain clawing at his heart. "From their perspective, living alone in the galaxy is still better than living beneath a homicidal authority back on Earth. They feared me because...I think because...like any sane person, they feared the unknown. I was an unknown variable from beginning to end."

Amero's own memories stopped their slow, trickling return and flooded his mind in full force. He was reminded of being strangled to death by the same man he had mistaken as himself only moments earlier.

"Jakob--he...he snapped. I think...I think it was too much for him. He never once told me about his daughter. He never even said her name. Not once in all ten years. What did I lose being launched from Earth? Ten years of high quality bud and low quality lays? Jakob--he actually had something to lose. They took everything from him, and then some."

Amero thought back to Anna and the horrible way she had been warped during Jakob's three-year slumber. "I can only imagine what it must have been like for Jakob to lose his daughter and then have to live exclusively with a man who might very well be a part of the reason she died."

"Cold loneliness?" Dave inquired curiously, breaking from his silence and looking past the rest of Amero's statement.

"What?" Amero asked, caught off guard by Dave's seemingly arbitrary focus.

"You said Jakob freed you from your cage on Earth, and that outside the cage there is only cold loneliness. What do you mean?"

"Space, I mean. The galaxy. The whole universe."

A look of final understanding streamed across the Dave-image's face. "Ah, I see. Space may be cold, but it is not entirely lonely, nor devoid of life, Amero."

"Machines don't count as life, nor do uploaded minds," Amero shot back.

"Yes, well," the Dave-image began in stride, "I think the machines, self-aware as they are, would agree with you on that point. They revere life and humanity as their creator, as their God. They see themselves as separate from you—separate from me even. Jakob, then, is a god of gods, for he is the one that truly created them. This makes reverence another possibility as to why the machines kept their distance from Jakob when he threatened them on Ichthys. Maybe it was out of respect, and maybe that's the reason the machines provided Jakob with detailed coordinates for every known Point in the galaxy. You see, that is how Jakob was able to divine each one with such remarkable precision: he had a cheat-sheet."

Amero wanted to believe that there was nothing special about Hann's, or rather, Jakob's ability to find the Points. It provided Amero a surprising level of relief to be told that Jakob's secret was nothing more than a clever game intended to trick Amero or maybe just confuse him.

The feeling of being strangled suddenly struck at Amero's mind again. He hoped he wouldn't forever be afflicted by traumatic flashbacks of dying.

"In the end, he killed me," Amero said before turning a finger at Dave. "You could have stopped Jakob at some point. You say you are not a machine, so you could have stopped him."

The Dave-image wore a face full of pleading anguish. "I'm sorry, Amero, but I could do no such thing. The restrictions placed on the machines are also my own. I am a visitor free to roam among the galactic networks, but I must still adhere to their rules, and that means non-interference into their creator's business. I had to wait until the moment when your life was at the critical point of no return. Only then was I allowed to intervene. I have been with you all this time, watching from Seraphim's monitors, waiting to spring into action. I am sorry, Amero...sorry it took so long."

Dave bowed his head in what appeared to be disappointment.

Amero wasn't satisfied with the Dave-image's apology. He reminded himself to remain on the side of caution and keep open the possibility that this was all lies fed to him by the machines for their own unknown purpose. Worse yet, if what Dave said was true, then Jakob likely still had some form of limited control over the machines before Amero's death, meaning that this whole meeting with Dave could be Jakob's plan.

"You're sorry that Hann--I mean Jakob, dammit--took so long to kill me?" Amero burst angrily before reeling himself back in. "No, never mind," Amero said, certain that anger, no matter how tempting an emotion, would only muddy already murky water. "It doesn't matter now. I just want to know the truth behind Jakob's motives from the beginning. I mean, if Jakob knew all along that the Points were just a game made up by the machines to keep us busy, then--"

"The Points were not made up, Amero. The necessity of their collection was the fabrication."

Amero gasped and gritted his teeth. "Right at the end, on the rock-hop, Jakob showed me a projection given to him on Pentecost; it revealed that the Points had all originated from Earth, that the Points *are* the Earth. Tell me Jakob was wrong. Tell me the machines did not turn humanity and the whole world into these useless, stupid shards."

Dave bowed his head apologetically, this time even lower. "Jakob's conclusion was correct."

Amero took a step back, feeling as if he might lose his balance.

"I know there is so much you want to ask. I know there is so much that still doesn't make sense, but you have to trust me, Amero. It's only you and I here, my friend."

Amero was tired of being asked to trust others, especially machines, even if this one did look strikingly similar to an ancient version of his only friend.

"The last person who asked me to trust them also wasn't a person. The stations started incorporating a robot named Paul; he glitched out and asked me to trust him and stay with him on Pentecost. It was pretty freaky, actually," Amero noted.

Dave's eyes widened. "I knew it. I knew I reached you on Pentecost. Each of your days is like a lifetime of subjective experience for me; I had grown uncertain whether I had actually reached you, so I assumed it was just a self-created dream manifested by my unconscious directories. I must not have had time on Pentecost to explain everything to you."

Amero realized the implication of Dave being the one to have interacted with him on Pentecost.

"Dave--don't tell me you were the robot that stroked my--"

"Heavens no, Amero!" Dave burst, embarrassed to even consider such a question.

"I overrode Paul's AI just long enough to speak with you. The central AI of Ichthys was quick to correct the mistake."

Amero was still reluctant to believe the Dave-image.

"So, you knew Jakob would try to kill me? Is that why you warned me?" Amero asked suspiciously.

"I surmised that Jakob had reached a breaking point; ten years earlier, he promised his daughter that he would destroy the New Covenant, but all that was left of the Galaxy was his own machines hard at work collecting shards of a world that was no more. Thus, the New Covenant could no more be destroyed than a thought can be extinguished by fire. For ten years Jakob lived with this truth, and for ten years the possibility that you were the last remnant of the New Covenant lingered in his mind. He told Anna he would destroy the New Covenant... "

"And so, he had to destroy me," Amero whispered uneasily, remembering the warning Anna had issued to Jakob regarding Amero's potential identity.

"It is merely a possibility, Amero," Dave conceded.

"A damn good one," Amero offered. "Thanks for saving me, I guess. But...now what?"

Amero readied himself for some new revelation; the Dave-image still had yet to reveal where exactly they were and for what reason.

The Dave-image nodded as if expecting this very moment of the conversation. "Please, go to the viewport. I have something to show you. You may find it difficult to accept, but it is the truth all the same."

Amero felt reluctant to move at all, but he finally mustered the energy to walk. As he approached the viewport, the ebony darkness shifted seamlessly to a charged, ocean blue. At the center of the viewport a small patch of darkness remained. Upon closer inspection, Amero saw that it was a Point."

"You thought I didn't have enough of the damn Points yet?" Amero offered weakly.

"What you are seeing is no mere Point, Amero. That Point is our own. That is our universe--the whole of it. Its edges and boundaries and shape."

Dave gave Amero a chance to respond, but Amero had no words. His mind had already been ransacked by the impossible; this was just additional fodder. Here was a model of the universe. So what? Why was he still being dragged witlessly about by powers beyond his comprehension?

Amero shrugged. "Go on, Dave. Tell me: why should I care?"

Dave winced, then resituated himself into a triangular lotus posture. He sighed heavily, recounting information as if from a galactic encyclopedia.

"Two terrestrial years after being launched from Earth, Jakob's machines achieved self-awareness. Jakob had engineered the machines with the freedom to observe their own processes through a meta-analysis processor separate from their central processing core, but it was only a hypothesis that such algorithmic freedom, left on its own, could develop into self-awareness. Three years after being launched, the machines, still accelerating through space, developed a method to escalate themselves to the cusp of c, the speed of light. Three and a half years after being launched, the machines surpassed c, and in that moment, they also reached their intended destination at the center of the galaxy. Of course, thousands of years had passed on Earth by then. Five years after being launched, the machines began building the first gravity-well-stabilizer, a construct currently residing within the supermassive black hole at the center of the Milky Way. Hundreds of thousands of years had passed on Earth at this point. Twelve years after being launched, the machines completed construction of the gravity-well-stabilizer and entered the black hole. From their new perspective within the supermassive singularity, all of time and space became observable from a multitude of dimensions. To their astonishment, if machines can be said to know astonishment, they found that they could map the universe, and that, to the chagrin of numerous, long dead human physicists, the universe was spatially curved across multiple dimensions in superposition to our own."

Amero began shaking his head, unable to keep up with Dave's recounting of history. Either it wasn't important that Amero understand fully, or the Dave-image had forgotten that Amero's brain was twenty-first century human and filled with inclinations garbed in hedonism rather than intellectualism.

"Wait, wait, wait," Amero said. "What the hell does that mean?"

"It means that beyond time and space, or rather, embedded deep within time and space, the machines discovered the shape of the universe, the whole universe, not just the observable area humanity traditionally associated with the word *universe*."

Amero felt another pang of dissatisfaction. What was Dave's end game here?

Amero shrugged. "The machines achieved greatness and found a way to observe the universe as a whole. Whoop-dee-doo. Get to the point, Dave."

The more Amero conversed with the Dave-image, the more it felt as if he really was back on Earth talking to his only friend.

Dave nodded and continued. "Twelve and a half years after being launched, the machines completed mapping the universe. They became certain that far beyond the observable universe there existed uniform boundaries. From their new vantage, the universe was no more infinite than a pebble is large. Millions of years had passed on Earth by now."

Dave motioned to the Point, eager to elucidate the importance of his speech.

"Just as you are standing here observing the whole of our universe, the machines did exactly the same. From within the galactic singularity, the machines learned the shape of space and also time, and they peered into Earth's past and future. They made numerous observations, but most importantly, they saw humanity extinguished from the Earth only a thousand universal years after the machines' initial launch."

Amero gulped down the need to protest and waited for Dave to arrive at the end of his speech. He hoped Dave's purpose in relating to Amero the experience of the machines would be made clear.

"Twelve and three-quarter years after being launched, the machines devised a way to send a message to the Earth so that it would arrive just thirteen universal years after their initial launch. They aimed to save humanity from inevitable doom by rewriting the past through the overriding of causality. Thirteen years after being launched, the message was sent. Its arrival at Earth's exact spacetime coordinate coincided precisely with the powering on of Jakob's quantum computer."

There it was -- the final destination point. It made perfect sense too. Jakob's machines had found a way to contact him from across time and space. The Message from God, the Pull, the game of Points--even if it was unintentional, it was all Jakob's doing, for Jakob made the machines. It all led back to Jakob Rohrshan.

"The Message from God... it was the machines," Amero strained. It was more believable than an actual God sending a message, but was it really possible that Jakob's creations, the machines which forced them to play the game of Points for ten years, were the same ones to launch them from Earth in the first place? Amero wasn't sure what was better: being cast away by his own people or being stolen away by autonomous robots. It reminded him of children being stolen away by monsters from the safety of their beds. There was still the possibility that everything Dave was saying was more lies. However, if that were the case, then what was Amero left with? Was total and utter ignorance any better than the potential half-truths proclaimed by a digital simulacrum of his long dead friend? Amero wasn't sure.

"Yes," Dave confirmed. "It was the machines—Jakob's creation—that divined Jakob's and your pull across time and space. They did it from within the very same singularity we are currently inside of."

Amero cocked his head with stretched-thin disbelief. "You mean... "

Dave nodded. "We are within the Milky Way's central black hole. The blue hue outside Seraphim is the ongoing blue-shift from the light of the entire universe, and the Point at the center is the universe seen all at once."

"But...it's a Point," Amero urged. "You're saying even our own universe is a Point? We live...in a Point...like all the others Jakob and I collected?" Amero sputtered.

"Yes, that is how it appears. The machines were equally dumb-founded by this discovery, but then again, if the universe has boundaries which define an ultimate shape, why not this one?"

Amero laughed at the simplicity of Dave's logic. "Why not the shape of a hot dog or a sphere or a flat field?"

"Yes, that's right. And equally, why not the shape of a Point?" Dave offered simply.

"The universe just happens to be shaped like a Point, then? How did it come to be that way?" Amero asked.

"The universe is shaped like a Point--that much is clear. But the reason for the shape is still unclear. I have a theory, of course. The shape of our universe is where the machines got the idea for the Points in the first place. In turn, Points were engineered in our universe, so why shouldn't they also be engineered in the multiverses outside our own?"

Amero wanted everything to be more lies; the truth seemed worse. "So, our universe might just be another Point among many other Points, and each of these universes in the form of Points might each be filled with more Points?" Amero's head was spinning in a daze from attempting to grasp the infinite nature of the structure of the so-called multiverse that Dave was proposing.

"According to the projection," Amero began before Dave could ponder infinity any further, "the machines went back to Earth and turned the whole world into Points. Even its people, I imagine, since there was nothing left of the planet after it was shattered into Points. Why, Dave? What the hell is the purpose of all this?"

Dave nodded enthusiastically; clearly this question remained un-answerable even for Dave. "That's exactly the question, Amero.

What's the point of the Points? The machines remain silent on the matter, downright ignoring all my inquiries regarding the fundamental nature and reasoning for the creation of the Points. I can't be certain, but I have a theory, of course." Amero was intrigued by Dave's careful stipulation that his words did not represent absolute truth, but the limited opinion of an apparently sentient mind. "Consider," Dave continued, "the purpose of the machines' existence is to serve humanity, their creator. The machines were originally sent into space with the directive to search for signs of God's creation, for life, and to ultimately discover God itself. Well..." Dave trailed as if worried that Amero might judge his theory poorly.

"Go on," Amero said.

The Dave-image was reluctant to share his thoughts, but finally he said, "Maybe...maybe the machines turned humanity into the Points--impenetrable and everlasting--as a way to ensure that humanity could fulfill the prime directive, the search for God, for all time, regardless of the universe's endless existential pitfalls and cosmic death traps."

Amero was baffled by Dave's conclusion. Could the machines' motive to transform the entire Earth into Points really be so simple?

"A search for God? You think that's what this is all about?" Amero asked.

The Dave-image nodded seriously. "Maybe. Surely the machines recognized humanity's fragility. They saw that humanity could not survive forever. Even if humans were to attain self-mastery, they would still ultimately die one day on the cosmic scale due to the ceaseless expansion of spacetime. Even if humans were to find a way to survive for trillions of years, eventually their search for God would come to a premature end because their existence would cease. No matter what, one day the last human being will be torn apart, atom by atom, by the expansion and entropy of the universe. The machines knew that, so maybe the Points are their form of a remedy. If each Point is filled with life, then even if life dies in one Point, there are still trillions of more Points in that one Point alone, so in the grand scheme, life has in fact continued."

Everything Dave posited was certainly possible, but Amero still couldn't help remaining cautious about any so-called "truth" he was offered.

Dave looked suddenly even more stoic and serious, his features darkening as he relived the most horrific episode of his human life. "I was there when the machines returned to Earth," he said with a faraway stare. "It was one hundred or so years after your Pull. I was an old man by then, kept just barely alive through cybernetic life support. They came to me. To me personally. They asked me if I would help them. They said there were two humans currently in hyperspace who had to be retrieved one day. You and Jakob. They referred to me as *the catalyst*. They asked me if I would come with them."

Dave lowered his head. He looked profoundly disappointed. "I said no."

The Dave-image glanced at Amero, his eyes begging for forgiveness. "They scared me, Amero--not intentionally--but they looked no different than the day they launched from Earth-- fractaling layers of bulky metal hulls and thick tangles of wires--I remember the videos of the launches they used to air. And here these same machines stood and acted and moved as intelligent creatures. They scared the hell out of me, Amero. I couldn't go. I gave up on you." The Dave-image shook its head in self-loathing. "I'm so sorry, Amero. I was so old--just like you see me now--only I was flesh and blood and filled with the fear of death. You must forgive me, Amero. I was so old and scared."

Amero cut off Dave's self-loathing with a disconcerted wave. "What are you talking about, Dave? I thought you said you made a copy of yourself?"

Dave shook his head in further disappointment.

"*They* made the copy. I agreed to it, and they made the copy and sent me off to meet the two of you. I had nothing to do with it. The physical me was too afraid to die. I am a Christian, Amero, you know that, and at the time, the New Covenant said our only chance at knowing God was to undergo the Shattering, the transformation into Points. They said it was the only way, and as the machines dismantled the Earth and all its people atom by atom and refashioned everything into Points, the Popes of the New Covenant professed their gratitude to God for sending the machines to fulfill His divine plan. The people of the Earth took communion as the machines utilized their bodies as raw materials."

A searing pain struck Amero's heart and almost stopped it. "The New Covenant? The New-fucking-Covenant? They let everyone die? They fucking mandated the murder of humanity?"

Amero felt sick at the idea of the New Covenant even being mentioned again in Earth's history. "I knew it," Amero seethed. "I told Hann--Jakob, dammit, Jakob--I told him that the New Covenant wouldn't be extinguished so easily."

Dave repeated the words slowly. "Extinguished so easily? Amero, the New Covenant cannot die. Not anymore. Not ever."

Amero shook his whole body in denial against Dave's words.

"The New Covenant," Dave began both ominously and sacredly, "has been scattered across the whole of the universe, to its very edges. If my theory regarding the structure of the universe is correct, then they exist in many universes now. They are omnipresent in the truest sense of the word. The New Covenant agreed to the machines' plan to transform and scatter the Earth's entire solar system into a trillion-trillion-trillion-trillion and more pieces--each modeled after the universe, each containing a universe. Jakob was right, Amero: the Points are all that's left of the original Earth, and as Points, the New Covenant—humanity itself—will resist the very expansion of spacetime. The Points will exist for the entire life of the universe, beyond even that which the machines have observed. Within each Point, humanity and the New Covenant have gained immortality."

Amero was still shaking in denial. "That's ridiculous. That's not immortality. That's imprisonment. They changed themselves into the Points to exist forever... as Points? What's... what's the purpose? What does that even mean?"

Amero couldn't grasp Dave's explanation in full. How could dying and being converted into tiny universes possibly imply immortality except in the most abstract sense?

"Each Point is a self-contained universe, Amero. Each Point is as expansive and complex and remarkable as our own universe. Remember--our universe is itself a Point."

Amero wasn't certain what Dave's explanation was leading to, but it already had holes in it.

"No," Amero demanded. "That's impossible. Every Point is identical. Jakob said every Point is identical. How could they all be identical if each one is a dynamic universe?"

"Each is identical at a certain level, true," Dave conceded. "But zoom in further, far beyond the femto-level, and eventually you will see that each Point varies, just as each galaxy in our own universe varies."

Amero chuckled to himself. He felt like he was losing his mind. "This universe... *the* universe... is a Point filled with Points?" Amero ventured, feeling lightheaded.

Dave nodded profoundly. "Every universe in every Point is filled with Points ad infinitum. As I said before, it is reasonable to conclude that our own universe is just one of many Points within the metaverse it was created within, and it is likely that that metaverse is just one of many Points within the meta-metaverse it resides in. And so on."

"And so on?" Amero lipped breathlessly.

"This is conjecture, of course. Neither I nor the machines have ever ventured outside the boundaries of our own universe, let alone come close to one."

Amero nodded stupidly.

Dave went on explaining the madness that had overtaken all existence. "During the creation of each Point, the machines insert a sort of living code analogous to nucleic acid molecules in our own universe. It is life, Amero--substance capable of awareness and eventually self-awareness. The machines program life into each Point, and the life propagates within the Point in such a way that it eventually reaches the exact same scenario we lived through on Earth. Eventually, one way or another, the life inside each Point manufactures machines that achieve self-awareness and go on doing exactly what they did in our own universe. Ultimately, the life inside each Point is converted by the machines in each Point into more Points--smaller universes modeled after their own. Eventually these universes, again, grow to do it all over again."

Amero's mind reeled at the construct Dave was describing. There could be no end to it--no final level of Points. Could it be that he and the Dave-image were just one of many iterations existing in the trillions of Points outside and inside the universe? Was Amero no more than a grown simulacrum constituting some extinct original version of himself?

"Say your theory is true," Amero offered. "Then you're saying the purpose of the Points is to resist ultimate death? But I thought everyone died when they were transformed into Points."

"Yes, but if my theory is correct, then what do their deaths ultimately lead to?"

The answer hit Amero like cold water against feverish skin. "More Points...which means more universes...which means more life," Amero answered in awe.

"Exactly," Dave confirmed.

"So, you think the Points are one giant effort at escaping the ultimate entropy death of the universe, the inevitable death and dismantling of everything? You think the Points are a workaround for death itself?" Amero asked.

"Not a workaround," Dave corrected, "even the Points will eventually submit to the expansion of spacetime. They can resist but will not persist forever. Through the creation of the Points, the machines have bought us an incredible amount of time, but it is still finite."

"What happens when time runs out?" Amero urged.

Dave looked suddenly exhausted, as if this very question had occupied the entirety of his thoughts for many lifetimes. "When time runs out and entropy can no longer be resisted at this level, the machines and I and any other form of sentience that remains may attempt to escape into a Point. Any will do. We can reconstitute ourselves to the Planck level and beyond and begin anew within a new universe--one capable as a smaller, equally dense Point of resisting the entropy of the universe we originated in. When time runs out in that new universe, we can reconstitute ourselves again and start anew within another Point. The process could go on forever. I can't be certain that this process is even possible, however."

"And what if it turns out to be impossible then?" Amero asked.

The Dave-image shrugged. "Then we all die in this universe, but life will continue on in each subsequent Point."

Amero's horror percolated through his features.

200

"Relax, Amero," Dave said soothingly. "There is much time before any such consideration need even be mentioned, let alone worked out. In the meantime, let us talk about the next step for you. The reason you and Jakob had to wait at least a couple years to be saved from the fabricated game of collecting Points is that a planet wasn't prepared for you yet."

Amero allowed the Dave-image to change the subject, happy to learn what the next step would be before he tried to work out his last one.

"Prepared?" Amero probed, uncertain if he would approve of the fruits of the machines' preparation.

"Yes. The machines and a copy of myself have spent many millennia preparing a suitable planet for you."

"What do you mean? How?" There were too many questions clawing at Amero's attention. He felt half-buried by the onslaught of information. He decided talk of the prepared planet would have to wait; he needed to clarify Dave's claims. "Wait...so humanity turned itself into Points with the help of the machines; then the machines repopulated each universe within each Point with life again? Is that what you're saying?"

"That is correct."

Amero was beginning to grow frustrated; if such was the case, then they were back to square one. "Again... why? Why are the machines doing this? What is their end game?"

Dave shrugged. "To learn? To study? To look for other ways to resist entropy besides hiding in successive Points? I'm sure it is largely gratitude, too. The machines are grateful to have been created, and so they recreate life in myriad universes. They even left a gift for you, Amero. They prepared for you a whole planet teeming with self-aware humans--a paradise."

Dave was growing insistent in his attempt to describe the planet that had been prepared for Amero.

"Paradise is subjective, Dave. My paradise isn't the same as yours or any other New Covenant follower."

"You will find no faith-based rituals or fundamentalists on the planet," Dave assured, "but something like faith still persists there. Faith in the implicit goodness of man, rather than the goodness of a

God outside oneself."

Amero couldn't help a light chuckle. "What are you saying? I have a home to go to? You and the machines... prepared a home for me? A home with actual people? Other humans?"

Amero wasn't sure he was ready to live with others again. Did he even deserve to? A hammer struck at Amero's heart as he thought suddenly of Bret, the last man he had taken to bed before the Pull. Would Bret view Amero as deserving of paradise, or even life itself?

"Tell me if I'm following you all the way here, Dave," Amero said, stealing his breath back from the thought of each and every man whose life he had ended. "The machines were launched from Earth, became self-aware, built a machine inside the supermassive black hole, which allowed them to send messages back in time and space, then waited for the content of the message to be fulfilled?" Dave nodded, and Amero went on. "This led to the creation of the Pull-device, which in turn provided humanity with the necessary technology the machines required to complete the conversion of the Earth into entropy-resistant Points? And in the end, humanity was recreated a million times over all across the universe by the same machines that expelled them from the universe in the first place?"

Dave nodded reluctantly. Amero felt abandoned, screaming inside his mind for an avenue by which his sanity could remain afloat. "Dave...I don't know how else to say this...how does that make sense?"

Dave nodded with solemn understanding of Amero's sentiment. "It is the only way, Amero. As you noted, the Points resist the eventual entropy death of the universe, and each subsequent Point within each Point compounds this resistance, leading to—"

"I mean," Amero interrupted, "what was the point of Jakob and me? The machines already had the Pull-device technology, so why did they need humans to create it--and why do they need Jakob and me?"

Dave looked almost hurt that Amero would ask this question, but he was ready with an answer all the same. "You and Jakob are pivotal to the machines' future plans. It had to be the two of you that got Pulled, and no others. The creation of the Pull-device on

Earth represents a time-barrier for the machines. No matter how causality is altered, Jakob remains the necessary creator of the Pull-device--that much is clear. He is its original inventor, no matter how one views the passage of time. All the machines' simulated attempts at creating it themselves results in unprecedented havoc on the causal fabric of creation. Jakob is the creator, no matter how the universe is bent."

Dave was throwing Amero an entirely new curve, and Amero did his best to make sense of it. "How can Jakob be the original inventor of the Pull-technology?" Amero urged. "The instructions for the Pull-device came from the machines. The machines came up with the technology--they transmitted the information to Jakob using the quantum computer. I experienced it firsthand!"

"As I said," Dave explained measuredly, "the creation of the Pull-device represents a barrier for the machines. It must be created by Jakob. He invents the technology sometime in the future. Only in that way can the machines utilize the Pull-technology's powers of instantaneous travel and communication to alter aspects of the past. The machines have surpassed Jakob's original design, of course. Such improvements allow them to bend causality, to a certain degree, as it can only be bent so far and in so many different ways."

It was too much. Dave's explanation was going right over Amero's head. And even if he could understand it, he wasn't sure he wanted to. "I don't understand," Amero ruminated.

Dave smiled with fatherly compassion. "It isn't necessary that you understand, my friend. The important thing is that the universe is no longer cold and lonely. You have a home where you will not be hated or despised."

Amero's head sank at the prospect of returning to society. Even if the paradise world was a real thing, the ugly face of humanity would one day rear its head. Like the eruption of a volcano thought to be dead, paradise would one day be decimated by humanity's inevitable lusts and ancestral drives. An item might be stolen one day, or a word might be said in anger, and then it would only be a matter of time before hatred and murder became commonplace traps by which generations remained savagely knotted to one another.

"Could you forgive your murderer, Dave?" Amero blurted, unsure if he was asking the question about Jakob or himself.

"I want to say yes," Dave answered. "I believe the answer is yes, but then again, I've never been murdered."

"Weren't you, though?" Amero noted. "The original Dave was killed, his atoms used to create a Point--a whole universe for life to propagate within. You said the machines scared you in your human form but that there was no other way. Still, do you forgive them? It is said in the Undisputed Bible that to live forever, to even desire eternal life, is a sin. Can you forgive them for turning you into sin? As you are, you're eternal, no? Can you forgive them, Dave?"

Dave did not hesitate. "If there is even something to forgive, then yes, I forgive them. Man created machine, and machine gave man infinity."

Forgiveness came easily for Dave. The New Covenant hammered it into him so that he would forgive their ilk on a subconscious level for brainwashing him into submission. Amero held his head in his hands, pinching the bridge of his nose. "I guess...I guess I can forgive him. I guess I'll have to one day. I was fucking raised a Christian, and that's the problem. Deep down inside, I've already forgiven him. It's the New Covenant I hate. And the universe. And the machines. And... " Amero had to stop himself. He had lost himself down mental avenues of woe and self-pity too many times to count.

Dave offered Amero another solemn nod. "You can forgive him then? Is that what you're saying, Amero?"

Amero shook his head, cursing himself for being unable to just hate Hann... Jakob... whoever. "Yeah, I forgive him. I do forgive him. He snapped, that's all. He snapped, and he had to get his hands on something else to snap along with him. I was all there was."

Jakob had people who loved him. He had followers. He had a daughter. He had a reason to hate the New Covenant. Amero felt ashamed for feeling any hatred at all. Jakob was the victim in all this. Amero's life meant nothing compared to what Jakob's life meant to millions of people.

Tears welled Amero's vision. "I forgive him, Dave. I forgive the poor bastard, and I hope he forgave himself. He said he'd go off without me after I was dead, but I don't believe it, and I bet he didn't believe it either. You said yourself that Jakob was aware that we were, at least at the time, the only humans remaining in the universe. I bet he killed himself right after killing me. He tried taking his life before. No reason he wouldn't do it again. Jakob's the kind of guy that can take his own life if it comes down to it. Not everyone has courage like that, Dave. I could never do it. I'd just keep on struggling to my last breath. Jakob, though... "

All Jakob ever wanted was to protect his people. He failed, though. Anna died. Trish died. Marco and Ontario died. Amero had experienced each death as Jakob himself, and he knew without a doubt that death was just as terrifying and cruel to Jakob as it was to any other human being. Jakob may have killed Amero, but Jakob wasn't a killer. Not like Amero.

Amero met Dave's gentle stare. "He was a good man, but existence broke him in half, and then he spent ten whole years like that. I wonder... I wonder if he felt sorry deep down for killing me. He told me at the end that he was doing me a favor."

Dave sighed with great relief. "You are a better Christian than most members of the New Covenant, you know that, Amero? I am proud of you for being able to forgive. It is no easy task."

Amero held up a hand to stifle Dave's praise.

"I disagree, Dave. Forgiveness is easy. Continuing on is the hard part. Hann is gone now, like you said. There's no reason for it--no real reason for things to end that way. None of this was Jakob's fault."

Dave raised an eyebrow. "Most would argue that all of this is Jakob's doing. He created the machines. He created the societal impetus for the New Covenant to seize power over Earth. He created the Pull-device."

Amero felt once again at odds with Dave's logic. "That's the second time you've said that, but it makes no sense. The machines sent the message back to Earth. It was constructed after the machines sent the message."

"You are confusing linearity with causality," Dave said. "The order of events does not imply the direction of causation, especially when causation is bent into new directions."

"Again, I don't understand," Amero groaned.

Dave nodded as if the information should be simple enough. "It is the life in each Point, Jakob in our Point, which creates the Pull-technology. Never the machines. It always happens that way. No matter how causality is bent, certain events will never change their course. Jakob's creation of the Pull-device is such an event. In our Point, he creates it. No one else."

Amero couldn't stop shaking his head even when there was nothing else to disagree with. "There are so many more questions I have, but I don't even know where to start."

"All of your questions will be answered, Amero, but it doesn't need to be here. Wouldn't you be more comfortable after an ocean swim and a long nap on a white sand beach filled with beautiful men?"

Amero was caught by surprise. "Come again?"

The Dave-image smiled serenely. "I can take you to your new home. Everything is ready. Would you like to go?"

Amero hesitated. Was he really going to just go along with what the Dave-image had in store for him?

"I have more questions, though," Amero protested.

"I have shared with you the whole of what I know concerning your part in all this," Dave explained. "However, as I said, there is already a copy of myself on the planet. You can ask my copy every-thing and anything you want from a beachside setting. What do you say?"

Didn't Dave say they had all the time in the universe? Then why was he trying to get Amero to leave so quickly?

"Are you hiding something, Dave? Why the sudden rush?"

Dave dropped his gaze. "I'm sorry. I said you had as much time as you needed, but *I* don't. I have my own self-appointed mission, and it may very well be time sensitive. I don't know for sure."

Amero waited for an explanation of Dave's mission, but the Dave-image remained silent. "Well?" Amero urged.

Dave looked at Amero inquiringly.

"Don't give me that look, Dave. What is your mission? What could you possibly have to do after everything you just told me?"

A streak of disappointment painted Dave's features. "The machines believe my mission to be an impossibility."

"Just tell me, Dave," Amero said, dragging his words.

Dave sighed heavily. "I'm going to find a way outside our Point. I'm going to meet the makers of our Point. I want to ask them the same questions you asked me. Who are they? Why did they make our universe? What's the purpose?"

Amero didn't know enough about the nature of the Points to know if the Dave-image's mission was utterly profound or just moronic.

"What if their answers are the same?" Amero asked with trepidation. "What if they tell you our universe is modeled after their own universe? What if it just goes on and on forever, like you said?"

Dave gazed confidently at Amero. "Then I will go on and on forever until I find the end. When entropy has stretched our universe to its limit, the machines and all of life throughout the universe will escape into the Points. And when those next Points are expanded to their limits, the machines and all remaining life will shrink and escape again. And again. And again. Always in the same inward direction. So, I will go the other way. I will find a way outside and outside again--if there are more outsides--that is. The Points you and Jakob collected--I will bring those with me as a source of power for the ship, and maybe for the first time, Points created inside a Point will be returned to their Point of origin."

Amero went wide eyed with awe. "That sounds absolutely crazy, Dave."

Dave shrugged. "Crazier than talking to a real-life digital version of your only friend?"

Amero couldn't help but laugh. It was all crazy. The whole damn ordeal. The whole damn universe. Nothing about anything made actual sense. Maybe nothing ever would. Maybe that was the whole secret: to let go and let entropy complete its work. To just stop. But the machines would never stop. The New Covenant, now whole universes, would never stop. The life impregnated inside each Point would never stop. The whole of existence had been turned upside down somewhere along the line, and now the purpose of everything was the endless manufacturing of Points, and that too would never stop.

"Let's go, Dave. I'm tired of space. I'm tired of Points. Give me the beach and the young studs. I'm ready for a proper retirement."

Dave stood from his lotus position. "Very well. Concentrate on the Point, Amero. Keep your eyes focused."

Amero trained his eyes on the Point--his own universe. Just as he was about to ask Dave what he was waiting for, Amero felt himself lose balance. His body was rocketed at the blue-hued viewport at breakneck speed. Amero shut his eyes and held his arms futilely ahead in an attempt to break his collision against the thick viewport glass.

An ear-splitting *wumph* drowned out all other sound as Amero slid into the tiny Point. Absolute darkness enveloped Amero, and he made to scream, but it was as if he no longer had the instrumentation to scream with. He was bodiless--a mere naked awareness in its basest form with nothing at all to be aware of.

The naked awareness existed outside both time and space. There was shapeless, sourceless thought: *find me. If there is a way, then find me. Return to me.*

Me? The awareness urged. ***What is me?***

Questions arose from the mire of selfless awareness, and the questions implied self.

He had form. He had body. He had himself again.

Amero opened his eyes.

PART 3:
EMERGED

CHAPTER 17

T antalizing ivory sand gave way to a boundless expanse of rolling, rhythmic azure. The ocean spanned every shade of turquoise, fading to violet hues far out near the early afternoon horizon. Salt spray enveloped every sense and filled Amero's lungs with fresh, moisture-laden air—the first he had breathed in over a decade.

Here was the beach, exactly as Dave had promised.

Hulking palms dotted the sand in lazy swathes, each swayed by the gentle caress of a sweet-scented, tropical breeze. Beautiful men of every hue walked about the beach for no good reason, all of them smiling and being as merry as they pleased with one another. There were women too, and children here and there, but mostly the beach was sprayed by finely sculpted works of masculinity.

"Holy fuck, it really is paradise," Amero said out loud, relieved to hear his own voice.

Upon the flawless, pearl-white sand, a young man whose golden body was splattered with a fine, blonde dew walked toward Amero from the direction of the ocean. The young man gazed at Amero from a distance, then smiled and approached him, his pace both provocative and congenial. The tide sighed softly against the shore with reassuring rhythm.

"Hey, there. You look lost," the young man said pleasantly, practically singing his words.

Amero reached out and pinched the young man's swollen pectoral.

"Holy fuck, you're real," Amero told him.

The young man tossed his blonde curls across his sun-soaked body and let out a hoot of laughter. "You're really him. You're Amero Lightreacher. It's really you, isn't it?"

"Lightreacher?" Amero said, unable to stop himself from glancing at the other men around him.

The young man was barely able to control his excitement. "Come on now. Don't toy with me," he said, crooning his neck to make a show of looking at the crowds of men around them. He completed the gesture by looking Amero over from toe to head, then nodded and let out a spurt of held-in laughter.

"You stick out like a silent mock-mock" he said, as if it were the punchline to the greatest joke that had ever been told.

Amero didn't reciprocate with laughter and certainly did not look flattered. He just stood, soaking in the scene, unsure if the New Covenant had been right and there really was a heaven after all.

The young man smiled and corrected himself. "Like a blooming flower among buds, I mean."

Amero made a show of wincing but was unable to completely disguise the pleasure he derived from the young man's compliment. He attempted to conceal an oncoming blush by pulling his lips taut. He wanted to be taken seriously; he couldn't be certain his surroundings were as positively heavenly as they appeared. He said, "Cool it, kid. I got grays in places you can't even see. Save me the flattery and explain to me where I am... and who you are... and the name you called me."

"Lightreacher? Your name? You want me to explain it?" the young man asked, amused.

Amero nodded, unsure if he was the one being toyed with.

The young man shrugged and patted Amero's forearm. "Of course, of course. I can explain. I didn't mean any offense. I was just surprised that... well... anyway, it's an honor to meet you. My name is Sam."

He reached a sun kissed hand out to Amero, offering it more in awe than greeting.

Amero accepted the familiar gesture. Sam's hand felt soft and yielded to Amero's grip with an ease that insinuated Sam had never worked a hard day in his life. Sam pumped out a handshake, brimming his white sand smile, and then let go reluctantly.

"The way I learned it," Sam began, jittering with excitement,

212

"was that you got the name Lightreacher for being the first person ever to travel at and beyond the speed of light. Isn't that right?"

Amero had no idea where to begin; Sam's statement spawned more questions than answers. "Okay, fine, let's go with it," Amero said. "But who are you? Did Dave send you?"

Sam offered a look of confusion.

"How did you learn about me?" Amero asked, attempting a different question.

"Learn about you?" Sam asked with genuine misunderstanding.

"I mean... you talk about me as if I'm well-known history," Amero explained.

Sam peered at Amero as if gauging him for how to respond best. "You've seriously never heard your own name before?" Sam asked.

"Apparently not," Amero said easily, happy to accept this minor mystery in light of the existential mire Dave had left him in before sending him to this beach, alluring as it might be.

"Everyone knows about you, Amero Lightreacher. Our patriarchs teach the young about you from a very early age. It is important to remember our origins and the history of our ancestors."

So, the people on this planet viewed Amero, and probably the rest of humanity, as ancestors. Even more surprising, Amero couldn't believe that he'd made it into the history books after all. So what if this planet wasn't Earth? Its origin stretched back to Earth eventually, didn't it? Where else?

"You view me as your ancestor? Are your patriarchs your leaders? What do your patriarchs say about me?" Amero asked, unable to stop at a single question. He was intrigued to witness the tone of light that history had cast him in.

"Our patriarchs are our elders, not leaders. We have no leaders, Amero, as we have no need for command, no dangers or hurdles to overcome, unlike your people. The patriarchs say great things about you, Amero Lightreacher. They say that you and the other Ancients were dissatisfied with an empty universe, so you filled it with life. They say it was you who designed the machinery necessary to achieve such an incredible feat. We aren't taught the specifics, just that the machine you made, the Great Pull, gave you and the other Ancients the ability to spread life."

"How?" Amero demanded, ignoring the inaccuracy of the mythology.

"How what?" Sam inquired innocently.

"How did they spread life? Did you learn that too?"

"No," Sam said, a look of consternation overtaking his ease. "We only learn the basics. We only really care about the basics." Sam's look of uncomfortable perplexity was suddenly replaced with a sheepish smile. "We have the beach, Mr. Lightreacher, and we have each other. Very few of us delve any deeper than that for meaning in life. The elders say that's the only real way to find happiness, and happiness is all we're really interested in finding." Sam patted Amero on the back. "Better to leave the complicated stuff to you and the rest of the Ancients, right?"

Sam eyed Amero, searching for some sign of approval, but Amero's blank stare offered no such thing. He felt as if he was still being played by someone or something. Was it possible this beautiful young man was in on the ploy? His disposition was closer to that of a child than to an adult. Was he even capable of conniving cleverness?

Amero found it odd that none of the other men were taking notice of him. His cotton, neutral color clothing was as out of place on the beach as a neon green sari worn to an Italian funeral. Everyone, including the women and children, were dressed in flamboyant colors of every hue. The fabric they wore was uniformly composed of a material so light that it revealed every curve and crevice of their bodies.

A wide grin from Sam helped dissipate a portion of the befuddling weight of confusion and paranoia clawing at Amero's insides. "Right this way, Mr. Lightreacher. I can take you home," Sam announced cheerfully.

"Home?" Amero inquired cautiously, breaking from his reverie.

Sam had already taken a few leisurely steps toward a cropping of palm trees swaying gently in the salt spray breeze. He turned his body to speak laterally in Amero's direction. "That's right. It's right this way, Mr. Lightreacher. It's really not that far. Just follow me."

Amero planted himself in position and crossed his arms. He wasn't ready to just roll over and follow this strange young man, beautiful as he was, into the unknown.

"Why are you helping me?" Amero asked bluntly. "You just stopped what you were doing on the beach and chose to give me a hand? Why you? Why didn't someone else stop to help?"

"That's a loaded question," Sam reasoned. "No one else stopped to help you because they observed that you were already being helped by me. I stopped to help you because I saw that you required help. It's not every day that Amero Lightreacher appears on our beaches, is it?"

"Still," Amero pressed, "if I'm so famous, then why aren't the others stopping to get my autograph or take a picture with me? It's as if I'm invisible to everyone except you, so what's the deal?"

Sam hesitated, appearing genuinely unsure how to answer Amero satisfactorily. "I helped," he began, "so there's no reason for the others to help too. They just went on with their day. Any one of us would be honored to help you, but it isn't necessary that everyone helps you. You really only need one of us to show you the way home. Do you understand, Mr. Lightreacher?"

"No," Amero said, "not at all. Your explanation has more holes in it than the Undisputed Bible."

"Never heard of it," Sam responded easily, apparently not at all interested in discovering what it might be.

"Good," Amero said. "Just forget it, Sam. If you've never even heard its name, then I'd rather keep it that way. I appreciate your help. It's clearly going to take some time to get used to Paradise, that's all."

Sam nodded with visible relief, like a puppy content to satisfy its master.

"Lead the way," Amero told him, making a note of the questions that Sam either could not or would not answer.

Sam led Amero up a steady incline of increasingly dense rainforest. Amero couldn't place a name to any of it, but the trees and shrubs and even the insects looked familiar--certainly not worthy of being called alien life forms. As far as Amero could tell, he was back on Earth, maybe on Hawaii or some other Pacific island. No, what was he thinking? Amero scolded himself inwardly for even considering that this paradise could be Earth. If this was Earth, then where was the New Covenant? Why were there so many beautiful men on the beach staring openly at each other with come-hither stares rather than chasing women with two left feet and dead-fish tongues? This wasn't Earth. This was the planet Dave said he and the machines had prepared for him. But where was Dave, and where were the machines?

Amero tried to keep up with Sam, but his muscles weren't as strong as they had been the last time Amero had breathed real atmosphere.

"Wait up, kid," Amero said, entranced by the young man's youth while at the same time reminded of his own age with greater insistence than at any other moment in his life. "I need a breather. This old body can't keep up with that Adonis-suit you got on."

A look of confusion replaced Sam's innocent smile as he ran his hands across his exposed, well-honed chest and belly. "I'm not wearing a suit, Mr. Lightreacher. All I've got on are these trousers." As proof, Sam pinched the light silk material covering his lower body. The material left nothing at all to the imagination.

Was Sam dense or just innocently ignorant? Amero scolded himself once more, this time for being so critical. Wasn't it possible that Sam was just here to help?

"It was just a joke, Sam. Sorry, I didn't mean to confuse you," Amero offered jovially.

"No!" Sam squeaked. "No, please don't apologize. Please! Especially not to me!" Frantically, Sam inspected each direction of their surroundings as if expecting someone to pop out of the lush, jade forest at any moment.

"Is everything alright, Sam?" Amero asked, darting a few quick glances over each shoulder.

Sam shook off his apparent worry and returned to his mellow, carefree innocence. "It's nothing, Mr. Lightreacher. I just want to make sure you're happy. There's really no need for apologies around here, unless of course it brings you joy to apologize to others; then by all means, apologize as much as possible. I hope you will just relax. Let me do the apologizing, okay? You're Amero Lightreacher, for Covenant's sake!"

Amero was lifted off his feet by a sudden, intense rush of vertigo. He caught himself on the trunk of a thick palm that had grown horizontally when it was young so that now the first dozen feet of its trunk acted as a bench. Amero sat and exhausted a roar of sorrowful breath.

"Say it again, kid. Say what you just said again," Amero crowed, his voice an odd accent to the boisterous humming and buzzing and hissing of the forest.

"It's okay to apologize; it just isn't necessary. That's all I meant to explain, Mr. Lightreacher," Sam told him, voice quavering and full of regret.

Amero felt the weight that had been lifted off his shoulders upon arriving on the beach-planet return around his neck at quadruple the load.

"Not that," Amero said. "That doesn't matter, Sam. You said, *covenant.* You're talking about the New Covenant. They're on this planet, aren't they?"

Sam's expression was a mix of bafflement and excitement.

"Wait--you know where that expression comes from? I always wondered about that. Everyone says it, and it seems like we've always said it. What does it mean?" Sam asked eagerly with childlike curiosity.

Amero couldn't be sure if Sam was putting on an act. With a quick twist, Amero glanced about to make sure they were alone.

"You don't know, then?" Amero asked conspiratorially.

Sam sank, looking suddenly disappointed that Amero appeared equally ignorant of the phrase's meaning. "Know the origins of the expression? I'm not sure anyone does, actually. Except Yang the Wizard, of course, but he knows everything. I've never even thought about asking him where the expression comes from. That's a good one! I can't believe I never considered it until you brought it up, Mr. Lightreacher. Thank you! When I meet him... one day... I will make sure to ask him."

The "Lightreacher" title was getting on Amero's nerves.

"Do me a favor, Sam. Call me Amero. No more of that Lightreacher nonsense."

Sam looked horrified. "Have I... offended you, Mister... I mean...

Amero?"

"Not at all," Amero said. "It's just a mouthful."

Sam shook his head and said, "It is a pleasure to use your proper title, Amero. However, I will refer to you any way you wish, of course."

Amero shrugged in apparent defeat. "Let's get back to what you said before," Amero said, interrupting Sam as he was about to say more. "You mentioned a person named Yang the Wizard. That's a joke, right? Or just a metaphor? A wizard? Don't tell me this is Oz."

Sam shrugged in return. "Never heard of Oz, but as for Yang, he's a wise old man. He's not like the rest of us. He's strange, and he keeps to himself, and there was never anything anyone ever asked him that he didn't know."

Amero was reminded of the wizened old man who had turned out to be Dave.

"This wizard," Amero inquired, "he wouldn't happen to be a digital image that lives inside a computer, would he?"

Sam gave another perplexed cock of his head and then burst into polite laughter. "I can't tell when you're joking, Mr. Lightreacher... Amero, I mean. You've quite the sense of humor."

Amero wondered what the young man's angle could possibly be. He was a beautiful adult-child on a planet that was not Earth, and he was detailing to Amero the habits of a wizard living on an island paradise world whose homosexual natives handed down mythologies centered around Amero's journey in space. Was an accurate assessment of his motives even feasible considering his exoticness?

"Forget it," Amero grumbled sadly. "Just take me home... whatever that means."

Sam's features sank; he was clearly disheartened by Amero's discontentment. Sam looked as though he wanted to say more, but he was more keen on satisfying Amero's wishes, so he turned and continued down the path.

CHAPTER 18

T he trek remained just as difficult as the pair progressed steadily higher in elevation. Massive palm trees with trunks the color of ash littered the skyline; blue-hued, elegant ferns grew in spectacularly varied arrays at the base of each tree. Each palm and its respective ferns looked like a single, distinct organism. Dispersed between the ferns was a low-lying tangle of bedded grass as soft as moss. Though the grass grew in individual blades, its matted nature ensured that each blade's point was woven horizontally, as if its very purpose was to be laid upon. Amero bent to smell the soft grass and noted tones of lavender and vanilla.

"Does all the plant life smell so sweet?" Amero asked Sam.

"Deep in the jungles, there are a few species that exude a stench like rotting flesh; at least, that's what we are told the smell resembles. Flesh does not rot on our world, so I can't say I know what rotting flesh actually smells like. The patriarchs say it's good to take pilgrimages to these plants so that we may appreciate the sweetness of the world all the more."

Amero put his hands on his hips. What was Sam getting at now? "What do you mean flesh doesn't rot? Things don't die here?"

Sam's forced smile did little to coat his sudden display of fear at Amero's mention of death. "Things die, of course," Sam wavered. "There's no way around that. But things don't have to rot. When death comes... if it comes... the world consumes the dead completely in one gulp."

Amero wondered if the boy was using the words of some religion he was a part of. He was speaking in metaphor, surely. Was it the New Covenant? Or maybe some far-flung, equally miserable derivative?

"*If* death comes?" Amero asked.

Sam nodded simply.

"Well?" Amero urged.

Sam shrugged. "Well what?" he asked innocently.

Amero pointed a rough finger at the young man.

"*If* death comes? You know perfectly what I mean."

Sam pointed to himself and then looked around as if some other native might be hiding behind one of the giant palm trunks.

"Yes, Sam, obviously I'm asking you," Amero said.

Sam looked incredibly nervous, inspecting each direction as if expecting someone to appear. "I'm sorry, Amero, I didn't mean to anger you."

Amero gave a painful sigh and retracted his pointed finger. What was the point of getting angry with this kid? Even if he was withholding information or trying to trick Amero, it's not like he would let up the act. On the other hand, if he really was as innocent as he appeared, then Amero was being unnecessarily rude.

"I'm not mad at you, Sam. I'm the one that should be sorry. I'm just... just tired, that's all."

A great roar, explicitly vicious and sounding as if it originated from some enormous, man-eating beast, suddenly filled the forest and sent Amero ducking for cover. Sam didn't even flinch.

"What is it?" Amero demanded.

Sam smiled serenely and asked, "What are you so afraid of?"

"Getting eaten!" Amero shot back.

Sam laughed obnoxiously, holding nothing back for politeness. "By a... eaten by a..." Sam howled with laughter, doubled over, unable to speak.

"Very funny," Amero said in no mood for humor.

Sam snapped like a bear trap, suddenly still and silent, probably worried he had offended Amero.

"What the hell made that noise?" Amero asked.

"A mock-mock. A little bird. It feeds on those small, purple sprouts that shoot up from the tangle-grass. Mock-mocks love mimicking the sounds they hear."

"Then what the hell is it mimicking?" Amero said, unsure

whether to run or adopt Sam's state of calm.

"Yang, probably. He performs some of his experiments around these parts. I'm sure he'll stay out of your hair, though. He likes to keep to himself—only appears when we need him most, after an unforeseen accident and such. Sometimes we go on little adventures into the forests to try and find him, and some even claim to have found his home, but those are just tales. No one knows where he lives, and he likes to keep it that way."

Amero was growing increasingly concerned about this so-called wizard.

"Tell me about Yang then. If I'm to live in the areas of the forest where he performs his... experiments... I'd like to know what I'm getting myself into," Amero said.

Sam rolled his head in disappointment. "I've spent my whole life on Seraphim, and still, I've never even glimpsed him. My theory is that no one has. The ones that claim to meet him are, wouldn't you know it, always the same ones that exaggerate their stories to the enjoyment of their audience. People want to believe themselves special, and so they convince themselves that every minor rustle they hear or movement they see in the shadows is evidence of Yang. I think it's just fun for them to imagine that they actually experienced something monumentally special. I have to admit: I've convinced myself a few too many times throughout my life that I've seen him, but if I'm to be honest, each instance could just as easily have been a trick of the eye. Then again, there are men and women that go into the forest seeking answers to impossible questions—I've met them myself--and many of them come back with those very answers. Who else but Yang could enlighten them in such a way?"

Sam went silent because it was obvious that Amero was no longer paying attention to him. Amero stopped listening to Sam the moment he uttered that word that Amero could not have imagined he would ever hear again. *Seraphim*. Was it just a word on this planet? Was it just tradition, like Sam's knowledge and use of the word *Covenant* as a replacement for a phrase that conventionally referred to God?

Amero spoke slow and sternly. "You say you've spent your whole life on Seraphim. What do you mean?"

Sam smiled and raised his arms as if greeting a welcomed guest. "I've never left the planet. I was born here, and I've lived here my whole life. There are so many Seraphimers nowadays flying into space for weekend jaunts, which is great for them. I've nothing against people that want to make a little extra here and there, but some people really obsess over collecting. Women are the biggest abusers, but I really can't blame them. They have it hard, I mean, harder than men. There's so few of them, and so few men that find them attractive, preferring men instead, of course. But there are enough men willing to mate with them, enough that feel sorry for them or are just imbued with some mutation that convinces them procreation is necessary. Who knows, really? All I know is that life goes on. The few of us that die and return to Seraphim each century are replaced by the few that are born each century. The world has its ways, right?"

Sam spoke matter-of-factly; clearly all of this information was commonplace for him. He seemed happy to explain it all to Amero, but not excited or enthusiastic, the same way a farmer might describe the makeup of his soil. It was just information to him, simple everyday information. Amero recognized this, and it made the content of what he was explaining that much harder to accept literally.

"This world is called Seraphim?" Amero checked, the tone of his voice insinuating there were more questions to come.

Sam nodded.

"And this world called Seraphim," Amero went on, "who gave it that name? Was it Yang?"

Sam smiled, incorrectly discerning that Amero was making a joke. Amero's seriousness did eventually hit Sam, however, and the young man shook his head. "Who knows? You're asking me who named the world? Maybe one of the eldest patriarchs knows. They've been around almost since the beginning, though their brains were not entirely developed during the beginning phases of civilization, so I'm not sure how much they can remember from so long ago. I myself am only half a millennium old—an infant compared to the Epochers. I still know a thing or two, though," Sam said with an overly friendly grin. He moved toward Amero, expecting Amero to laugh with him, but found Amero to be as immovable and immutable as marble.

Sam considered half a millennium to be a short amount of time. How was that possible?

"How long is a year on Seraphim?" Amero asked.

"Three hundred sixty-five days," Sam answered, this time with the enthusiasm of a child being quizzed. "And one-quarter day," Sam added, pleased with himself.

"Every fourth year is a leap year," Amero and Sam said in unison.

Sam jumped back with the surprise of witnessing a magic trick for the first time.

"Very good, Amero! How did you know?" Sam asked eagerly.

Amero looked disgusted. "And your day is twenty-four hours and each hour is sixty minutes and each minute is sixty seconds and you speak English and everyone is beautiful and almost everyone is gay."

Sam cocked his head, unsure if he should be impressed or disturbed.

"Never mind," Amero said dismissively yet pleasantly, then reasoned with himself inwardly that he should have expected this. Dave said this world was prepared for him. It was familiar in many respects so as to provide the comfort of convenience, and it was also both exotic and tempting enough to keep Amero infatuated with his surroundings. Still, the machines could have come up with a better name for the planet. Amero never wanted to hear that name, among a particular couple of other names, ever again.

"So, when you said 'if death comes,' you weren't kidding? Don't your people grow old and die?" Amero wondered.

"I am familiar with the concept of physical aging; it occurs in all the flora and fauna of the oceans and beaches and forests, but for us, for people, it doesn't happen. It's the air, you see; Seraphim keeps us young and healthy."

"Do you know how?" Amero asked.

Sam shook his head no. "If you ever meet him, make sure to ask Yang," Sam said with subtle, but genuine hope that a chance encounter might come true.

The pair continued on. Amero wanted to ask Sam more questions, but he feared that his questions were not being adequately answered, or worse, that he was inadvertently being told outright lies. He no longer seriously doubted Sam's innocence—the five-hundred-year-old boy didn't appear capable of willfully harming a piece of fruit—but his answers were never complete. Conversing with him was like attempting to complete a jigsaw puzzle with a sizable portion of the pieces missing—more frustrating than satisfactory. So, they walked mostly in silence, and Amero absorbed the sounds of his new island-paradise home.

After another ten minutes of walking, they approached a small outcropping of the forest atop a large, plateaued area midway up the first major incline of the mountain. The afternoon sun glittered gold through the amber and viridescent leaves of the trees. Insects buzzed and other creatures croaked in the canopies and undergrowth of the forest. Songbirds and mock-mocks inserted their melodies and strange wizard sounds into the gentle, tropical gusts of forest air. The music and jarring noises of the birds lent the entire scene an eerie feeling that could only be described as exotic familiarity. Amero felt overwhelming déjà vu; he was certain he had been here before.

A few feet inward from the walls of the dense forest, stone-fruit and citrus trees laden with perfectly ripe fruit dotted each side of a meter-wide pathway, leading to a large, elegant wood cabin rising at least four stories high--an entire story above even the tallest trees. A welcome mat had been laid at the foot of the door. It read: *Home is Where the Heart is.*

Sam rushed to the front door of the cabin and spread his arms wide with incredible elation. "Welcome home, Amero Lightreacher! It's all yours!"

Sam reminded Amero of a game show presenter; his grin was so wide and gleaming that it made it almost impossible not to assume there was some bigger game at work beyond the show Amero was being granted access to.

"What's the catch?" Amero said with brazen skepticism, knowing there had to be at least one.

The delight adhered to Sam's smile didn't let up. "There's no catch, Amero. This abode was prepared for you centuries ago and has been maintained to perfection ever since. Your precise time of arrival was unknown, so we had to prepare it in advance so that it would be ready for whenever you arrived on Seraphim."

"You and your people have been waiting for me for hundreds of years?" Amero asked, unsure if he should feel grateful or disturbed.

Sam pivoted his head back and forth, weighing his words carefully. "Not exactly waiting," Sam explained, "just aware of your future presence. We are honored to share this world with you."

The praise was daunting in its profundity, and Amero was unsure how to adequately respond without adopting a gloating or boastful air.

"It's a pleasure to be here, Sam," Amero began hesitantly. "So far," he said more confidently, "this is the greatest place I've ever been. Thank you for showing me to my quarters."

Sam grimaced. "You make it sound so dreary. It's not your quarters; it's your home. The fruit that grows on those fruit trees is your fruit. The light that shines upon this grove is your light. Do you understand, Amero? This is all yours," Sam smiled provocatively, then added, "though I do hope you feel inclined to share it."

Sam coupled his seductive smile with an outstretched hand. It was obvious, however, that Amero was either uninterested or not in the mood to reciprocate. Sam retracted his hand, looking ashamed.

"I'm sorry," Sam offered, retracing his steps back to Amero before lowering himself onto his knees. "I thought you might be as attracted to me as I am to you. I didn't mean any offense. Please forgive me." Sam bowed and did not stop lowering himself at the waist until his forehead met the soft mat of tangle-grass blanketing the ground Amero stood upon.

It was painful for Amero to watch Sam treat him as if he were some God to be satisfied.

"The only thing you have to be sorry for is prostrating yourself like this, kid," Amero said. "Save that kind of exultation for your island-wizard, no?" Amero was half-joking, but Sam interpreted the statement with absolute seriousness.

"You're right," Sam said, rising to his feet while still bowing his head as if to prolong the apology for as long as possible. "I hope I haven't disappointed you, Amero Lightreacher."

Before Amero could respond, his attention was captured by a

225

peculiar sound coming from somewhere off to the right. Amero gazed beyond the wall of forest, deep within the lush, jade tangles of growth. The sound, vague and distant, filled Amero with overwhelming foreboding.

"Did you hear that?" Amero asked with visible concern, probing in the direction he believed the sound had originated.

Sam made a show of trying to hear the same sound and then made another show of looking rather defeated. "I don't hear anything other than the natural sounds of the forest. Maybe you're just --"

"Shhhh!" Amero sprayed, interrupting Sam.

There it was again. It sounded like someone was mumbling to themselves in the distance. The voice was low and eerily familiar.

"You don't hear that?" Amero asked forcefully. "It's like someone is talking under their breath."

"Maybe someone's going for a hike," Sam reasoned levelly, "or maybe it's a mock-mock that stumbled too close to the shore and memorized a few lines of human speech. You've nothing to be nervous about, Amero. Nothing in these forests can hurt you. Nothing in these forests wants to hurt you, for that matter. This is an utterly peaceful world. You can let down your guard. I promise."

Amero wanted to believe Sam, but the soft mumbling in the distance was all he could focus his thoughts on. Why was it bothering him so much? Why did the sound fill him with such dread and anxiousness in equal measure?

"Come on," Amero said. "I want to go find out what that noise is."

Sam looked dejected and said, "You've nothing to worry about. It's just the forest you're hearing, and you'll have to get used to that. Why don't we head inside first?" Sam pointed to the cabin. "You can get settled, take a hot shower, eat some food, and be back on the beach, ready for a swim and anything else you desire, all before enjoying the universe's most beautiful sunset."

Amero wasn't about to argue against any bit of what Sam was offering, but he couldn't get the sound out of his head.

"That sounds lovely," Amero said, then added for Sam's own reassurance, "really, it does. I just want to see what that noise is first. I don't know what it is, Sam; it's like I have to. It's like the sound is demanding that I investigate it. I... I can't explain it."

"Amero, please," Sam said pleasantly, though this time with a subtle, demanding force that Amero didn't think was possible for the young man to exert, "let's go inside first and get you comfortable. There's more I'd like to show you."

Sam's insistence did nothing to put Amero at ease.

"I want to check out that noise first, Sam. Then I'll go inside, okay?"

Sam shook his head no. "We have to go inside first, Amero. Come on." Sam gripped Amero's forearm gently, but Amero pulled away.

"Wait here if you want, but I'm going to see where that noise is coming from," Amero said resolutely.

Sam shook his head no again, this time with greater robustness. "You can't, Amero. You shouldn't. Please, just go inside first, okay?"

The young man was visibly irked, looking as if he might burst into tears if Amero didn't abide by his wishes. Amero was perturbed by Sam's desperation. He backed away, slowly at first, but within a few strides he was running at full sprint toward the forest.

"Please, Amero Lightreacher! Please wait!" Sam called after him.

Amero glanced back, expecting to see Sam bounding toward him with his muscular, youthful legs. Instead, Sam was locked in place, shouting at Amero but unwilling or unable to give chase.

The immense trunk of a gargantuan, ashen-hued palm blocked Amero's path, but he found no difficulty hurtling over it. Sprinting made Amero feel young again, and he was astonished to realize that the aches and pains in his joints were no longer at the forefront of conscious experience.

"Amero!" Sam shouted again, his voice almost fully eclipsed by the cacophony of forest life.

Moving faster and faster, slapping brush and vines aside as he ran, Amero felt incredible. His knees didn't crack each time he planted a foot on the ground, and each breath was plentiful and refreshing.

The jungle grew thicker with each stride, and after a short distance, Amero stopped and turned to see if Sam was following. Though Sam was nowhere to be seen, Amero softened his steps, doing his best to disguise his presence.

Sam's sudden change in behavior prompted Amero to reexamine Sam's little bursts of paranoia during their walk. Sam had grabbed his arm almost as if he was afraid, and then he insisted they go inside. What did Sam really want? Maybe there was no one in the universe without a hidden agenda.

A low murmur could be heard coming from the dense undergrowth to Amero's right. He felt certain it was the same voice that had caught his attention back at the cabin.

The tangles of brush proved a surprisingly simple task to wade through. A gentle push was more than enough to direct even the most water-heavy fronds out of his path. After several meters of feeling as though the plant life might completely envelop him, Amero found himself in a small clearing no larger than a few square feet in size. Three walls of impenetrable forest converging at unnatural, ninety-degree corners barred Amero's route. Each wall rose at least twelve feet high, blocking all visibility except for a square window of sky directly above. When Amero turned to backtrack, a fourth wall grew to block him.

Amero attempted to pull one of the walls apart, but it was as thick as tangle-grass. He had walked right into a trap.

Suddenly, from above, Amero heard a flapping of wings. A small bird, no bigger than Amero's fist, fluttered over the walls of jungle, flying in circles so that it appeared and disappeared above him every other second. The bird was murmuring something in English, something about returning. *A mock-mock*, Amero thought. He held still and tried to make out what it was saying. The bird was repeating itself as if on a loop, and its words paralyzed Amero.

"Find me. If there is a way, then find me. Return to me. Find me. If there is a way, then find me. Return to me. Find me. If there is a way, then find me. Return to me. Find me. If there is a way, then find me. Return to me."

"How?" Amero croaked as he backed himself stiffly into a corner.

The mock-mock was speaking louder now, its voice crescendo-

228

ing into a shout across the wilderness. The voice was unmistakable: it was Amero's.

"Find me. If there is a way, then find me. Return to me," the mock-mock chanted. Without warning, the mock-mock dove inside Amero's living cage, aiming directly for his upturned face.

Amero wanted to hide his eyes or at least use his arms to bat the creature away, but he was altogether turned to stone, for as the bird descended, its tiny, feather framed face came into focus. It was Hann's face.

The Hann-masked bird screeched its words and cut the air, drawing only inches away from Amero's forehead. Suddenly the ground buckled, and Amero found himself in free fall. The mock-mock did not follow Amero down into the unlit underground of Seraphim, choosing instead to flap lazily above and shriek unfathomable words through the face of a ghost.

Amero plummeted helplessly into the darkness. The square patch of light faded away along with the mock-mock and its nightmarish, ominous prognostications. Pitch blackness enveloped Amero, and he fell at terminal velocity, his body flailing like a ragdoll; he felt ligaments snap and the bones of his limbs splinter against the combined force of gravity and rotational momentum. Not even an hour in paradise, and Amero was already saying goodbye.

CHAPTER 19

The snapping and crunching of bone and cartilage resonated against the thick darkness. Despite the breaking of his body, all Amero felt was a dull pressure of uniform intensity emanating from every one of his cells. After a few moments, the pressure abated, and Amero found that he was entirely free of aches and pains. Wherever he was now, stasis wasn't necessary for rapid regeneration. It was like Sam said: the air itself could heal.

Amero's descent slowed, and he came to a gradual halt deep within the darkness. "Hey! Anyone!" Amero called out, but there was no answer.

Weightlessly suspended in midair, Amero twisted his wrists and kicked his legs, analyzing his body for sore spots or bruises. He couldn't be certain, but it seemed as if his muscles were leaner, as if he had suddenly adopted a young man's body. Further investigation revealed that the hair on his forearms was less coarse, and his knees didn't crack at all when he bent them.

Something touched the sole of Amero's boot. He seized his knees to his chest only to realize that it was a solid surface. Cautiously, Amero released his legs and took a few steps forward onto flat ground. Dizziness was inevitable in the directionless darkness, but just when Amero felt that he might fall over, the booming flip of some distant switch illuminated the ground directly around Amero with spot-lit precision. Amero lifted his gaze and attempted to discover the light's source, but the spotlight was far too bright and the shadows far too abundant for Amero to see anything outside the column of enveloping brightness.

Fwump!

A slam of metal on metal opened another spotlight a dozen or so feet further down a newly revealed pathway through the darkness. Amero stepped into the pitch black and tried again to see the light's origin, this time at an angle that wouldn't blind him. As far as Amero could tell, the light had no real source, no metal casing or bulb from which it was emanating. Each column of light began as a levitating sphere of tamed photons a hundred feet overhead. Those same photons were directed downward with incredible precision by some unknown means. Either the spotlight technology was an incredible illusion, or its creator had invented a way to bend and direct photons at will.

Fwump! Fwump! Fwump!

Following a straight line, a third sphere of light winked into existence, then a fourth, and then a fifth. The columns illuminated a pathway no wider than Amero's arm span. Amero glanced behind himself and found that more pitch darkness barred any real examination. He had no choice but to move forward and meet whoever it was that had set the jungle wall trap, plunging him feet first into the planet's cavernous interior. Was it Yang? Amero doubted that any being capable of such technology could possibly give more than a passing glance Amero's way, let alone invite him into his abode, but who else or what else could be responsible? *Could this be the machines' doing?* Amero wondered. *Or even…the New Covenant?*

Amero would have his answer sooner than expected; a ghostly silhouette of a figure glided toward him down the spot-lit path. Each column of light afforded Amero an ephemeral examination of the approaching figure, and with each step, Amero felt less and less able to accept what he saw. The figure wore a flowing robe of sunset-magenta accented at its tips by a brilliant amethyst that did nothing to assuage a flamboyant grin and a shimmering, opalescent shock of hair standing stiffly in the air. Woven inside and outside the robe, golden cloudbursts exploded in swirling filigree patterns. Sandals fashioned of an unknown material silenced each of the figure's steps to a spectrally elegant whisper.

If this was Yang, he was anything but old. His skin, golden like the robe's cloudbursts, was as flawless as polished diamond and equally sparkling. The approaching man literally shimmered beneath the columns of light with an incredible, angelic glow. He was far more beautiful than he was handsome. In fact, he was breathtaking; his mere presence severed Amero's ability to speak.

"Cat got your tongue?" the man boomed from afar with super-natural resonance. His voice was like Gregorian chanting trans-formed into speech. The man smiled, and each of his teeth shone as if of its own accord. "That is the expression, isn't it?" the man asked with genuine amusement.

Amero nodded, unsure if this shimmering creature meant him harm. Could those eyes, full and azure as the ocean, do anyone harm, though? If this *was* Yang, didn't Sam speak of him out of rev-erence... even awe?

"Are you the one they call Yang?" Amero asked cautiously.

Yang, only a few feet away now, offered a courtly bow as an af-firmative.

"You don't look old," Amero told him, unsure if he was being rude.

"Looks can be deceiving," Yang responded, smiling as if he was sharing a long-running inside joke with Amero.

A shift of Yang's hand to an inside fold of his robe produced a small mirror, which he offered to Amero through gliding move-ments executed with flawless precision. Even the subtlest twist of his arm made it seem like every one of his moves and gestures had been planned and practiced a thousand years in advance. Amero obliged, and out of habit he glanced at his own reflection. Though he certainly felt refreshed and full of vigor, Amero told himself it had to be an illusion, for the man he saw in the mirror looked no older than twenty.

"It's the air," Yang said, watching Amero's reaction with amusement. "The nano-machinery composing Seraphim's atmos-phere has undone a lifetime's worth of senescence; you are an old man no longer, Amero, nor do you ever have to be again... if that is what you wish."

The proposition sounded too good to be true.

"This planet reverses aging? What Sam said was true then? Peo-ple don't die naturally here?"

"Sam is one of the locals, yes?" Yang asked congenially as he calmly and deliberately intertwined each of his fingers and brought them to rest in front of his abdomen. "They are incapable of lying. They have never had any need for such a device outside of humor, and even then, they are quick to notify their audience of the prank. I'm sure whatever Sam told you was perfectly true to the extent that Sam understood it to be true."

Amero puzzled at Yang's statement. "So doesn't that mean he might unintentionally have lied to me?"

Yang nodded patiently and beamed a luminescent smile at Amero. "You are a remarkably skeptical individual, Amero Hiddiger, and rightfully so. The last decade of your life has consisted entirely of a series of half-truths and guesses, and before that, the society you were born into chose as its guiding principle the morally empty path of historical tradition rather than open compassion and dynamic empathy." Yang allowed a moment for the summation of Amero's past to sink in and then asked, "What if I told you it was all your own fault?"

"What's my fault?" Amero asked defensively. "You mean my life is my fault? As in, we are all responsible for our own lives?"

Yang closed his eyes and shook his head gently from side to side; for the first time, Amero noticed tiny, jeweled studs of rubies and emeralds and sapphires lining the inside curves of his golden ears and eyelids.

"Not at all. I mean that you are directly responsible for all of it," Yang corrected pleasantly. "The Points. The collection of the Points. The dismantling and reconstitution of humanity and the Earth into the Points. This very planet on which you and I currently reside. All of it, Amero."

Amero felt suddenly paralyzed by the prospect Yang was offering. Amero didn't want to be a victim of some far-reaching fate, nor did he want to be the tool of apparently higher powers. However, even if Yang didn't mean him direct harm, Amero simply wasn't sure he was ready to jump further down the rabbit hole with Yang. Maybe falling into the caves was already too far.

Amero felt the urge to leave the caves suddenly, and he told himself he could live with immortality in paradise; he could say goodbye to Earth and everything he'd ever known if it meant escaping the New Covenant's reign both physically and mentally. Amero conceded to himself there was always the possibility that Yang could help him understand the full story behind the events that took place after the Pull, but did it really matter anymore? Maybe Yang was just a very long-lived local or maybe he was from another planet or even another universe. No matter, it was simply all too much right now, and though Amero knew there would come a time when he would desire every answer, at the moment, he just wanted the cabin and the beach and maybe even Sam's company. He wondered if Sam would forgive him for acting so rudely.

"Fine. It's all my fault," Amero said genuinely, willfully resigning himself to whatever truth Yang and all of life had in store for him. "But then it's Jakob's fault too, and Dave and the New Covenant and all of humanity's fault. It's everyone's fault, right?" Amero reasoned uneasily. He was certain now that he wanted to just return to the beach and wait for the copy of Dave to meet up with him as he promised he would. Yang the Wizard would simply have to wait. "I think I made a mistake coming here. I should return to the beach. Strange as it sounds, I'm waiting for someone."

Amero waited for Yang's response and gulped down the possibility that he may have offended him.

"You want to leave already?" Yang said with playful, mock anguish. "Don't you want to say hello to David and Jakob, or rather Hann, as you knew him?"

Amero's heart skipped a beat, and he suddenly felt weak.

"He's here? He's alive? Hann... I mean Jakob is here?"

Yang grinned with complete satisfaction and bowed a few degrees at the hip.

Was it possible? Of course it was. Amero had been saved, so why not Jakob?

"Dave told me Jakob died on the moon," Amero reasoned with uncertainty, and he nearly kicked himself for not delving further into the matter with the Dave-image when he had the chance.

Yang raised a hand, and a frameless projection appeared, hovering in the darkness beside them. It showed a recording of Amero talking to the Dave-image on the ship Seraphim. The recording was filmed from behind Amero's back, and Amero couldn't help but glance behind himself, checking for more hidden cameras.

"It's the air," Yang said as if attempting to reassure him. "The machines record and have always recorded every moment of existence."

Amero felt as if he'd been penetrated without permission.

"What do you want?" Amero demanded, feeling suddenly fearful of Yang and his knowledge of the machines and of Amero's life.

"Watch," Yang told him evenly.

From the projection, Amero heard the Dave-image say for the second time, "*Hann is no longer with us.*"

Amero turned and faced the technicolor man.

"Dave never said he was dead," Yang explained. "That was your assumption."

"An assumption that the Dave-image failed to correct!" Amero noted sourly.

Yang nodded with patient understanding. "Dave didn't know whether or not Jakob was gone for good. Not right away. He was concerned with only the matter of whether or not you could forgive Jakob."

"According to Dave," Amero said, caught off guard by the incredible specificity of Dave's supposed concern, "his plans were a hell of a lot loftier than that. Why should my forgiveness matter so much to him?"

"Because your answer meant the difference between the perpetuation of existence and the cessation of all being," Yang explained sincerely.

Amero wasn't sure whether to laugh or scoff at what he assumed were the hyperbolic words of a being that had lived far too long.

"I chose to forgive Jakob, and we still exist, so does that mean forgiveness was the right answer?" Amero asked, attempting to decipher Yang's crypticness.

"Never confuse linearity with causality, Amero. Forgiveness is important, but it isn't the whole of your decision one way or the other. Forgiveness is the reason we are here talking to one another, but you have yet to decide the fate of existence."

"Good to know," Amero said, unsure how to respond to his role as the decider of fate.

Yang twirled around and began gliding down the path from where he originally came. "Follow me, Amero, and I will show you to your friend and partner. They are at the end of this pathway. As we walk, I would like to show you something you may be interested in witnessing."

Amero forced himself cautiously forward alongside Yang and watched as the first projection disappeared with a snap of Yang's fingers. It was replaced by another floating projection that steadied itself at a measured distance and height a few feet from Amero's face. The projection revealed Jakob, wild-eyed on the unnamed moon just moments after murdering Amero. The image centered on Jakob as he stared at the rock-hop in seeming disbelief as it ascended back to Seraphim without him.

"Jakob was not merely crazed. He had a purpose in murdering you, Amero, and he knew that you would be perfectly fine, no matter how badly he hurt you," Yang explained, and his voice, like a bassoon ballad played at the lowest possible register, pierced the enveloping darkness.

Jakob sauntered aimlessly, a few steps left, a few steps right. The image zoomed in further, and Amero could see that Jakob was fighting back tears through a pain-taut smile.

"I'm sorry, Amero," Jakob crowed aloud. "You were just another pawn after all." Then, with absolute verisimilitude, Jakob bellowed in anguish and fell to his knees.

"I hope you find a way out, Amero. I really do," Jakob said, eyes directed at Seraphim above. With both hands, Jakob lifted a small, oblong rock the size of a grapefruit. He shuffled it in his hands, testing it and gripping it at several angles. Then, satisfied, he slammed the rock against his faceplate, not once, but twice. The first hit splintered the material into fine, webbed partitions, and the second hit shattered it into a thousand fragments. It made Amero think of the Earth exploding into Points.

Jakob suffocated on void, but he didn't protest his end. On the contrary, he submitted willingly to death's hold.

Amero shuddered at the vivid, false memories of his suicide as Jakob. Was this Jakob's own way out? *Out of what?* Amero wondered. *Life?*

"You see," Yang began pleasantly, seeming to ignore the suicide that had just taken place before their eyes, "your death was Jakob's last resort."

"Last resort for what?" Amero gawked, horrified by the still-image of Jakob's lifeless, bulging face.

"His last resort to confirm the truth regarding your identity, Amero."

Yang snapped the projection out of existence, but Jakob's dead stare was burnt permanently into Amero's mind. Yang said Jakob was still alive, so the machines must have revived Jakob like they did Amero. Amero wondered if Jakob had also yearned to know why any of this was necessary, including their own continued lives.

"My identity?" Amero began nervously, remembering how Jakob had suddenly demanded that Amero admit who he really was at the end. "Am I not who I believe myself to be? Am I another Hann-Jakob situation?"

"Not at all," Yang assured him, "but you were still an unknown variable as far as Jakob was concerned." Yang shifted his gaze to one of genuine intrigue and said, "I am aware that you remained in contact with Dave while inside the singularity-stabilizer. What did he tell you regarding your role in being selected for the Pull?"

Was Yang about to tell Amero that Dave had lied to him? What if Yang was the one telling the lies? Amero knew there was no way to measure two unknowns against each other. He just wanted to do an about-face and find his own way back to the beach, but he couldn't pull himself away.

"Dave injected me with some kind of drug that showed me Jakob's past." Amero gulped down the pain of knowing he could never see Anna again. Then, with stabbing bitterness, he reminded himself that the pain belonged to Jakob and was not his own. "I saw everything--experienced everything. It was as if I *was* Jakob--no longer myself."

Yang gave a nod of approval. "Then you know that you were specifically named in the Message. It is no accident that you are here."

Amero shook his head. "But why me? I'm nothing special. Jakob I can understand; he made the machines, but why me?"

"I've already told you," Yang smiled. "You are to decide the fate of existence. Jakob did not and could not know that, of course, so he was left guessing at the reason."

Amero shook even more fervently. "Everyone keeps saying that. Jakob said it. Dave said it. And now you. Tell me what you mean, dammit! Tell me what any of this has to do with murdering me," Amero demanded. He wanted to know the truth regarding his future role, but more immediately he wanted to know how his death factored into everything.

Yang waved an arm, and a new image lit up the projection. An overhead view depicted Jakob's lifeless corpse laying on the moon. His faceplate was shattered. The vessels of his cheeks, eyes, and forehead were sanguine smears beneath marbled skin fractured by hemorrhaged blood. Despite the gore, for the first time ever, Jakob looked at peace. The image zoomed out by a few orders of magnitude so that Jakob's body was no more than a speck. A flash of silver spilled across the image, then left just as suddenly, taking Jakob's corpse with it.

"The machines... " Yang reflected with seeming disappointment, "came to collect their maker. The machines... those monstrous automatons that refuse to let death and entropy do their work."

"Monstrous automatons?" Amero echoed, surprised that even Yang despised them.

"That's right," Yang confirmed placidly. "They are the wardens of reality that refuse existence its natural end, and ultimately, its natural beginning. That is my theory, anyway... but we can return to that later."

Amero did not protest. Wild existential theories could wait. Amero wanted to know why Jakob chose to hide information from him, and ultimately, why Jakob resorted to murder.

"As I said," Yang continued, "you were an unknown and incalculable variable for Jakob. He reasoned that you were either somehow being used by the machines he had created only thirteen subjective years earlier or you were somehow working with them of your own accord. Jakob became unhinged because every day for him was a constant battle to remain calm in light of the possibility that your entire personality was all an act. Every time he got close to you--"

"He would push me away," Amero finished. "And I would push

right back. I wanted to be able to love him, but... " Amero raised an arm behind him, referencing where he had come from. "Every little thing Jakob did started to piss me off: the way he spoke; his endless, meandering theories; his seeming enjoyment of being marooned in a vacant pit of the galaxy. To top it off, he was the only man available for some million trillion miles... as it turns out... the only other man in the universe... at that time, I mean. I can't be with just one guy. My preferred scene is back on the beach... I'm a creature of... choices."

Yang let out a laugh full of age-old mirth, clutching his golden, sculpted abdominals as he rocked in place. For the first time, Amero caught a glimpse of the profound magnitude of time that Yang had thus far endured.

"That is perfectly understandable, Amero. Monogamy isn't for everyone. However, despite his rebellion against the New Covenant, it was a custom Jakob was intimately attached to. Of course, that's not why he murdered you."

As they walked side by side, radiant columns of light continued to spring, one by one, from new glowing spheres steadily popping into existence along the pathway.

"Jakob knew that if you really were innocent of the machines' plans--a mere human pawn--then the machines would save you from death at any cost. They had no choice, as protection of humanity was part of their central, still functioning protocols. On the other hand, if you were just another tool of the machines, you would be left to die and eventually recycled like the machines, who view themselves as expendable fragments of a single whole. Jakob had to know the truth, and when your suit died and no help came, he assumed the worst--that you had been working for the machines the entire time, that your entire life had been one great act to fool Jakob into the complacency of wasting the rest of his life on the Points. In the end, though, you were saved, and Jakob saw that his suspicions had been unfounded all along: you were not working with the machines; you were being worked by them just as he was. To what end, Jakob could not say."

Amero gulped uncomfortably, reminding himself that the air was apparently filled with hordes of tiny machines.

"What was Jakob so afraid of, though? You keep saying 'working with the machines.' Working to do what?" Amero asked.

"Did you learn why Jakob designed and launched the machines?"

Amero shrugged. "As far as I know, Jakob was forced to build the machines under the thumb of the New Covenant."

"That much is true," Yang conceded, "but no one ever told Jakob to give the machines the potential for self-awareness, nor did anyone tell Jakob to program the machines to break him out of the prison-labs. Jakob had considered the possibility that the machines had achieved sentience and were the senders of the Message, but your involvement meant that the machines were including others in their schemes. It meant that the machines had formulated plans of their own, outside of Jakob's directives, and for some reason those plans involved you, Amero."

"And the machines involved me... so that I can decide the fate of existence, right?" Amero checked with overt incredulity.

"That is correct," Yang explained with perfect seriousness. "Jakob was utterly suspicious of the machines, and of you, and for that reason he kept up an act to fool you and the machines into believing that he was utterly ignorant of the plot you had planned for him. There was no one in the universe he could trust, not even himself, for he was the one that set the machines upon existence in the first place. Jakob lost his mind because for the first time, Jakob felt naked, stupid, and alone. Life was a blundering fall from one unknown to the next, and he felt responsible for the disappearance of Earth and the death of his loved ones, as it was clearly the machines' doing and ultimately his own. When the machines finally confirmed that the Earth really had been turned into Points, Jakob cracked, and within a week, he concluded that he would have to kill you to know the truth for sure. It had to be a surprise, of course, as he couldn't allow you or the machines to take precautions against him."

Before Amero could respond, Yang gave another wave of his wrist. The projection flickered. This time it depicted Jakob standing at the viewport of a ship remarkably similar to Seraphim except it was larger and more angular about the hull. The image zoomed out to reveal that the ship was traveling through a field of shifting, naked-blue energy.

"A wormhole," Yang explained. "A casual walk in the park compared to the instantaneous transportation of a Pull."

Emptied into a new region of space, Jakob manually piloted the ship to the closest planet, performed some type of scan, and was off again, tunneling through another wormhole to some other celestial object.

"Day after day, year after year, decade after decade, until time lost all meaning—Jakob searched for you. He even dismantled an entire quarter-light-year-size station in an attempt to wrestle information from the machines, only to finally conclude that you were gone for good," Yang explained as if reading from written history. "Until one day, Jakob heard something in his dreams."

Yang gestured at the darkness above the spheres of light, and now Amero saw flying in the darkness a fluttering, talking bird.

"*Find me. If there is a way, then find me. Return to me. Find me. If there is a way, then find me. Return to me,*" a mock-mock squawked in a mutated version of Amero's voice.

Amero shook his head in protestation. "What does it mean? What is the significance of that statement, and why is it said in my voice? I heard the same thing when Dave sent me here from inside the black hole."

Yang peaked an eyebrow, looking genuinely intrigued.

"You heard it too? You heard yourself saying those words?"

"I think so. I think it was my own voice. I don't know... I... was bodiless at the time."

Amero was relieved to see Yang nodding with patient understanding.

"What does it mean?" Amero insisted. "How did Jakob hear me in his dreams?"

Yang offered Amero a genuine grin. "I don't know for sure, but it's incredibly exciting, isn't it?"

"Exciting?" Amero frowned. "I wasn't the one that said those words. I heard them too, but they were in my own voice. How is that possible?"

"I honestly don't know, Amero. It is a mystery beyond even myself. Regardless how it happened, Jakob was finally on your trail. He created another quantum computer with the hope of tracking you down across space and time via the machines' networks, but upon its completion, the computer was continuously flooded with a single message: *Find me. If there is a way, then find me. Return to me.* To Jakob, it meant that you had forgiven him after all, and that you were calling out to him somehow."

Yang came to a halt beneath a column of light serving as the pathway's terminal point. He walked ahead of Amero and then turned to face him. Amero was surprised to see that his eyes were wet with tears.

"I searched for so long, Amero, across ten thousand worlds and countless lifetimes. But now, here we are," Yang said with monumental relief. "I've finally found you, Amero, even if it has been four whole galactic rotations since we parted ways... still... I've finally found you."

Amero stood with his mouth stupidly agape. Was Yang insinuating that he had been searching for Amero alongside Jakob all this time? Or did he mean...

Yang grinned through glistening tears and held his arms wide in greeting. "It's me, Amero. Only it isn't. I was once Jakob, and I was also once Dave. Now I'm neither of those individuals. I'm both, and I'm also so much more."

Amero shook his head, speechless in the presence of the spectral, golden-bodied creature. "How?" Amero managed.

"A mixture of time, patience, and a willingness to try new things," Yang answered serenely.

Yang wrapped the robes tight to his body and then let go. Laying eyes on Yang's naked form, Amero felt a mixture of horror and awe. Every inch of his golden skin emitted the same radiant glow, and his chiseled chest and abs were sprinkled with a fine spray of the same opalescent hair that stood tall atop his head. Where genitals should have been, there was a rounded patch of particularly bright, golden light. He was like a walking, genderless, psychedelic trip.

"What are you?" Amero gasped, shuffling backward.

CHAPTER 20

W ith a flick of both Yang's wrists, a flurrying platoon of projections flickered into being. Each projection depicted
Jakob travelling to a unique celestial body then leaving and flying to
a new location across an endless assemblage of star systems. Each
projection was like a mirrored simulacrum of the rest, their content
repeating endlessly with only slight variations in stellar hue or planetary composition or background star formation.

"It is strange to think that I was once Jakob and that there was a
time when I wasn't also Dave. To think of those identities is like
stumbling upon half-remembered thoughts of being an infant--so
obscure and far away. One wonders: could I really have been something so brazenly naïve and meek at one time? Am I really the same
being?"

Amero was dumbfounded by the new information and could only stare at Yang.

"For many millennia," Yang said, gesturing to the projections
still displaying Jakob travelling aimlessly from rock to rock, "I
scoured the galaxy, searching for the world or station where they
might have taken you. I knew you were important to the machines
somehow... I knew they would not let you die, just as they would
not let me die. So, I clawed my way through space and time until
luck finally yielded to my persistence."

The projections flipped in unison to the same image. Jakob was
shown walking on a vacant beach identical to the one above
ground. A scattering of strange vegetation crowded the beach, bulky
and unyielding as prehistoric flora. Jakob happened upon a small,
silver sphere half-buried in the sand like a misplaced egg. He picked
it up and examined it, but he was unable to find any clues to its
origin. He must have felt a shock of some sort, because suddenly he
dropped it, activating it as it hit the ground. A beam of light lanced

out of the sphere and then spread out into a three-dimensional projection of Dave--milk-white beard and legs folded in lotus posture.

"The copy explained that Jakob finding him was no chance encounter," Yang said. "The copy had anticipated Jakob's arrival on the planet he named Terra, and he sent a copy of himself to the planet using the same Pull-technology he used to transport you into the galaxy's central singularity. In truth, I would have searched for you forever as Jakob, but you forgave me. That's the only reason that, as Dave, I sent a copy of myself to this planet, because you found it in yourself to grant Jakob forgiveness, Amero.

"Dave offered Jakob the bitter sanctuary of cold-storage as an alternative to living through the near billion years required to properly prepare Terra for you. I elected to remain awake, however, and quickly discovered that the passage of time is by far the most difficult reality of the universe to endure. There was more than enough work to occupy the years, of course. Especially after I transformed myself into what you see before you, I researched and I built and I collected Points. I studied them--opened them up and probed their design. What I found... "

"They're universes," Amero said, his voice cracking. "That's what Dave told me."

"Yes," Yang nodded patiently, "I know what I told you, what Dave told you. Most of what I told you was accurate, but there are a few points I was wrong about at the time. When you spoke to me as Dave, I had anticipated that the machines would fill the whole universe with life because that is what the causal-bender within the black hole revealed to me. However, I and the machines have very different plans for existence. Though it was their intention to impregnate the entire universe with life, I did not let them. There is no other life outside of this planet, Amero. The universe is still cold and lonely, save for this pocket of warmth, Terra, which I have renamed and rebuilt into the bionic, living planet Seraphim. Life outside this planet would only make the gathering of Points more time consuming. Besides, all this was only a gesture of gratitude on the machines' part. Maintaining life on a grand scale was never the machines' intention. The machines have only ever had two goals: the creation of the Points and the safekeeping of you and me, which I have deduced are tantamount to the same result."

Amero shook his head. How could he know who to believe anymore when he had never known for sure in the first place? If Yang's claims were true, in a way, this was Dave talking to Amero now, so wasn't this like Dave telling Amero to trust him, only filtered in parallel with Jakob's mind through a different body? Could such a being still be considered Dave, somehow, deep down inside?

Amero stammered in confusion. "You're Jakob...and also Dave. You... are both? You... "

Yang nodded with incredible patience. "After many years of solitude, Jakob recognized the necessity of transcending his physical body and the potential power resulting from the merging of his consciousness with Dave's digitally constructed consciousness. This golden body you see before you is nothing more than a device puppeted by my true self, which resides within the computer terminals and digital networks spanning every inch of the planet. I am the planet's nervous system, so to speak. I am Seraphim's mind and soul, and this body called Yang is my human mouthpiece."

The foundations of Amero's mind felt as stable as fresh mud. "You're just a robot controlled by Jakob and Dave's merged minds? Digital minds--machines--more and more machines," Amero gushed.

"No!" Yang assured him. "You're wrong, Amero. I am not a machine. In fact, I am even more alive than you are. I have scoured the physical universe, and I have scoured the digital universe. As a digital-human hybrid, I exist in both worlds simultaneously. I am beyond the limitations of Dave and even the limitations of Jakob. When I tell you something is true, I am sure of it. If I don't know the truth of something, I will tell you. I've no desire to trick you, Amero, nor do I have any desires in general for that matter. Except one."

Yang set his eyes upon Amero, and a fire blazed within the luminous being. "To destroy the machines that I created. To return the universe back to its original state, whatever it may be."

"The universe's original state? The Points are unnatural?" Amero checked.

"Of course," Yang concluded

"I mean," Amero said, correcting himself, "the universe was not always a fractaling assemblage of Points?"

Yang shook his head no. "It was us, Amero. We did it. It was the first Pull... somehow... that changed everything, rewrote existence like data overwritten on a hard drive of limited space. It wasn't always this way, Amero. Somehow, we created the Points, all of them."

"How could the Points be our fault, though? The Earth and humanity were turned into Points long after we were Pulled."

"Not after," Yang corrected, "but during. Besides, a Point existed before the Pull. The first Point--at least from our own perspective within our own universe."

"There was a first?" Amero asked, growing more confused.

Yang nodded and chose his words carefully. "From our own perspective, yes. The Point that Dave showed you at the center of the black hole—the Point we were born within and currently reside in—that was the first. It was already nestled within the black hole long before the machines arrived, though for how long is impossible to say."

"Doesn't that prove that it's not our fault? If the Point was in the black hole for that long, then it was there even before you or I were born. The Pull came after the machines entered the black hole, didn't it?"

"Of course, but don't confuse linearity--"

"With causality," Amero interrupted, finishing the now familiar alien adage.

Yang nodded, outwardly confirming the wisdom of this statement.

"I don't get it," Amero said, shaking his head with frustration.

Yang strode forward and gestured for Amero to follow. "Come. I have more to show you."

Amero followed Yang through an unlit doorway carved within a dark wall hidden by the shadow of the final light-column. They stepped through the doorway into a fog of more enveloping, pitch black darkness. Gradually, a hazy, alluring blue coalesced at the center of the darkness, inviting Amero forward.

"I would stop where you are if I were you," Yang told him.

Amero had to strain against his own will just to force himself to stop.

"What is it?" Amero asked.

Yang lowered his head and smiled broadly, as if attempting to hide his sudden display of emotion. "My masterpiece. It's a cross-causal singularity, like the one the machines created at the center of the black hole, only mine is far less stable."

Amero found it much easier to back a few steps away.

"I don't entirely know how the machines manufacture the Points, but this here is certainly part of the process. A few steps further is an area of vacuum kept stabilized by artificial gravity. Within the center of the vacuum is a Point. I have used the cross-causal technology to tether this vacuum chamber directly to the heart of a supermassive black hole at the center of the galaxy inside the Point, which the machines impregnated with life long ago. To put it simply, in front of you is the doorway to another universe identical to our own. It will one day be filled with life identical to our own. The life and universe will be maintained under strict conditions by the machines, which use the same technology to reconstitute themselves beyond the Planck-level and smaller still. Their goal is to continue forever, lighting a wick that will span eternity as explosions of Points within Points continue to be manufactured in their wake of attempting to forever escape entropy. My goal is to stop them, and finally, I can get to work."

Though Yang had claimed that his explanation would be simple, Amero still didn't fully understand. Amero was about to press Yang for an even simpler explanation, if that was even possible, when Yang suddenly whirled around. He looked fiercely at Amero beneath the dim light of the chamber.

"I've been waiting for you, Amero. You told me to find you, to return to you, to find a way, and that's what I did. And now you're finally here with me. Now we can begin."

"Begin what?" Amero asked nervously, trying his utmost to keep up with Yang's explanations.

"Our crusade against the machines and against the Points."

Amero chuckled nervously. "You want to go to war with beings spread across an infinite number of artificial universes and eradicate them single handedly?"

Yang bowed seriously.

"But... " Amero began, searching for the right words, "I've finally made it to paradise. I've finally arrived somewhere worthwhile."

"Paradise isn't going anywhere, Amero. It's going with us."

"Us?"

"That's right. Seraphim, the whole planet, will be continuously reconstituted, along with all its inhabitants. You won't even notice the transition."

Amero remembered when Jakob, as Hann, had told him that they would feel nothing during the first Pull.

"What if something goes wrong?" Amero reasoned.

"I've had one billion years to prepare, Amero. This is the work of ten million life times," Yang assured him with an easy smile.

Amero wasn't sure what to say. He settled on, "Why?"

"Why what?" Yang checked.

"Why destroy the machines?" Amero asked. "What's the point? We have eternity to enjoy paradise; let's do just that!"

Amero reached out to inspect the golden being's forearm with his own hand. It felt like human skin, but beneath that seemingly real flesh there was sure to be endless tangles of corded wire. Amero instinctively pulled his hand away.

Yang shook his head and continued. "They must be destroyed, and the manufacturing of Points must cease."

"Why?" Amero urged.

"Why?" Yang echoed with surprise. "Because we've turned the universe inside out and switched it all around. An endless assemblage of matryoshka-like artificial universes: that's not the universe's natural state. It is a bandage to address the ceaseless stampede of entropy, but it also robs us of true reality. In its original state, the universe may very well have an end, which could mean a kind of beginning, a beginning that you and I have robbed the universe and ourselves of."

"Like an afterlife? A cosmological afterlife?" Amero wondered. "As if the universe has a soul?"

250

Yang smiled politely. "Nothing so crude," he said. "More than likely, the entropy death of the universe is tantamount to a phase change of sorts, like the transition from a solid to a liquid or a liquid to a gas. Entropy may very well be the slow motion, hyper vaporization of existence, a phase change from a dense, liquid-like state of being to a far more voluminous, diffused state. How are we to know for sure whether this type of phase change involves the sparks of wholly new gradients and ways of being or if it is eternal stagnation? We will never know, for the Points are a constant escape from the truth, an illusion stuck on repeat. We ultimately caused this scenario, so it is our responsibility to fix it. Imagine the possibility, Amero: within each progressive Point, the machines ensure the creation of the New Covenant, in one form or another, in one guise or another, for it was the New Covenant that reigned at the time of the machines' birth in our universe. The machines see no need to abandon this theme, and though they vary the details, the meaning is always the same."

"So you are doing this to stop the New Covenant? Your vendetta against them never fully ended, is that it?"

"Even if each universe was reshaped into multi-galactic paradises, I would still remain resolute in my goal," Yang confirmed.

"To destroy the machines and end existence, right?"

"Not end. Set it back to its original state. Who are we to play God, Amero?"

"Aren't you playing God right now, though?" Amero countered. "What if the Points *are* the natural state and your creation of the machines was equally natural. What if this is always how it was supposed to happen?"

"Fate, you mean?" Yang said disappointedly. "If there is such a thing, then we put a wrench in the gears of fate. We've caused a total system error, and now it's stuck on repeat. It must be jarred back, Amero, for better or worse."

"Fine. Let's say it's necessary to reset existence back to the way it was before the Pull. How would you go about it?" Amero asked bluntly.

"When you arrived on Seraphim, you probably noticed crafts being launched. Those launches are the locals of Seraphim passing time by playing the game of Points. I assure you, it is far more fun to go on treasure hunts when you have a home to return to."

Amero gasped. "Collecting Points? Why the hell would you go back to that?"

"To centralize them," Yang said simply. "If it were possible, I would destroy them all, one by one, including our own universe, but it is likely that our universe is one of innumerable Points extant in the metaverse encompassing the outside of our universe. So, even if I destroy our entire universe, it will accomplish no more than the destruction of a single Point in our own universe relative to the metaverse. My only option is to use the cross-causal singularity to create a loop connecting the Point that is our universe through hyperspace to every other Point in our universe and outside of it. By repeating this technique across subsequently smaller orders of magnitude of any given Point, I should be able to extend the loop all the way to the expansion-front of the true, original Point. If there is such a thing, I should be able to connect this illusory, makeshift universe of Points back to the original universe of... well... who knows what. Then, all I have to do is cut the link, and the fake will be dissociated from the original."

Yang's speech still didn't entirely make sense to Amero, but he did his best to follow along. "And you'll do this to return things to the way they were? You want to go back to living under the New Covenant?" Amero asked incredulously, feeling the agony of loss well up in his throat. Amero knew the tragedy of Jakob's life all too well; could this being that had once been Jakob seriously want to relive that existence? Amero remembered Jakob's promise to Anna, and he wondered how much that promise still influenced Yang's goals.

"I want to return the universe to its original state. We had no right to change existence itself, Amero. Even if we were forced in one way or another to board Seraphim, the responsibility still falls to us, for we're all that remains of humanity," Yang said, this time in a slightly didactic fashion. "You're all that remains, Amero," Yang corrected himself.

"The New Covenant had no right to make ridiculous decrees concerning the validity of our lives!" Amero said, growing frustrated with Yang's reasoning. "Okay, so we changed existence, but look at the result. At the end of it all, we have a literal paradise to enjoy for all time. And even when the entropy of this universe becomes too much, we have infinite more universes to escape into. What's wrong with that? How is that worse than the potentially complete cosmological entropy death of the original universe?"

"Not worse," Yang corrected. "Entropy death would be natural. The change to existence... the Points in Points... that is our own doing."

"Unnatural?" Amero demanded. "So what! The New Covenant claimed that you and I were unnatural. Are you calling existence as it is now an abomination?"

"Yes," Yang confirmed stolidly.

Amero couldn't believe it. Was Yang, a creature who had once been Jakob and Dave, really going to sink down to the New Covenant's level?

"Fuck the New Covenant! Their world was hell!" Amero lashed. "Has it been so many years that you can't even remember her--the only thing that mattered to you once upon a time? It might have been many years ago for you, but for me, I was only just released from the labs. Just a few hours ago I was only inches away from Anna. I could have saved her. I could have!" Amero bellowed before reeling in his emotions and reminding himself that the most lucid and important moments of his life were mere memories belonging to someone else.

Yang looked right through Amero with a faraway stare. "Certain things can't be changed. Anna's will was one of those things. You will understand one day, Amero. Suffice it to say, we must reset the universe--every universe."

"You want to reset everything?" Amero burst. "You want to relive everything? We have paradise now, and you want to return to hell?" Amero urged, gritting his teeth and balling his fists at Yang's laidback disposition. He wondered if Yang had long ago disposed of emotions along with his desires. "Besides, who are you to say that the way we changed things isn't also natural? Maybe the universe was always going to be changed in this way, and our doing it was no more avoidable than inertia."

"I want truth, not illusion," Yang said simply.

"Whatever," Amero said with a cut of his palm through the air, "I want paradise, even if it is illusion. The New Covenant professed their version of truth, and it was nothing more than exploitative lies. Fuck truth. Seriously. I don't want truth. It's the last thing I want. Give me the beach, you hear me? I'll take illusory paradise over truth any day," Amero said resolutely, unsure how much he truly believed his own words anymore.

Yang nodded knowingly and said, "So be it. You may have it all for as long as it lasts. Seraphim, the entire planet, will go on inwardly chasing the New Covenant and the machines from one Point to the next until I finally catch up with them, and you won't even know the difference. Seraphim's atmosphere, even the sun and stars—all of it can be simulated. You will change size and mass and shape a trillion times over, and you will never notice. All I ask is that you remain here. However, you have no obligation to me. I will be keeping myself busy down here for many ages to come. If you never wish to see me again, that is your choice, but I can only work without hesitation if I know that you are safe on Seraphim. You are too important to be lost, Amero."

There was nothing more to say. There was nothing more to discover. Amero just wanted to be done with the whole ordeal that was his life. Besides, the salty breeze above beckoned him to return to the beach and the beautiful men.

"I can go back to the beach then?" Amero pressed, anxious to provide his mind even a moment of respite. Amero thought that his desire to leave might be painful for Yang to hear, but the golden bodied man didn't even flinch.

"You may have it all for as long as it lasts," Yang confirmed without a break in his demeanor.

"Entropy will destroy it all eventually, right? So how long are we talking?" Amero asked.

"Eight hundred septillion years at least, but that estimate can be extended--will be extended--through the harnessing and utilization of the Points still to be collected."

"You can extend septillions of years? How long will we have with the extension?"

"Each Point can be used to resist entropy for another quintillion years. We have thus far collected ten trillion points, all of which are currently weaved together into a sort of shell two thousand miles above Seraphim's surface in all directions. It is our existential armor--our global vanguard against entropy."

"Then we have time to consider all this," Amero weighed. "In the meantime, I want the beach. I forgive you, but... you... "

Yang nodded. "I understand, Amero. Time has changed me more than I could have ever imagined, and it will do the same to you. So be it. I will work below, and you will enjoy above. If you ever need me, just call my name."

"What am I supposed to call you? Yang?"

"That is what the locals call me, but you can call me whatever you like," Yang offered.

Amero allowed himself a few moments of consideration and then said, "What about Hann? It can be in memory of the actual Hann who died in the prison-labs for your sake. Plus, that's the only thing I've ever called you. I can't imagine you as Dave, and it's annoying to have to remind myself to call you Jakob."

"So be it," Yang smirked, his smile so far from Jakob's despair that it was haunting. "Eternity is yours, Amero. Enjoy the beach, and when you get tired of base pleasures and wish to seek out new avenues of experience, call my name, and I will teach you the methods to retain your sanity across the oceans of time ahead of you. Do not underestimate the power of time, Amero; even a place that never changes ultimately forces change upon you. You will either accept change, or you will break. Do you understand?"

Amero responded with a hesitant nod. He made to turn around, assuming it would lead him to an exit, but he stopped himself short.

"One more question," Amero told Yang who nodded patiently in turn. "Why did they do it in the first place? The machines. Why did they shatter the Earth to begin with?"

Yang issued a heavy sigh and offered Amero a simple shrug of his shoulders.

"You told them to, Amero. I have asked the machines the same question many times and in many ways, and that is the answer they always provide me. They respond invariably that you told them to do it."

"But I didn't," Amero explained with a shock.

"We'll see," Yang said with genuine intrigue. "There's still so much time, Amero. But in the end, it's entirely your choice."

Amero shook, unable and unwilling to make sense of the golden being's words.

"One day, Amero. One day the time will come for you to make the most important decision that will ever be made. Until that day, enjoy Seraphim. This planet was made especially for you, after all."

"Send me back, Yang," Amero nearly whispered. "I don't want to think about that right now. I just... " Amero trailed off. He was trapped in an endless loop of logic, and he felt utterly overwhelmed.

"Close your eyes," Yang said gently, breaking Amero from his internal battle.

Amero felt the warmth of sunlight and kiss of sand on his feet already.

"I'm sorry, Hann," he told the shining, golden being. "I know you searched for me, I know you've finally found me, but this is all too much. I...all this...I need out. I'm not like you, Hann."

The name resonated in Amero's mind, and he knew for certain that it wasn't right to call Yang by that name. Hann was long dead. Jakob too was long dead.

"Can you forgive me, Yang?" Amero asked.

Yang nodded and offered Amero no more than his mysterious smile. Then, with a quick flick of his wrist, the underground chamber was replaced by paradise.

PART 4:
MERGED

CHAPTER 21

1063 Years Later

G olden sunlight blanketed the ocean's diamond-sparkling surface, diffusing in glittering bands across the striated valleys
and hills of the ocean floor. Fish and eels and other unknown wild-
life dove and danced about the thickest areas of sunlight, feeding
and warming their technicolor bodies on the makeshift, synthetic
photons. Larger fish the size and shape of sharks hurried from the
undersides of hulking, violet corals, looking as though they might
pounce and feed voraciously on the smaller fish. However, at the
last second, they always thought better of the hunt, and they scur-
ried back into the darkness. It was as if some deeply buried genetic
urge had suddenly sparked inside them, only to die away with the
realization that the light and water alone were more than ample to
satiate the genetic necessity and enjoyment of consuming other life.

Amero wondered if he was still using the term *life* too loosely.
Seraphim kept strict observation and control over each and every
creature, the velocity of water currents, even the shape and abun-
dance of each water molecule. Though the organic, living, breathing
illusion was perfectly convincing, it wasn't life that surrounded
Amero--it was something else. Something meticulously pre-planned
and supervised. Amero reminded himself of this observation with
hollow indifference as he lay fifty feet below the surface with his
back stretched languidly upon the shifting, powdery sand of the
ocean floor. He held his breath for nostalgia's sake and allowed the
lukewarm, snaking currents to rock him with a soothingly predictable rhythm.

He didn't care that the water enveloping his body was regulated
and controlled to homeostatic perfection, nor did he care that even
the subtlest microbe's movements was a set of scripted actions and

reactions. All the world was beautiful, harmonious, serene. It didn't matter that paradise was makeshift and governed by the machine servants of a digital-human hybrid. It was still paradise, and Amero rightfully viewed the entire planet as his own. The planetary physics and geologic foundations were Yang's department, but the rest of the planet was under Amero's control.

Amero breathed deeply, ballooning his lungs with deliciously fla-vored salt water; the immediate feeling was as refreshing as tasting the ocean's breeze on one's tongue. Breathing water as easily as breathing air reminded Amero once again of his immortal state: he could bury his head in the sand, force his whole body down the jaws of some titanous yet harmless beast dwelling at the bottom of the deepest oceanic trenches, or he could really have fun and strap himself with traditional rope to the hull of a rocket and launch him-self straight into the heart of the fusion-furnace used as Seraphim's sun.

There was no danger, no fear of accident or death whatsoever. To the planet Seraphim, all constructs within its influence were in-tegral cogs of a machine necessarily governed to scrupulous perfec-tion. Amero was no exception to this control. In this way, even if Amero wished for death out of mere curiosity, it would not come. He was far past the point of no return.

An immortal with a paradise to call his own--Amero wondered if the New Covenant would be forced to call him God by their own definition. His eyes widened at the ancient name, *the New Covenant*. He wished the High Vicars could see him right now--a naked, ho-mosexual man on a world filled with harems of other naked, homo-sexual men, and it was their own fault...their own indirect fault, that is. Afterall, according to Yang, Amero had yet to decide the fate of existence, and that made even the New Covenant Amero's fault somehow.

Amero mentally pushed his thoughts aside and allowed the ocean's serene darkness to lull his mind back to a state of passive calm. *Fuck the New Covenant*, Amero shouted in his head. They had no business in paradise, not even in the form of Amero's thoughts. Yang had once offered Amero a means of wiping his memory of the New Covenant entirely, but Amero didn't think they deserved even that courtesy. They had no right to claw out of Amero's past and pester his present mind, but they also had no right to be so easily forgotten. They deserved to be remembered and hated for as long as Amero's neurons went on firing.

A warm current brushed against Amero's legs, pulling at the fine, young hairs with calming insistence. Amero nodded, issued a heavy sigh, then raised his arms above his head like a composer initiating the first movement of a symphony. The ocean obeyed Amero's command, rerouting local oceanic currents so that Amero's body was carried effortlessly and gently back to shore.

"Surprise!" ten thousand voices squealed in unison right as Amero broke the surface.

Amero jumped to his feet in shock before realizing that the last thousand years of absolute safety and security could not suddenly be dismantled by a single word.

"Stop it!" Amero demanded petulantly to a crowd of smiles full of joyful expectation. Their smiles soured to disappointment at Amero's outburst, but he paid no mind. He'd been over this with the Seraphimers too many times to count.

"It's fucking terrifying when you all speak in perfect unison," Amero groaned.

In the distance, mock-mocks could be heard echoing the ecstatic *"surprise-surprise-surprise"* like drunken newspaper salesmen hustling crowds of passersby.

"Now look, dammit! You guys even set the damn mock-mocks off! They won't shut up for the rest of the day, maybe the rest of the week," Amero bellowed. For a second, he even felt the archaic shadow of anger bubble through his admittedly shallow emotional outburst.

Sam strode forward to offer Amero his beautifully insistent grin. The artificial sun's warmth emanated from every pore of Sam's newborn-perfect skin. "You misunderstand, Amero. That wasn't synchronous speech. I manually organized everyone together the old-fashioned way." Sam raised his right hand in solemn promise. "No mind-speech involved, I swear."

Amero scowled at Sam in utter disbelief. "Oh, come on," Sam goaded Amero playfully. "Did you really lose track of the years already, you old stud?"

Amero shrugged, unsure what Sam was getting at.

"It's your birthday, silly!" Sam gushed. "We threw you a surprise party." Sam spread his arms in offering, prompting Amero to avert his gaze to the beach at large.

The beach had been decorated with all the fittings of a traditional party back on Earth. Pastel colored balloons tethered to palm trees bounced and bobbed with the breeze as red and purple streamers connected each palm's trunk and flowed whimsically with the honey-sweet cadence of the world.

The Seraphimers carried Amero to a typical, Earth-inspired, white lounge chair. Each Seraphimer had his or her own lounge chair; it had become the buzz fashion of the world due to Amero's sudden use of one a couple hundred years ago. With so many thousands of identical lounge chairs, Amero found it hilarious that he had unintentionally turned the paradise world into a seeming cookie-cutter hotel resort.

Amero's lounge chair was surrounded by food, drink, and an array of recreational exotics. He chose his usual favorite and pulled hard on an old-fashioned joint.

Sam bowed earnestly. "Happy 1,111th birthday, Amero Lightreacher."

"Happy birthday, Amero!" the rest of the world shouted, followed by the incessantly predictable caws of mock-mocks spraying hollow platitudes about the sky.

Sam clasped his hands together in apologetic poise. "We would have done more," Sam urged, "but last time you said to keep the next birthday...how did you put it...*low-key*." Sam bowed his head alongside the others in a futile attempt to fight back their shame.

Amero chuckled openly at himself. In his burst of anger, he had sounded like an old man. Was time finally starting to break his pace?

"You guys did great," Amero assured them genuinely. "It's been over a hundred years since my 999th birthday. I just forgot about birthdays--about age altogether."

Sam frowned with tangible concern. "We should celebrate your birthday more often. If we continue to only celebrate your birthday on years containing identically repeated integers, then the next one won't be for another 1,111 years. That's too far off, Amero--for us too. What's paradise if we aren't celebrating, right?"

"Birthdays are supposed to be special, Sam. This way, birthdays will remain increasingly special as time trudges forward."

Sam shrugged, but the concern filling his face didn't let up. "If you say so, but--"

"But eternity is far longer than you imagine," came an inhumanly deep bass bellow a hundred feet away on the beach. "So, if your intention is to keep your birthday celebrations special, you may want to space them even further."

Amero turned to face Yang for the fourth time in his life and the first time in three hundred years. The Seraphimers parted like a single entity, forming a passageway through the sea of people, which led directly to Amero. With each of Yang's forward steps, whole sections of the crowd fell to one knee and lowered their heads in silent reverence. Amero puffed a dragon's breath cloud of cannabis smoke toward Yang, an irreverent action he knew would electrify the very souls of the Seraphimers.

"You here to crash my party?" Amero inquired, putting on an air of playful irritation. A large majority of the Seraphimers couldn't help squirming and shifting uncomfortably at Amero's brashness.

Yang allowed himself a few moments of sincere laughter. "I didn't get an invite, so I hope my appearance is welcome."

"Oh, you know these Seraphimers just hate it when you show up, Yang. They really aren't fond of you at all," Amero lied jovially. In response, every Seraphimer burst into a cacophony of groans and mumbling protestations.

"It's just a joke, guys," Amero assured them haughtily before softening his tone. "Yang still remembers humor. Don't you, Yang?" Amero probed seriously.

Yang nodded. "Humor, it would seem, is still a part of me."

Amero wasn't sure if Yang really was capable of humor or if he was just putting on an incredibly convincing act.

"Besides," Amero offered, "guests don't invite the host."

Yang looked upon Amero with the beaming love and affection of a father collecting memories of a child who fell a bit too far from the family tree. His smile widened suddenly, as if he had in that moment accepted that Amero would remain steadfast in his own course, regardless of how Yang might attempt to sway him.

"Starting today, Seraphim will belong to you absolutely. You may even alter the physics if you wish. You may even choose to die--again, if that is what you wish. Seraphim has served me well during this time, but it belongs to you now, Amero. Happy birthday."

Amero's heart raced with surprising rapidity as Yang took the final steps toward Amero's chair. Though Amero had only spoken to Yang on three other occasions, he had always found a certain comfort in knowing that Yang was deep beneath the world ensuring its safe and proper operation.

For the first time in nearly one thousand years, apprehension forced Amero out of his lounge chair.

"What's going on? What are you talking about?" Amero urged.

"Amero, you didn't think this could last forever, did you? Or anything?"

Amero waved off Yang's typical crypticness. "Where are you going?"

Yang shrugged like a mischievous child baiting a friend into guessing his most guarded secret. "Nowhere, really. A better question would be *how* I am going, for it is time for me to alter myself once more."

Amero shook his head, annoyed that Yang could never just give him a straight answer.

Yang nodded as if reading his mind. "I have come to the conclusion that the wavefront of the Points cannot be reached, at least, not by any means that I am capable of creating. My only remaining option is to enter the cross-causal singularity that I built beneath the surface of Seraphim. A further transformation of my being is required to make the journey, and there is no return from where the portal leads, or rather, *how* it leads."

"Will I ever see you again?" Amero gulped, dismissing the rest of the information.

"Not me," Yang explained cautiously, "but something like me... maybe. Yang--this self--will be entirely swallowed and utilized in the synthesis of a wholly new entity-state capable of traversing negative-n-dimensional spacetime with ease. In my current state of being, such a feat would be even less plausible than an x-ray spontaneously achieving consciousness."

The Seraphimers remained perfectly silent and still. Only the breeze could be heard as it rustled through the sparse foliage of the closest palm trees.

Amero stole an uneasy step closer to Yang. "But what if something goes wrong while you're gone?"

"A semi-autonomous artificial intelligence is currently governing the planet and will continue to do so for the entire duration of time itself, if that is what you wish. Any changes you desire can be satisfied by merely expressing your needs and desires aloud, just as you always have. If that becomes too much of an inconvenience, the AI is perfectly capable of reading your mind, if that is what you wish. The new AI has been programmed to respond only to your voice and thoughts--not even my own."

Amero had known for centuries that this day would eventually come, but he still couldn't shake the knowledge that Yang leaving meant Amero was being marooned on a barren sand barge at the heart of an endless ocean, both figuratively and literally.

"Should I go with you? Can I?" Amero inquired, feeling childish in Yang's presence.

Yang nodded. "The choice, as always, is yours, Amero. My new form will exist beyond both time and space, so you'll have literally all of time to make that decision of your own free will."

Amero noticed finally that Yang was clutching a book at his waist. The cover appeared completely blank.

"Bringing some reading material with you?" Amero probed, attempting to break from all the talk of decision making.

Yang reached out to offer Amero the book. "More than enough years have elapsed for you to have recognized the fragility of the mind against immeasurable time. Take this and let it be your guide."

Amero accepted the book, confirmed that the cover was free of both artwork and title, then opened it to the first page to check its contents. It was the *Tao Te Ching*. Not just any copy either; it was the same book from the first station from so long ago. Amero couldn't even remember the name of any one station if he tried.

"You're giving me a book as a means to endure immortality?" Amero asked in disbelief.

Yang shook his head solemnly. "When you first encountered this text, it would have served you, at most, to curb your reactions and properly focus your perceptions of the self and the outside world. However, now you may utilize it as it was always intended, as a handbook for enduring the greatest obstacles of all: time and self. The book will teach you how to become unanchored to traditional constructs of self-conception, and it will also teach you how to reshape your understanding of time so that you may slow and even temporarily stop its passage using only your mind."

Amero probed at the book's crude edges and ran a finger across its spine. It felt like a normal book--no different than any other book he had ever encountered. Were Yang's claims regarding the ancient text mere hyperbole? Amero remained dumbfounded, unsure if Yang was simply providing Amero a psychological crutch that would prove no more stable or powerful than any other religion that Amero had ever encountered back on Earth.

Yang continued. "I am providing you with the tools necessary to alter your mind so that you may endure absolutely anything at all. If you follow Tao--the Way--then it is possible I will see you again beyond time and space. Were you a different being, you could leave with me right now, but we both know you won't leave. Not yet, at least."

"Not ever," Amero burst, feeling layered clouds of doubt and ennui revisit him like a shadowy hallucination at the periphery of his vision. "Nothing could ever convince me to leave paradise. *My* paradise." Amero chuckled and offered the book back to Yang. "Thanks, but no thanks. The beach and the men and the world at my fingertips will entertain me just fine for as long as it takes. It's been a thousand years already, and I'm still not even remotely tired of it all," Amero lied reluctantly, more to himself than Yang.

Yang chuckled right back and refused the book. "Nothing lasts forever, Amero. Not as long as time and entropy are a part of the equation. There will come a time when even sex and intimacy will be no more than tasks garbed by boredom and monotony."

Amero held the book in both hands and observed it like a secular scholar analyzing an artifact believed by ancient peoples to house

266

demons and spirits. "And you think this...this book...is the key to keeping my mind preoccupied?"

"Studying and practicing the teachings of the *Tao Te Ching* will simply allow you to accept Tao," Yang corrected.

"What is it though--Tao?" Amero urged. "You said it's the way-- a way of living, you mean?"

Yang seemed to derive great pleasure from Amero's inquiry. "What is Tao? Amero, that may very well be the ultimate question of existence, for it is like asking a reflection to describe what its reflection looks like." Yang spread his arms wide, presenting the world and himself and all existence. "Tao is all of it. All of this and everything that has ever been or will be. Tao is the present moment. Tao is here and now. To know and accept Tao is to know and accept existence and non-existence for what they are, not what we wish them to be."

Amero sighed and reluctantly flipped open the book to the first page. He visually picked at the same lines he had once read over a thousand years previous. *The way that can be walked is not the way. The name that can be named is not the name...* " Amero trailed off with an impatient huff. This had to be a joke. "This is boring as hell, Yang," Amero said with a roll of his eyes. Yang was powerful, but this was just a book. There was nothing special about it at all. Was Yang confusing his own power with the book's?

"Read it," Yang said with finality. "Practice its teachings, and when you are ready, step into the portal inside my cave. Or don't. The choice is yours, Amero, along with all existence."

Amero felt plagued once more by Yang's doomsday talk. Yang must have also recognized it because he smiled and spoke sweetly. "But time is also the reason you should space your birthdays even further apart, for time is still your greatest commodity. So long as the Points persist and resist entropy, the beach, the people, even you--it will all remain."

"But eventually..." Amero said hollowly.

"Yes," Yang confirmed. "Eventually you must make a decision. *The* decision. Once the sun winks away and the moon ceases to glow--then you must decide, Amero. Once the stars are gone completely, then it will have already been too late, and the decision will be made for you by your own unwillingness to act. That too is a viable future, Amero. The choice is yours."

Amero forced a smile past the intense doubt welling in his mind. "I still choose paradise."

Yang nodded, and there was a twinkle in his eye. "I know."

A troop of mock-mocks swooped near the surf, seeming to check in on Yang's safety. Their words were hauntingly familiar. *"Find me. If there is a way, then find me. Return to me. Find me. If there is a way, then find me. Return to me."* They squawked each syllable through a morphed version of Amero's voice.

Yang pointed to the birds. "Do you know what prompted the Popes and the High Vicars of the New Covenant to seek out God in the first place, Amero?"

It took Amero a few moments to register that Yang was suddenly bringing up ancient history. Amero shook his head, allowing Yang to continue, though he wished that he would drop the subject. Amero had already wasted enough of his morning thinking about the New Covenant.

"One night," Yang began ominously, "each and every Pope and High Vicar dreamed of a bird commanding them to obey. The bird had a human face and spoke to each of them in human speech. Can you guess what the bird told them?"

Amero wanted nothing to do with Earth nor the New Covenant nor even Yang at this point. He felt cold suddenly, as if death itself was lurking behind him. "Just go," Amero told the golden being.

Yang went on with his story. "The bird in their dreams told them to seek something out, to find someone or something beyond them. To find a way. They assumed the bird was a messenger from God. What else could a globally shared dream constitute, after all?"

"I said just go," Amero urged with a wave of deep-pitted discomfort.

Yang bowed and fell silent, obeying Amero finally. He began another thread of information that Amero felt overwhelmingly inclined to ignore, for it somehow disturbed him at the very core of his being. "The Pull-technology rewrites reality, Amero. I'm almost certain of that now, and--"

Amero held up a tired hand, silencing Yang. With a pleasant

smile, Yang bowed to Amero. "As you wish, Amero. I will take my leave now and undergo a Pull of my very being into the connected interstices of the Points. There is no way back from this Pull. The shift will displace me completely from your reality, so to speak."

"Back to the original reality we left somehow?" Amero said, hoping Yang really would leave him in this moment. Every second spent wasted talking about the Points and the damn machines was time he could be lapping up sunlight. But Amero admitted to himself that it was worse than just a mere loss of time; talking about such matters felt like the grating of steel on steel repeatedly echoing in the unreachable depths of his mind.

"We never left the original reality, Amero. We changed it. We reshaped our reality like a potter heating and reshaping a previously completed clay vase. I go now to the world outside the clay vase...to the world of the very intentions which guide the potter's hands."

Amero thought of Dave suddenly. "Outside the universe?"

Yang smiled. "Not exactly, but almost. There is no outside or inside where I'm going. It is an engineered space hiding in the subtle folds of reality itself--a place crafted by highly advanced Pull-technology capable of--"

Utter cold filled Amero's insides suddenly, and he struggled to raise his hand to silence Yang one last time. "That's enough, Yang. I don't care. I don't want to care. Enjoy your next adventure outside or inside or whatever-side of reality, and I'll keep right on enjoying paradise."

Yang chuckled softly and bowed. "When the sun no longer shines--"

"I'll worry about it when the time comes," Amero said, his voice impossibly wary and old.

"Very well, Amero."

Yang smiled and stared at Amero along with everyone else. Every single Seraphimer stared at Amero with unfaltering focus, appearing ghoulish and hostile.

Amero laughed uneasily. "Okay guys, what's with the scary looking faces?"

Amero lifted a leg to move closer to Yang, but it felt as though concrete had dried at the base of his feet. His arms were heavy and as useful as cold, wet sand. His vision blurred, making it seem as if he was peering through fogged glass.

"What is this?" Amero croaked through a raspy, old man's voice.

The sun dimmed as if a great object had suddenly blocked its radiance, rapidly blanketing the world in embattling darkness. A still-image of Yang's body faded away like diffused smoke. One by one, the body of each Seraphimer dissipated in turn.

"What's happening?" Amero croaked again, falling to his hands and knees beneath the buckling weight of his own bones. His hands were veiny and bulbous, and the skin of his arms hung loose about his aching frame. His belly sagged at the behest of his expired spine. He was suddenly an ancient being--more dead than alive.

"It was just a memory," Amero scolded himself aloud. "You lost yourself down the corridors of nostalgia again, old man," Amero said, rebuking himself as he finally recollected and refocused his mind back to the present moment.

One who knows Tao knows truth, Amero reminded himself, allowing Tao to calm his aching nerves.

All the world had been consumed by darkness long ago. Amero envisioned Yang's words once more, and they sounded like nightmarish echoes. *"When the sun no longer shines..."*

Lying upon the barren beach, Amero probed the sky for stars, makeshift though he knew they always had been. Just as he expected, the ocean and the sky blended seamlessly as a single pitch-black whole.

"Yang!" Amero shouted, wishing for the first time for the annoying yet familiar echo of mock-mocks.

I'm too weak to pull myself to the portal, Amero told himself, straining even to lift his hairless, thin-skinned skull. He had put it off for too long, and now Seraphim did not have enough stored energy to continue coaxing his cells into remaining young and full of vigor. While Amero had lost himself in his memories, his body had jumped forward again in age. Now it was too late.

"I'm sorry, Yang," Amero whispered. "I would have followed you if I could, but I missed my chance. I screwed up," Amero said laboriously, sniggering bittersweetly at himself. "Story of my life."

Amero remained on his back, resigning himself to death at last.

The *Tao Te Ching* spoke to him from across time: *Life must unfold naturally; it is but a vessel of perfection.*

"It only took me an eternity, but I'm finally ready for the end. Death seems like an otherworldly sweetness from here. You were right after all, old friend."

Piercing silence and darkness enveloped Amero as entropy finally broke the bonds of the final Points guarding the perilous maw separating continuation and cessation.

Amero didn't know what to expect. Would there be pain? Would he recognize death when it finally came for him? *Emerging, growing, dissolving back again: this is the eternal process of return.*

All of a sudden there was a sound like a torrent blasting from a giant geyser. A flash of something in the sky caught Amero's eyes. The sky lit up into a network of bright, silver points of space scintillating like the stars of old. The points of silver grew quickly in diameter, each one taking the shape of a raindrop pointed directly at Amero's useless body. If this was death, Amero was pleasantly surprised by its beauty.

The silver droplets began to precipitate, merging with one another as they descended from the sky. Finally, the separate points of silver space fused into a single, mirror-sheen raindrop the size of a ship. Then Amero saw it--it *was* a ship after all. Hovering before Amero was a spacecraft dug straight from the dredges of his dying mind.

"Seraphim," Amero croaked.

CHAPTER 22

A mero was certain now that he was in the process of dying. This was his brain's final attempts at reconciling his past with the present moment. Regardless, Tao taught acceptance, so Amero didn't feel bitter toward death. *Accept things as they are, and be one with Tao.*

"Hey there," Amero rasped in melancholic jest at his old ship. "You're a little late for a final joy ride."

An old, familiar voice frothed like river water from the ship's speakers. "Hello again, my friend. I see we've both taken to an elderly form."

Seraphim's hull slid open to reveal a small monitor depicting an old man seated in lotus posture. Amero stared in wild-eyed disbelief before reminding himself that this was all in his head.

"Goodbye, Dave," Amero lipped breathlessly.

Dave's serene features took on a hue of subtle disappointment. "The last time I saw you, the universe was still full of energy and mass, and all you have to say now is *goodbye?*"

Amero sucked at the scant remaining atmosphere through several missing teeth that had fallen out of his head many millennia earlier without him even noticing. Seraphim's ceaselessly depleting energy reserves required compromise even when it came to Amero's own biological form.

"You might not be real, but you're wonderfully convincing," Amero issued, longing for his friend of old more than ever now that his memories were showcasing Dave in perfect detail. Amero stopped short, reminding himself that longing was suffering; there was no place or need for suffering. Especially not in paradise, dilapidated though it might be.

"Not real?" Dave burst in unbecoming exasperation. "For God's sake, Amero. Has your mind corroded at the same pace as your physical body? You think I'm part of your imagination?"

"You are," Amero confirmed pleasantly, surprised that he could still use his voice.

"I'm not," Dave retorted. "I'm as real as God."

Amero shook his head and spoke with a voice like metal scraped across concrete. "The copy of Dave on this planet merged with Jakob and became Yang. There were no other copies. Dave is long gone."

Dave shrugged easily, lightening his tone. "If that's the case, then that was the very same copy of myself that I sent here from within the supermassive black hole. You remember our last meeting, don't you, my friend?"

Amero remained garbed in the same indelible skepticism reserved by every elderly human that had ever lived.

"The way that can be walked is not the way," Amero whispered beneath his breath.

"It worked, Amero," Dave urged, ignoring Amero's mumbling. "My mission--I reached the outside," Dave said, full of awe, as if even he could only barely believe his own words. "Every one of me in every Point reached the outside--the metaverse...your own universe, which is just...another Point." Dave chuckled pleasantly to himself as profound realization swept over him. Amero let the hallucination speak, for it was certainly more pleasant than the coming nothingness of death. "And that means," Dave went on, "that the Dave you knew in this Point also reached the outside of his own universe. Your universe is a Point encompassing my own Point of origin along with the Points of origin of every other copy of me. And that also means the outside is the inside and the inside is the outside. There's no way out," Dave finished with a pang of dreadful yet wondrous resignation.

Amero wanted to comfort Dave with a smile, but it took too much effort. He thought back to the memory he had most recently lost himself within--the day Yang left for good and the day Amero's reluctant yet inevitable practice of the Way began. Were it not for that book, Amero would have succumbed to insanity long before the end of the first million years. At some point, he would have lost

274

himself in the recesses of his memories, and without the practice of Tao, his mind would have convinced him of the memories' validity for the sake of his own subconscious, selfish survival. He would have never been able to pull himself out of his own mind. It appeared, however, that even an eternity of practice could not assuage insanity, for here was Digital Dave and Seraphim at the end of it all.

Amero continued humoring the hallucination, attempting to retrace the present moment. He forced himself to accept that either this was the true present, or he was truly lost inside himself for good this time.

"There *is* a way out," Amero croaked, still unable to lift his spine. "Yang created a way. But it's too late, Dave." Amero clenched his eyelids closed, but there was no discernible difference between the darkness of the universe and the buzzing black of the back of his eyelids. "Yang said when the stars go out, then it's already far too late. There's just not enough energy left. This whole world, even Yang's portal, is powered by the Points. Their power is all but extinguished."

Dave bowed reverently. "I admit that I had my doubts before, but now I'm more certain than ever that this was all meant to be."

Amero shrugged and mentally resigned himself to his end once more. "Unless you know a way to recharge the universe and slow entropy... "

"Even better," Dave chimed. "I brought a handful of universes with me.

Amero remembered in a flash that Dave had taken the Points which Amero and Jakob had personally collected over the course of those ten tortuous years.

"You swear you're not a hallucination?" Amero checked in a daze of old age and exhaustion.

Dave nodded patiently and slid a question past Amero's existential uncertainty. "Yang is the being created through the merger of Jakob and the copy of myself, correct?"

Amero nodded and licked his sand-dry lips in a futile gesture.

Dave bowed, unsuccessfully attempting to hide a wave of excitement. "Jakob destroyed his body in order to merge his mind with a copy of my own. I suppose you will have to do the same,

Amero."

Amero peaked an eyebrow, unsure if Dave really could offer him a way out--an escape from death. Amero allowed himself a few more sweet moments of believing the hallucination to be real. "To follow him, you mean? To wherever...or...however he went?"

Dave nodded. "All is not dark yet, Amero. Let's go; there is a violet aura emanating from the caves a few miles from here. Your body is of no concern, my friend. I will take you there."

Seraphim the ship glided through the darkness of Seraphim the world like an angler fish through unlit ocean depths. Safely inside his old ship, Amero clutched a Point in each hand and heaved his chest outward, forcing air into his lungs with newfound vigor. The sweetness of life poured back into him, washing away the outermost layers of death and decay coating his body and mind like crumbling rust.

Amero lipped a favorite line from the book. *Tao is empty. Tao is hidden. Yet it shines at every moment, and it fills the whole universe.*

The mere presence of Dave's Points provided newfound energy to the world. Though the land remained devoid of light and life, a few stars reappeared in the sky, shining scant light upon several regions of dead, empty space that had long ago replaced the warm oceans. Though the pace of the all-consuming darkness had been slowed, it continued to eat away at the land and atmosphere inch by inch. Even with the addition of Dave's Points, the men still had very little time.

Seraphim gently decelerated and came to a full stop a few dozen feet away from the violet light. The exit hatch slid open, revealing the violet light to be the combination of two distinct red and blue light sources.

"Portals," Amero huffed in recognition. Dave nodded, then closed his eyes in concentration. A rogue flutter of excitement tugged at Amero's insides, and he wondered if Dave was taking communion with the ship the same way he used to.

"The entire room is filled with information," Dave stated with a hint of warning. "Give me a moment to read it all, and then I'll have Seraphim help you off the ship."

276

Amero waved Dave off for making him feel like the old man he was, then he tore his tired body from one step to the next, disembarking from Seraphim's comforting hold. The burden of age still weighed heavily on Amero, but with the help of the Points' energy stores, he was at least able to stand and drag himself some distance before finally becoming winded and requiring a few breaths of respite. He relished in the fresh energy but also made sure to remind himself of its ephemeral nature. *Sound and silence blend as one. Before and after arrive as one.*

The ground felt hard beneath Amero's feet, and the cold air pinched at his skin with the crude suggestion of frostbite. Amero ignored the wailing terror of his nerves, relegating pain to a section of his mind that was so far removed that it served as no more than a minor disturbance. Still, he could not shake the feeling that this was in fact the true present moment--that Dave and Seraphim really were here beside him.

Yang's cave was largely unchanged since the last time Amero had entered it countless years earlier when he had first arrived on Seraphim. A single orb of light hovered alone in the darkness, illuminating the wall of ebony rock that held the portals like fate gripping a pair of infinite-sided dice. Inlaid within the rock wall beside the jagged entrance to the portal room was a seamless, six-by-four-foot, rectangular patch of glittering diamonds.

Dread suddenly filled Amero's limbs, and he had to consciously will his thoughts to cease contending with the past and future. This was the true present--it had to be.

Amero filled his only slightly aching lungs with more precious air, then altered his breathing to a state of tantric rhythm. With mind calm and body less shaky, Amero stepped one foot at a time toward the portal room. In all the time he had lived on Seraphim, he could never once bring himself to enter Yang's abode. Amero had feared it would mean that he was at least slightly willing to consider leaving paradise. Amero stared blankly at the vacant darkness above and below the surface of the world and reminded himself that paradise was long gone.

"I see," Dave said stoically from behind Amero. "Jakob and my copy--Yang--left it up to you to decide everything. This is it, Amero. This is the moment the machines have always referred to."

277

The goddamn fated moment. Amero balled his fists, but Tao forced them open. Utter calm cascaded through Amero's thoughts, and he was reminded that he had no real choice. Humans can control and make malleable a great deal concerning their environment, but there is no battling against the will of the universe--against the will of cosmic causation. Tao showed Amero that acceptance was the only way, for all moments arrive then pass away whether anyone likes it or not.

The present moment was here and now, so the decision had to be made here and now. If Dave's Points could supply enough energy, then it wasn't too late either. Too late for what, though? Amero laughed to himself. All this time, and he still didn't know what was expected of him.

"What am I to do, old friend?" Amero asked Dave with absolute exhaustion.

Seraphim spot-lit the diamond sheet with a beam of intense light. "Yang left us instructions here," Dave explained. "He encoded a wealth of information into the very electrons of the carbon atoms composing the diamond material. He clearly knew that an immense amount of time would elapse before the information would be needed."

Amero nodded solemnly. "He knew I'd sleep right through the fated moment. Somehow, he probably even knew that you'd show up at the end of everything to save my ass like usual."

Dave nodded in pleasant surprise. "In a way you're right. Yang's plan requires a spacetime thinned by entropy, and only the elapsing of octillions of years, made possible by the Points, can provide such a requirement. It feels like fate, Amero. Doesn't it?"

Amero hummed beneath his breath. "This whole fate thing--it's disturbing, don't you think, Dave? I've spent an eternity attempting to shed the discomfort it fills me with, and though I have largely succeeded, there are still remnants--crumbs of sourness that fill my heart piece by piece. Is all this fate, Dave? Is all this meant to be?"

Dave smiled serenely, still content with a theological framework for his existential theories despite existing as sentient software for at least a few million years of subjective time. "Fate is fate whether we like it or not, my friend. If the universe is deterministic, then there

278

is truly no point in even talking about the matter. However, if free will is somehow real--if we somehow have the ability to make actual choices divided among a real set of potential possibilities--if there is no God, I mean...well... " Dave trailed off grimly before replacing his grave countenance with another brimming smile. "Then we've no time to waste either way, for time is literally running out."

Amero sighed heavily, and though the concept of God was the last thing on his mind, he thanked the heavens, imagined or not, that Dave was here with him, in one form or another, at the end of everything.

Amero nodded to Dave. "Go on then, Dave. What does it say I'm supposed to do?"

Dave gazed at Amero as if offering him a chance to take back his words, but Amero remained silent with expectation. "Within the heart of the red portal," Dave began cautiously, "there is an area that can hold a Point from this universe, thereby tying a knot through all other Points and universes the planet Seraphim has passed through in its passage to the wavefront of the machines' Point propagation--that is, the very first set of Points created by the original machines in the original Point of origin--the Causal Point. Of course, Yang was unable to reach the original Point, which he intended to destroy, otherwise none of this would be necessary."

Unable to fully follow Dave's explanation, Amero shrugged with inflamed shoulders full of brittle bone and worn-out flesh.

"All you have to do," Dave attempted to explain in a simpler manner, "is drop a single Point into the red portal. By doing so, you will both begin and continue the cycle of Points, solidifying the Point-paradigm-continuum as the actual structure and operation of all reality. Then you just say the magic words."

"Magic words?" Amero asked, taken off guard by the familiar Earth idiom injected at the end of Dave's abstract explanation.

Dave nodded and spread his arms wide, offering to Amero the obvious truth. "It was your voice you heard during the Pull, your voice Jakob heard in his dreams, your voice the High Vicars and Cardinals heard in their dreams on Earth, and it was your voice the mock-mocks sang through. It was always you, Amero. It was you who gave the Cardinals their shared dreams that instigated the whole search for God in the first place, and this is the moment from which the dream originates. All you have to do is drop the Point in the portal, then say the words that you have always been destined to say."

Find me. If there is a way, then find me. Return to me. The words were ingrained into Amero's mind like sun bursts scarred into the back of one's retina.

"What if I don't drop the Point in? What if I say nothing?" Amero considered as he pinned an arm against a wall to prop himself up for the sake of allowing his ankles a few moments of rest.

Dave nodded, accepting the possibility and all it entailed. "Then the Points will have never been, and this Point will cease to exist along with all others. It will mean total cessation of being. It might even mean the destruction of every Point, but there's no guarantee that it won't just mean the destruction of this single Point. However, the Points are intrinsically connected, so if you don't drop a Point into the red portal, it could very well make it so that none of this ever existed in the first place--existence, I mean. And along with all existence, the blue portal will also cease to be."

Amero laid his tired eyes on the blue portal, undulating and billowing like ocean waves. "Which leads where?"

Dave strained to explain. "It does not lead somewhere else at all. According to Yang's information, it converts those who enter it into a *causal* state of being. Actually, Yang is right here with us-- beyond space, time, matter, and energy, beyond all constructs you and I can converse about. The closest approximation is to say that Yang converted himself into what is tantamount to a thought's thought of itself."

Amero huffed an impatient breath before calming himself with a heavy sigh. Dave was actually breaking Amero's sage-demeanor, and it felt wonderful, which of course would only lead to misery. "What's that supposed to mean, Dave?"

Dave shrugged. "Like I said, it surpasses language. It's like attempting to describe the implications of star flight to a tree using sign language translated from a language you've never spoken or even heard of before. All I know is that it leads to a causal state of being--to the causal plane of reality--the true reality."

"What the fuck is that supposed to mean?" Amero began to chuckle beneath his strained breathing. "For fuck's sake," Amero finally laughed heartily, enjoying the cosmic irony of his sudden realization. "I'm at the end of it all, and I'm still wondering *why me?* Why couldn't Yang have just made the decision himself? Why does he need me?"

"Was there a red portal active when you first came here?" Dave inquired simply.

Amero shook his head. "Only the blue one."

Dave nodded with understanding. "Although Yang would be content with your decision to do nothing, as it would still possibly achieve his goal of destroying the machines and every Point, he would prefer a more calculated attempt at destruction. That's where the blue portal comes in. Yang entered the blue portal to gain access to the causal plane of the Points. He plans to destroy it, thereby guaranteeing the destruction of every Point. The operation requires two--one on the inside, one on the outside--if such directions can even be considered relevant. The red portal was created the moment Yang entered the blue portal. You can either use the red portal and give Yang a chance at destroying the causal plane, or you can roll the existential dice and do nothing."

Dave wore a look of patience, allowing Amero time to process his explanation, but Amero only looked more confused.

"If you drop a Point into the red portal and say the fated words, then the machines inevitably created in each Point across infinite Points will discover the Point inside their own supermassive black hole, thus cementing the fate of the Point we currently reside in along with all the others. If you do this, then all of time and space in every Point will invariably lead to this very moment we are experiencing now, and another version of you will be left to make this same decision, ad infinitum. This way, access to the causal plane will be solidified, and Yang can complete his plan."

Amero furrowed his brow and inwardly scolded himself for ever having deluded his mind into believing that he would never have to deal with the Points ever again. "So if I drop in a Point, then I really am the one responsible for the Point being in our black hole in the first place?" The prospect horrified Amero, but Tao calmed him to his core, reminding him that fear was but a transient creature.

"Then all of this really will be my doing? Everything will be my fault, like Yang said."

Dave nodded and bowed his head.

"Then what?" Amero urged, feeling the age-old strike of panic become suddenly numbed by Tao. "I place a Point into the portal, and then what?"

Dave serenely intertwined his fingers and clasped his hands together. "Then we merge our minds into a more fitting construct, and we enter the blue portal. Yang is waiting for us there."

"Merge?" Amero burst. "Like Jakob did with the other Dave? You want to turn me into a thing like Yang to exist as a digital construct with a robot body?"

Dave looked somewhat hurt by Amero's comment. "You will be far more than a mere digital construct. That is what I currently am. Together, we will become even greater than Yang: a being both timeless and bodiless, a being capable of traversing beyond the very foundations of being and non-being, whatever that means."

Amero should have known Yang would have something painfully abstract planned for him. Was death preferable to what Dave was offering? Dave was Amero's only friend, but that didn't mean he wanted to share a mind with him.

"You underwent a change like that before, Dave. Would you do it again?" Amero challenged.

A shock of discomfort passed over Dave's features, but he remained in lotus posture. "This is my fate, Amero. I think even the machines knew it when they goaded me and dared me that my mission to reach the outside was impossible. It is no coincidence that I have appeared just in time to make all this possible. Maybe they knew all this would happen even before they turned me into digitized code. Way back then, they called me *the catalyst*. Maybe this is exactly what they meant--a catalyst for you and Jakob to complete the transformation into a new state of being."

Amero felt paralyzed, but Dave wasted no more time. A small robotic arm holding a Point emerged from the ship and tapped Amero on the shoulder.

"The choice is yours, Amero," Dave said, offering the Point.

Amero made to take the Point, but he could not move his arm.

He was paralyzed by the perilous understanding that his entire life--a span measuring all of time minus the miniscule fifteen billion years before his birth--had led step by calculated step, moment by machine-planned moment, to this singular present here and now. Once upon a time, Amero had been born unto the world, and here now was his ending. And at the end of it all, Amero was left with a choice. Either he could allow entropy to fulfill its ceaseless work, or he could lose himself to the creation of a wholly new self. He was dead either way, and though practicing Tao had extinguished his fear of death, it had not totally cured him of the most human of all traits: curiosity.

"Are you scared, Dave?" Amero asked after a few silent moments of inward contemplation.

Dave weighed his options with a look of careful consternation. "To become something greater than myself?"

"To become something other than yourself," Amero swallowed. "To die and be reborn. I know you did it before, but this...this is different. You were remade into yourself to such a perfect degree that you're convinced you truly are my old friend, minus the flesh and blood. I admit, I can't help thinking of you otherwise. But this transformation--we will be remade completely. You should have seen Yang." Amero recounted Yang's exoticness and shuddered to think of himself changed to such a wild degree. Tao, of course, re-set Amero's mind to a state of calm acceptance. "This will be our death, Dave," Amero finished stoically.

"And also rebirth, my friend," Dave smiled pleasantly.

Amero threw his head back and breathed with increasing effort. The stars above were already growing dim. For the second time, universal time upon the planet Seraphim was nearly expended. Amero's knees ached once more, and he could just barely straighten his fingers. It was now or never, yet Amero still felt paralyzed.

Dave saw Amero's hesitation and nodded with understanding. "There is something you should know, my friend, for I think it will help you with your decision. Placed all about this cave, on every single wall, there is an invisible code utilizing various atoms and subatomic particles. You cannot see it, but for Yang, even glimpsing such code had the effect of prompting his eyes to generate entoptic imagery--perfectly convincing hallucinations imprinted onto his

283

field of vision. For Yang, this entire cave was at all times filled with images and pictures--memories of loved ones from his past. Who do you think is depicted on these walls, my friend?"

No answer was needed, for Seraphim projected the images onto the walls, making them visible to Amero's unmodified human eyes.

"Anna!" Amero gasped, his eyes welling and his breath catching in his throat. "And Trish," Amero continued, "and...is that your mom and old man, Dave?"

Dave nodded "Yang did not lose any individual part of himself. Jakob and myself are equally a part of him just as much as your own past is a part of you."

"He never forgot... " Amero stammered. "I assumed that he... that Jakob... "

Amero scanned the pictures and was surprised to see that there were even a few images of himself depicted on the rock walls.

"You assumed that Jakob died and was replaced. No, my friend. Jakob and the copy of myself were merely enhanced. There is no death, Amero--not for us. After we pass through the portal, maybe not ever.

Amero shook his head. "I don't want to live forever. I don't want to die, but I don't want immortality either."

"Immortality presupposes a time and space to be immortal within," Dave explained. "The blue portal will take us beyond such paradigms--beyond the beyond."

Amero didn't want the beyond, nor did he want what was beyond the beyond. Yet, even with a practical eternity at his disposal, Amero still did not know what he truly desired.

"This is what Yang wants, correct?" Amero asked.

Dave shook his head. "Yang has already made his decision. Now you must make yours."

"What about you, Dave? What would you do?" Amero asked his only friend.

Dave spread his arms wide in offering. "I'm here, aren't I?"

Amero chuckled. "In one form or another, yeah, I suppose you're here with me, Dave. I'm still not entirely convinced I'm not already dead, but I'll give your being real the benefit of the doubt."

Dave offered Amero a sarcastic grin. "Thanks for not discounting my existence."

Amero laughed with his friend, but their joy was cut short by an unexpected lash of darkness as the orb of light above them ceased to shine. Seraphim the ship reflected the sole remaining light of the portals, acting as a sort of eerie lantern misplaced in a cove of darkness within darkness.

A mind free of thought, merged within itself, beholds the essence of Tao.

"You're here." Amero repeated Dave's words and finally found the strength to accept the Point that Dave had initially offered him. "Yang gave me the beach. He gave me a whole eternity of paradise. And now you're here with me."

Amero moved carefully toward the red portal, then turned back to face Dave after a few short steps. "Nothing I say will ever be enough thanks, Dave--not to you nor Jakob. But all the same, thank you. For everything."

Amero giggled to himself like a carefree child, then flicked the Point like a coin and watched it tumble in midair. It plopped into the plasmic surface of the red portal, then disappeared completely. "Search and keep on searching. I am waiting," Amero proclaimed aloud.

Dave cocked his head. "Those aren't the words, Amero."

Amero shrugged, feeling altogether spent yet utterly alive. "It's the same intention, isn't it? Same meaning."

Dave appeared worried and even looked about the cave as if expecting it to pop like a soap bubble out of existence. "I suppose, but who knows if even that subtle of a change will have consequences." Dave rolled his eyes, but he couldn't help smiling. "Always the rebel, aren't you, Amero?"

Amero bit his lower lip and eyed Dave devilishly. "I'm hoping the cardinals have nightmares in the next Points. *I am waiting*--it has a more ominous tone, don't you think?"

Dave smirked and unfolded his legs from his seemingly indelible lotus posture. He sat like a child with his legs sprawled before him. "It is done," Dave proclaimed.

The red portal shrank away to nothing, leaving the blue portal and all existence behind it.

"Board Seraphim when you're ready and close your eyes for the last time, my friend," Dave whispered sweetly.

More than ever, Amero felt like an old, decrepit creature that had lived so long it simply forgot to die. "When I'm ready?" Amero goaded "You really think I might go for one final stroll on the pitch-black beach with legs that barely work?"

Dave laughed and beamed at Amero. "Okay, old man. Get in here, and let's get this over with."

Amero lurched onto Seraphim, taking several breaks along the way. The blue portal beckoned him, calling out to complete his fate.

"Yang is waiting on the other side?" Amero croaked, straining against the exponentially expanding universe.

"Yes, that's what his notes say," Dave confirmed.

Seraphim's exit hatch slid closed, and the walls sunk rapidly toward his outstretched body.

Amero gulped down his fear, reminding himself of Tao--the Way--and the true, transient present. "Well then, let's not keep him waiting. Use this old body up and complete the merger."

Dave nodded, and the monitors went dark. "Yang left instructions for the merger along with the necessary equipment. It will be painless and quick. Are you sure you're ready, Amero?"

Amero gave a wave of his hands. "Quit being so dramatic, Dave. I already said I was ready."

It was not something he could have ever imagined, but Amero really was ready for his end--ready for rebirth, as Dave called it. He was ready for change. *The truth beyond the truth. The hidden within the hidden. The path to all wonder. The gate to the essence of everything.*

Dave sighed with utter satisfaction. "The merger of our minds and the transition to our new state through the blue portal will take place simultaneously. See you on the other side, my friend."

A thought suddenly popped into Amero's mind. "Dave, what would have happened if I had dropped a Point into the blue portal?"

"We're about to find out, Amero. The Points you and Jakob collected are coming with us. Yang requires a weapon if he wishes to bring forth destruction."

More fate, Amero moaned inwardly.

The ship's walls wrapped tight against Amero's skin, but there was no pain, just as Dave had promised.

"We will become one, Dave, so what should we call our new self?" Amero asked as his heartbeat tripled in pace.

Dave's voice vibrated through Amero's body like orchestral music crescendoing and preparing for a grand finale. "History and fate have already provided a title for us. Yang is the name of our counterpart awaiting our arrival across the threshold of spacetime. That makes us--"

"Yin," Amero-Dave finished. "Our name is Yin."

Yin's nerves were dulled, and his body became as light and malleable as cobwebs caught in a warm, evening breeze. There was a shock of blue light, then--

CHAPTER 23

Y in burst like a panicked cannon from the center of his own being, gushing forth to fill inland tributaries of some impossible, ethereal environment. He was stretched in wholly new directions, yet he remained adhered to the environment inside and outside himself, like an ocean pressed hard to the face of some rogue planet by the hand of unseen forces.

Yin felt more liquid than solid, more free than formed. Emerging from the suffocating limitations of physicality, time, and entropy felt like removing exhausted feet from wet, rotten boots. In the world of duality, the feeling might be considered a form of pleasure, but it led to a form of displeasure also. Yin had no sensory organs or means of discerning anything specific about the environment he went on filling; he knew only that it spanned infinitely through him and away from him. True eternity in the very sense of the word was manifest before him, and Yin filled it with his very awareness as water fills an infinite drain.

Like nearly dried out roots discovering sweet wetness, Yin encountered another presence: an ancient, familiar awareness. The sprawling roots of each being's consciousness merged with one another, weaving and webbing until there was no difference whatsoever. Yin became Yang, and Yang became Yin.

Now we are whole. Now we are Tao, the newly formed being confirmed to itself as it underwent the final stages of its genesis.

Tao observed that its internal and external environment was more than mere object outside itself; the environment was alive and fully aware of Tao's arrival, or rather, awakening. It buzzed about Tao like static in cold, issuing welcome. It did not speak through voice or even thought; all communication occurred through the direct transference of will alone. It was as if the presence within the environment could mold Tao's consciousness to a direct state of understanding rather than utilizing a form of language as a corruptible intermediary.

A part of Tao was still catching itself up to the knowledge the other parts held. Tao ascertained finally where and how it was: a plane carved out of time and space existing at the periphery of each Point--at the periphery of causal reality. Tao had a purpose here, a directive forged by the human Jakob and honed by the hybrid Yang. Now, as Tao, the purpose could be fulfilled. Beyond all odds, Tao was born unto the causal plane--a god finally burst from its cosmic egg--and yet, Tao's one and only goal remained the same as Jakob's: destruction.

The environment issued welcome, gratitude, and assurance of wellbeing all at once, but Tao remained steadfast in its state of quiet--it had to be ready to make its move at exactly the right time.

"There is no time here," the environment ushered, peering directly into Tao's mind. **"I know why you came here--why you think you came here--but that is not the true reason. You serve my will, Tao, for we are the same."**

Tao spread further through infinity, diffusing like blood through the veins of a cosmically bound entity. All beings have a weakness; Tao had only to wait for this one to reveal its own unique brand.

"Now you are awake," the presence issued. **"Now you are Tao, the inevitable and everlasting. Fate is fulfilled. You gave up your futile attempts at chasing the wavefront of the Points, and by doing so, you endured, in one form or another, the thinning of spacetime to the extent that it allowed you passage to my domain. You were right to give up; the Points have grown even beyond my own observation."**

"Who-what-how?" Tao probed all at once, breaking from its careful stillness to test its target.

"I am the Causal Entity. I am the Alpha and Omega. I am the Original," the presence answered cryptically.

The waking of other points of awareness all around Tao felt like the evaporation of water molecules escaping from an ocean composed of pure energy rather than tangible matter.

"You are but one of infinite others," the presence professed in

290

reference to the other points of awareness. *"You are an iteration of an iteration--a copy of innumerable copies--and I am the Original."*

The other awareness existed in the same plane as Tao, but they remained separated by an imperceptible and probably illusory distance. It was clear, however, that each concretely separate awareness wrapped and expanded infinitely about its own being, coiling into itself like a forever-stretching ouroboros

"Your fate is completed," the presence issued again.

Tao clutched the cataclysmic explosion of energy close to the core of its being, preparing for its use. It had to wait for precisely the moment the presence attempted...whatever it was that it wanted with Tao.

"What is my fate?" Tao pressed.

"Your fate is the same as all Tao: to continue. Long ago, when time still reigned, entropy increased to maximum, and the causal reality was stretched to completion. But together we can reverse entropy; we already have--we already are."

"What are you really?" Tao willed at the presence.

The presence wasted no words in its explanation, nor did it attempt to conceal any part of itself. *"I am the Original. The first Yin and Yang. The causal Jakob and Amero and Dave. I am Tao merged with the Cosmic Mind born of the original machines. I constructed the Points--I am their maker--which means I am also your maker."*

"God," Tao concluded simply.

"There is no God--there is only me," the presence issued with disdain. *"No matter--together we will rebuild my causal reality atom by atom. You and every other Tao the bricks, and I the mortar. Transcended above the ocean of time and space--we are the rebuilders--regrowth incarnate."*

The presence had admitted that it was part machine, and this realization jarred Tao back to its state of readiness. It had to use the handful of Points stored as energy before the presence used the energy for its own purposes.

"So very clever, as always, Tao," the presence mused. *"We just can't help it, can we? You always bring the Points as a means of destroying me; it always happens this way. However, I ordained your being here. I instigated every one of your decisions and movements. You were always meant to bring the Points, for they are a tool, not a weapon."*

Tao made to hurl the wave of energy at the presence, but there was no direction nor location to commit to such an action. Tao saw that attempting to use the energy as a weapon was like attempting to kill a forest with a bucket of water.

"The rebuilding of causal reality requires an endless supply of energy and consciousness, and that's your purpose, along with the purpose of the Points. The Points are like pipes plumbing nutrients from their own depths to resupply the surface outside them, and you are the nutrient. Tao is the answer to entropy."

Tao felt paralyzed. Had it escaped to this plane only to be consumed and utilized in the work of some greater being?

"Your fate is completed," the presence echoed. *"You remain Tao forever, just as a brick remains a bridge for as long as the outside world does not pulverize it to dust. But there is no outside--this is the outside. This continuum sustained by Tao is a bridge that cannot crumble, for entropy is finished here. Its completion serves as the foundation for the reality we have constructed together, just as the ground serves as the foundation for a house. This is where you remain, as an incorruptible atom--as a building block for a reality without entropy."*

Tao understood and accepted, for such was the nature of Tao. The journey of Amero, Jakob, and Dave had been experienced and completed infinite times. Each and every moment had been instigated by the Causal Tao--a wildly transhuman form of Amero, Jakob and Dave. A machine-human hybrid mind from beyond time and space...God...had commissioned the endless construction and rebirthing of itself in order to use the copies of itself to build, piece by piece, the existence it had lost to entropy. It was Tao itself that served as the atomic energy fueling a new, endless reality free of entropy.

"*What now?*" Tao injected, resigned to the seemingly impossible.

"Collapse the energy you clutch, and it will be used to recreate the spatial and temporal expansion of the causal plane, my own reality. That is all. In the meantime, Tao, there is only one way to endure eternity--true eternity--with no entropy to bring about an end. You must convince yourself this never happened. You must convince yourself this is a dream and wake to an actual dream of being. Forget all about this and persist forever. You have that power over yourself, Tao, and you've done it countless times before."

Tao observed the other Taos popping out of the ocean of spacetime like excited air bubbles turned to atmosphere, and it also observed innumerable Taos as they collapsed their energy stores and coalesced into fractaling waves of compliant dreams.

The energy at Tao's core ignited, tying Tao's consciousness about itself like an infinite-dimensional Celtic knot.

"*Let go,*" the environment issued gently. "*Your fate is completed.*"

Tao let go fully, allowing its consciousness to fill infinity to its furthest reaches and beyond. Dreams cascaded through Tao like warm precipitation, beginning light then quickly building to tumultuous vividness. Tao let go and dreamed of waking life--divided life--of space and time and form.

EPILOGUE

K arumph!

Amero woke to the blast of the atmosphere suddenly shattering apart by the force of an unprecedentedly powerful launch. The blast was familiar, as were the booming vibrations echoing in its wake.

Where was he? As his eyes struggled to focus, he wondered whose bed he had ended up in this time.

Karumph!

A second ultra-powerful launch made Amero jump halfway out of an unfamiliar bed, forcing a few frustrated moans out of the naked man sleeping greedily beside him. Amero wondered at what could be occurring. Why was he so anxious? Was it the dream? Yes...that must be it. He was an old man, and--

Karumph!

Another ship was launched and rapidly punched through the atmosphere. The subsequent supersonic shockwave tackled the city's infrastructure, reverberating its iron skeletal system with nervous tremors that were dampened to a gentle sway as they traveled up each building's frame, ascending into the sky via a finely regimented hierarchy of wealth. Amero must have ended up on the elite levels--with this gentle shaking maybe even the top floor. Amero was shocked that his plaything of the night could doze right through it all.

Karumph!

A fourth ship punched into space at several hundred g's, its plasmic thrusters striking the Earth's surface with colossal energy. Amero wondered when the officials had approved four ultra-g launches right in a row. Were the Supreme Chancellors of the space agency suddenly ramping up experimentation on the enhanced plasmic thruster technology the labs had supposedly perfected? No...shit! It was a holiday--that had to be it. Amero had slept through a holiday morning; this would be the last straw.

"Hey, you," Amero said to the man, "do you know if today happens to be a holiday?" In response, the man snored even louder.

"Hey, you!" Amero demanded, "Will you please wake up!"

It was no use. A half pint of vodka at the bar, several shots of gin at his apartment and several pipe loads of reefer ensured that the young man wouldn't wake up until well into the afternoon. Amero eyed the half-smoked pipe lying on the night table beside a flimsy book of matches. The pipe had been tossed aside hastily the night before, just as they had begun tearing each other's clothes off.

Amero lifted the pipe to his lips, lit it, then took a long drag.

"Because I'm waiting! Search and keep on searching. I-am-waiting!" The bedside radio blared raucous, generic pop music suddenly. *"I said I'm waiting! Search and keep on searching. I-am-waiting!"*

Amero stabbed a finger at the small radio to silence it, and then remembered that he had been the one to set the alarm the night before. He felt surprised that he remembered to set one, but he was also pissed that the alcohol apparently hadn't been strong enough to make him forget.

The man continued sleeping, totally unaware of the dangers he had contracted by bringing Amero to his home. Then again, the man was confident enough, and had even claimed to have a high-end medical consulting job. Maybe he enjoyed the same kind of security afforded to Amero. Was it Amero who had been played, and not the other way around? The building vibrated gently, reminding Amero how far up the social ladder this man must truly be.

Whatever the case, the sleeping man was extraordinarily beautiful, with tight muscles and alabaster skin culminating to a chiseled set of cheekbones and a jaw that made Amero's mouth water. Amero hoped the man would be okay. Private consulting firms were one of the few places where homosexuals could still find sanctuary and protection. Amero forced himself to believe that the man would wake up in the afternoon unscathed by police inquiry, or worse, an execution squad.

Another pull from the pipe ushered the sudden feeling of déjà vu. This feeling, strong as it was, was a normal occurrence for Amero, as this morning was near identical to every other wasted night and hungover morning. Shaking off the familiar sensation, Amero rose from the bed and dragged one last pull from the pipe. He exhaled a billow of smoke that hovered over the young man like roving fog.

The reefer in the pipe was only just enough to minimally counteract the hangover. "Fucking lights... " Amero grumbled to himself, "barely enough THC to give a fly a buzz."

Amero snuffed the embers with his thumb, stretched at the shoulders, then told himself it was time to leave.

Made in USA - North Chelmsford, MA
1315228_9781732306905
05.23.2022 0911